D1370622

# Forty
# Rod
# Road

# Forty Rod Road

**A young man's tale of adventure and discovery**

## GROVE N. MOWER

## ACKNOWLEDGMENTS

My sincere gratitude to my readers and supporters:
Brooke Hummer, Ned Mower Chapin Mower, The Mitchell Family,
Chapin and Jennifer Mower, Chris and Vicki Mower, Emily Mower,
Amy and Ted Mower, Bill Lederer, Jay and Martha Mittelstead, Philip
and Lynn Hummer, Elizabeth Hummer, Becky Parr, Ryan Ross, Bryan
Gruley, Tom Kiernan, Nick Lefferts, Madonna and John Merritt,
Angus Vaughan, David and Lauren Gorter, Chris Gorter, Taylor
Gorter, Jim and Audrey Gorter, Mary Krey, Jim Smith, Channing
Smith, Will Carney, David Parry, The Kaiser Family, Helen Feid,
Charlie Feid, Steve Feid, Hurley Ryan, John Ryan, Anne Coyle, Hank
and Francie Ashforth, Peter McMillan, Chuck Pass, Nancy Weltchek,
Jeanette Sublett, Langdon Neal, Merrill Smith, Sandy Fencik, Roger
McEniry, John Fornengo, Ann and Steve Bartram, Steven Bartram,
Christina Robert, Barnaby Thompson, Christina Gabetti, Jill Riddell,
The Martin Family, Carol LaChapelle, Amy Krouse Rosenthal, Jason
Rosenthal, Alicia and Tim Mullen, Sheri and Jim Passalino, Jeff and
Ann Walters, David Paton, Patsy and Gunny Harboe, Brory Harboe,
Graham Harboe, Jeff Cicurel, Cari Cicurel, Joe and Tracy Merrill,
Olly Merrill, David Zaycek, Joel Goldsmith, Wyatt Cohen, Matthew
Kinney, Tracey Biedron, Chris Walker, Mirja and Ted Haffner, Will
Haffner, Bob Horne, Leslie and Jamie Rachlin, Susie Braman, Mindy
and Ken Bauman, Jane Everham, Patty Grier, Kathy Buck, Scott
Colmery, Larry McCarthy, Katherine and Kirk Baldwin, Ted Sulger,
Aley Hall and Her Book Club, Michael Friedman, Dale Hernsdorf,
Mary Jo Reenders, Kelly Ketchum, Claire and Michael Walshe, Floyd
Siegel, Brian Siegel, Cloe Ott, Lorraine Walker, Richard Kosarak, Sara
Sereda, Elliot Silver, Robert Joynt, Jessica Day, Jim and Barb Corbett,

Ed Watkins, David Watkins, Andrew Rosenheim, Dan Rosenheim, Betsy Blumenthal, Michelle and Tim Turner, Susan Barclay, Scott and Julie Kleberg, Janet Lane, Connie Lane, Linda Bearman, Georgia Cady, Elliott Buck, Ginny O'Neil, Bill Wallace, Mary de Compiegne, Gigi Mortimer, Penn Newhard, Jerry Adelmann, Jeanne Park, Cynthia Crawford, George Gowen, Jean Riegel, Pat Coyle, Sandy McCandless, Ellen Bates, David Paton, Pat, Carter Sullivan, Sarah Zimmerman, David DeCamp, Lija Fisher, Carol Bodine Lloyd, Lydia Mower, Jim Stein, Walker Richardson, Tessa Richardson, David Sweet, Susie Garvin, Jim Johnson III, Marcy Oliva, Erica and Ned Janotta, Cliff Gately, Chip and Anne von Weise, Warren von Weise, D.J. Patenaude, Susan Wright, Phoebe Chandler, Ed Chandler, Susan Grant Slattery, Larry McCarthy, John Clatanoff, Mike McCarthy, Scott Williams, Ann Merritt, Wendy Browder, Karl Kusserow, Steve Helms, David Paton, Kim Barnes, Dave Mueller, Monika Kedzierawska, Jelena Jovovic, Kelly Manchac, Jennifer Marlowe, Gary Lenhoff, Terry Scherck, Googan Bunn, Wendy Browder, David and Rusty Browder, Jill Soderberg, Amy Hensold, Georgia Martin, Fred Klein, Genetta Townley, Rip Everett, Roger and Mary Hawk, Bill Schilling, Jim Stansell, Elise Paschen, Margot Rose, Joe Eskey, Amory Cummings, Liz Parker, Michael Parker, Chris Ksoll, Jackie Sedlak, Jim Sommerfield, Tom Hale, Rick Wholey, Dave Poitras, Cecelia Brunetti, Halina Batko, Tina, Conor Skea, Tom Hale, Liza Voges, Monika Verma, Elizabeth Kaplan, Elizabeth Scharlatt, Elise Howard, Mike Rorick, and Ragdale.

Lastly, to my editor, James Harrison, who took me on, guiding me with a steady and patient hand, believing in me and Forty Rod Road, my deepest appreciation.

# Prologue

*August 25, 1977*

*Dear Professor Gurney,*

*I realize that I did not do my best at following directions or completing the final writing assignment in your English Comp class, which resulted in you giving me an incomplete (and thank you for not flunking me because if you did my GPA would have fallen below the minimum for being asked back next year). So after our meeting I wrote down all you said in my journal so I would not blow this assignment, which was to "write a compelling story about a meaningful life experience."*

*Two days after our meeting at the end of the school year, I was offered a summer job in Wyoming working as a ranch hand. I took this job for many of the same reasons I was flunking your class and a couple of others: In a nutshell (hah), as you know, I was AWOL and spinning out of control. (You were nice enough to talk with me about this, giving me encouragement.) At first, I was worried about writing this story because I didn't think of myself as a writer, and you* said – and I wrote it down – "Hogwash, boy. I've heard you tell stories, now just organize them and write them down. You've got the ear." That was good advice.

So, I kept a journal, then organized my thoughts and wrote a story about the events leading up to and my time spent on the ranch. But a story has to be about something and that's where I struggled, so I went back to my roommate's notes from your class and you said that any good story should be about redemption. I tried to do that with *Forty Rod Road* – I just hope there's something redeeming about this story for you.

The characters are all real – I couldn't have made them up. I did use a little "artistic license," as you said I could sometimes, in dialogue and descriptions so as to smooth out the edges a little. I also tried to be "honest and truthful and find my voice and not write like somebody else."

I know you will want to talk with me about the ending of the story, and please don't tell anybody, because it's true. And I'm still a little shaken up by it, so maybe we could meet and talk about it at the Faculty Club – they gave me my job back. Dennis, the manager, called me last week and said the members were complaining about the new bartender; that he didn't know how to make a good martini or Manhattan, or remember what all the faculty members and their wives drank. (You like a Manhattan straight up with a cherry, light on the sweet vermouth, and Mrs. Gurney likes vodka on the rocks with a splash and a twist of lemon – a splash because the doctor told her to. Funny what you remember. You always said I had a good memory and a good ear for nuance – I never knew what that meant until I looked it up.)

If I am allowed to stay in school, I will be coming back a little late because I had to have some dental work done on account of a broken jaw (this is part of the story I have to talk with you about). Anyway, it doesn't hurt so bad anymore, but

*I do have sort of a crooked smile.*

*I hope you like my story, so I can pass your course, so I can come back for my sophomore year, so I don't end up bartending for the rest of my life.*

*Sincerely,*
*Henry (Hank) Chandler*

# Chapter 1

## WAKE-UP CALL

I'm not well. I felt like killing someone. That sounds insane, I know. It's not like I ever willingly killed someone; at least not by myself. At the moment, what was driving me crazy was my goddamn phone; it would not stop ringing.

Rinnnnnnnnng!
Rinnnnnnnnng!
Rinnnnnnnnng!
Rinnnnnnnnng!
Rinnnnnnnnng!

I let the first five go then prayed it would stop. The next ten had me guessing: Was it Janie wanting to get back together? My mother calling to confirm I'd be home for some debutante party? Or, my father wanting to know why the college had me on life support? By the twentieth ring I was *really* pissed – who was calling this early and why wouldn't they let up? I slithered to the floor, still in my sleeping bag, on a mission: Kill it before thirty rings (motivation is weird). I found the phone cord, reeled the ringing thing in, then spit out *Hullo.*

Nothing.

After two more gluey *Hullos*, a husky cigarette voice answered: "You the kid wants a job?"

I looked at the phone like it was a prank call.

My bedside clocked flipped to 9:12.

I brought the phone back to my ear, the pieces falling into place. Back in January when my father asked me what I had planned for the summer (meaning did I have a paying job), I told him I had written a letter to a rancher in Wyoming after Luke died, inquiring about work. My father dismissed the idea, calling it a "long shot" and asking "what qualified me for that type of work." He was right on both counts. I had forgotten about the letter, writing it off as just another disappointment in my freshman year of college.

I scrambled back onto the bed and kicked off my sleeping bag. My dorm room was dark and it reeked of me, the party the night before, and a mound of dirty clothes. I told the caller to hold on a second as I fingered my hair behind my ears then rearranged my underwear. I cleared the beer bottles off my trunk, threw my Marlboros into my desk drawer and shoved my roommate's spanking new *Playboy* under my mattress, then used his T-shirt to wipe the ashes off the trunk. When I told the caller *Yeah, I'm the kid*, it got me to worrying: I pretend to be spontaneous because that's what guys believe makes you cool and girls think makes you cute. But really, I'm sort of cautious. That's why I didn't answer him right away about the job offer. The caller became clearly irritated by my stalling because he growled at me: "Well, you want the job or not?"

I rubbed my temples feeling trapped. "Sure...sure," I said – about as convincing as a guy being asked if he wants to be the next to jump out of the plane.

He asked, "When can you start?"

*Start*. Shit, I had hardly finished flunking my exams. I scrambled around for a calendar. "When would you like me to start?"

He said, "As soon as you get out here."

*Out here? Out where?* I barely knew what day it was. I found a calendar and flipped to June. All I could remember was that Luke had always flown in and out of Jackson, that Wyoming was a big squarish state with mountains, and that Jackson was on the left side near Yellowstone. I told him I guess I could fly to Jackson in a week, Friday, June 3. Was that okay?

"Whaaa?" he drawled. "Can't you git here any faster?"

I told him sorry, I couldn't. I had to finish up school then fly home to Chicago.

"Where you at?" he asked, obviously not recognizing the area code he had dialed.

I looked down at the 401 on my rotary phone as if I was unsure. "Providence," I said. "Providence, Rhode Island."

He grumbled like he may have understood the distance between Providence and Jackson was about 2,500 hundred miles. "Okay, then," he said. "Call this number and let Eleanor know when you're coming. She'll get ahold of me. Her ranch is just up the road from mine. You're bunking with Clete in the trailer. He'll meet you there in Jackson." He gave me a telephone number, which I scribbled on the inside cover of my Econ 101 book, then had him repeat it so I had it right. Tapping the pen on the hard cover of the book, I asked him, "Who is this?"

"Huh...Whaa?" he replied.

I addressed him like my mother would when she calls the club to make a reservation: "To whom am I speaking?"

"Buzz Stifel," he said, pronouncing two names as one.

Before I could introduce myself, *Henry Chandler, most call me Hank*, Buzz Stifel hung up. *He hung up.* That left me sitting on the edge of my bed looking at the receiver, the front part of my brain hammering to get out. I was tired, hung over (not unusual) *and* now confused about what I'd just done. Here's what had led up to this: At the end of last summer, just before college started, my boarding school friend Luke Danforth died while rock climbing with his longtime girlfriend, Polly Hamilton, at the Hamiltons' wilderness camp in Wyoming. Luke had sometimes talked about that camp; he had spent four summers there when he was growing up and had been working the last two years as a counselor.

At Luke's funeral, I was anxious to meet and talk with Polly about Luke and how he had died – to be honest, his death had left me hanging (sick as it is, I love that metaphor). But something was not right; Polly wasn't at the funeral. *She didn't come to his funeral.* Also, Luke's family had been all tight-lipped and weird. So I wrote Polly a letter asking for names of ranchers who might hire me for the summer so I could go out and see for myself where Luke spent those summers and talk with Polly about Luke and how he died and close the chapter. In the mix was my desire to do something a little outrageous, like pretend to be a cowboy, because my current situation was circling the drain. So Polly wrote me back and sent me Buzz Stifel's address, and I'd written Buzz a letter in January inquiring about a job, but I'd not heard back.

Until now.

I was a little nervous about all of this. It's one thing to talk about it, it's another to have to go through with it. That's why I fiddled with the phone, unscrewing the plastic cap, removing the mouthpiece, then putting it back together. I scrounged around and lit up the last of a joint and lay back on my bed, thinking it over: I could ditch. Tell the guy I didn't know I was allergic to horses and hay. Or, I just got a job offer from IBM. Covering my eyes with one hand, I took a couple of deep drags then dropped the roach into a beer bottle jammed with butts and shook it. I rolled over, pulling my sleeping bag around me and went back to sleep.

I'd think about it later.

# Chapter 2

## JANIE * ANDY * POOLSIDE WITH MY PARENTS * O'HARE

When I woke up I was still foggy from the joint and whether I could pull off going to Wyoming. These were the facts: I did not know where I was going; I was clueless about working as a ranch hand; and I had no idea what this guy Buzz was all about, only that he had the telephone manners of a two-year-old. I lay back and stoked up a Marlboro, reasoning I'd written the letter and couldn't back down, couldn't disappoint my dead friend Luke or his girlfriend Polly. Most of all, I think, I wanted to prove to my parents, to Janie, to myself, that I wasn't a big wuss. (Smoking a little dope can make you creative and do stupid things.)

I squeaked through exams and hung around for a day hoping to see Janie, my freshman year crush that crushed me. Jane Stewart Wallace is from Perrysburg, Ohio. She's tall, lanky, sexy, a free spirit with long, dirty-blond hair and an outstanding pair who wore her pants slung low over her narrow hips and little butt. A nose with a cute bump made her even sexier. Best, she talked out of the side of her mouth, which drove me crazy. I fell in love with her standing in line for registration, and we had a solid thing going until spring break, when she went to Florida.

When she came back, lug nuts started flying around and our wheels came off. I don't know what happened and she wouldn't tell me. She just gave me the sincere cold shoulder and avoided me like a bad rash. If you ask me, and I think most would tell you, soon after we deflowered each other, she blossomed with pretty power and I wilted under the weight of first love. After a few at the bar, I asked her girlfriends about it but they dummied up, which meant it was another guy – duh! (Never tell a girl you love her because she'll bank it and move on. Trust me.)

A couple days later, just before I left for home, I spotted Janie sunning on the college green with her girlfriends. Approaching, I fantasized about her telling me: *Don't go, Hank. I love you. I'll miss you too much. Stay with me; or, I made a mistake, Hank, but I'll be here for you when you get back and I'll count the days until we're together and you're back in my arms.* Either way, we would end up back at her room hot under the covers. But the reality was I was not going back to her room, and that confirmed that I had to leave for Wyoming because I dreaded the thought of pining away for Janie Wallace all summer while stuck in the bubble of Lake Forest, Illinois.

She saw me coming and starting acting odd, talking real fast, looking around while her friends picked at the grass or twirled their hair. Once she settled down, I told her I was going to Wyoming to work on a ranch, spicing it up when her friends asked if I was going to be riding horses. I never really liked her friends so I told them this guy Buzz gave each ranch hand his own horse, a new pickup truck, and fifteen hundred dollars a month because it was extremely hard and dangerous work. Her girlfriends cooed *Oh cool* and *That's a lot of money.* Janie didn't believe my bull; that's why I liked her; and that's why I was dying to talk with her alone, to find out before I left what the fuck went wrong. When I broke down and asked her in a puppy-doggish way to drive me to the airport, she said – *get this* – "Gee" (she said Gee). "Gee, I'm sorry, Hank, I have to type a Religious Studies paper."

I wanted to scream an inch from her face, *Gee...gee, I'll type your goddamn paper on my lap in your car on my Smith Corona while I drive a hundred and ten down I-95 if you can explain to me what the hell went wrong and where do I go from here.*

But I didn't.

Instead, Janie stood up and sister-kissed me, hugging me like an aunt. She said stay in touch, write, give me your address, I want to hear about everything, especially you riding horses in Wyoming. I checked my watch, an uneasiness building behind my eyes. I turned to go, saying *see you around* as coolly as I could, then kicked my feet back to my dorm with my hands jammed into my pockets and my Cubs cap pulled down so nobody could see my face.

The next morning, I flew from Providence to Chicago, fantasizing about rolling around in the hay – literally a haystack – in Wyoming with Janie. My older brother, Andy, met me at O'Hare and we headed home to Lake Forest in his VW Rabbit loaded down with my two gigantic duffels and a backpack. When we were rolling through a tollbooth on the Tri-State, Andy calmly and astutely impressed upon me:

*"Are you crazy? Going out to Wyoming to work on a ranch? You don't know anything about being a ranch hand. Nobody in this family ever did anything like that!"*

I didn't make any excuses; I told him I had to. I'd written the letter and owed it to Luke and Polly. I also told him I had to get out of Lake Forest. My brother understood and shut up. He punched the radio stations, trolling for a song. He asked, "How much are they paying you, Hoss?"

Boy, was I stupid. I didn't know; I hadn't asked. So I bluffed, trying to sound like Clint Eastwood in *The Outlaw*

*Josey Wales*: "The guy who ramrods the outfit said goin' wages."

Andy said, "And who's this ramrod?" sounding like my father interrogating me about my D in Spanish.

I said, "His name's Buzz Stifel. He called me three days ago. Asked me if I wanted a job."

"What does this Buzz do?" Andy asked, again in Daddy-speak, turning up Bruce Springsteen's "Rosalita," following a truck I would have blown past.

"He's a rancher."

"Why'd he hire a greenhorn like you?"

"Needs more brains in the outfit, I suppose."

Andy smiled. "Seriously, what are you getting paid?"

I was honest, I told him I didn't know.

"Make something up for Dad," he said, flipping on his left blinker to pass a Caddy with Wisconsin plates, the driver puffing on a stogie, the windows rolled up and a Boxer staring out the back window. A soft rain had begun to fall, one of those early summer storms that's like a quick rinse in the morning, so Andy turned on the wipers. I looked out the window listening to the slap-slap of the blades, a hollow feeling building in my stomach. I thought: *What a total dumb shit I am. I didn't even ask what they would be paying me. My father would wonder about that...wonder about me...like he has been half my life.*

To be honest, my first year of college had not been what either of us expected. I wasn't on track – his track. Then there was Janie dumping me, Luke's death, and a low level of post-high-school-nineteen-year-old depression that compounded it all. What's kind of hard, because you don't want to sound cry-babyish, is explaining to your older brother that you feel unglued, and all you want to do is curl up in the fetal position and pull your sleeping bag over you. Which is what I had done for most of my second semester.

Pathetic, I know. Boo-hoo, right?

Andy knew I had had a rough go, so he took it easy on me. He broke the silence, not taking his eyes off the road because the rain had really started coming down. "You know where Wyoming is?"

"The United States," I said.

Andy – sounding like the old Andy again, not my father – coaxed me. "Which part?"

"I think the West."

"Can you give me three states that border Wyoming, and you can't say Montana?"

I confidently sat up. Starting with my thumb, I counted: "California, Canada and Montana."

"*Not Montana.*"

"Guam then?"

Andy socked me in the arm. "You'll make a fine ranch hand."

We exited at Old Town Road heading east to Lake Forest. The rain had suddenly stopped, and as we drove closer to Lake Michigan, I spotted a rainbow on the horizon.

I think it was a rainbow.

Ten minutes later we turned into my parents' driveway and parked between my father's Mercedes and my mother's Volvo wagon. My parents are great, *really*. It's just that they were born upright and uptight. My father's not a bad guy, it's just that he's paid a lot of money to be an ill-at-ease asshole – and he's good at it. Think a tightly wound Ward Cleaver in Brooks Brothers. My mom – *I love her* – is all about appearances, parties and charities. Think June Cleaver wrapped in Neiman Marcus.

They're a cliché, but so am I.

Andy had me pretty well coached: My job was to convince my parents going out to Wyoming was a good idea. He told me to state my case, fudge it a little, clam up, then hold my ground – he'd supply air cover.

Outside by the pool, in shorts and polo shirts, with Andy as my wingman, settling in with a cold one, the sun casting long shadows on the eighteenth green of The Bogey Club an easy seven iron away, I proceeded to screw it up big time.

"Luke told me about Buzz. That he's a great guy and has a really cool ranch, and if I ever needed a job to write him. I wrote him after Luke died." I addressed my father: "Buzz said at the funeral if I ever wanted a job to write him. We've been in communication since February...me and Buzz have."

"You mean Buzz and I," my father said, correcting me in his legal way. "And I thought you told me you wrote a letter in January. That you didn't know anyone. That Luke's girlfriend gave you his name...this Buzz..."

"Yes, sir," I said. "Polly Hamilton...Luke's girlfriend... gave me his address..." I fidgeted, peeling the label off my Stroh's bottle, my story leaking air fast.

"What type of ranch?" my father asked, sipping his Johnny Walker Red on the rocks with a twist, his free hand rubbing the head of Winston, our black lab – cliché, I told you.

"Big cattle ranch with some horses," I said.

Andy nodded.

My mother was dying to ask so she could tell her friends, "How big a ranch, dear, and where is it?"

"I think south of Jackson. How big? I'm not sure. I think Luke...or Polly...said about fifteen thousand acres. It's right next to the mountains. A really big beautiful spread. Lots of elk and moose."

Andy cleared his throat with a pipe-down frown.

My mother said, "How exactly did Luke know this man, honey? What's his name again? How do we know you'll be safe? Is he reputable? What exactly will you be doing and how do we get in touch with you?" This was typical of my mother, wanting to know if what I'm doing and whom I'm hanging out with is okay by her and my father. That's why I'm sure they set me up with Luke when I first went to boarding school, because he came from a family that was one of *us*, if you catch my drift. Turns out, my father had known Luke's dad through business and my parents had hobnobbed with them on some junkets, so when I was shipped off to school, they made sure Luke and I connected.

Now I was stuck. I reached for the mixed nuts. I started to squirm and sweat, my thighs sticking to the pool furniture. I popped a nut into my mouth looking to Andy for backup. He's a great bullshitter, Andy is. My parents always believe him, even when he's yanking their chain. "Don't worry, Mom," he said, reaching for her near-empty wineglass. "I'm sure Buzz's family goes back to the *Mayflower* and he has a second house in Hobe Sound. Let me freshen your drink."

She looked up, squinching her eyes in that mother-loving way, oozing out a "Thank you, sweetheart."

Andy went inside, the screen door brushing behind him. The mechanical pool cleaner broke the surface of the water then snaked back near the diving board. Turning to my father, my mother broke the silence saying, "Peter, do you suppose this Buzz knows the MacKenzies or the Wentworths?"

My father looked up, caught off guard. He's a brain at finessing the deal, but socially he's retarded. He can't relax.

"Doubtful," I said butting in, "but I'll be sure to ask when I'm out there." Making it sound like this was a done deal.

My fathered cleared his throat of legal brief and said, "Are you sure this is a good idea? As I've pointed out previously, you know nothing about working on a ranch. Wouldn't it be wiser to work at the firm in some capacity?"

My mother brightened. "Peter, that's a splendid idea. Could you make that happen?"

*Could he make it happen?* Of course he could – with a call and a grunt. I heard Andy's voice pounding in my ear, *Hold your ground*, so I dug in, knowing if I caved I'd be hoeing my father's row the rest of my life. I said, making it sound definitive, no turning back, "I can't, Mom. I already committed to Buzz Stifel for the summer."

An awkward silence descended. I watched Winston

sniffing his way around the pool fence, marking his territory on the begonias. I was dying to do the same to my father – mark my territory – so I gave him a rock-hard stare, holding it like he would when he was being a hard-ass, and said, "Dad, you understand: *I have to honor my commitment. I signed a verbal contract.*"

My father missed the humor – or more likely chose to ignore it – instead returning to sip his Scotch, mulling over I'm sure if I was ever going to amount to much. Then he looked up at me and demanded, "What are you being paid?"

I was prepared for this on account of Andy telling me to be ready. I shot back, "Eight hundred for the summer is what he told me."

My father said, "You could make three times that at the firm if you worked hard."

I shrugged my shoulders in defiance like money wasn't important, which really must have cut him to the quick.

When Andy came back and handed Mom her drink, she said what a disappointment it would be that I wouldn't be coming to the Cape this summer.

"I know," I said. "I'll miss it. But a commitment is a commitment."

My father shook the ice in his glass, nodding, his lower lip sticking out – a rare indication of satisfaction.

"But I want to take you shopping for clothes," my mother said.

Andy flew to my rescue. "Mom, all he's going to need are boots, jeans, work shirts and a blue jean jacket. I'll take care of it *and* get him a haircut – "

"Short this time," my father interjected.

Andy continued: "The best thing you could do, Mom, is wash his sleeping bag, *and make sure he's not in it.*"

Andy leaned back, grinning.

I said that would be great, not realizing you could wash a sleeping bag. My mother promised she would have Verna do it first thing in the morning. And for me to leave all my dirty laundry in the basement so Verna would not have to trek up to the third floor; she just turned sixty-seven.

On my last night at home, Andy and I stayed up late drinking beer, smoking a little pot and lots of cigarettes, and washing my new work clothes so I wouldn't look like I'd just come out of a box. Because I didn't want to go to sleep, I made Andy stay up so I could talk with him about school and stuff. I didn't tell him about Janie (what's the use?), but I did let on how Luke's death was still weighing on me and that what had happened at his funeral was bugging me. He agreed I was doing the right thing going out to try to find out what happened to Luke, and that working on a ranch would be a good break for me, a way to clear my head.

As brothers, Andy and I are more alike than different. We look pretty much the same – longish noses, Irish complexion and sandy hair. Where we differ is he's three inches taller than my five-ten and definitely more handsome, while I'm still what the girls call cute. Beyond that, we're well-mannered, good dressers and solid backyard athletes, the product of having been raised on a steady country club diet. The big difference between us, I suppose, is Andy's a whiz; nothing really bogs him down. And he's gotten to be a neat older brother after being quite a dick to me growing up. He used to do shit like fart in my face, embarrass me in front of my friends, and force me to play goalie so he could shoot pucks at me. One time he even strong-armed me into riding his mini bike down the driveway wearing ski goggles so he could shoot BBs at me from his perch in a tree. Now he's twenty-four and has a job at a company that makes pumps and valves, and my father's always telling everybody at the country club, *I don't have to worry about Andy.*

When he asked if I was going back to school next year, I gave my hand a *comme çi comme ça* waggle, not wanting to admit I had been an empty chair the whole year. I told him I was borderline, had an incomplete in an English composition class, but had it taken care of. I didn't mention the story I had to write to be asked back for sophomore year, because I didn't want to suffer through a lecture about making sure it got done. It was late. And I really didn't want to go to bed. Andy understood. He said he'd set up a smoke screen for Mom and Dad when my grades came in. Assure them that the Wyoming gig was a good idea. "A good résumé builder" is what he'd tell Dad. And a good way for me to get back on track.

A few hours later, curbside at O'Hare, before I got out of the car, Andy asked, "You need any money?"

I said in a froggy voice, "No, I'm good until payday."

Andy laughed in a phlegmy way, "When's that?"

I cleared my throat. "As soon as we round up the herd and punch some dogies."

"Seriously, Hank," he said, "do you need money?"

I told him no, I was fine; I still had a hundred dollars from my bartending job.

He said, "Did you give Mom your phone number out there?"

"I forgot."

"Give it to me."

"I don't have it."

"Do you know where you're going, Hank?"

I glanced at my ticket inside my dog-eared copy of *The Catcher in the Rye*. (Yeah, I know.) – now stuttering like a spaz because Andy was treating me like a child – "*Ja...Ja... Jackson, Wy..Wy..Wyoming.*"

Sounding like our mother, Andy said, "Call us when you get there? And be careful!"

Sure thing, I told him with a hand salute, grabbing my knapsack and my backpack (with my newly cleaned sleeping bag attached) from the back of the car. I leaned in the passenger window to shake his hand good-bye, my new cowboy hat pulled down over my still-long, curling hair, just a little neater and cleaner-looking after my haircut, but long enough to tuck behind my ears.

Andy gripped my hand. "You look mighty stupid, cowboy."

I stepped back and looked at my reflection in the car window. I flung the hat in the back seat, agreeing with him.

Funny thing about Andy, he said the same damn thing when he picked me up two months later. Only difference was I was walking with a limp, had a bandage across my jaw, and I was wearing Buzz Stifel's hat.

# Chapter 3

## CLETE ✳ FORTY ROD ROAD ✳ BUZZ

I boarded my flight, slid into a window seat, opened my journal and penned, *June 3, 1977 – Andy dropped me off at the airport.* After that, I laid my head back, closed my eyes and fantasized about me and Janie in our underwear (just the bottoms) watching *All My Children* in her dorm room.

Three hours later – still only nine o'clock in the morning because I gained an hour flying west – the stewardess was shaking my shoulder saying I had to get off or buy a ticket back to Chicago. I looked up and peered around an empty plane with guys in red coveralls vacuuming and pushing around big metal boxes on dollies, flirting with the stewardesses, bragging about an elk they'd bagged and jerkied (lucky them). I took my time getting up. I must have still been dreaming about Janie because I was pitching a tent. When the coast was clear, I slung my knapsack over my shoulder and slumped up the aisle, then down the stairs, yanking my Cubs cap over my eyes because the sun was bright as hell. At the bottom, I pivoted –

Wow! The mountains I was looking at were amazing. The Tetons, I guessed. I took a deep breath of air that felt to me like it had been cut in half – there was a sign on the side of the shoe box-size terminal that said JACKSON, WY, ELEVATION 6,237 FEET – and looked around the empty tarmac; all the other passengers were already inside. I slowly zigzagged toward the terminal with self-doubt nagging me, seriously thinking about what the stewardess had said, that I could buy a ticket back to Chicago and flush this ridiculous brain fart of working on a ranch, take a job at the firm, play golf all summer, then go to the Cape. At the terminal door I looked back at the jet being refueled and quickly calculated how much shit I'd have to eat, mostly my own. I took a double deep breath and stepped inside.

After a quick trip to the can, I lined up behind a mother helping her kid at a drinking fountain. I bellied up and stuck my whole face under the cool stream, forcing myself to wake up. Then, sitting against a column, I watched and waited for my pack to come out, on the lookout for somebody who looked like they might be Clete. Once the place cleared out a bit, he wasn't hard to spot. Not because he was a gangly six-foot-three in soiled jeans and a ripped red flannel work shirt. Not because he was wearing well-heeled cowboy boots and a high-crowned black cowboy hat splattered with mud. No. I thought it was Clete – or at least I hoped it was – because his smile lit up against his sunburned face like a neon sign. He was joking with a gaggle of Japanese tourists, assuring the group he was indeed a real cowboy as he threw his arms around them, mugging for their cameras.

Once the Sea of Japan departed, I closed in and stuck out my hand. "Clete?" I said, half asking, half introducing.

He stammered, "You..." pinching a scrap of paper from his shirt pocket, un-crumpling it and reciting, "you...Henry Tornton Shandler?"

I winced. "Thornton Chandler. Yes, I am," I said.

He balled up the paper and tucked it back into his pocket. Still smiling like he'd won the lottery, he shook my hand, almost yanking it off. "Clete Nicholson. Pleased to meet you."

Wanting confirmation, I said, "You work for Buzz Stifel?"

"Have for a few years," he replied.

I turned and looked out the double doors into the parking lot. "Where're we going?"

His voice was like the innocence and exuberance of Christmas morning. "To the Lazy T."

"That's the name of the ranch?" I asked, barely shielding my disappointment, the Lazy T not conjuring the Ponderosa or *The High Chaparral.*

"Yep. The brand too," Clete added.

Shouldering my pack, I gave Clete a dumb-cat look. "The brand...?"

Clete grabbed my knapsack and we walked out, with me trying to keep up. "Sure, a brand is what they burn on a cow's hide so you know which ranch they belong to. During the summer the ranchers push the cattle up in the mountains so the grass can grow and we can hay. Then in the fall we round 'em up by their brands and bring 'em back down."

That made sense.

It was also reassuring – his manner and consideration – explaining in big block letters and broad brushstrokes. I immediately liked him. He reminded me of Eb on *Green Acres.*

In the parking lot, Clete pulled open the driver's door saying, "Henry, just throw your gear in the bed."

Wheezing a bit, I swung my pack into the back of a red 1960s Chevy pickup. I asked, "Clete?"

He looked up.

"How far is the ranch from here?"

He gauged the traffic coming down from Yellowstone Park. "About two hours," he said.

I was rabid. "All right if I have a quick smoke before we go?"

"Hell, yes," he said, grinning. "What're you smoking, Henry?"

"Marlboro."

"That'll do by me. I'll join you." He let the tailgate down. "Set here."

We sat. I shook out two. We lit up.

We smoked and watched the traffic, me feeling slightly retarded in my Lake Forest Lacoste uniform and long hair sitting next to Rowdy Gates fresh off the trail. I was also still insecure about Buzz hanging up on me. I pointed to his pocket for an answer: "Did Buzz write my name on that piece of paper from the letter I sent?"

Clete shook his head taking a drag. He exhaled. "Buzz couldn't remember your name…he lost your letter. That's why Hope scribbled it down for me. She found it." Clete leaned back and pulled out the balled up piece of paper, his cigarette pinched between his teeth, smoke getting up under his hat and in his eyes. "She copied your name from your letter so I wouldn't forget. Said it was real beautiful stationery." Clete pulled apart the scrap of paper, pointing. "Is that really your name?" he asked.

I leaned over and saw my name neatly crafted in a woman's script: *Henry Thornton Chandler III*. That's my full name, what you find on my driver's license, passport and birth certificate. It's also what was embossed on the stationery my grandmother had given me, which I had stupidly used to write that letter.

"It is," I said, slightly embarrassed.

"That's a mouthful."

"Yes, it is," I agreed, my head down, my tennis shoes now toeing at the gravel.

Clete said, "What are those three sticks at the end for?"

I said, "That means I'm the third."

"The third what."

"I'm the third to have the name."

"Who else had it?"

"My grandfather and great grandfather before him."

"Must like the name." Clete took another drag. "Must be confusing when family gets together...all them Henrys running around."

I squinted through the sun and said, "The other two are dead."

"Just you now?"

"Yeah, just me. And you can call me Hank."

"That'll work," he said. "Hank sounds like a hand's name. Henry sounds more like a banker." He balled up the paper again and gave it to me. (I was glad that he did, because I saved it and later taped it in my journal above *June 3, 1977 – Andy dropped me off at the airport.*)

I ground out my cigarette and stood facing Clete. The sun caught his face as he peered up at me and smiled for no reason, his big right front tooth crooked and partially obstructing the tooth next to it. Besides the honesty of Eb on *Green Acres*, Clete also struck me as sincere and wise, like the scarecrow in *The Wizard of Oz*. I put my hands in my pockets, rolled on the outside of my tennis shoes, and asked, "So Hope – Buzz's wife – found my letter?"

"That's right."

I was confused. "So she's the one who hired me?"

"Yep. Buzz ramrods the outfit. But Hope runs the books. Hired me, too." Clete flicked his cigarette butt down the parking lot. "Let's get a move on. Hope wants us back by dinner." (Just so you know, in Wyoming, the midday meal is called dinner and the evening mean is known as supper.)

Before we pulled out, Clete hung his hat on a spring-loaded contraption on the ceiling of the truck that held the hat upside down so it wouldn't get mashed. I looked at his whitewalls and big ears as he ran his hand over his lopsided, Depression-era cut. He said, "Hope has some clippers. She does a pretty good job on all the hands."

"Really?" I said, curling my hair behind my ear like I was protecting it, praying the barber's chair wasn't a condition of employment.

Clete also reached under his seat and brought out a holstered Smith & Wesson 357 and placed it on the seat between us. I was in awe and a little worried as I asked if it was loaded. Clete said it wouldn't be any good if it wasn't. I kept staring at it like it would start breathing or moving.

Clete asked, "You ever shoot one?" eyeballing the handgun.

"No," I said, eyeballing it too.

"Want to?"

"Yeah!" I exclaimed. What boy wouldn't? I looked at Clete with a big smile. I'd been duck hunting and shot skeet with Andy and my dad. But nothing like this, never a 357.

He said, "We'll set up some beer bottles behind the trailer after supper and blow off a bunch of rounds. If you have trouble with the kick – she's a lot to handle (here he mimicked throwing up his hands together) – you can use my twenty-two pump that I use to shoot prairie dogs."

That sounded fine to me.

We headed out, driving south through Jackson, listening to Jimmy Buffet singing *Margaritaville* on the truck radio. As we wheeled our way through town, we hit a Dog n Suds for something to hold us over until dinner. (I had not eaten since I couldn't remember when and Clete, I found out, is always hungry.) On the outskirts of town, winding along the Hoback River, I went quiet. The bright sunshine, the altitude, the motion of the truck and the Dog n Suds, were all mixing with my hangover and doing a rumba in my gut. I think nerves were in the mix, too. Anyway, I was reaching for the handle to roll down the window, preparing to get sick, when I slapped my hand over my mouth and barfed up a little. I burped out, "*Clete, please pull over.*"

Clete saw I was green at the gills so he swerved off onto the shoulder. I pushed open my door and – with a healthy heave, careful not to get any on myself – spewed out my Dog n Suds.

As I came up coughing and spitting, Clete was kindly

saying, with a hand on my back, "*Whoa there, Hank,*" handing me a rag from the dash. "Try not – will you – to get any on the truck."

An hour later Clete slowed, downshifted and turned off onto a gravel road. I had fallen asleep but was now awake, still not feeling great. I sat up, dry swallowed and looked around.

There was not a cloud in the sky, nor a tree in sight, just scrub. It was like the surface of the moon – flat, barren, colorless, full of rocks and looking like it lacked oxygen. The only hints of vegetation were scraggly bits of grass and shrimpy, bluish-green plants Clete said were sagebrush. It didn't look like much of anything grew around here except misery, and the only movement were the semis, campers and pickups whizzing to and from Jackson on the highway we had just turned off. We slowed to a crawl as we bumped over a cattle guard. I rolled my window all the way down. "Where are we?" I asked as I peeked at my watch, now 12:30 in Chicago. I reset my watch for Mountain Time and took a deep breath through my nose to clear my head.

"I'll show you," Clete said. (Clete, it turned out, was good at explaining stuff to me as if I was a little slow, which I was, considering my background.) He stopped the truck in the middle of the road, then reached across into the glove compartment and pulled out a Wyoming map you'd buy at a gas station, this one worn and dirty. He opened and folded the map to the quadrant that showed the upper left corner of Wyoming and pointed: "Here's Jackson. The airport's north of town." He moved his finger from the airport, down through Jackson, tracing our route south on Highway 191. "You got sick right about here," pointing to a spot not far from town. Now we're here." He tapped on the map near 191 where a road – two barely discernible parallel lines – ran east and west between 191 and the next highway east, 352. I knew enough about maps to know that meant the road was not paved. I said, pointing at the two lines, "So this is Forty Rod Road?"

"Yep," Clete said. "It's about five miles long. Runs pretty much straight over to 352, which runs north and south and reconnects with 191 just a little south of Cora." He fingered the map at the junction. "That's how you get to Pinedale, which is right there, a few miles farther on." He circled his finger around a slightly bigger dot on the map.

"That's the nearest town?" I asked.

"Yep. About twenty miles from here. That's if you don't count Cora."

"What's Cora?"

"One-horse town on 352 about three miles south of Forty Rod. Just a post office and a small general store."

I said, "So where's the ranch from here?"

"Here," he said pointing to a spot about third of the way along Forty Rod. "About two miles ahead." Clete put away the map saying, "You can just see the windmill, the roof of the house and the top of the barn." I leaned forward squinting. "Where?" All I could see was a mountain range in the distance that ran diagonally along the horizon with snow on the highest peak. "So those are the Wind River Mountains?" I asked.

Clete said, "Yep. That's right. And that big one there with all the snow is Gannett Peak, tallest in Wyoming." Clete carefully picked up a little speed, maneuvering around potholes and rocks, talking about all the people being stupid enough to climb that mountain, and how he didn't see the purpose *'cause all you did was turn around and hoof it back down.* I pretended to listen but what I was really thinking about was how Luke had bragged to me about making it to the top of Gannett Peak. That it was dangerous, that he loved the thrill of being up high.

Luke liked heights (I'm not crazy about them). One time in our junior year in boarding school, I found him sitting on the window ledge in the bathroom of our third-floor dorm. When I asked him what he was doing, he told me to come out and sit on the ledge with him. I climbed out one of the two windows and squeezed in next to him, but kept one hand wrapped around the frame that separated the windows. Luke had his hands in his lap and he kicked his feet like he was riding a Ferris wheel. We talked for half an hour or so and the only thing I can remember is Luke telling me about Gannett Peak and how he had climbed it. All I wanted to do was to get back inside. Luke wanted me to stay, and I always did what he told me.

He wasn't an easy guy to like, and was even easier to misunderstand. He didn't have a lot of friends and that didn't seem to bother him much. He was the first kid I had met at boarding school and I imprinted on him like a baby duck would, me being green and insecure from the Midwest and him being cool and experienced from the East – Greenwich, Connecticut, to be precise.

Luke was the bad boy you could not stay away from. He was handsome, athletic and had a dark, brooding side that wouldn't let you in but was hard to escape. Why did he tolerate me? I think it was because I always did what he said and willingly went along, whether it was sitting on window ledges, breaking into the dining hall, or going skinny dipping in the school pool after midnight. (Once he dared me to join him in jumping off the balcony that hung over the swimming pool – I admit I *was* the puppy running after the big dog but I *did* have limits.)

My attention drifted back to Clete, who was now packing in a wad of Red Man, using his tongue as a plunger. He slowly let out the clutch and we started bumping over the washboard gravel, going less than ten miles an hour. He told me with a cheek full of chew how Buzz and Hope homesteaded the ranch back in the 1950s, how they built the log cabin barn and house themselves while living in a trailer on the property, how they irrigated the land with a series of canals and ditches they dug so water could flow and hay would grow. He told me how they had about a hundred head of cattle, which were now in the mountains grazing for the summer, along with their three horses, except Buddy, who was Buzz's horse. Clete spit a long red stream out his side window, a drib hitting the mirror. He said, "You'll like working for Buzz."

I didn't know what to say.

Clete blinked a couple of times, then reached out his window and thumbed off the tobacco spit. "He'll watch your back, knows his way around machinery and stock. Don't you worry.,,"

I then interrupted and said something stupid: "So he's a real cowboy?"

Clete blinked again, this time hard like he was squeezing out tears. He rested both hands on the steering wheel. "Yep. Real as they come. Used to ride broncs on the circuit with his friend Sonny Skinner after Korea. I've been with him in the saddle before, but Buzz don't cowboy much anymore. He's still slick with a rope, though. Can handle any horse. And he'll ride a buckin' horse when he's up to it. Most folks around here are ranchers…think of themselves as cowboys… but they ain't really. My way of thinking…Buzz's always been a cowboy who's had to scratch out a living being a rancher."

"How old is he?"

"Forty-seven," Clete said with a grin. "And tougher than a two-dollar steak…sneaky quick with his hands too – I've seen him slap around younger hands in town who didn't know better. Drop 'em faster than a honeymoon nightgown."

I asked another stupid question. "What's he like?"

Clete rolled the tobacco in his mouth: "He's quiet. Mumbles a lot, even when he's telling you what to do. Likes to play his guitar. Mostly minds his own business. But be careful, he'll pull one over on you…so watch out." Clete stopped the truck, got out, picked up a Coke can from the road and flipped it into the bed, then climbed back in. "Damn hippies – smoking dope, littering up the country."

"What about Hope?" I asked wetting my lips, tasting the dust from the road.

Clete goosed the truck into gear keeping his hand on the stick. He said, "Best I can tell you is don't bullshit her. Smart. Reads a lot of books. Makes mean biscuits...best cowboy chow in Sublette County. Wired the house and put in the plumbing..."

He paused. I could tell he wanted to say more. He pushed the truck into second, then placed both hands on top of the steering wheel as he said, "I think she gets lonely out here sometimes. No telephone. Away from town and her friends. Away from Bit."

"Bit? Who's Bit?" I asked.

Clete pulled on his ear. "That's their daughter... Elizabeth. She lives in Pinedale...a real pistol." I perked up at the mention of a girl who was a pistol and imagined erotic possibilities. Clete stopped the truck in the middle of the road, just before the entrance to a small ranch (it was no problem stopping a truck in the middle of Forty Rod Road because, as I came to learn, there were few cars or trucks and only three ranches along the five-mile stretch: Hope and Buzz's, Eleanor Pfisterer's and Sonny Skinner's. What traffic there was was mostly logging trucks or occasionally tourists with campers short-cutting across from 352 to 191 to get up to Jackson).

I looked around. In front of me, through the windshield about twenty miles to the east were the Wind Rivers. To my right were hayfields lined with irrigation ditches. Wherever water could flow, I quickly learned, brown and rocky terrain could be transformed into green and grassy hayfields. To my left, hanging high and slightly crooked, suspended between two tall posts with wire, was a weathered wooden plank burned with child-like lettering: *The Lazy T.* With the *T* angled on its side.

I looked over the homestead, maybe about two acres. About twenty yards beyond the entrance was a crude log cabin house with yellow insulation bulging out between the logs. A big bay window faced the mountains and the hayfields. The roof was covered with rough green tarpaper; smoke drifted from a cracked and blackened cinder block chimney that had a twisted-up, rusting TV antenna banded to one side. There was a covered front porch stacked high with firewood. The house faced three pole corrals that were connected with each other with swinging gates. A solid-looking barn constructed of big square logs sat near the back of the property with an open air work shed attached to the side of it. Scattered in front and around the house was a yard sale of ranch machinery: small red tractors, a horse trailer, a front-end loader, hay rakes and mowers. A slowly spinning metal windmill in front of the corral, about fifteen feet tall, pumped water from the ground into a long metal tank that looked like a coffin. At the far back of the property, just beyond a small ditch that had been formed by irrigation runoff, was an ugly green trailer that Clete told me was where the ranch hands slept. (At this point I wasn't stupid enough to ask Clete about moose or elk or riding horses, but I did manage to ask him if he knew how much I was to be paid; and he told me the *going wage* was three hundred a month, plus room and board; and during haying season you made more because you got paid by the day and according to what piece of machinery you could handle. And, he said, if you didn't go to town too much, you could save a little and get ahead.)

Honestly, the whole setup looked pretty dreary and a far cry from my wild-eyed fantasy of *Bonanza*, which had now gone up in smoke. This was not what I had expected. What spread out before me was *Green Acres* with a mountain view. All of this gave me an *oh-fuck-what-the-fuck-have-I-gotten-myself-into-now* feeling. I half-considered sending Andy an S.O.S to have him call Buzz and Hope and tell them that my parents had been in a bad car crash and that I had to go home.

Clete interrupted my depression, pointing down the road. "There's Buzz's pickup – he must be patchin' fence."

We drove on for about a quarter mile – me still half-mulling over an exit strategy – then pulled over to the wrong side of the road and parked, facing the grille of a faded blue Ford 150. Buzz was on the other side of a ditch, doing something to a barbed wire fence with a pair of pliers. Still bent over, he looked up at us from underneath his hat. As he straightened up he pulled off his gloves, stuck them in his back pocket, then hammered his pliers into the top of a post, leaving them stuck there as he edged down into the ditch, then up the near side, heading toward us.

Clete shut down his engine.

Through the dust and glare of a bug-stained windshield walked the man who ten days ago had asked me if I was the kid who wanted a job. I sharpened my focus. He moved effortlessly in a well-oiled and loosely hinged way; his upper body still, all movement coming from his hips and slightly bowed legs. He had an athletic build with a narrow waist and wide shoulders, a shade under six feet, I estimated. His face was mostly hidden by the shadow of his dark hat and the downward tilt of his head. He came to stand beside the truck, his head bowed looking at the ground, listening to Clete explain where we'd been. Buzz suddenly jerked his head up and said in a raspy growl: "Whaaa...he did whaaa?"

"Tossed his lunch," Clete said, attempting to whisper.

I leaned forward, feeling the need to defend myself. "It was food poisoning," I said, "and the altitude." I left out the nerves part.

Buzz squared himself to the truck, his arms now resting on the window, looking around Clete at me. I locked onto a pair of piercing blue eyes, finely polished and sparkling, set back and shooting out from under leathery eyelids. His nose was big and must have caught a lot of sun over the years because it was redder than the rest of his face. He was clean-shaven and his hands were thick, callused and etched with ground-in dirt and grime. He glanced down at the ground, then back at me, his face now fired in an unforgettable cheek-to-cheek grin. He mumbled softly in a low gravelly tone that I still hear to this day: "Well, you feelin' better now?"

# Chapter 4

## THE FENCE

Clete and I drove back to the house and lugged my gear across the yard, over a plank that had been laid across the small ditch, to the green trailer that was to be my home away from home. Inside, Clete kicked away boxes of clothes and got me set up on a thick bed of saddle blankets, then said to meet him in the house as soon as I got settled in. (He later gave me one of his pillows after Hope had washed the cover. She also gave me an old lamp to read by. Compared to dorm life this really wasn't going to be all that different, except here I could pee right outside.)

I nosed around the trailer like a dog inspecting a house for the first time. It was a beat-up abortion, with a sagging double bed (Clete's) in the back bedroom and a bunch of built-in closets running along a ten-foot hallway that had lots of ranch clothing hanging up or just stuffed inside. A small bathroom, with no door, was dirty and useless because the sink, vanity and toilet had been ripped out and boarded over. Salt licks were stacked in the tub, collecting dust. In the front where I was to sleep were those boxes of clothes, the cracked vanity from the bathroom and a makeshift workbench, below one of the two windows, where Clete re-loaded his shells for his Smith & Wesson. If my parents' housekeeper, Verna, could have seen this place, she would have quit; if my mother and father knew where I was to sleep, I'm positive they would have recalled me. That made me smile as I ran my finger along the grimy windowpane.

I made my way to the house, passing by farm machinery that I lightly ran my hand across. Inside, Clete had kicked back with a smoke, sitting by a wood-burning stove that had three good legs and a two red bricks as a fourth. The house was compact, everything within spitting distance: a small kitchen, two bedrooms and a bathroom; an island separated the kitchen from a small sitting area with a couch covered in Indian blankets and a TV with rabbit ears that sometimes got three channels. Against the wall, next to the wood stove, was a table that seated five. The log cabin was mostly lighted by a bay window in the sitting area, and that's where I first saw Hope, her back to me, looking out with a pair of binoculars. She turned around, the binoculars now hanging at her chest, studying me as if I was what she expected all along, no surprises. I took off my baseball cap and fiddled with my hair, nervously waiting for her to say something.

Hope was of medium build and well-kept; she wore moccasins and was dressed in jeans and a chamois shirt with some cool Indian-looking jewelry that had claws on it. Her mid-length hair was salt and peppery and stylishly framed a slightly pitted but youthful face. Holding the binoculars were hands and wrists that that had wired, plumbed, hammered and sawed. Her look was mixed ("some Cherokee" is what Clete told me later), which made her that much more attractive and tough. Inscrutable, too.

Before I could say *My name is Hank Chandler. Pleased to meet you,* she pivoted around and aimed the binoculars out the window again, focusing with the little wheel, speaking in a voice serrated by cigarettes, "Don't get too comfortable, Clete. Buzz's coming down the road. I want you to take his truck and run over to Eleanor's place. Henry, you go with him. There's a phone there. You need to call your folks and tell them you arrived safely. Clete, don't forget to ask Eleanor if I have any messages. When you get back we'll have dinner; then you boys can get to work on that fence."

Clete stubbed out his smoke, put on his hat, and gave me a nod.

I'd not said a word. I followed him out.

After dinner, Clete and I started building a cross buck fence along the western perimeter of the yard, from the trailer to Forty Rod Road – about a hundred yards – in order to keep out livestock. (This was to be our summer project when we were not irrigating or haying or just had nothing else to do.) Clete handed me a crowbar and had me yanking nails out of some old pieces of lumber so we could reuse them. I quickly built up a sweat, tugging and grunting, reciting under my breath Andy's work mantra that he had drilled into me during the ride to O'Hare: *head down, eyes and ears open, mouth shut.* Oddly, I should have been more tired than I was, staying up late with Andy, the flight out, and getting sick and all. But I was doing okay. Nervous energy I suppose, and not wanting to disappoint anyone on my first day on the job.

Out of the corner of my eye, I watched Clete pack in a wad of Red Man then methodically begin notching fence posts with effortless swings and swipes of his long-handled ax. He had me hold up one end of a notched pole that was going to be a side rail while he swung a claw hammer, sending home a nail in four swings, the vibration ringing in my ears. He hammered again, the bottom pole now in place. We hung the middle and top rails the same way. Before long I fell into the hypnotic routine of the scraping of the ax, the hammer banging nails, the wind gently rounding my ears and the occasional splattering of Red Man. Once, my head popped up when a semi rumbled by headed west in a cloud of dust on Forty Rod Road; Clete raised up, spit and said it was Shorty Johnson hauling a load of lodgepole pine to Jackson

Soon after, Clete called me *Squirrel.* (That evening, sitting on the stoop outside the trailer having a smoke before going to bed, he explained how younger ranch hands are called Squirrel because they had to do all the running around. He'd been called Squirrel by Buzz and other cowboys. It was part of the pecking order, and I took it as a compliment. That night Clete also told me about himself. He was twenty-three, an only child, single, but had a girl down home in Florida, which was where he was from and where he lived with his dad when he wasn't in Wyoming. His father was a fireman; his mother was dead from cancer. He came to Wyoming because he wanted to cowboy more. He hooked on with Buzz and Hope and had been with them for three summers, and wouldn't work for anybody else, even if he was paid more and lived in a real bunkhouse. He'd found a home at the Lazy T and wouldn't change it for anything. He said when the snow flies in November, he heads south, then returns again in April when branding season starts.)

"Squirrel," Clete said, "scoot your end up a cock hair so it's plumb." He handed me the hammer and a nail. "Now drive it home."

I did my best. After bending two nails, I finally sank one. He said, "That'll hold her."

I checked my work against his. I had a ways to go.

I figured that this was how it was going to be for most of the summer. Me working harder than I had to because I didn't know what the hell I was doing, but always trying to please, wanting to be a good ranch hand; and Clete being patient with me, telling me to slow down, showing me an easier way.

After about an hour, Clete stopped doing what he was doing; said he was going to get his water jug and for me to take a break. When he returned he handed me the jug and paid me a strange compliment. "You're a sight better than working with Asshole Pete."

"Who's that?" I asked.

Clete said, "Pete Farnsworth. He was a ranch hand here. Only lasted three months. Buzz had to run him off." Clete looked up at the sun and clear sky, wiping the sweat off his face and the back of his neck with a red checked bandana. He folded it and slid it in his back pocket saying, "I grew up with Pete down around Lake Okeechobee...didn't care much for him. His old man was tall hat, no cattle."

He stopped to take from me one of the nails I'd pulled out of an old plank. Drove it hard into a pole.

BANG!

He said, "They moved up here to start over. Farnsworth – that's the old man – hired on as a deputy in town. He became sheriff when his boss died driving drunk coming back from one of them titty bars in Rock Springs. Then old Farnsworth hired his son...that's Pete...after Buzz fired him."

BANG! BANG! BANG!

"Pete's the sheriff's son?" I asked to make sure.

BANG! BANG! BANG!

"Yep, that's right. Pete's his son. I gave him the 'Asshole' part. Can't stand that boy."

BANG! BANG! BANG! "Bad seed just like his dad," Clete said, bent over lining up another nail. "Worthless as tits on a bull."

BANG! BANG! BANG!

"His mother...Dorothy...she was from Savannah, I think. Polite-like and educated...but no pushover. That's why I think she and Hope got along so well. Too bad she drew a weak card with Farnsworth...had to bite the bullet and move here."

BANG! BANG! BANG!

"Problem started when Dorothy and Hope became friends."

BANG! BANG!...BANG!

Clete stopped hammering, his head bowed, the last BANG an obvious punctuation point, his voice now heavy with regret. "That's when Dorothy caught Buzz's eye." He dropped his hammer and picked up the ax. He hacked away at a pole, slimming it to the point that it was useless, throwing it aside. He went for the water jug and took a long swallow, mulling something over while I busied myself pulling up new poles for him to notch. He thumbed the ax blade, not looking at me, and said, "I'm telling you these things, Hank, 'cause you'll be here awhile and need to know the lay of the land. It ain't no secret Buzz'll shoot at a stray shot of leg when he goes to town. When Dorothy couldn't stomach Farnsworth no more" – here Clete's voice turned arrogant: "*Acting high and mighty 'cause he's Johnny Law in town* – they split up. Farnsworth didn't want it but Dorothy couldn't stand him anymore. That's when Buzz started giving Dorothy a steady poke in the whiskers. But I wouldn't be surprised if he'd been doing it before."

Clete addressed me, now serious, "Now you gotta be careful, Squirrel. Farnsworth and Asshole Pete are on the warpath against the Lazy T. They'd like nothing better than to run Buzz in...or any one of us. They're a bad lot. I've heard about boys who ended up in his jail because of being drunk or disorderly, 'accidentally' falling and hurting themselves, or punished for starting something they didn't do." Clete looked over the hayfields at the top of Eleanor Pfisterer's house a mile away, set way back from the road, and said, "Eleanor told me about how Farnsworth and Asshole Pete dragged her husband, Gene, out of his truck one night coming back from town 'cause he was drinking and refused to walk the line. They beat him up bad on the side of the road just past the Cora store turnoff...nobody'd see 'em do it way out here – who was he gonna tell anyway? Soon after, Gene got the cancer and died. Eleanor told Hope that when they laid him out at the funeral parlor, his whole body was still black and blue."

Taking a breather, Clete leaned back against the fence. Thank God he did, because I was frothing, desperate even, trying to take in all this information, reciting it back to myself so I wouldn't forget names, places and events. It was like I'd just been plunked in the middle of a dime-store Western. I looked at him, buying time, slowing it down, asking, "How's all this set with Hope," flashing a glance at the house.

He handed me the hammer and three nails and let me "put-out" on my own. He reset his hat, looking over the fields, his voice softer now. "She tries not to show it, but I know it makes her empty inside. She'll let loose on Buzz, but he don't fight back. Just figures it's better to duck, let it blow over. Buzz's a tough guy to hate. He treats her good. Bit, too. Gotta lot of friends and respect around town. This's been going a long time. Bit told me there'd been fights and a couple times Buzz had guns pulled on him – "

"*No shit*," I spit out, bent over and hammering.

"That's what I heard," Clete said picking up the next pole, eyeballing it to make sure it wasn't warped.

"Did they shoot?"

"Heard they did. Must not been good shots."

"Who was it?"

"Not sure. Husbands, I s'pect."

This was getting more intense by the moment, certainly not what I expected when I wrote that letter to Polly. Sure, I was angling for a western experience to solve my problems, but this was way different from what I'd bargained for. *This was real, not fiction. And they were using live ammunition. This was great.*

But...the infidelity part bugged me. It wasn't something I was used to. I hardly knew Hope but I immediately felt sorry for her. I motioned toward the house asking, "Why would somebody do that? Run around with other women when you have someone like that? I don't get it."

Clete nodded agreement, his brow furrowed, saying he'd never known a finer woman and didn't understand Buzz's running around either. Then he straightened up to his full six-three and looked down at me, his taut expression evaporating into a goofy smile that exaggerated his crooked front tooth. He pushed back his hat and giggled:

"But wait 'til you get a look at Buzz's pecker."

# Chapter 5

## FIRST NIGHT ✳ FIRST DAY ✳ PRAIRIE DOGS ✳ BUZZ'S CANNON

The first night I went to bed about an hour after sundown, which, it turns out, is what we did most nights, because we were beat. Before we'd turn in, Clete and I would usually hang around outside the trailer, sitting on some beat-up lawn chairs with our feet up on the stoop, listening to country music from an old radio, smoking, talking about ranch stuff or comparing how we both grew up (we never judged each other and I think that's why we got along so well).

That night, after scribbling down as much as I could about my day, I snuggled in and lay still listening to the wind blowing through an open window while staring into a patch of deep blue sky with so many bright twinkling stars that you'd swear they were fake. I closed my eyes for a second, now fully aware of where I was on a map of Wyoming, settling in on my bed of saddle blankets, picking up hints of cow dung, diesel and sagebrush.

When I turned off my lamp and said good night to Clete – who was reading a Louis L'Amour novel that Hope had given him, his light shining down the hall to my "bedroom" –

he said, "Good night, Squirrel. Make sure that door's pulled tight. We don't want to be bunkin' with no varmints."

*No shit* I thought, and scrambled out of my bag to check the door.

Sleep was impossible. The altitude – and me being nervous about not knowing anything about anything – kept waking me up; so I'd punch my pillow and twist around in my bag, wondering what time it was. Just after daybreak, I shot up in bed, eyeing the doorknob gently turning. (Oddly enough, I'd been having a dream about bears outside the trailer trying to get in.) I peeked over the top of my sleeping bag and saw the door slowly open. There was Buzz's grinning face with his finger pressed over his lips signaling me to keep quiet.

He tippy-toed back to Clete's bedroom.

I wondered *What the hell?*

The tippy-toeing stopped.

Sheets and blankets rustled and were ripped away.

Clete screamed, *"Goddamnholyshitwhat'sgoingon?"*

"Drop your cock," Buzz bellowed.

*"Buzzwhatthehell?"*

"Grab your socks."

Clete pleaded: "Give me back them covers, Buzz."

"Time to go to work, Clete," Buzz said, laughing a little.

Sheets and covers rustled again.

"Goddamn, Buzz" – Clete now out of breath – "Sneaking up on me that way. Jesus Christ, I'd swear you was Apache."

Buzz danced back down the hall sing-songing, "If I had *any* Apache, Clete, I'd had you scalped, dangling upside down roasting over a slow-burning fire."

Buzz stopped. He saw me hustling to get dressed. He rubbed his hands together massaging his fingers. (Buzz was always massaging his hands and fingers, I think because of the cold winters and working on machinery all his life.) I could barely make out what he was saying because he now spoke to me facing out the open trailer door, mumbling as he often did.

"S'pose this morning," he said, "I set you up irrigating, then this afternoon you and Clete keep putting out on that fence." He rubbed his chin and cheeks as I buttoned my shirt, my fingers fumbling from the morning chill. "You know how to drive a tractor?" he asked, now picking at a blackened fingernail, looking at the sun coming up over the Wind Rivers.

"It's been a while," I said, tucking in my shirt, almost out of breath.

Buzz stood in the doorway still looking out. "Clete," he yelled behind him. "Get him set up on the Scab Ass." Then he launched off the stoop, adding, "And milk that cow before breakfast."

Pulling on my jeans jacket and baseball cap, I yelled to Clete who I could hear getting dressed, "Okay if I go behind the trailer?"

Clete said, "Free country."

When I came back around after peeing, Clete was outside the trailer brushing his teeth, holding a plastic milk jug half full of water. He spit a foamy white stream then wiped off his mouth saying, "Okay to go anywhere, but if you have to crank a duke" – he pointed with his toothbrush toward the outhouse inside the corral – "go there. The bathroom in the house is for Hope and Buzz and Bit...and company when they come over." He screwed the cap back on the jug. "Let's get a move on, I can smell Hope's biscuits from here." He buttoned his jeans jacket with one hand asking me, "You ever milk a cow?"

I tucked my hair behind my ears, tugged on my cap then jammed my hands in my pockets while rolling on the outsides of my new boots. I winced. "It's been a while."

Clete gave me a tap on the shoulder; he knew where I was coming from. He said he'd take care of it this morning and give me a lesson that evening.

In the house, Hope was cooking breakfast and Buzz was sitting on the couch by the bay window reading an old Jackson paper. My nose perked up: I could smell eggs and bacon frying; coffee brewing; burning pine from the wood stove; fresh cigarette smoke; and odors of the morning dew mixed with sagebrush and the corral that wafted in through the open door.

Clete and I washed up at the kitchen sink.

Hope said, "'Morning, Henry," not turning around, just poking at the bacon. "Coffee's on the island and cups are hanging up."

Clete and I settled in with hot mugs of coffee, warming ourselves by the wood stove. We ate breakfast at the small wooden table beside the stove, a tight but cozy fit, Hope helping us to all we wanted. After breakfast, we all lit up and kicked back a little. I took a deep drag of my Marlboro and held it, slowly releasing the smoke as if I was sighing. The whole setup wasn't anywhere near what I had imagined, but I was warming to it.

Outside in the yard, Clete gave me a driving lesson on the Scab Ass, which was a small Massey Ferguson diesel tractor with some burlap sacks substituting for a long-lost seat cushion. He rounded up irrigating boots for me – think thigh-high waders like you use for duck hunting – and rigged up a shovel down one side of the tractor with some wire. Next he tied a jug of water to the back of the seat with some baling twine. Before he sent me off, he went to the trailer and came back with one of Buzz's old cowboy hats, a sun-faded tan color, splotched with dirt and grease. Clete told me it would keep the sun off my neck and face better than my baseball cap. It was a comfortable fit, and I felt really cool wearing a *real* cowboy's cowboy hat. Clete dug in his pocket and gave me his beat-up Old Timer folding pocketknife because he said I would most likely need a knife around the ranch and in the fields. (I played with that knife all summer, pulling it open, clicking it shut, feeling it wrapped in my palm, sharpening it on a whetstone, cleaning my fingernails, scrapping shit off my boots.) Last, he made sure I was fixed for chew, then spit a stream of reddish brown goo in the dust saying he'd just bought a whole carton in town if I wanted more.

I climbed onto the Scab Ass and carefully puttered across Forty Rod Road to the hayfields. I could see Buzz in the distance walking with a shovel on one shoulder. Humming the theme song from *Green Acres*, I drove around the irrigation ditches that ran through the fields to where Buzz had parked his tractor. It was after 9:00 and the day was warming up so I took off my jacket. Buzz was on top of an embankment, unfurling a big piece of blue canvas that was attached to a long pole. He placed it across the ditch to create a dam. He pointed at some big rocks for me to fetch so he could put them on the canvas to hold it in place. With the dam secure, he told me to sit tight and left to turn the water our way.

The water came in a rush as I stood on top of the ditch and watched it flow against the canvas dam, then out through a cut and onto the field. The water turned the sun-bleached ground dark, and I noticed that some of it was disappearing down a bunch of little holes.

Soon little furry wet heads popped up, looked at me, scampered out, hightailing it to a dry hole.

I turned and said to Buzz, "They're cute."

Buzz looked at me and said, "Prairie dogs. *Git your shovel.*"

I did as I was told and joined Buzz, who was poised with his shovel high over a cluster of holes that were quickly filling up with water. Whenever a head popped out and the prairie dog made a run for it, Buzz popped it.

*Ding.*

I turned, not wanting to watch.

*Ding.*

*Ding.*

When I turned back I saw three flattened prairie dogs and Buzz carving a little valley to a bigger hole, helping the water along. I looked over the field at the rolling water slowly saturating the earth. I could see that wherever the water could get to, grass would grow.

I asked, "What're you doing?" using my shovel to help him scratch away earth and rocks.

Buzz stopped and straightened up. "This is a badger hole," he said, tilting back his hat. "Badgers dig holes near the prairie dogs because they eat 'em. Problem is you can drop a tractor wheel in these holes or a horse can break a leg. But they go deep and hold a lot of water, which is good for the grass" he said banging his shovel on the ground making a vibrating sound. "This goddamn earth's so goddamn hard and rocky the water'll just run off. It needs to soak in." He watched the water run down the hole mumbling softly, "Hopefully we'll flood out one these buggers. They're wily. Harder than hell to kill." Buzz bent over scooping away more dirt. "Hope makes jewelry out of the claws. Goes around your neck."

I understood what Buzz was saying and I appreciated it, just like when Clete had explained to me about cow brands. For sure, what I was doing wasn't quantum physics, but I appreciated Buzz and Clete going out of their way to make me feel comfortable, explain shit so I didn't feel like I had my thumb up my ass all the time. Because of their patience and my desire to learn, I adapted pretty quickly, and was irrigating on my own by the second day. It was a solitary chore for a month – walking the fields, checking on the dams, digging trenches for the water to flow. A lot of time spent spitting tobacco or chewing a long piece of grass, waiting and watching the water do its job. Looking at the mountains. Following the occasional truck cut across Forty Rod Road. Watching the clouds. Thinking about Luke. Throwing rocks at my shovel stuck in the ground twenty yards away.

Thinking about Janie. Wondering what Andy was up to. My parents, too. Emptying out my head. Liking Buzz and Hope and Clete more and more. Writing this story. (Once I knew how to irrigate, I snuck my journal out to the fields by hiding it under the burlap sack on the seat of the tractor. Truth be told, it made the ride a little more comfortable and the time go by faster.)

Now, Buzz stood still with his hands on top of his shovel watching the water spill into a badger hole. After a long silence, he reached into his breast pocket and took out a small cotton pouch with a drawstring along with a pack of rolling papers. Inside of fifteen seconds he'd fingered and rolled the ugliest smoke I'd ever seen, and had it on his bottom lip as he hunted around in his pockets for a matchstick that he swiped up the back of his blue-jeaned thigh, lighting the smoke. He puffed hard, the cigarette burning unevenly and hot. It hung out the side of his mouth as he went to work opening up the neck of another badger hole. A few drags later he put it out by pinching off the coal with his thumb and forefinger, sticking what was left behind his ear.

Buzz pointed to a where the water was rushing down a new cluster of holes and told me to get ready.

*Batter up*, I thought, taking up my position, shovel poised and ready. When the first cute little head surfaced, I swung awkwardly and missed – I think on purpose (I'm not big on killing animals).

Buzz yelled, "Here comes another one."

*Ding.*

I had made my first kill, whispering *Sorry.*

*Ding.*

I nailed another.

*Ding.*

*Ding.*

Two more.

When I saw no more heads popping up, I stopped. I

looked at Buzz who was scooping up carcasses and pitching them into the tall grass by the ditch. I did the same, begging the good Lord for forgiveness with each fling. When Buzz went to clean his shovel in the ditch, I looked around for a spot to pee. I edged over to the tall grass for cover and unzipped. Being a little self-conscious, the flow was slow in coming. I spotted Buzz out of the corner of my eye, also unbuttoning.

I snuck a peek.

*Holy shit.*

I angled away, fingering my snub-nose .38, willing myself to release, faking a whistle.

Clete was right. The man packed a cannon.

# Chapter 6

## FARM ANIMALS * THE OUTHOUSE * TOBACCO

There were three animals on the ranch: Blue, the dog; the nameless three-legged cat; and Buzz's horse, Buddy, who's as calm as a turtle.

Blue is a medium-size cow dog, maybe thirty-five pounds. Buzz takes Blue along when he has to move cattle in the spring and fall and needs help keeping the herd in line. Now that it was summer and the cows are in the mountains, Blue would follow us to the hayfields and lie under the truck, out of the sun, or else just hang back at the yard and be lazy.

When I asked Buzz about his breed, he told me in his raspy sort of way, *whatever jumped over the fence.* He didn't know for sure and neither did the guy selling the pups for five bucks a throw from the back of his pickup outside the Cowboy Bar in Pinedale. Buzz's best guess, judging by the dog's snout and ears and bluish coat, was that he was a mix of Australian shepherd and blue heeler. When I stupidly asked him why he named the dog Blue, Buzz growled at me like he does when I'm not doing something the right way or irritating him by asking too many questions: "'Cause he's blue, goddamnit."

(Buzz wasn't being mean, that's just the way he is. Besides, I appreciated him naming his dog after its color, like he was taking a minimalist approach – that's an artsy-fartsy term I learned from Janie, along with *juxtaposition* and *derivative*.)

Most dogs I know you can suck up to by petting or bribing them with treats, like our black Lab, Winston, who would give you the keys to our house for a Milk-Bone. Not Blue. He couldn't be bought. Blue only followed Buzz. When Blue was in the yard, he would usually be hiding somewhere – behind the wood pile, under the porch, in the shadows of the work shed – waiting for Buzz's whistle, which was a quick, shrill blast (no fingers, all bottom lip and tongue). This was Blue's signal to load up into the truck for a ride, which he could do from anywhere in the yard in under three and a half seconds. Sometimes all Buzz had to do was lower the tailgate and Blue would make a beeline and jump in. There were times when Blue would hear Buzz's whistle coming out of the house and he would beat Buzz to the truck, making the leap – not always cleanly, sometimes ass over tea kettle – into the bed. But he'd always pop up panting, wagging his tail with his feet up on the rail waiting for Buzz to scratch his ears and mumble in his throaty way *Goddamn good dog.*

Once – and Clete confirmed it because he was in the truck – Buzz forgot to whistle and was driving away when they heard a *thump*: Blue had run and hurled himself into the back of the moving pickup. Buzz had turned and said to Clete in disbelief: "*Goddamn dog got some kangaroo in him, too.*"

Besides being his shadow and companion, Blue was also Buzz's alarm system. As long as Blue was in the bed, nobody would consider heisting anything from that truck. And, if you surprised Blue by sneaking up on him, he'd lunge out and growl, make you jump two feet up and three feet back like he did to me one day when I walked by and surprised him. Buzz clearly saw what happened and explained calmly with his hand on my shoulder (I could see he was holding back a grin) that Blue was just protecting the truck, don't take it personally, but be careful sneaking up on him because he might take a chunk out of your arm – like he once did to Asshole Pete.

The three-legged cat belongs to nobody; she just showed up one day about three years ago and never left. She has no name, is colorless, ugly, fat, mangy. She lives in the barn and hobbles to the house for water and food scraps that Hope puts in a bowl. Nobody knows how the cat lost her front right foot – Hope thinks it got caught in a trap – but it doesn't slow her down much when she's darting after mice or after Blue when he's trying to sneak leftovers out of her bowl. The cat hissed at me the first time I got close to her so I never tried to be friends. Hope told me, *She's meaner than a snake, but a good mouser and she doesn't cause any problems.* The cat had found a home and stayed on account of Hope.

Buddy is Buzz's big, black workhorse that any kid would love to ride and hang around with. He's slow and friendly and never gets riled and always has a smile on his face and he listens to you when you're knocking around his stall killing time, talking to him about your problems, and you know he can keep a secret.

## MILKING A COW

I never imagined I'd milk a cow in Wyoming – every day in fact, morning and evening. I thought you only did that in Wisconsin, and more likely with a machine, not your hands. It sounds simple and easy – milking a cow – but it's not. It's a tedious chore that requires strength, stamina, balance and practice. Here's how I explained it to Andy in a letter:

*Here's how it works. There are three participants in milking a cow: me with a pail and stool; the calf who is hungry; and the cow who has four teats and is willing to let me pull on two as long as she is satisfied with her bucket of honeyed oats and her calf is happily suckling on the other two. So the deal is I get two teats and the calf gets two teats. Even Steven; fair enough.*

*Now imagine me balancing my butt on a T-shaped milking stool with a seat no wider than a two-by-four, my forehead pressed against the cow's flank for stability, and I'm squeezing my knees around a large metal milk pail, keeping it steady and tilted toward her udder. And then I start pulling on these things that are like large, soft dill pickles lubricated with this shit called Bag Balm (think sticky Vaseline), aiming the spray between my legs, shaking out my cramping hands, racing to beat the cow before she finishes her oats and wonders what the hell I'm doing back there yanking away like a fourteen-year-old while her calf has already drained his two teats and is bellyaching for more.*

*So the calf butts his head against her udder for more milk and noses over to my side and slurps his slobbery pink tongue on my two teats. Then Clete – that's the cowboy I work with – yells at me: "Sock the calf in the nose, don't let him slobber on your teats." So I do...WHAM-O. Which causes the calf to freak out and start running around the stall. Then the cow goes batshit and begins snorting and pawing at me for whacking her calf. I fall backward off my stool into a pile of piss and manure. The milk pail spills. I jump up not wanting to get trampled. And Clete – who's been coaching me all along – busts a gut laughing, spits tobacco juice at the milk pail, hits it with a ding, assuring me: "Almost had 'er, Squirrel."*

## THE OUTHOUSE

Getting comfortable using an outhouse takes time; in my case it wasn't until the end of my second week that my morning constitutional became rhythmic and routine. After breakfast I'd waltz out to the corral with a steaming cup of coffee, wearing my blue jeans jacket because the mornings are nippy, climb three stairs, fling open the door and leave it open. The outhouse is inside the corral and faces the mountains, so nobody can see you unless they are in the corral or they sneak up you like Clete did a bunch of times, one time surprising me with a *Hey there, Squirrel. Whatcha doing? Shaking hands with the bishop?* And I wasn't, believe me, but his surprise still caused me to fumble my cigarette into my crotch, making me jump up and dance around with my pants down while holding the cup of coffee. Clete loved it. He had to tell everybody at the dinner table and at the bar. Really embarrassing, I know. So what did I do? I rigged up a piece of baling twine to the door and pulled it closed whenever I sensed Clete was in the neighborhood. (I was learning quickly how to jerry-rig everything with anything. That's what you do on a ranch.)

Anyway, once in the outhouse, I'd do an about-face, drop my drawers and back in. I'd settle my lily-white buns down on the cold wooden toilet seat – mercifully shaped and sanded down – trying to ignore the stench coming from below (in fact not much worse than the corrals in front of me). Settling in, I'd stoke up a Marlboro and look out over the hayfields and the foothills toward the Wind Rivers, the morning sun warming my face. It's a beautiful view and that's why I preferred the door open – my thoughts constantly running to Andy and my other guy friends and how I couldn't wait to tell them about this whole experience. So I would sit there, smoke, sip my coffee and then catch up on my outhouse reading: *Popular Mechanics* (March 1965); *National Geographic* – the issue where the sixteen-year-old kid takes off and sails his boat solo around the world (I must have read it thirty times); and the 1972 Sears catalog – the women's underwear section earmarked and slightly soiled.

## TOBACCO

Everybody smokes on the ranch, and Hope smokes the most, but I figure she's alone a lot in the house while we're working, and it's sort of lonely out here which makes you reach for a cigarette more often because you have a lot of time to think. Also, Hope is a big reader; she often leaves a fresh smoke snaking in the ashtray when she's in the middle of a page-turner.

Buzz rolls his own cigarettes because they're cheaper than store-bought smokes and you don't have to worry about having your pack getting smashed or anybody bumming one from you at the bar. Buzz could roll a cigarette faster than I could draw one out of a pack; all it really took was no more than a shake, three twists and a lick. (Clete challenged me one time after dinner to roll a smoke, and I did, making a nice tight cigarette that oddly resembled a joint, which Clete pointed out to Hope and Buzz. They just laughed, but I was embarrassed.)

Clete and I smoked Marlboro out of a box – box instead of soft pack because, as I had learned, a box is harder to crush in your pocket when you're working in the fields. Buzz called them factory cigarettes. Clete called them lung bleeders. I called them heaven. They just tasted so much better out here after a long day putting out (western term for working hard). Most nights after supper we'd settle in outside the trailer with a cold beer and a smoke, our feet up, watching a deep blue dusk turn to an inky black, listening to country music on the radio, looking for shooting stars, thinking about nothing more than the shit on the end of your boot.

# Chapter 7

## BIT

From the time Clete told me, on the ride down from Jackson when I first arrived, that Hope and Buzz had, in his words, a pistol for a daughter, I was hoping she would stop by the ranch so I could check her out. A couple of times, I innocently nosed around before and after meals looking for photographs of her. No luck. So during dinner after I'd been there a few days I nonchalantly said to Buzz and Hope, "Clete said you have a daughter and that she lives in Pinedale."

Hope said, "That's right. Elizabeth...we call her Bit."

I couldn't exactly ask to see a picture of her; that would have been a little creepy and obvious. So I asked how old she was and what she was doing in town. Hope told me she was my age, nineteen, and had been working for a year as a veterinarian's assistant at a clinic south of Jackson – a long commute. When I said she must like animals (duh), Buzz said she was good with horses and had done some barrel racing in high school. That's when I asked, "Wow, cool. Barrel racing. I've never seen barrel racing before. Do you have any pictures?" (Academically, I'm not that strong; but given a complex social problem, I can figure out how to get from point A to point B, even if I have to go through C and maybe D.)

With that, Hope looked at Buzz who was chewing on a chicken wing, and said, "Buzz, will you grab that picture on our bureau of Bit riding Blaze last year in the rodeo? That's my favorite."

Bingo.

Buzz mumbled *Sure*, wiped his hands on his napkin, pushed back from the table, clomped into their bedroom, and came back with a 5x7 black-and-white photograph in a wooden frame. He handed it to me as Clete was saying, "I don't know if I've seen that one."

"This one?" I said turning the picture around and showing it to him across the table.

Clete studied it and said he had not seen it before. I turned the frame around, careful not to smudge the glass. The photo was perfect because it was so simple. Simple because it told a story of a girl who grew up on a ranch on Forty Rod Road in the house where I sat. A little girl who grew up around horses, taking care of horses, now riding one to perfection as she rounded a barrel at a rodeo. Now a young lady with a full, muscular lower body; her torso still and poised leaning into the turn; her face partially obscured under a weathered straw hat but her expression confident; her single black braid floating an inch off her back. If I ever wanted one photo of Elizabeth "Bit" Stifel, this would be it. (And eventually I would end up getting it.)

Occasionally, Bit would stop by on her way back from Jackson after work, and a bunch of times after the haying season began, which was around the second week in July at the Lazy T, she'd come out and help – usually riding a mower and cutting hay – pocketing a little money, which was always handy, she told me, to pay for gas because her commute to Jackson was over a hundred miles round trip. I once asked Clete how she could afford a car on her wages (I knew that a vet's assistant barely made more than a ranch hand) and he told me that Buzz took on extra work in the winter pushing snow around for the county to help her with the payments and insurance.

After Bit's first visit I stayed up unusually late writing in my journal. She had given me a lot to think about concerning my friend Luke and his girlfriend Polly Hamilton, who turned out to be a good friend of Bit's from high school. Small world, huh? Welcome to Wyoming. Here is my journal entry for June 7, my fifth night at the Lazy T:

*Bit came out to ranch tonight while Clete and I were still in the fields. We saw a car coming from 191 and Clete said he knew it was Bit because of all the dust her camel-colored El Camino was kicking up. Apparently, she has a lead foot and drives fast even on Forty Rod Road, which is pretty torn up, but he said she knows the rough spots so well that she can weave around them, using both sides of the road. Anyway, I was anxious to meet the girl in the photograph because I had become infatuated with Buzz and Hope and wanted to meet their cute daughter. And I wanted her to like me. After having dinner with her tonight, I can confirm she is cute, and I think she thought I was okay, even though she made a few cracks about my long hair and being from the East Coast, even though I kept telling her I was from Chicago. Where the conversation really turned interesting was what she told me outside after dinner as we were sitting on the front porch looking out at the Wind Rivers.*

*Bit: "Mom tells me you know Polly Hamilton."*

*Me: "Not really. She was the girlfriend of a friend of mine who died."*

*Bit: "Yes, I know. Polly told me. That was sad – what happened to him. I'm sorry."*

*Me: "It is sad. He was a good guy. We were friends for four years at school."*

*Bit: "That's what Polly said, that the two of you were roommates back East."*

Me: "We were. How do you know Polly?"

Bit: "High school and riding – we barrel raced against each other in high school. I wish I saw her more, but in the summer she's up at the camp in the mountains on Silver Dollar Lake. Now I'm working in Jackson and she's in college. Anyhow, accidents like that are hard to explain to folks."

Me (intrigued): "What do you mean?"

Bit: "The Hamiltons were worried about the reputation of the camp and Luke's family." (Here Bit looked down as if she knew she'd made a misstep.)

Me (coaxing):"What did you hear happened?"

Bit (matter-of-factly): "That he died rock climbing."

Me: "Where exactly?"

Bit: "Polly told me it was just north of the lake. She said there's an easy climb there where they teach the kids."

Me: "An easy climb where they teach kids, and he fell?"

Bit (dodging): "Did you talk with his family?"

Me: "About the accident?"

Bit: "Yes."

Me: "No. Nobody really talked about it. Nobody wanted to. And I didn't want to pry. But it was like there was an elephant in the room at the funeral."

Bit: "No wonder."

Me: "Why?"

Bit (abruptly): "It was not an accident."

Me (focused): "What do you mean not an accident? Who told you that? Polly?"

Bit: "Are you going to see Polly?"

Me (sitting up): "Yes, as soon as I can. Why?"

Bit (sitting back): "Good."

(That's all she said: Good.)

(Period.)

I eased off of my questioning because I didn't want to come across too strong and be thought of as a jerk. But this *was the main reason I had come out here in the first place, right? To get to the bottom of what happened. And I was getting somewhere. That's why I let our discussion cool for a moment, instead asking her about growing up on the ranch and what it's like to be a vet's assistant. Flirting with her a little; getting to know her. I asked her about Buzz and Hope, where they were from and how they met. She said her mother's family was originally from Minnesota (Norwegian stock and she an only child) and that Hope's maternal grandfather was Lakota Sioux (not Cherokee, as Clete had said). Hope's parents had originally been sodbusters in South Dakota who before the Depression migrated to Jackson to start a ranch and raise cattle. Hope had told Bit it was a hand-to-mouth existence, but that that's the only kind of life they knew.*

*Buzz grew up down in Greeley, Colorado, the fourth in a family of thirteen, and came to Jackson to get out of the house and to cowboy and rodeo. He met Hope at a rodeo in 1950, when she was 19 and he was 20. They were married three months later. The rodeo is also where Hope and Buzz both met Sonny Skinner – he was riding broncs alongside of Buzz. Bit intimated that from the start Sonny had had his eye on Hope, but Hope had her eye on Buzz. Bit said she was born after Buzz and Sonny came back in 1953 from serving in Korea and after her parents had homesteaded the Lazy T.*

*When Bit turned the conversation to me, asking me about my parents, then my first year at college, the conversation took an unexpected turn that made me question more than ever how Luke died.*

*Bit: "Did you like your freshman year of college?"*

Me (lying): "It was okay."

*Bit: "Polly just finished up her first year, too. Down in Laramie. She and Joe are having fun being together."*

*Me (alarmed): "Joe? Who's Joe?"*

*Bit: "Joe Alexander. He lives a few miles from here, just south of Cora. He and Polly have been going steady since their junior year in high school. He's a cowboy on the University of Wyoming rodeo team. It's a good bet they'll get hitched."*

*Me (taken aback): "Married? Really?"*

*Bit: "Why?"*

*Me (naively): "Because I'd thought Luke and Polly were going steady."*

*Bit (shaking her head): "No, don't think so."*

*Me: "Did Polly ever mention Luke being her boyfriend?"*

*Bit: "No. Just said he had a crush on her. Came out here as a camper during the summers and they became good friends. But nothing happened. I don't think. She said he was good looking and a nice guy...but..."*

*Me: "But what?"*

*Bit: "She said he was a nice guy and all, but you know... he was a little weird about her. Sort of suffocating, is what she told me. Couldn't leave her alone."*

*Me: "Do you know if Polly ever told Luke about Joe Alexander, that they were going out together?"*

*Bit (sincere, but serious): "I don't know. I really am sorry about your friend, Hank, but you'll have to ask Polly more about it when you see her. She knows."*

What Bit had said – *She knows* – was enough for me to be pretty sure that Luke had been responsible for his own death. I had thought about that possibility, of course, especially after the messed up funeral with Luke's uptight and repressed family acting as if *they didn't know* what happened, just that Luke died rock climbing. That would make sense if you were trying to brush something under the carpet like suicide.

During the rest of my stay at the Lazy T, Bit and I innocently flirted with each other at the ranch and a couple of times in town at the bar. I didn't make any moves on her and she wasn't exactly trying to get me in the hayloft, but there was something there, something innocent and fun and not worth spoiling. We figured out quickly enough how to kid each other about our different lifestyles and upbringings. She couldn't believe I could play golf (and was actually good at it), and I couldn't believe she could shoe a horse. I loved that she was a western girl in her father's mold and had the keen instincts of her mother. She liked that I enjoyed working with her parents and pretending to be a ranch hand. The only times we ever touched were when we danced at the Cowboy Bar and later when she gently hugged and kissed me good-bye before I went home (now more than just friends). She also kidded me about my well-worn baseball cap and anyone would name a team the Cubs. Bit wasn't stupid; she had me pegged as a novelty that would soon disappear just like all the Eastern dudes did. And I didn't want to start anything that would screw up my time at the ranch. That was more important to me. But it was still nice snuggling into my sleeping bag at night and kicking Janie out.

# Chapter 8

### FIRST TRIP TO TOWN ✳ SONNY SKINNER ✳ DOROTHY FARNSWORTH

By my third week at the ranch my hands were scratched, rubbed raw, sunburned, mosquito bitten and scabbed over. Clete showed me how to cut off a piece of Hope's aloe plant for the cuts and burns and how to rub tobacco spit on the back of my hands to keep the mosquitoes off and stop the itching. Everything we did had something to do with machinery – trucks, tractors, mowers, rakes, balers – and figuring out how to fix it, which meant our hands and fingers were always getting in the way and taking a beating. Quickly, I learned the difference between a standard screwdriver and one with a Phillips head. How to remove a sparkplug and change oil. Flush a radiator. Pull off a timing belt. Change a tire. I may not have been riding the range punching dogies like I thought would be, but this was just as good because it was macho gear-head type of shit that I could brag about when I got back to school.

One morning, just before dinner, I busted a U-joint on my hay rake – not my fault, things like that happen all the time on a ranch. And because haying was to begin in a week and

I wanted to be prepared, I'd asked Clete to give me lessons so I'd be ready. Sort of like reading ahead in class, which is something I never did. At the noontime meal, Buzz told me he didn't have any more U-joints, so he'd have to make a run to town this afternoon. Hope gave Buzz a sour look that told me something was up. (Clete saw it too, later describing it to me this way: "Squirrel, did you see that look on her face when Buzz said he'd have to take off for town in the middle of the day? I swear you couldn't have pulled a pin out of her ass with a tractor.")

After thinking about it awhile, giving her Marlboro 100 three taps on the ashtray, Hope said, "Take Henry with you."

Buzz swiped the ash off his cigarette with his pinkie, complaining like she was pestering him. "Why do you want me to do that?"

Something was brewing, the air between them thicker than when my parents would stop talking at the dinner table after arguing about my mother's younger brother, Homer, a philandering drunk who borrowed money from my father, cheated at golf, couldn't hold a job and wore loud sport jackets.

Hope said, "Think on it, Buzz. When's he going to get to town? You may as well take him along so he can wash his clothes."

She was right. I was a mess. My work clothes were long overdue for a spin. Wearing them three weeks straight had numbed me to what clean clothes felt like or looked like...and it really hadn't bothered me.

Hope took a deep drag from her cigarette and powered the smoke out of her nostrils like a dragon. "Buzz, I need you to pick me up a twenty-five-pound bag of potatoes at Farsons, two boxes of baking soda, four loaves of bread, aluminum foil and two boxes of matches." She took another hit of smoke and blew it out, "You remember all that?"

Buzz nodded, mumbling back her grocery order. He went for a toothpick, pushed back from the table so he could cross his legs, then dug at his teeth. We sat in silence for more than two minutes – I know because I timed it by the second hand floating around the face of the electric clock above the stove. After Hope stubbed out her cigarette, Buzz stood, palmed his hat from the counter, opened the door and walked out. I looked at Hope as she moved to clear the plates, dumping them into the sink, turning on the tap, her expression dank as the dishwater. Clete slid a toothpick into his breast pocket and followed Buzz. I hesitated, not wanting to be rude. I inched slowly toward the door. Hope put her hand in the water then squeezed out some green goo from a bottle of Palmolive, swishing the water to make it soapy.

"Henry," she said, not looking up, strands of hair falling over her face, "make sure Buzz doesn't forget my groceries."

"Sure thing."

In the trailer, Clete and I rounded up our dirty clothes and jammed them in a big canvas bag with a drawstring that Hope gave the ranch hands for runs to town. I swung the bag into the back of the truck – careful not to hit Blue, who was already there – imitating an Olympic hammer-thrower, making Clete laugh. In the cab, Buzz carefully turned the ignition key like it was the first time. I buckled up, then saw he hadn't, so I slipped mine off. Through the bay window I spotted Hope washing dishes, her head down and shoulders slumped.

On Forty Rod, well past Eleanor's house, Buzz moaned, slowed, downshifted. I looked up (I'd been daydreaming about taking off Janie's bra again). Ahead was a big dip in the road where three horses were drinking from a small pool of rainwater. They pricked up their ears and swished their tails, not budging. Buzz rolled to a stop on the decline in front of the horses. I would've laid on the horn. Instead, Buzz turned off the engine and pressed down the parking brake. He curled his hands around the steering wheel, gazing out at the horses like he had planned all along to come here and watch them take a drink.

When Buzz talks, he pushes out what he wants to say, then pauses.

Push...

Pause...

Push...

Pause....

He uses words like he'd paid for them. He also lets them breathe.

Buzz said, "Those are Sonny Skinner's horses...

"Buys and sells 'em to the dude ranches 'round here...

"Lives there," Buzz said, nodding toward a dingy red shack with a porch and four windows about fifty yards ahead, set back from the road. To one side I could see an aluminum watering tank, a bunch of salt licks, two falling-down corrals and an outhouse. A bare yellow bulb shone above a punched-out screen door. No truck around. Nobody home.

Buzz pulled out his "makings," quick-twisted a smoke and stuck it on his bottom lip. He swiped a match across the dashboard, leaving a curvy white scratch next to dozens of others. He sucked in and blew smoke in the direction of Sonny's house.

"I got after Sonny about fencing his place...

"Forty Rod ain't the same, I told him...

"Not like when we homesteaded...

"But he don't listen."

I stared at the house imagining what this Sonny guy looked like. The horses clomped around and put their heads down for another drink.

"Road commissioner finally come down on him when one of Emerson's logging trucks hit one." Buzz rubbed his eyes with his thumbs, his cigarette resting on his bottom lip. "Almost killed him."

"The horse?" I asked, now tuning in to the story.

Buzz dusted the ash out the window with his pinky. "No. The driver."

I was confused. "What happened to the horse?"

"Sonny had to put her down...

"Horse wasn't worth a damn with Peterbilt stamped on her belly...

"Sonny wanted Emerson to pay, claimed the plug was his most prized thoroughbred." Buzz's eyes twinkled.

I sat as still as a fish in water – this was the most Buzz had said to me in two and a half weeks. He was opening up and had my rapt attention. I asked, "Didn't Emerson know the horse was just a hay-burner." (I had heard that expression from Clete and had been dying to use it.)

"Sure. Hell, we all knew." Buzz inspected his smoke, as it was burning hot down one side. "So Sonny hauled her away." Buzz chuckled. "Buried the evidence way back of his place with my front-end loader."

"So after that how was he going to prove that the horse was his prized thoroughbred?"

Buzz rolled what was left of his smoke between his fingers, the paper, tobacco and embers drifting to the ground outside his window. "Sonny had it figured...

"Had a photograph of him alongside a good-looking filly taken at a dude ranch...

"Had Hope scratch on the bottom, 'Me and Buttercup, My Favorite Thoroughbred, 1976'...

"Horse wasn't even the same color...

"And Snook Ewing....

"Who'd been driving the rig...

"Couldn't swear what the nag looked like because it was dark and he'd come up on the horse quick...

"Problem was Sonny told everybody at the bar, even the judge. Claimed no one in the state would rule against a cowboy on disability whose prized horse was run down."

The horses started to move away from the road, their flanks leisurely bumping up and down.

I asked, "Why's Sonny on disability?"

"Rodeo accident," Buzz replied. "Got kicked." He pointed to the side of his head.

"And he's okay?"

"Mostly. He's got a small dent – he'll show it to you."

Buzz started the engine, then took off the parking brake. We drove up the far side of the dip.

"How long ago was that?" I asked, sitting back, now following two stories.

"'57. Down in Big Piney...

"Had a tough draw...

"Got hung up in a stirrup...

"Then got throwd and kicked hard."

Again, I asked, "And he's all right?"

"There's a few who think he's nuttier than a shithouse rat," Buzz said rolling up his window. "'Specially when he's drinking...

"Which is most of the time...

"Lucky he ain't a vegetable. Doc Evans said it could've gone either way."

I returned to Sonny's scheme: "Did Emerson pay Sonny for his horse?"

Buzz chuckled. "No...Emerson never cowed to Sonny. Told him his horse almost killed Snook...

"Snook kissed the windshield pretty good...

"Flattened his nose so everybody in town could see...

"You talk to Snook now and he sounds like a busted pump...

"Hard to make out what he's saying through his wheezing...

"Wife told Hope he's hell to bunk with...

"Hope said if she was his lawyer she'd have gotten his wife on the stand crying to the judge that her life's ruined because she has to sleep two counties away with earmuffs."

Buzz chuckled, scratching the stubble on his cheek, making a sound like coarse sandpaper on rough wood. I did the same – rubbed my cheek – but came away with nothing. Like velvet buffing silver.

I said, "Sounds like Hope would make a good lawyer."

"Good horse sense," he said. "Knows when to hold 'em and when to fold 'em."

"So what finally happened between Sonny and Emerson?"

"Sonny caved. Never filed suit. Him and Emerson called it a draw and got drunk at the Cowboy, mostly on Emerson's nickel, is what I heard...

"That happens a lot around here. There's a dust-up then it settles...

"After a time nobody can rightly remember."

We rolled to the blacktop of 352 and stopped. The sun was high in a crystal blue Wyoming sky with wavy, wispy clouds. Buzz bumped his hat back and looked left...then right...thinking about something, no cars around as far as the eye could see. What he'd just shared with me gave me a rush just like when Clete gave me the lowdown about the soap opera at the Lazy T. My entire freshman year I never felt connected to a class or took an interest in any book – that's why I never took notes. It all seemed remote and foreign and useless and stupid. But not this. This was real. I'd been looking for a story, a narrative, something to latch onto so I'd feel like I wasn't just bobbing around in the ocean. I felt a surge of confidence like you do when you really like a teacher and his class, and you want to participate because he's turned you on to something.

"Buzz?" I said in a confident tone.

"Whaa...?" he mumbled back at me.

"Don't forget your blinker," I said, trying to sound like him. "Clete told me the sheriff's a real hard-ass."

From the corner of my eye I could see his teeth twinkling under the shadow of his black hat. He thumbed the red bulb of his nose. He looked both ways again then flipped his blinker and drawled, "Smart-ass kid."

What he said – *Smart-ass kid* – and how he said it, was heaven to me, like welcome to the club. I'd passed a test. I was in. From that moment on I felt a part of it.

On the outskirts of Pinedale, where the speed limit drops from fifty-five to twenty-five faster than a safe falling four floors, Buzz warned me: "Gotta be careful 'round here. Sheriff likes to hide between them semis in Johnson's Trucking...

"Got one of them new speed guns."

Buzz imitated a women's voice: "*Buzz, you was going thirty in a twenty-five. Look here.* Then he shows you the ass end of this gun with red numbers that prove it."

"That's the sheriff?" I confirmed, craning my neck around to see a brown police cruiser tucked back between two big rigs like a crab in a hole waiting to spring.

"Yep," Buzz said. "He's the law in town. Tough job with all the roughnecks working the oil rigs south of here moving in...

"Hired his boy to help him."

I said, "Pete, right?"

Buzz nodded, the truck now puttering along at twenty-five.

I said, "Clete told me Pete used to work for you. You had to run him off." I repeated what Clete told me because it sounded funny. "Told me Pete Farnsworth was dumber than a fence post, couldn't find his ass with his hands in his back pocket."

Buzz ignored me like I wasn't even beside him in the truck. He turned into the Napa store and nosed in and parked between a tandem-wheeled Chevy with its bed full of square hay bales and a dusty Ford Bronco with Idaho plates and a bumper sticker that read *Gun Control Means Using Both*

*Hands.* Buzz shut down the engine and went into the store. I followed, feeling foolish, a full five steps behind.

Inside, I found Buzz at the parts counter rolling a U-joint in his hands. He asked the clerk, "This the last one you got?" putting it back in the box and closing it up.

"Afraid so," the clerk said taking a pen from behind his ear and writing out a bill of sale on a metal box. "That's it until after Rendezvous. Overnight won't ship unless they got a half-trailer full." He turned the box around to sign, then gave Buzz a receipt asking, "You riding Buddy in the Rendezvous celebration?" (This is a huge party that happens at the end of July where the whole town dresses up, parades around and gets drunk.)

Buzz folded his receipt: "Got to…

"Only day of the year Buddy gets to drink legal at the Cowboy."

The clerk filed his copies of the receipt, then said to Buzz, "You know, Sheriff Farnsworth's been telling everybody in town that anybody rides a horse in a bar this year he's running them in."

Buzz inspected the U-joint box, thinking for a moment, then mumbled with a wide grin, "Goddamn…is that right?" He opened the box and took out the U-joint, then tried to put his fist in the box, like he was sizing it. "How you suppose Buddy's gonna fit in one of them puny cells?"

Buzz and I drove down Main Street to the Laundromat, set the laundry to tumbling and then went on to Farsons for groceries. On our way back through town, Buzz said, rubbing his chin and cheeks with his free hand, "There's Sonny's truck. Let's go have a beer." We parked in front of the Cowboy Bar alongside an algae-green truck speckled with white spots, a mess of straw, burlap sacks and mixed tools in the bed. On the truck's mashed-up bumper was a weathered and peeling *America, Love It or Leave It* sticker; a side mirror was still attached on the driver's side, but badly cracked.

Without a word, Buzz reached across in front of me and pulled out a bottle of Aqua Velva aftershave lotion from the glove compartment. After a twist, a splash, and a slap, he replaced the bottle and stepped out, heading for the barroom door. I slowly got out and went to the back of the truck for a jug of water, poured some into Blue's bowl, then scratched the dog's ears and neck – his tongue hanging out dripping, his coat shiny and hot – as I looked up and down Main Street. Not much to Pinedale, Wyoming. No traffic lights, three bars, one restaurant, one greasy spoon, the Western Shop, Wind River Sports, a Sinclair gas station at the end of town next to Farsons general store and the Laundromat.

Above my head was a neon sign of a cowboy on a bucking horse. At night it would glow red with the cowboy waving his hat over his head. Floating in the bar's windows were neon Budweiser and Coors signs; and through a rickety screen door came the sound of Willy Nelson crooning. I strolled into the bar, trying to imitate Buzz's walk, and was immediately assaulted by a cocktail of bar smells and B.O. Around the large rectangular room hung western relics in shadow boxes too numerous to mention. On the right was a pool table; in the back was a dance floor and a small bandstand, and off to one side were the restrooms, marked *Standers* and *Sitters*. To my left, running the length of the room, was the bar, near the end of which Buzz now sat, hat off, talking to the only other person in the place.

Sonny Skinner.

Plopped down like a two hundred-pound-plus sack of grain, his hands clasped together and head slightly bowed, Sonny appeared to be either praying or taking a nap. A cigarette burned in an ashtray beside a pack of Camel straights. He wore weathered jeans and a short-sleeve cotton shirt with watery brown pit stains. His forearms and biceps were the same circumference, just one continuous girder of hairy flesh that strained against his shirt. With a strong chin, chiseled head and thinning sandy hair, he was Robert Duvall's larger, older brother. (I was curious about that dent in his head that Buzz mentioned, but was always too afraid to ask him about it.) His beat-up cowboy boots were enormous. (Size thirteen, is what Clete told me. He also told me Sonny was a big, gruff bear, harmless until you spooked him.)

I eased in next to Buzz, hearing Sonny gargle, "Buzzy Stifel, what took you so long getting here?"

Buzz said, "I'd been here sooner if I wasn't slowed down on Forty Rod by your horses...

"When you gonna fence 'em, Sonny?"

Sonny took a poke of his Camel then stubbed it out with an index finger the size of a big toe. He rubbed the smoke from his eyes, irritated. "Buzz, you sound like that govment man...what's his name?"

"Hawkins?" Buzz said, looking around.

Sonny spat out, "*Pissant!*"

Buzz reached for Sonny's pack of Camels. "Mind?"

Sonny thumbed over his dented Zippo. "Knock yourself out."

Buzz lit up, fingered a piece of tobacco from his tongue and tapped his cigarette on an ashtray. Looking around again, he asked, "Where's the bartender?"

Sonny smirked. "She saw your truck. Went to put on her war paint. Told me to watch the bar."

*Oh shit, was I hearing right?* She, *I was sure*, was Dorothy. *And Aqua Velva mixed with war paint spelled trouble.* Now I understood what Hope had been so upset about when Buzz said he wanted to go to town and why she wanted me to tag along. I needed a drink and a smoke – *quick*. Since Sonny was in charge of the bar, I said to him, "Can I get a beer?"

Sonny looked around. "Sure...cost you a buck. *Who are you?*"

I put down two one-dollar bills, told him my name, said

I worked for him – pointing to Buzz – and asked Buzz what he wanted.

"Whatcha getting?" Buzz asked.

"Coors," I replied.

Buzz nodded. "Same."

As I stepped around the open end of the bar, Sonny barked at me, "While you're back there, junior, grab me another." I slid back the heavy metal cover of a cooler and dug out three bottles of Coors, popping the tops off with a bottle opener on the side. I slid Buzz and Sonny their beers, then drained half of mine. I asked them if they knew where I could find a pen so I could write down the stuff that I'm writing down now. Sonny said to check in the drawer underneath the cash register. I pulled it open, gently rummaged around for a moment or two, fingering through some papers and tools with no luck. Shutting the drawer and looking up, I found myself face to face with a woman with her hands on her hips giving me a what-the-hell-are-you-doing-here look.

Dorothy Farnsworth.

She'd snuck up on me; and I could see out of the corner of my eye that Sonny and Buzz thought it was funny.

I quickly sized her as petite and pretty in a simple gingham dress with straps that showed bare shoulders and good boobs and other curves. I figured her needle close to fifty, her features slightly stretched but still fine – feminine with a tensile strength. On her small feet were white tennis shoes she'd have been okay wearing on a sailboat, and her full head of brown hair was pinned up and back with combs like the ones my grandmother used. Around her neck, on a chain, hung a pair of cat-eye glasses. Her makeup was fresh and she gave off a nice scent of *eau de* something. When she asked me what I was doing, she sounded like a schoolmarm, suspicious but not scolding. I told her I was looking for a pen. Moving closer to me, she glanced back at Buzz and Sonny saying in a conspiratorial tone, "You ask them?"

I whispered back, "No ma'am." (I don't normally say ma'am, it just came out because I remembered she was from the South and I thought she'd like it, which she did.)

A twinkle lit her eye. She slyly winked, which made me relax. "Wouldn't done any good," she said. "Men can't find anything unless there's hair around it." Then she handed me a Bic pen that was beside the cash register. "This'll work."

"Thank you," I said, scooting back around to my stool in the front of the bar, now scribbling on a napkin the first thing that came to mind: *She was a roughneck in a debutante's body.*

Dorothy Farnsworth faced the three of us and addressed Sonny like Miss Kitty on *Gunsmoke*. "All those drinks paid for? You know Courtenay counts his beers, and they're for sure not coming out of *my* wages." (Courtenay was the owner of the Cowboy Bar – had been for twenty years – and was also the judge and jury for many of the minor squabbles that happened around town.)

Sonny pushed the three dollars her way. "All there, Dorothy. You can count it."

She rang the cash register, head down. When she looked up again, she wasn't looking at Sonny or me. I wasn't feeling great about this. What I was feeling was complicit and traitorous: I hadn't bargained being part of a tryst when we first set out for town to get a new U-joint. Dorothy caught me staring at her as I was thinking about Hope's arms elbow deep in dirty dishwater. In the time it takes to pop the top off a Coors, Dorothy switched from Miss Kitty to Miss Scarlett, addressing me in the southern lilt of ladies having tea, saying sweetly, extending her hand daintily across the bar, "I'm so sorry. You must be Hank."

"Yes, ma'am," I said, gently taking her hand.

"Dorothy Farnsworth," she replied. "A pleasure to meet you."

We held hands for a couple seconds too long. That's when Buzz, looking down at his boots and rubbing his hands, said in his raspy way, "That washing's about ready to dry. Take the truck and I'll meet you back here in about an hour."

# Chapter 9

## LETTER FROM JANIE

The mail wasn't delivered to the Lazy T; it had to be picked up at the Cora store, which we did every three or four days. Just after the Fourth of July, even though I'd written Janie a number of times since I got here, I'd not heard from her. Nothing. (I guess I was still hopeful – and more than a little naive.) Anyway, after dinner on a day there'd been a morning cloudburst – Clete described it as raining harder than a cow pissing on a flat rock – I scrawled a quick letter to my parents and asked Clete if he would drive me to Cora so I could mail it; that I would make it worth his while by buying him a Coke. Clete said sure and Buzz okayed it, telling us to take Blue along.

We pulled out with Blue running around the bed of the pickup, barking, then we barreled out onto Forty Rod. A fine drizzle misted the windshield, but the sun was beginning to break through. As we neared Sonny's place, Clete slowed for the dip in the road – no horses around this time – and gave a toot as we passed the house. Sonny's truck was parked in front and the yellow porch light was on. After we reached the 352 blacktop, and with no cars in sight, as always, Clete gunned it, devouring the three miles to Cora in no time. I looked back at Blue through the rear window; he was squinting with his ears blown back and his fur lightly dusted with the swirling drizzle.

When we reached Cora, Clete slowed, not signaling to turn (what was the use out here?). He angled across the highway, bumped along twenty-five or so yards of washed-out gravel, and parked in front of a sign that said Cora Store and Post Office. I gave Clete some money, and while he went in to post my letter and buy two Cokes, I stayed outside with Blue, not wanting to get my hopes up or let Clete know that I was dying for a letter from a girl. I pulled down the tailgate and sat facing some corrals and chutes across the road that were used to load cows, watching the clouds break low over the mountains. It was still cool from the rain, so I kept my jeans jacket buttoned up. Blue came over, sniffed, then sat down next to me.

When I heard *Lookie what we got here*, I turned to see Clete backing out of the store's screen door with a Coke in each hand and a letter sticking out of his breast pocket. He came and sat beside me, handing over a tall cold bottle of Coke with condensation dripping down the sides. He wiped off his hand and carefully withdrew the letter from his pocket. He held it up to the sky, examining it like a doctor would an X-ray: "Looks like cooter to me."

I bit my lip, sipped my Coke, not rising to the bait.

Clete rubbed the letter between his thumb and forefinger. "Feels like cooter."

I continued trying to look disinterested. I stood, cleared my nose and throat, and spat a wad of phlegm as far as I could. I sat back down and looked up at the sky. "Looks to be clearing soon," I said. "Maybe we should get back and put out on that fence."

Clete wasn't buying it. He ran the letter under his nose

like a fine Cuban. "Smells like cooter, too." He gave it another whiff. "I wonder who it's from."

I offered up a possibility, "Maybe my mother." I slipped my Coke between my knees, readying for a grab.

"I...don't...think...so," Clete said slowly. "The handwriting's feline – I can see that." He held the letter at arm's length, pretending to have bad eyesight, then brought it up closer to his eyes. "It says here it's addressed to the Long Dicked Stud at the Lazy T."

I gazed away at the mountains and mumbled, "Must be talking about Buzz."

"No," Clete said confidently, showing me the letter. "There's these three funny sticks with lines on the top and bottom, that means the third." He pointed at me: "That'd be you."

"You're sure?" I said in mock surprise.

"Sure as I'm sitting here jawing with you." Clete held the letter at arm's length again jabbing at the return address. "Says here from Jane Somebody from Somewhere in Ohio –"

My arm shot out. I grabbed the letter out of Clete's hand. Carefully, so as not to tear it.

The letter was wafer thin – not a good sign. If it had been fat, I wouldn't have opened it then and there; I would have waited until later, lying on my bed, reading it over and over by the light of Hope's lamp.

Clete dared me: "Open it, Squirrel. Let's hear what she has to say."

All right, I thought. I wanted to show I was better than whatever the letter had to say and the girl who wrote it – to act as if I didn't give a shit. I tore off one end, blew it open and shook out a piece of paper you'd barely blow your nose on. From the side of my mouth I read the whole thing to Clete, top to bottom. To limit the pain, I'll paraphrase what she wrote:

*Dear Hank,*
 *How are you? I am fine. I really like you but you're sort of a loser. Believe me when I say it's me. Take care, and I hope you find what you're looking for. Wherever you are.*
 *XO,*
 *Janie*

Say what you will about Jane Stewart Wallace from Perrysburg, Ohio, with her slinky body, long dirty blond hair, great breasts, and adorable nose – she's honest. I folded the letter over and shoved it in my back pocket so I could read it again a couple of times before putting it in my journal with my other notes, now officially part of my Wyoming story.

 Clete and I just sat on the tailgate for a while, finishing our Cokes and not talking. Finally, Clete stood up, put his hands on his back just above his rump and did a slight backbend looking up at the sky. He said, "Squirrel...weather's breaking. What'd you say we mosey on back and put out on the fence for the afternoon." He tapped me on the shoulder. Knew where I was coming from.

# Chapter 10

### CONVERSATION WITH HOPE ✳ CONFRONTATION WITH FARNSWORTH ✳ NEWS OF LUKE'S DEATH

On the day I was to see Luke's girlfriend, Polly Hamilton, I knocked off work at three in the afternoon and went into the house to clean up. Hope was sitting on the couch reading *One Flew Over the Cuckoo's Nest*. I asked if it was okay if I took a shower. She folded down the corner of a page of the book and stood up, brushing ashes from her jeans. She removed her reading glasses and said, "Buzz said you're taking his truck to see Polly Hamilton up at their camp."

I fidgeted, rolling on the outside of my boots, wringing my clean clothes in my hands. I asked, "Is that all right?"

"What time will you be back?"

I told her I'd be back by eight, before dark.

She gave me a snake-eyed look, but didn't mean any harm; she just wanted to know: "You know where the turnoff to the camp is? It's easy to miss."

"South of town," I answered, "about a mile past the Sinclair station on the left is what Polly told me this morning when I called her from Eleanor's. She said from the road it's about a half hour and to be careful because the road is steep in parts and washed out.

Hope said, "That's right. The sign used to say Silver Dollar Lake but it's all beaten up, so look for a white arrow." Hope sat back down and gazed out the window, following Clete's progress cutting hay on his mower. "The Hamiltons run a good operation," she said. "Always have."

I didn't know what to say so I said, "*Really?*"

Hope turned and looked at me standing there. I was certain she was thinking about something that had to do with me. Frozen, watching her look me over for a few seconds, I thought back about what Buzz had told me, how he thought Hope would have made a good lawyer. I sensed she knew what was on your mind and how to size you up while staying two steps ahead. She said, "I'm sorry you were surprised to hear about Polly and Joe Alexander."

"That's okay," I said cutting her off, uncomfortable with the subject. I looked down at my boots, wishing for the conversation to be over.

But Hope kept talking, now tracking Buzz's progress on the baler. "I knew Polly and your friend...what's his name?"

"Luke," I said. "Luke Danforth."

"I had heard that Polly and Luke were...good friends, too. I called Polly after Buzz received your letter to ask her about you." Hope paused. "It must have been confusing for you."

"It was," I said, opening up a little to her, "and it still is." I was beginning to understand that Hope knew more than she was willing to tell me. I said, "Luke's death was one of the reasons I came to Wyoming." Here I stammered, "To see Polly...his girlfriend...at least that's what I thought. And see their camp. See where Luke spent his summers. See where he died." I didn't say *figure out how he died*, but that is what I was thinking.

Hope said, "It's damn hard losing a good friend so young. I'm sorry."

I didn't want to talk about that – losing a friend –

because I was still very much lost by it all. I gently steered the conversation away, asking Hope how she knew Polly and her family.

She said, "I've known Polly's family a long time. Wyoming's a big state but it's like a small town. And Polly and Bit, as you know, went to high school together. Don't see the Hamiltons much between spring and fall because they're up there at that camp and very busy, and we're the same down here. We're more likely to see them in the wintertime because then they live in town.

"Polly's grandfather, Corey, began outfitting back in the late 1940s, leading pack trips during the summer and hunting trips in the fall. Then he started the wilderness camp with his two sons, Charlie and Willy, about fifteen years ago. Both his boys went to Laramie and graduated with degrees in education. Polly's following in their footsteps is what I understand. Corey never went to college. He was just tough as nails...one of the last mountain men around here worth a warm bucket of spit. Self-educated. Old school. But always sweet to those kids." Hope looked up at me. "He'd ask Buzz up to the camp to sing cowboy songs to the kids...make them less homesick." She looked away. "Outfitting and running a wilderness camp is hard work...harder even than ranching. It was sad when Corey couldn't saddle up anymore." Hope looked back out the window again. "I don't think he knew what to do with himself. Took to drinking. Then when that didn't work he put a shotgun in his mouth. Did it on April Fool's Day." She turned back around with what appeared to be a sinister grin on her face. "Except he wasn't foolin'."

I shifted from one foot to the other, caught a little off guard by her dark humor, and said, "I guess he wasn't a practical joker."

"No," she said, "not when you eat two barrels of twelve-gauge. That's the way they did it back then. Put yourself down or have somebody help you if couldn't do it by yourself."

I remembered the photograph of Ernest Hemingway, head down in a cap with a snow-white beard, kicking a beer can down a road in Idaho soon after he was diagnosed with cancer, before he killed himself. "Like Hemingway," I said, offering what I thought was a scholarly connection Hope would appreciate.

Hope agreed. "I admired him. Knew when to fold 'em."

Out on Forty Rod a pickup pulling an Airstream trailer slowed and picked its way around a pothole. Hope watched the vehicle for a moment, and as she shooed me away she said, "Go take a shower," she said. "Get back before dark or I'll burn your eyebrows. Those mountain roads are tricky and not well marked."

I quickly cleaned up and headed out, babying Buzz's truck down Forty Rod, feeling Hope's binoculars boring a hole in the back of my neck. As I neared the outskirts of Pinedale I slowed down, making certain I was under the speed limit, remembering what Buzz told me about Farnsworth and his radar gun. Sure enough, there was the brown nose of a cop car lurking between two big semis as I passed Johnson's Trucking. When I next checked the rearview mirror, my heart skipped a beat. The cruiser had pulled out and was now tailing me. The driver – and I knew who it was – was hatless with a big square head and jaw, Wayne Newton-like hair, silver reflective glasses and a big sour puss.

*Farnsworth.*

He followed me the whole quarter mile of Main Street. I knew what he was doing. He was sending a signal to the Lazy T. At the far end of town he turned off and spun around in the Sinclair station, kicking up gravel and dust. His way of telling me *he* was the boss in town. Clete had been dead-on about Farnsworth: he had it out for Buzz and the Lazy T; and worse, he was playing with a deck stacked in his favor, being sheriff and with his son Asshole Pete as his partner in the game. I didn't like it at all.

South of town, I clocked one mile and turned off and headed east into the mountains just past an old piece of wood painted white and hacked into the shape of an arrow pointing the way to Hamiltons' camp. I rumbled across a cattle guard and snaked up a treeless, rutted road passing boulders the size of Volkswagens. Soon the road grew steeper and more washed out.

I took my time, being careful with Buzz's truck, my mind now drifting back to when I first got the news about Luke's death.

*It was two weeks before school started and I was on the tenth tee of the course near my home with my friend Scott Hodges, collecting myself after having shot a pedestrian forty-four and losing the front nine, facing a two-shot deficit for the match we were playing. Scott pointed to a fast-moving golf cart approaching with what looked to be my father behind the wheel. What had I done now was my first thought; he certainly had not come out to join us on the back nine (my father and I rarely played together because of the not uncommon toxic chemistry of father and son together on a golf course).*

*My father parked twenty yards back of the tee – ever diligent about golf course etiquette – and waited for us to tee off. Scott had the tee and proceeded to carve up the fairway with a blistering drive right down the middle. I stepped into his tracks and – with a hurried swing – hooked my ball down the left side into some high grass. After mumbling* shit *and pounding my tee into the ground with my driver, I walked back to where my father was sitting. His hands were wrapped around the wheel, his head hanging down as if he was hung over – a rarity. He looked up at me briefly, his eyes confused-looking – even more of a rarity. Obviously, something was up. He asked me to climb into the cart with him. He then forced out the words, "Luke Danforth's father just phoned to tell me..." He hesitated, lips quivering, then stammered:*

"Luke...Luke has had a bad accident."

I sat still as a stone, calculating the possibilities of what had been the cause, only two being realistic: car or climbing. "Climbing?" I asked.

"Yes," my father confirmed.

"When?"

"Yesterday."

"Is he...dead?"

"I'm afraid so."

"With Polly?"

"He told me she had been with him – yes."

"Is she okay?"

"Yes."

"What happened?"

"I don't know," my father said shaking his head, his eyes now misty and reddening. "I didn't ask him. David... Mr. Danforth...just said it was an accident. He was rock climbing somewhere out west."

I didn't feel like crying. I didn't feel like yelling or pounding my fists against something the way you see in the movies. Frankly, I was stunned. I didn't know what to think or do (an odd feeling for a know-it-all eighteen-year-old). I only knew that I wanted to go home to my room and be alone. I got out and walked over to the cart Scott and I had been using, unstrapped my clubs, and said to Scott, "Do me a favor, will you?"

"Sure," he said. Clearly, this was not normal behavior.

"Pick up my ball if you can find it," I said. "We'll finish up tomorrow."

Scott asked, "Is everything okay?"

"No," I said. "Some bad news. I'll tell you tomorrow." With my hands shaking a bit, I cinched my golf bag tight. My body felt weak and my head light as if I'd not eaten for a couple of days. I got into my father's cart and we headed back to the clubhouse.

*That drive across the golf course was the closest I'd ever felt to my father, even though not a word passed between us. His emotional display over Luke's death was more about me. Even though I was sort of a screw-up, and he would remind me of that, for that brief moment I knew deep down he cared about me in a way only father can about a son, and was now struggling with how to show it. It would have been way out of character for him to have thrown his arms around me, telling me how much he loved me, that if I died he wouldn't be able to stand it or live without me. That was my mother's role, which she immediately fulfilled as soon as I stepped into the house.*

*After my father and I left the cart at the pro shop and began walking home, it was I who touched his shoulder with slight squeeze, just long enough to thank him, let him know I got the message.*

# Chapter 11

## POLLY HAMILTON AND THE TRUTH ABOUT LUKE

A half hour after leaving the highway I pulled into the Hamiltons' camp. There was a large clearing and I could see a decent-size lake through the trees. In front of me were a bunch of white canvas wigwams tucked among a grove of pines, a work shed garage, what looked like a dining hall and a horse corral. There was also a big open fire pit ringed with tree stumps. It looked just like what it was – a base camp from which the Hamiltons ran trips up into the mountains. There were no kids around: Polly had told me to come up between sessions so she would have fewer distractions and we'd have more time to talk. A portly girl with a bad Dutch boy haircut in a soiled apron came out of the dining hall. I asked her if she knew where I could find Polly. She pointed inside.

I edged past rows of crude pine tables and benches to the kitchen in the back. I thought I would be nervous about our meeting, especially given I was not sure what to say or where to start a conversation about Luke. I mean, I couldn't just waltz in and say *What the hell, let's be honest. I've come a long way and I just want to know what the fuck happened. Please tell me the truth so I can turn around and go back to the Lazy T, go home, bury this mess and shelve my purgatory.*

That would have been the cool way. But I didn't have the balls.

Also, I couldn't be high and mighty, because meeting Polly Hamilton for the first time, I was smacked in the face by the simple fact that had it not been for her helping me get a job at the Lazy T, I would have been shit-out-of-luck, sucking my thumb in Lake Forest, working as a grunt in a law firm, hating my life, and most likely not returning to college. As it was turning out, Polly was my savior – my savior now stirring something inside a dinged-up stainless steel pot, dressed in an oversize red-and-black lumberjack shirt with a blue T-shirt underneath, khaki hiking shorts and boots. (She was hot – think a jockish Ali McGraw in *Love Story* or *The Getaway*; and definitely hot enough to make me a little nervous and flushed.) She mouthed a *Hi Hank*, fished out a steaming strand of spaghetti and slurped it onto her tongue, fanning her mouth and smiling at me at the same time. I tried to stay focused because *finally* I was standing face to face with the girl in the photographs that Luke had kept hidden for four years under his blotter at school. Seeing Polly in person made me think I would have done the same, kept those pictures hidden from all our drooling schoolmates.

There were two 5x7s, one was of a thirteen-year-old in braces and frizzy hair pulled back in a ponytail that Luke had taken his first year at the camp. Polly was posed, standing on a rock ledge with a lake behind her, smiling, her hip jutting out in a girly pose, looking Cracker Jack cute. The second – Luke had shown me this picture in our senior year – was Polly at eighteen, now with wavy dark hair floating on her shoulders, the same lake behind her, athletic, sitting cross-legged and looking up at the camera with a captivating smile. Any boy could stare at that second picture for a long time. At least that's what I did when Luke wasn't in his room.

Anyway, after Polly stopped fanning her mouth, she wiped her hands with a chewed-up blue towel and shook my hand with a soft palm and a firm grip, saying, "How was the road up?"

"Not too bad," I replied.

"Want something to drink?"

I nodded my head yes.

She pulled open an old Frigidaire and reached inside. Flipping her hair around, she caught me staring at her butt. "Coke or 7 Up?" she asked. I looked down at my boots and picked at my nicked-up knuckles, my face turning redder than it already was. "7 Up, please."

It didn't seem to bother her.

We sipped our sodas, talking about Bit, Buzz, Hope, Pinedale, the ranch. Small talk. I was doing most of the talking, and while I did, I sensed she was studying me. When I stopped, Polly asked, "How did you and Luke become friends?" sounding as if she wanted the truth, not a tossed-off reply like we met playing lacrosse.

That caught me off guard. I had planned on asking the questions, but instead Polly was the one who was getting down to business. That was fine with me. I finished my soda, crumpled the can in my hand and put it on the counter. I always wanted to open up to somebody about my friendship with Luke but I was too embarrassed. If there was anybody, Polly was the one I could trust because we shared Luke. I quickly went through my litany of: He was the first kid I met at boarding school. His parents knew my parents and we were encouraged to get to know each other. Difference was I was from the Midwest; he was from the East. I was insecure and self-conscious; he was confident and cool. I grew my hair long like his so I could tuck it behind my ears and wore the same preppy clothes as he did – with a western bent. And while I'd edge around the locker room with my towel wrapped around me, he would parade about naked, snapping his.

I told Polly how Luke knew the ropes; knew the hotshots around school; knew where trouble was and how to talk his way out of it. And he didn't care about what others thought about him; nothing seemed to bother him. He had no fears and was a little inscrutable – that was cool. Not like the rest of us who were more transparent and obvious. He also kept you off balance: you never knew for sure where you stood. He could be your best buddy, then shut you down, leaving you either elated or deflated. Also, I sometimes worried about his getting wasted, being reckless, taking risks. Lastly, I told her that I thought it was ballsy that he could be independent enough to come out here to Wyoming...leave home all summer. I wanted to be like that. Leave everybody and everything behind. Cut my own swath; not give a rat's ass what others think.

When I stopped talking I noticed I had been addressing the refrigerator and Polly was studying me with a solemn expression like a shrink, her head slightly angled. I was nearly out of breath. That was the most I'd ever talked to anybody about my relationship with Luke and how I idolized him. (That's a tough thing for a guy to admit, even to himself.) My rambling had left me a little off balance, which got me to thinking about the time. I eyed a Timex on Polly's wrist – just after five o'clock. I needed to step it up because I wanted to see the camp, especially where those pictures had been taken. I said, "Can you show me around?"

"Sure thing," she said, putting her 7 Up back in the refrigerator. I picked up my crushed can and with a set shot launched it into a large metal trash can, metal on metal ringing as we walked out.

For about twenty minutes we kicked around on a two-bit tour of the camp as Polly told me the history of the place, the mountaineering and survival skills the kids are taught in the summer, and the outfitting trips the Hamilton brothers – Polly's father and uncle – guide for hunters and fishermen year-round. When it seemed to me the tour was winding down, I asked her if she would show me the spot by the lake that Luke had talked about. Polly instantly knew. "Table Top. Sure. It's just about ten minutes from here. Silver Dollar Lake is about a half mile long and Table Top is at the far end of it."

We walked single file along a path through the woods with Polly ahead of me, neither of us talking. She stopped once, holding back a branch, and said, "You know Buzz comes up here to entertain the kids. We set up a big fire in the ring after supper and he plays and sings. Have you heard him? He's really good. The kids love his deep gravelly voice and his funny country songs and lullabies."

"A little," I said, taking the branch from her, accidentally snapping it off. I had been distracted, looking around through the trees wondering where Luke had fallen. I had thought about asking to see where he died but chose not to. Why? So I would not look up and say *Wow! He fell from there? That's crazy.*

Once we reached Table Top – a large, flat outcropping that rose about ten feet above the water – we sat cross-legged, facing each other. Like we were having a two-person powwow. After spilling my guts back in the kitchen and not wanting to hide behind pleasantries or proper etiquette, I went for broke:

"Can you tell me the truth about Luke?"

Polly calmly said, "You already know half of it."

I said, "What do you mean?"

"What you told me back in the kitchen."

"That Luke was inscrutable, fearless and moody?"

"Yes."

"What's the other half?"

She rocked from one side to the other, her voice now steady and measured. Polly was my age but seemed ten years more mature. "Luke was troubled when he first came out here when he was thirteen. His mother had recently died and his father couldn't handle him."

I added what I knew: "I know that Mr. Danforth remarried and that Luke didn't like his stepmother."

"Yes. And what my father and uncle were concerned about was whether Luke could handle it out here."

"Why?"

"Call it his other half."

"Tell me about it."

"Obviously, he was having problems with his mother's death and his father's new situation, and he was diagnosed with having signs of depression."

"How did you know?"

"Like any camp, we have to have a doctor's physical and evaluation."

"Did you know about this then?"

"Me? Oh, no. Not until three or four years later. My parents warned me of his problems when I was about sixteen. But at first we were like two chipmunks, running around playing with each other. It was all innocent and platonic."

"I always wondered if he loved you," I said. "Although he never said it in so many words. I know he thought about you a lot." Here is where I fumbled. "He was almost..."

"Obsessed?" Polly said, tensing a bit.

I recalled what Bit had said about Luke not leaving Polly alone, suffocating her. "Yes, I guess that's right."

Polly relaxed. "There was another side to him, Hank. He was vulnerable. Confused. What started off as innocent and fun – our friendship – became twisted and complicated."

I leaned back on my hands and looked up into the mountains. "What changed?"

Polly brushed a strand of hair from her face. "Me."

I understood immediately. She had grown up. There must have been a lot of Joe Alexanders around wanting to rope her in.

I said, "Did Luke know about you and Joe Alexander?"

Polly replied, "I managed to keep it from him because we were up here and Joe's down in Cora. But our senior year, when Joe and I started getting serious, I had to tell Luke. I told him about two weeks before we were to go to college."

"Did you ever go to bed with Luke?"

"No. We just made out. Kissing and petting, that sort of thing. And it was fun. For a while. Then it wasn't."

"Why?"

"It wasn't natural."

"You weren't attracted to him?"

"Physically I was – you know how good looking he was – but…"

I waited for her to finish.

"I could tell he was more interested in having others believe we were going out. He wasn't comfortable with the physical part. He just wanted to be with me and talk about his life and problems. But it became uncomfortable, so my father and uncle did their best to keep us apart in our counselor duties. They would purposely send us on separate expeditions in the mountains. That saved me."

I inhaled three shallow breaths, then said, "So what happened?"

Polly said softly, "The Sunday before he was supposed to go home, when the kids were all off on a day hike, he suggested we go for a climb and take lunch. He had smuggled a six-pack of beer up from town and stowed it in the lake for a summer-end celebration. Anyway, the climb was on an easy face, only about sixty feet. We use it for practice for the older kids. We made the climb, ate lunch and were drinking the beers, just hanging out at the top, dangling our feet over the edge, talking about college. How he was leaving soon to go back East. End-of-the-summer stuff. Horses. Kids. Staying in touch..."

"Then?"

"Then I finished my second beer, collected the empties, and got up to pee. Coming back from the trees I stopped in my tracks."

"Why?"

"Luke was lying on his back right by the edge. His hands were folded over his chest."

Polly bowed her head, her eyes misting. "He looked at me then up at the sky. I could see he had closed his eyes. I asked him, 'What are you doing, Luke?'" Here Polly choked up. "And he said, 'Resting.' Then he...rolled himself over the edge."

You might think I would have said *I can't believe it,* or, *Why did he do that? What was he thinking?* Instead, I asked, "What did you do then?"

"I rappelled down as fast as I could – "

"He was still alive?"

"Yes, but unconscious. I wrapped him in everything I could spare and ran for help. He died on the way to the road."

The breeze off the water was giving me a chill. I felt my teeth beginning to chatter. Polly asked, "Hank, are you okay?"

Again, you'd think I would have said something like *I can't believe this,* or *Poor Luke, he didn't deserve this* or, *How could this have happened?* Instead I said to Polly in a soft sincere tone, "I owe you."

She said, "For what."

I said, "For what you did."

"What do you mean?" she said, looking at me with a soulful and caring look.

"For getting me out here," I said, waving an arm around. "To figure this out."

Polly said, "Hope told me that Buzz had lost the letter. Bit told me her mom was fit to be tied. Fortunately, she found it and Buzz called you just in time."

I picked at my hands to give me something to do. "How'd you convince Hope to take me on?"

Polly said, "Outside of my family, only she and Bit know the truth about Luke. When you wrote me about working on a ranch after Luke's death, I spoke with Hope and explained the situation. She understood..." Polly's voice trailed off. "That's just Hope. And I'm so glad you came out and I got to know you, Hank."

"Me, too. Me, too," I said softly. I stood up and kicked my feet about. "I won't say anything about this to anybody." I reached down to help her up.

Polly said, "Thank you. I know you won't."

Then she gave me the lightest kiss on the cheek I've ever had.

On our walk back to the camp, Polly explained to me that Mr. Danforth and the Hamiltons had cut a deal concerning Luke's death. They agreed to say it was an accident and Polly's father and uncle and Luke's father would sign a document absolving the Hamiltons of any negligence. Luke's father insisted there be no investigation or speculation as to the cause of Luke death. So, "Rock climbing accident" was what the Hamiltons convinced the coroner to type on the death certificate.

As for Luke's funeral, Mr. Danforth said that it was not necessary for Polly to travel to Greenwich because of the memorial service the Hamiltons had given for Luke in front of the whole camp (Polly made it sound like he didn't want her there, so she didn't push it). Polly told me the creepy irony that the minister from town told the gathering on Table Rock that this is where Luke was the happiest and it was fitting this is where he should be *resting* in eternal peace.

# Chapter 12

## THE COWBOY BAR

After meeting with Polly, I went quiet for about a week thinking about Luke and how he had died. Even though I'd suspected something for a long time, it was still a lot to digest. So I kept my head down, working around the ranch and talking a little more than usual with Buddy in his stall. When Clete asked me if something was wrong, I lied, saying I just needed to go to town. Clete said he knew the feeling and told me he'd ask Hope for a hall pass for that Friday night. Hope agreed to Clete's request – I knew she knew the truth about Luke, and she could read from my face that I was a little twisted up by it all; so she said Go, even giving us four roadies for the drive to town.

In the truck, tapping our fingers to country music with the windows rolled down, Clete and I smoked and gulped down our first beer, pitching the empties out the window and into the bed of the truck. Popping my second cold one, quickly lapping at the foam so it would not drip in the truck, I asked Clete, "Does Bit have a boyfriend?"

Putting his beer between his legs so he could shift,

Clete said, "None I know of. Plenty of cowpokes circling, but nothing steady."

I asked, "You ever thought asking Bit out?"

Clete squinted. "Thought about it? Hell, I think about it every night. That don't mean it's gonna happen."

"Why not?" I asked, flicking some ash out the window.

Clete sighed. "I like my job, Squirrel, and Hope's cooking, too." He gave me a poke in the ribs. "Besides, I think she likes you."

I said, "Fat chance," looking away to hide my satisfaction, squirming a little in my seat.

We passed Sonny Skinner's place. No truck around...the house dark...the yellow porch light on. Up ahead four antelope scampered across the road, with the smallest one hotfooting it to catch up with his friends. I'd been wanting to ask Clete more about Bit but chose not to while we were working at the ranch because I thought it would be disrespectful to Buzz and Hope – Clete too, if he had his eye on her. Now well into my second beer, feeling a little high and confident, I said, "Tell me more about Bit."

Clete punched the radio for another country station. When he landed on Freddy Fender's rambling "Wasted Days and Wasted Nights," he said, "She's feisty...clever, too. Pretty much everybody gets along with her – she's like Buzz and Hope in that way. Buzz never says much about her... Hope neither. Except I see their eyes light up when she's around." The corners of Clete's eyes crinkled as he let out his toothy grin. "And she's a looker. Packs a lot in those jeans"

I nodded agreement but purposely canned any crude comments.

Again Clete poked me in the ribs, catching me off guard because I was looking out the window thinking about Bit's packed jeans. "Don't tell me," he snickered. "Bit don't give you the feeling of jerkin' the gherkin."

I didn't know how to answer. I pretended as if I hadn't

heard him, sipping my beer and hot-boxing the last of my cigarette. I'd *never* talked about masturbation. Not with Andy. Not with Luke. Not with my other friends. It made me nervous and self-conscious. I always tried to be very careful. Dreading the embarrassment of being caught... always careful to return my roommate's *Playboys* under the mattress of his bed...placing them exactly as I'd found them, in the right order and facing the same way. Looking out the window, I caught myself in the side mirror anxiously scraping my lower lip with my upper teeth. I flicked my butt out.

Clete saw I'd become uncomfortable, so he gently coaxed me, "Come on now, Squirrel...I heard you rustling around in your sleeping bag like you was wrestling a boa constrictor with both hands." We approached the blacktop of 352. Clete braked and downshifted. He looked both ways and blinked his eyes twice like he was squeezing the sun. He grinned at me, resting his hands on the wheel. He said, "My pappy once told me 99 percent admit to shaking hands with the bishop. The other 1 percent lie. How about you?"

*Shit. Shit. Shit.* Clete had me trapped. I couldn't lie, but I didn't know how to tell the truth. I drummed my fingers on the outside of the truck, quickly turning this over. Letting my breath out slowly, I confessed, "It's been awhile."

Clete howled and pounded the steering wheel.

Relief washed over me.

After he pulled out onto the road and powered past a loaded-down, dusty red Eldorado packed with a family of six, I changed the subject, now shouting above the air rushing in the truck windows. "How does Hope put up with it?"

Rolling up his window, Clete said, "You mean Buzz getting a stray shot of leg?"

"Yeah," I said pulling out the Old Timer knife Clete had given me, fiddling with the blade, opening and closing it.

"I suppose," he said, "thick skin and stuck on him."

I said, "That sounds like a country song."

"It is a country song, Squirrel."

"What's that make us?"

"Singing harmony, I guess."

"If you were married, would you ever cheat on your wife?"

"No," Clete said.

"How do you know?"

"The woman I want to marry would shoot me between the eyes – or legs. What about you?"

I said, "I was raised that it was wrong."

Clete said, "You was raised right. You just ain't seen enough."

I knocked my knuckles against the door. "Does Buzz worry about Farnsworth?"

"Doesn't let on if he does."

"Does Bit know about Buzz…" I didn't know how to correctly finish the question.

"…fooling around with Dorothy Farnsworth?" Clete said, reading my mind.

"Yes."

Clete scolded me. "Squirrel, Bit grew up on a small ranch, in a small town, in a small house. It's hard to hide anything."

As we slowed down, approaching the outskirts of town, I asked, "How does she deal with it? The infidelity."

Clete gripped the steering wheel – he was annoyed with me. "Same way I do. Same way you should, too. Mind your own business."

I shut up, feeling small and stupid. I looked over Clete's shoulder as we passed Johnson's Trucking. No patrol car.

Clete saw me looking. "He won't be setting there on a Friday night. Too much going on in town."

I took my last swig of beer and placed the empty under the seat. "Clete, can I ask you a question?"

"Shoot, Squirrel."

"Doesn't it worry you?"

"What's that?"

I knew I was being melodramatic, but I laid it out rationally: "Farnsworth's the law, he's jealous and dangerous. He followed me all the way through town when I drove up to the Hamiltons' camp, sending us a signal. He's tracking Buzz and he's gonna catch him. You told me yourself how Eleanor's husband was beaten up by Farnsworth and Asshole Pete, and how bad things happen all the time in Farnsworth's jail. *Something is going to happen, Clete!*"

We wheeled into the back parking lot of the Cowboy Bar. Clete turned off the engine, then tucked his Smith & Wesson under the seat. I got out and checked my hair and teeth in the side mirror. I looked around the parking lot whispering over the hood, "Aren't you worried there could be trouble?"

Clete came around and cupped the back of my neck, giving it a gentle tug, guiding me toward the back entrance to the bar, his neon smile lighting up. "Naw, Squirrel. Not at the Cowboy on a Friday night. But I'll keep an eye peeled for those two. Come on, first drink's on me."

Clete bought me a Budweiser and a double Turkey and Coke for himself. The place was jammed three deep at the bar. Cowboys and roughnecks were packed around the pool table holding cues, waiting for a game, and the dance floor was spinning counterclockwise with two-steppers. I spotted Sonny Skinner resting his head in his hands at the end of the bar as if he was snoozing, a fresh cigarette burning between his fingers. I didn't see Buzz (his pickup had been gone when we left the Lazy T so I figured he was in town somewhere, and I noticed Dorothy wasn't working the bar).

Clete ditched me for a cowhand who owed him some money. That left me wondering what to do, so I quickly downed my beer, ordered another, then pushed my way through the crowd and set up camp by the jukebox. I pretended to blend in, keeping my head down and not making eye contact, watching the cowboys and roughnecks shoot pool, the tension between them palpable, waiting for trouble to start.

And it didn't take long.

Fur flew right in front of me when a roughneck and a ranch hand got into an argument over whose quarter was next on the pool table. No punches were thrown. The roughneck with his Billy Gibbons beard – a full head taller and two sizes larger than the ranch hand – calmly settled the dispute in a business-like way with the thicker end of his pool cue, whacking the cowboy over the head, dropping him to the floor like a sack of flour. Everybody stood back, leaving the roughneck standing over the cowboy, the splintered end of the cue still in his hand. Before the roughneck could deliver a kick to the ribs of the recovering cowboy, he was jerked around by the beard and growled at by a voice that didn't back down: *"Not in my bar, rig trash. Take it outside or I'll make you eat what's left in your hand."*

Sonny Skinner had woken up.

I checked to see if Sonny still had a burning cigarette in his hand, worried the roughneck's beard would go up in a flash. Fortunately the butt was pinched between his gritting teeth, the coal flaring as Sonny breathed in and out staring down with dead dark eyes. The roughneck stared back, his head twisted upward at an awkward angle, his eyes wide in terror. He wisely let the pool cue drop, then weaved and lumbered out the door into the night, leaving the cowboys and roughnecks on opposite sides of the pool table warily sizing each other up like two packs of wild dogs. Finally, somebody racked new balls and the band kicked in swinging a Bob Wills song. Courtenay, the owner – with a thankful hand on his shoulder – sat Sonny down and bought him a round. My hand shook as I lit myself cigarette. I nervously pounded my beer, worried another fight could break out and somebody would decide to wipe the floor with my preppy ass. Just as everything seemed normal, and I was breathing easy, a hand caught my shoulder and spun me around.

My stomach hit the deck.

"*Jesus,*" I whispered loudly.

There, face-to-face, eye-to-eye, nose-to-nose, stood Bit, about three beers deep, her voice a smidgen loud. "About time you showed up at the Cowboy, Hank. Learn any new eight-dollar words tonight?"

*Here* was a girl with thick black hair floating across the shoulders of a purple cowboy shirt with mother-of-pearl snaps. *Here*, north to south, was firm real estate evenly distributed with a bottom snugly packed in a pair of well-worn jeans with split knees and frayed bottoms, all standing tall on new buckskin boots.

Her skin glistened.

Her nose glowed.

Her slightly drunken smile killed me.

"No new words," I said, greatly relieved, now trying to sound professorial to hide my nervousness. "But I did firmly grasp the concept that it's easier to swallow your pride than a pool cue."

Bit smiled at me without showing her teeth. All she said was, "Mom's right."

"About what?" I asked.

"You're a quick study," she said tapping me lightly on the shoulder with her bottle of Coors, then tilting her head to the side like girls do when they think you're okay. She asked, "You really like it out at the Lazy T?"

Acting cool, I said, "Yeah, it's okay."

"When are you heading back East?"

"End of haying."

"How's it going with Clete?"

"No problems. Taught me a lot. He's a great guy."

"He is," she said. "Mom and Dad really like him. He's a good hand."

I said, "You know, he's saved my life a few times." I was trying to be funny, but it wasn't far from the truth.

Bit took a big hit off her beer – she drank just like a guy – eyeing me and said, "He said you got a girlfriend."

"Had a girlfriend," I said, looking around a little embarrassed. "It's been over for some time. I was bucked off a long time ago" – lamely mangling a western metaphor – "I was just trying to hold on."

Bit inched closer to me so a waitress with a tray full of drinks could pass. "Nothing wrong with that," she said with a breezy Coors breath that I didn't mind.

I shrugged.

"So get back on," Bit said, tacking on to my western metaphor, "take a new draw."

I couldn't tell if she was hinting at something or giving me free advice. I didn't care. I just liked her standing close to me; unfortunately, close enough to freeze my vocal cords.

Bit saw I was a little tongue-tied so she changed the subject. She asked, "How'd things go with Polly?"

That made me even more uncomfortable. I didn't want to talk about Polly and Luke. I said, "Good." Nothing more. Period.

Bit got the message.

We looked over each other's shoulders for a few seconds, then I caught Bit's brown eyes twinkling at me. She was hiding a smile.

"What?" I said, being coy.

Bit said, "Mom says you make her laugh. Says you can talk a dog off a meat wagon."

I had to think about that for a second and decided to take it as a compliment. I said, "I like your mother a lot. She's no bullshit." That's a weird way to compliment somebody's mom, but that's what came out.

"She is," Bit said, giving me another look that made me look away because I could feel myself blushing. I had to say something fast. "So's Buzz," I said. "No bullshit, I mean." Quickly I became a puddle, melting like a ten-year-old describing a major league ballplayer he'd just met. "He's...

he's a real cowboy. I mean...he really is. The way he walks and talks and...rolls his own cigarettes...and plays the guitar...and rides bucking horses...he's really cool and..." I was running out of steam when Bit saved me:

"He likes you, too."

"*Really?*" I choked out.

"Yeah," Bit said, squeezing close to me again so an older couple could make their way to the dance floor, our noses nearly touching, the scent from her neck something wild and sweet. "He says you try and you tell them what you don't know. And you work hard and don't complain." I think she batted her eyes at me when she said, "That's a lot from a college boy."

God, I wanted to kiss her – on the lips, right then and there. But that was not going to happen. Instead, I rolled my Budweiser bottle around in my hands peeling off the label, words stuck in my throat. We didn't talk for a little, which dragged on long enough for Bit to have this confused look on her face, which I interpreted as *are you gay or are you going to ask me to dance.* I looked over the dance floor and was just opening my mouth when she grabbed my hand and asked *Wanna two-step?*

Before I could respond she had me on the floor, placing my right hand on her hip just where it curves into her butt and my left one up high – as if I'd never been to dancing school – and started pushing me around the dance floor. She giggled and gave me a slap on the shoulder saying, "Loosen up, Hank, you're as tense as a dog on a vet's table. Don't they teach you anything at that college?"

She pulled me closer, our noses now brushing. Again, I inhaled wild and sweet. I followed her lead feeling the rhythm of the music, stealing glances and imitating other couples as we flowed around the floor. I spun Bit once and gently took over the lead. We danced round and round – not effortlessly, but not spastically either. The song lasted what seemed like a long time. We didn't talk until it was over. The band took a break, and we walked side by side off the dance floor, Bit swerving into me a little and I swerving back.

Reaching the edge of the floor, I said, "Thank you."

Bit said, "Mom's right. You *are* a quick study."

A minute later I lost Bit to a drunken lovesick cowboy she knew from high school. It didn't bother me. I went looking for Clete and found him curled around his fifth Turkey and Coke blubbering to Sonny at the end of the bar. I decided not to have anything more to drink because I was the one who was going to be driving back to the ranch – plus I was paranoid about Farnsworth and Asshole Pete. I sidled onto a barstool beside Clete. The band sounded tired. In the mirror behind the bar I could see that the crowd was thinning out. I wanted to tell Clete to drink up so we could go but figured he was having a good time talking with Sonny. So I nursed a Coke while scribbling down notes on some napkins. When I heard the screen door squeak open, slam shut, and a big pair of boots stomp in, I turned around wondering who was coming into bar at this hour.

Farnsworth.

He stood still as a statue with hands on his hips. No hat, black hair high, his six-two two-thirty squeezed tight in law-and-order brown, like sausage. His nose was boozy red with pores as big as potholes and he oozed dumb and dangerous. He brushed his jet-black mustache with his index finger taking inventory of the bar, walking around like he was wearing spurs. I kept my head down, anxious for him to leave. When he finally did, I followed him through the bar windows as he checked the pickups on the street – I'm sure looking for Buzz's. Ten minutes later I hauled Clete out to the truck, got behind the wheel and slowly eased out of the parking lot. I stayed off Main Street as I headed out of town.

With Clete snoring off a snoot-full I kept one eye on the rearview mirror and the other on the speedometer the whole way back to the ranch, worrying that Buzz was with Dorothy and that Farnsworth would find them. At the ranch, the first thing the truck's headlights hit was the back of Buzz's truck. I shook Clete out of his slumber and helped him to the trailer, wondering whether I was just being paranoid. Like maybe my imagination was running away with me. Like I was the only one worried about all of this.

# Chapter 13

## WRANGLING AND TRAILERING HORSES

Rendezvous is a big Western celebration, and Clete loved it because there were country bands, cowboys, pretty girls and oceans of booze. Hope was a little more precise, explaining that it's an annual celebration on a Saturday in late July that commemorates the time when, years ago, fur traders, trappers, mountain men and Indians would get together, swap supplies and stories and whiskey (and I'm sure a few squaws) and get down-and-dirty drunk for a month. Nowadays, the townspeople and ranchers in the area dress up in Indian and mountain-man garb, have a parade, reenact the event, and party as if it were spring break.

At the supper table on the Thursday before Rendezvous, Buzz said that he had told Sonny he'd help him out by trailering some of his horses into Pinedale early the following morning. (Buzz was already going to trailer Buddy in on account of he was riding him in the parade.) Seems Sonny had cut a deal with three townsfolk who needed horses to ride in the parade. Sonny was getting sixty-five dollars a pop. That was enough, according to Buzz, for Sonny to park himself at the Cowboy for at least two weeks. Buzz told Clete and me we needed to be up early to get over to Sonny's so we could help them wrangle and load the horses, and Sonny would give us a ride back to the Lazy T. It was no surprise then early the next morning around five I heard Buzz enter our trailer and rummage around for his buckskin leggings, beaver vest, and furry mountain hat, telling us to stop whatever we were doing and get dressed, grab some breakfast and hitch the trailer to his pickup while he fetched Buddy.

I got dressed, then stood outside in the cool, dark morning, my breath streaming out. I blew a few smoke rings. The wind was blowing big fluffy clouds across a fading full moon far down in the west of the wide Wyoming sky, creating a slow motion kaleidoscope of light across the earth. Clete came up beside me buttoning his jacket, checking his pockets for knife, chew and cigarettes. I did the same. We headed to the light in the kitchen, Clete striding over the plank across the ditch with no hesitation, hands in his pockets. I gingerly followed with my hands outside my pockets for balance. Inside, Hope was up and moving around; a Marlboro burning, as always; dressed neatly, as always. She had laid out cereal, biscuits and coffee.

Clete and I hammered through breakfast then pushed our chairs back – Clete grabbing two toothpicks, handing me one – thanking Hope and hustling out the door to help Buzz. Hope waved us off, shutting the door behind us, telling us to say hello to Sonny.

Clete backed up the blue Ford to the trailer with me twirling my hand, guiding the hitch over the ball mount, securing the connection with a metal pin and a solid kick for good measure. Clete inspected my work. "That'll do 'er, Squirrel," he said. From the open corral gate Buzz appeared, leading a head-down, sleepy-looking, slow-moving Buddy. Buzz walked him into the trailer and tied him up at the front, keeping one hand on the horse's back as he walked out of the trailer. He then went back to the barn and returned with Buddy's saddle and tack. Clete took it from him and hoisted it into the bed of the truck, the stirrup clanging against the wheel well.

Buzz unlatched and eased down the tailgate. He looked around flexing his tongue against his lower lip to whistle, but Blue beat him to it as he raced out of the shadows and leaped into the truck. He jumped up on his hind legs with his front paws on the side of the bed, panting, tail wagging. Buzz took Blue's face between his hands and mumbled softly, "Goddamn good dog."

He latched up the tailgate, giving it a push and a pull to make sure it was secure. "Let's not keep Sonny waiting." He looked east down Forty Rod Road toward Sonny's place, the early morning sky just beginning to turn a pale blue. "We're running a little behind."

We squeezed into the truck with me in the middle, my legs straddling the stick shift (that's where the *Squirrels* had to sit when you rode three abreast). Buzz carefully pulled out onto Forty Rod testing the load of the trailer with Buddy aboard. When I asked why Sonny couldn't use his own truck to trailer the horses, Clete chortled, "Squirrel, Sonny's truck couldn't pull two dogs apart – right Buzz?"

Buzz didn't say anything. He just kept staring down the road into the darkness and the swath of the truck's headlights, swinging carefully around chuckholes, slowly picking up speed. I asked another question: With his horses spread out over Forty Rod Road, how did Sonny round them up? Clete explained all Sonny had to do was leave the corral gate open with a busted bail of fresh hay and a salt lick inside and they'd come home. I then asked where he got the hay, because from what I'd seen, Sonny didn't have any hayfields, just open range. Buzz mumbled real softly so I could barely hear him even though I was sitting next to him, that he'd made a trade with Sonny years ago: Sonny helped him in the winter feeding his cows in exchange for hay for his horses.

Buzz shifted the stick into third gear, up and away from my crotch.

Just before Sonny's house, Buzz down-shifted and eased our load into the dip in the road then gunned the blue Ford into Sonny's front yard – Clete and I goofing around, pretending we were riding horses, leaning forward, urging the old truck on. The truck's headlights landed on Sonny, standing on his front porch in a clean T-shirt with his arms extended over his head holding onto the eave of his porch, rolling a toothpick in his mouth. (He may have been the town drunk, but Sonny Skinner, even in his late forties, was still cut like a tight end.)

Sonny grumbled at Clete through the open truck window, "Where ya been? Putting on your makeup?"

Clete said excitedly, "Buzz said you're having a party, Sonny. Where're all the white women at?"

Sonny replied, "Why don't you ask Buzz, I think he keeps them locked away in his barn."

Sonny walked over to the truck and scratched Blue. "How much you want for this dog, Buzzy Stifel?"

Buzz pushed open his door saying, "You ain't got enough, Sonny Skinner."

"You're right about that," Sonny said, now resting his forearms on the hood of the Ford.

Buzz, now opposite Sonny, asked, "Which ones we trailering?"

Sonny said, "The mare, the Appaloosa and the gelding."

Buzz asked, "You been paid?"

"Cash on the barrel."

"Which one rides next to Buddy?"

"Take the App – that mare will bite the shit out of Buddy in a trailer. She's better off with the gelding."

Buzz took out his makings and rolled a cigarette, then flicked his thumbnail across a matchstick. The cigarette flared up as he puffed out, "Most females are."

We moved to the corral, Buzz and Sonny with lariats, testing and coiling their ropes. Clete and I stood outside the gate by the trailer, ready to help. In the center of the corral the two cowboys swung loops over their heads, gauging wind and distance as eight horses circled the corral in a pack, something spooking them.

I said to Clete, "What's got the horses so riled?"

Not taking his eyes off the ring, Clete said, "Most likely the moon and the clouds. You. Me. Blue. There's a lot up their nostrils. Buzz and Sonny'll settle 'em down. These boys know how to throw a loop. Watch now and be quiet, Squirrel."

Side by side, about ten feet apart, Sonny and Buzz homed in. Buzz said, "I've got the gelding."

Sonny said, "I'll take the App."

I shut my mouth and watched in awe. It was like Joe DiMaggio gliding across center field, Bobby Orr in an end-to-end rush or Gale Sayers breaking free. I'd never considered cowboys athletes until now: Buzz and Sonny were poetry in motion, two cowboys calmly positioning themselves, hampered by darkness and wind, tracking a spooked pack of thundering horses around a ring, poised, patiently waiting for an opening.

Sonny threw a perfect loop over the App. He quickly set the rope behind his back, using the full force of his six-three two-thirty to bring the horse to rest. He led the now-calm horse out of the corral and handed him over to Clete to halter and lead into the trailer. Buzz was close behind with the gelding, which I stepped up to take. Clete had shown me how to put on a halter, and I walked him into the trailer and tied him off.

That left the mare.

Buzz and Sonny stood in the center, recoiling their lariats.

Sonny said, "That mare can be a bitch."

Buzz asked, "You want her?"

"All yours," said Sonny.

Buzz threw a loop over his head. "You cut the others out so I can get a good look."

The mare was fast and dodgy, hiding behind the others in the pack as they circled the corral. Buzz threw a few loops but they fell off her neck. Sonny yelled for Clete and me to jump in and help. We did, running around waving our hands, trying to cut the other horses away, but that only stirred them up more. Sonny kept yelling at us while Buzz tracked the mare around and around the ring. Suddenly they bunched up and one horse let out a shriek I had never heard before and don't care to hear again: a small white horse with brown markings had gone down on three legs. The horse had broken a leg by getting it caught on the bottom pole of the corral, snapping it at the knee joint.

"Aw, Jesus," Sonny shouted. Turning to me he said, "Get my gun, junior. Back of the door. It's loaded and the safety's on."

I ran fast to the house, found the twelve-gauge and brought it back. Buzz had roped the mare somehow and was leading her out. Sonny and Clete were shielding the down horse from the others. I inched closer to Sonny with the shotgun pointed to the sky, expecting him to take the gun.

The horse's nostrils flared, his breathing erratic and labored.

"*Shoot him,*" Sonny ordered.

I looked around to Clete and Buzz for help.

"Both barrels," Sonny shouted, waving his arms, trying to keep the other horses away.

I lowered the gun. Sighted. Froze.

"Get closer," Sonny commanded.

I edged to two barrel-lengths away, the stock against my shoulder, feet firmly planted, the way you would if you were shooting skeet.

Sonny shouted, "*Shoot, goddamnit. Shoot the goddamn thing. Put him out of his misery.*"

I thumbed off the safety. I willed myself to pull the trigger. The horse jerked around on his bloody splintered stump, his eyes electrified pools of pain and terror. I jumped back, now pointing the gun in the air.

From behind, Sonny grabbed the gun and pushed me aside. He lowered the weapon and fired, the horse's neck becoming a red-speckled mess.

Sonny shoved the gun back into my hands. "Break it down. Load it with the shells on the table in the house. Put it back of the door with the safety on. Next time, don't think on it too much. That'll get you in trouble out here." He turned to Buzz who was walking back into the corral. "Right, Buzzy?"

Buzz had his gloves off and was picking at a bloodied finger. "Damn rope burn," he said sucking the blood off. "Gotta get me some new gloves." He looked at the dead horse and said matter-of-factly to Sonny, as if it were just another chore, "I'll bring my front-end loader over. We'll plant him next to Buttercup."

# Chapter 14

## RENDEZVOUS

Rendezvous lived up to Clete's billing as being the wildest day of the summer. With the haying season winding down, it also marked the end of my time in Wyoming. Clete and I watched the parade in the morning – Buzz, in his trapper's garb, rode Buddy with an old single-shot rifle across his lap.

After the parade the day quickly descended into a sort of western-themed Mardi Gras, with the traffic on Main Street slowing to a crawl because of all of the revelers. Farnsworth and Asshole Pete did their best to keep things under control, which for the most part they did – except for a few fights and the occasional rifle fired into the air. Hope had nixed attending, claiming that she been to too many "Rendezvouses" and couldn't stomach dressing up yet once again as a Sioux squaw. That sounded reasonable, but I think Dorothy Farnsworth had more to do with it.

Dorothy was there. She was working the bar at the Cowboy and was, in her words, busier than a one-legged man in an ass-kicking contest. I talked with her briefly and over-tipped her and she thanked me with a wink. (I felt a little guilty about that, but what was I to do?) Sonny was plopped down at his regular spot at the end of the bar and I bought him a round, more than expecting him to buy me one. But when he didn't, I moved on to the next bar, the next jukebox, the next country band, always avoiding the crowds around the pool tables.

The long day was a blur. I just knocked around not knowing anybody, feeling out of place. Occasionally, I checked on Buddy in the trailer and Blue in the back of Buzz's truck, talking with them because they had become good friends. I purposely keep a lid on my consumption because I wanted to avoid having my butt kicked. (I really should've gotten my hair cut short, because after almost two months it was longer than even I was comfortable with, and I didn't want to have to defend it or my preppy looks.)

Once during the afternoon I spotted Bit and talked with her a little. Clete too, but I didn't want to tag along after them and be a nuisance because they knew a lot of people and really looked like they were enjoying themselves. Buzz seemed to split his time between the bars and the street, always with a beer in his hand (there was no problem about carrying alcohol around in public during Rendezvous).

Toward eight o'clock, Clete and I had settled in at the Cowboy, he banging back Turkey and Cokes while I slowly nursed my Coors. I did at one point do a shot of Jack Daniels with Bit and swung her around the dance floor before a stuttering cowboy with a handlebar mustache and a large hunting knife attached to his belt stole her away, pleading, "Let's fi...fi...fi...finish the dance we started last year." (Bit gave me a wink and a helpless *Sorry, I gotta do this* look.)

Around ten o'clock, when the night seemed to be peaking, I spotted Buzz heading toward the rear exit of the bar and out into the parking lot. I followed him, having an idea what he was up to. I asked, "Need any help, Buzz?"

Shushing me with a finger to his lips, he whispered,

"Don't want Farnsworth to know what I'm doing." He then disappeared into the horse trailer and I could hear him talking to Buddy. Soon he backed out the horse, still saddled from the parade.

I held Buddy's bridle. I could see that Buzz was weaving a little as he grabbed the horn and cantle and swung himself into the saddle. Rocking side to side, he looked down and asked me, "How do I look?"

I stared up at a cowboy I'd read about, dreamed about, wanted to be. I stared up at him with my eyes nearly misting. I wanted to say so much more but didn't know how, so I defaulted to what my father would say to my mother at the front door when she would ask how she looked as she checked her hair and makeup in the mirror: "Like a million bucks," I said.

He tipped his cowboy hat, which was not his normal workaday one. This was his Saturday-night-going-to-town special, set just at the right angle, looking real sharp.

"Stetson?" I guessed, pointing toward it.

"Nope. Akubra," he said, touching the brim, winking, nudging Buddy toward the bar with a gentle rein. I moved on ahead, holding the door open and flattening myself against the side of the building as Buzz ducked his head under the exit sign.

Buddy stopped – half in, half out – tail swishing.

From the other side of the door I heard someone bark, "*Buzz, stop!*" his voice shaky and unsure. "You can't bring a horse into the bar."

I peered around Buddy's flank and saw that the voice belonged to Asshole Pete. He was wearing a law-and-order brown shirt, tin star, and a stiff straw cowboy hat.

Buzz complained, "Whaa...why not?"

"Because there're laws."

"Whaa...there are?"

"Wyoming law forbids bringing a horse into a bar."

"But I'm not – "

"Then what're you doing, Buzz?"

"Buddy's bringing *me* in."

That brought a chorus of chuckles and guffaws and one loud *That got him, Buzz* from the crowd, which was moving in closer to watch the action. Still holding the door, sandwiched between the wall and Buddy's flank, I tilted my head down to avoid his swinging tail, noticing more and more pairs of boots congregating inside the door.

Asshole Pete said, "Buzz, the sheriff won't let you bring him in."

"Where's he at?" Buzz asked.

"He's busy, Buzz. But if he was here he'd tell you that you can't bring that horse into this bar."

"You saying Buddy ain't legal?"

"Yes, I am."

"Well...he is *too*. Just check his teeth."

The bar crowd roared, everyone in on it now. Asshole Pete warned Buzz he'd run him in if he brought Buddy all the way into the bar. Courtenay joined the fray, ripping Asshole Pete a new one, making it clear it was *his* bar and that if Buzz Stifel wanted to ride a bull elephant buck-necked through his bar on Christmas morning, he could. So get out of the man's way so he can have a drink.

Asshole Pete said, "The sheriff won't be happy about this, Courtenay."

Courtenay barked back, "He won't be too happy if I have to charge his tab for Buzz's drink. And while you're at it, *tell your dad his tab is two months overdue.*"

That stirred up more whooping and hollering and *You tell 'em, Courtenay,* which sent Asshole Pete packing and Buzz bumping Buddy all the way into the bar. I followed along, then joined the crowd and watched as Buzz was handed his congratulatory drink. The band was on break and the jukebox had been turned off, so Buzz-on-Buddy was the only entertainment. Buzz downed his drink in three gulps, waved his Akubra high, acknowledging the recognition of the rowdy crowd. Then he carefully turned Buddy around and headed back toward the exit. Running on ahead I again held the door, Buddy passing by shaking his mane and flubbering his lips at me, like *What's the big deal?*

In the parking lot, I held Buddy as Buzz dismounted, took off the saddle, and heaved the tack into the truck bed, being careful not to hit Blue. I unbridled Buddy, put on a halter, led him into the trailer and tied him off. When I joined Buzz by the side of the truck, he was petting and mumbling to Blue, who was curled up on Buddy's saddle blanket. "That goddamn Sonny Skinner wants to buy you. He knows a good goddamn dog. Might-a got his head dented by that bronc, but he ain't all that dumb."

Buzz looked at me through rheumy red eyes, beat from the long day of celebrating. I was worried about him driving back to the ranch hauling a trailer with Asshole Pete and his father on the warpath, *especially after ignoring Asshole Pete's warning about riding Buddy into the bar.* I said, "Let me drive you home, Buzz. I'll go get Clete. Let's call it a night."

Buzz looked at the trailer, then at the bar, then at Clete's truck, then down at the ground, rubbing his fingers and hands. I think he would have done it – let me take him home – if just then a male voice hadn't crooned from the back door of the bar: "Buzzy, somebody's here wants a dance before the night's over."

Buzz perked up. "Be there in a minute, Boone." He turned sideways, leaning against the truck, took out his makings to roll a cigarette, and said to me, "No...no. You get Clete home safe – I don't want him driving. I'll trailer Buddy and Blue back." He licked his fingers, unable to grip a paper. I helped him. But when he went to shake out some tobacco, most of it landed on the ground.

I pulled out my smokes and handed him one, then swiped a matchstick three times up my thigh before it sparked a sizzling blue flame. I waited for it to turn yellow. Buzz pinched and cupped the cigarette between his thumb and forefinger, taking three quick drags, then rested the Marlboro in the corner of his mouth as he dug and rubbed the exhaustion from his eyes with the pads of his thumbs. He asked me, "You had a good time out here?"

"Yeah. Really good," I said.

"Think you'll come back?"

"I'd like to."

"It's a hard way to make a living – "

"I know – "

"I got no complaints."

We smoked together.

I was restless and worried. "Please let me drive you back to the ranch, Buzz."

He shook his head. "No...no," he dragged out, now slower and deeper, "I gotta go back in."

I knew I wouldn't have another chance to be alone with Buzz before I left, and I was a little drunk myself. What I told Buzz I won't repeat here because it was a lot of drivel. (Think about pouring out your heart to your favorite high school teacher at graduation, and what a mess that was.) But it was not what I said that mattered.

It was so simple.

In his slow smoky drawl, making it sound like I'd earned it. He said, "You're a good kid."

Buzz rubbed his eyes again as he looked around at the door to the bar. He tapped me on the shoulder before he strolled back in.

Those were the last words he spoke to me.

# Chapter 15

## BUZZ

The next morning just after nine (Hope had told us we could sleep in; she'd milk the cow because of our long day and late night in town), Clete and I rolled out of the trailer to find an empty yard and house. No Hope. No Buzz. No Blue. No Buzz's truck and trailer. Only the three-legged cat hobbling through the yard, stopping to lick her stump. In the corral, the milk cow was pissed off and mooing, wanting to feed her bellyaching calf in the barn. Clete's truck was gone too. That was really odd.

We speculated (optimistically) that Buzz may have broken down, maybe a blown tire or the Ford finally gave out because it had nearly 100,000 miles on the speedometer and was not great at pulling a trailer.

We milked the cow then hung around the house and yard not knowing what to do. After a while, Clete set to sharpening sickles in the work shed while I greased and lubricated some machinery. After that, we lackadaisically worked on the back fence, which was nearly complete. Just after noon we were going to the house to fix ourselves dinner when we saw what looked to be a dust storm coming down Forty Rod from the direction of Pinedale. Turned out to be a caravan with Sonny in the lead driving Buzz's truck with the trailer, followed by Hope in Clete's truck and Bit in her El Camino. Clete and I stood on the porch and watched as they all pulled in and scattered around the yard. Sonny hopped out of Buzz's truck and immediately led Buddy out of the trailer and into the corral. With heads down and blank expressions on their swollen red faces, Bit and Hope silently shot past us into the house. We followed them in. They stood by the bay window staring out at the hayfields and the sky. Bit had her arm around her mother.

Nobody said a word until Clete rubbed his chin and asked softly, "Where's Buzz at?"

Hope spoke up after a few seconds sounding like she was reading from a newspaper clipping. "The postmaster found Buzz this morning lying beside his pickup outside the Cora store. Sheriff Farnsworth said it appeared to be assault and robbery. Two men...he thinks...jumped Buzz when he stopped to relieve himself. They stole his money and tack and beat him up. In the scuffle Buzz must have fallen and hit his head. He was taken by ambulance to the hospital in Pinedale where Doc Evans put him on life support."

"He's going to be okay?" Clete pleaded.

*"No, he's not,"* Sonny growled, now standing in the doorway. *"He's a goddamn vegetable."*

I reached for a chair.

Hope lit a cigarette.

Bit crossed her arms and rocked a little, looking down at the floor.

Sonny poured some coffee. Clete said he could use a cup, too.

I was in disbelief and feeling guilty. "I told Buzz I'd drive him home," I said softly.

Hope, not turning around, said coldly, "Don't blame

yourself, Henry. Buzz *chose* to stay at the bar."

I said, "What about Blue? Where's Blue? He was in the truck when Clete and I left Buzz at the Cowboy."

Sonny took a gulp of coffee not looking up, said they found Blue in a culvert nearby, his tongue hanging halfway to Cheyenne and the back of his skull missing.

Nobody spoke.

I watched the second hand on the electric clock over the stove circle once, waiting for any one of them to state the obvious; what Clete had warned me about on my first day when we were building the fence: Farnsworth and Asshole Pete had it in for Buzz and the Lazy T. And hadn't Buzz challenged Farnsworth by riding Buddy into the Cowboy Bar and then stayed around for a dance with Dorothy? Why were they covering this up? This was much more awkward than the elephant in the room at Luke's funeral. I was certain Buzz hadn't been robbed. He'd been followed, pulled over and jumped just like old Gene Pfisterer had been.

Unfortunately, I opened my mouth and let loose with, "You can't let Farnsworth and Asshole Pete get away with this."

Bit spun around, a furious look on her face, her body rigid. She raised her arm and slowly pointed her finger square between my eyes. Sonny banged down his coffee mug, hissing, "*Don't be poking that skunk, junior.*" A cigarette now flared between his gritting teeth as he came at me with open hands, grabbed me by the shirt, lifted me off my feet and slammed me into the wall. "*This is none of your goddamn business, college boy. So butt out or I'll take you outside and make a three-car garage out of your asshole. The sheriff says that Buzzy Stifel was jumped and robbed and they killed Blue too. That's it and there's nothing gonna change it.*"

Sonny released me. I slumped into a chair.

Hope had not moved a hair, still staring out the window, over the fields, into the mountains.

Soon after, Hope and Bit put on clean clothes, said they were heading back to the hospital, dropping Sonny off at his place on the way. Clete and I hunted around for some leftovers for dinner, then went back to the yard to finish up the fence. We didn't talk much, and I didn't say anything more about the Farnsworths. We went to bed soon after dusk.

About three in the morning I was having a smoke trying to get back to sleep when I heard a truck pull into the yard, stop, shut its engine down, then came the creaky metal sound of a door opening and closing. Boots crunched through the yard and thudded across the plank, quickly approaching the trailer. You might have thought I would have been scared, thinking maybe it was one of the Farnsworths coming to finish us off. But I was oddly calm. Just going with the flow. Like I knew this wasn't over. The door was flung open and a flashlight's beam stung my eyes as I sat up. I dropped my cigarette butt into a Bud bottle as Sonny grunted at me, then stomped back to Clete's bedroom in his size thirteen boots. I couldn't make out what they were saying, only the rustle of bedding and Clete ending the conversation with *I got 'er*, meaning he knew what to do to get it done.

I was sitting up when Sonny headed out the door, ducking his head, his shoulders brushing the doorjamb, Budweiser with a nicotine chaser following him out.

Clete barked, "Get dressed, Squirrel."

"What's up?" I barked back, kicking off my sleeping bag.

"Going to town."

"Why?"

"Get dressed. We're going with Sonny – in my truck."

"Why your truck?"

"Can't chance Farnsworth or Asshole Pete seeing Sonny's truck in town."

"What're we doing?"

"Just get dressed."

I jumped up, tripped over some stuff on the floor, turned

on Hope's light and put on whatever was closest, then stood by the open door buttoning my jacket. I followed Clete out, briskly walking across the yard to his truck where Sonny sat in the passenger seat. I climbed in on the driver's side and slid over into the middle, not saying anything to Sonny, remembering how he had slammed me into the wall.

Clete spun the truck around in front of the house, passing Bit's El Camino, then headed out onto Forty Rod. The house was dark; not a single light on. I glanced over Sonny's shoulder toward the bay window and spotted the red coal of a cigarette flare up behind the glass.

On the way into town Sonny didn't say a word, not even a grunt. He just stared ahead as if in a trance, smoking and drinking and looking at the headlights' beam on the road ahead.

In town we parked in the darkest corner of the lot behind the hospital. Sonny told Clete to sit tight, then he slapped me on the thigh and said, "Let's go, junior. Buzz told me you was a good hand."

*A good hand?* What the...? I wanted somebody to tell me just what was going on. But I had an inkling: Sonny wanted me to go with him and help him put down Buzz. I looked at Clete. The look on his face and his nod of *just go* confirmed that thought. I slid out and followed Sonny across the parking lot to the rear door of the hospital. Sonny tapped it twice. The door opened and we were quickly ushered inside by an older, heavyset man of about my height with a full gray mustache and wire-rim glasses.

Doc Evans.

The hall lights were low. Doc led us into a dimly lighted room right next to the door where we'd come in. I was pretty sure nobody else had seen us. There in a bed was Buzz, a plastic oxygen hose taped over his face and into his mouth.

Doc said, "He's breathing, but he ain't alive. I numbed him up pretty good so he can't feel much." He reached for the door and said he'd be outside. I heard a chair being pushed against the door outside and his weight plop into it.

I peered at the person I could hardly recognize as Buzz, attached to machines that pumped and beeped and wheezed and bled ragged lines on a couple of green-screen monitors. I stood ramrod straight next to Sonny, who still smelled of the corral and the bar. His breathing was slow and steady like the machines, his voice honest and innocent like he was kneeling at the church rail explaining to the good Lord what he had to do. He stared straight ahead at the lump in the bed. "Buzz and I talked about this in Ko-rea when we saw them boys come back from combat all maimed and messed up. And when we were rodeo-ing...when someone would get bucked off hard and end up not right.

"Said we'd never let it happen...

"We took an oath with a drink...

"Buzz saved me from that...

"Being a vegetable like this...

"He jumped in the ring and pulled me out before that bronc could stomp me again...

"He saved me...

"And I swore I'd save him too if the time ever came."

Here Sonny's tone turned dark and threatening: *"Goddamn Farnsworth, he did this to Buzzy. And Hope and I agreed we won't let Buzzy Stifel be a trophy for that sonofabitch."*

So I had been right. Buzz had been jumped by Farnsworth and Asshole Pete. Sonny and Hope just didn't want a snot-nose kid like me pointing fingers and mucking up the works. They wanted everybody to believe the sheriff's story of Buzz being robbed and hitting his head in a fall. And, now they wanted to pull the plug on Buzz quickly and quietly so he wouldn't be Farnsworth's trophy, an example of what happens when you cross the law in his town. (I immediately recalled Hope reading *One Flew Over the Cuckoo's Nest,* and what happened to McMurphy when he crossed Nurse Ratched.) Also, with Buzz dead and the story surrounding it history, I reasoned, any street corner justice meted out on the Farnsworths would not result in accusations of revenge. Hope had thought this through. And now I knew Bit was in on it because that's why she had pantomimed shooting me between the eyes. She didn't need the college boy telling everybody the obvious.

Now, Sonny glided over the linoleum floor as if he was dancing at the Cowboy. He picked up an extra-large pillow from the bedside chair.

A pillow? *NO!* I wanted to scream. Just kick out the plug!

But Sonny wasn't looking to kick out the plug. *He was going to suffocate Buzz.* I considered suggesting to Sonny an easier way but he shut me up as he held the pillow to his chest, hissing at me: "As soon as you get your thumb out of your ass, sweetheart, you mind giving me a hand?"

I pointed to myself and mouthed, *ME? You want ME to give you a hand?*

Sonny said, "Come on, he's dead. You heard Doc. So let's not keep him waiting."

God, this was twisted. Even though this was not in my job description of being a ranch hand, Sonny *did* need a hand and I couldn't let him down – nor Hope, nor Bit, nor Clete, nor Blue, even Buddy. Most of all, Buzz. So I sent up a quick message to Whomever was keeping score, praying that this was okay – I was in Wyoming where they played by a different rulebook and hoped it wouldn't count against me later.

Sonny shook me from my reverie, barking, "Let's get a move on, junior." I jumped and was now staring more closely at Buzz's heavily bandaged head and grossly swollen right eye. He had purplish bruises around his cheeks and eyes and his neck was scratched raw. His hands were swollen and the skin was scraped off the knuckles.

Looking at Buzz, Sonny said, "I once seen him whup two men in a fair fight. This warnt fair."

Holding the pillow to his chest with his left arm, Sonny crossed himself, then reached over and placed his right hand on Buzz's face and ripped off the tape and oxygen tube and fell forward over Buzz's face with the full weight of his body. It was a couple of seconds before Buzz kicked and scissored his legs.

I gawked helplessly.

Sonny growled: "Don't stand there looking pretty. Hold his legs down."

I also fell forward over Buzz, same as Sonny had done, which wasn't the brightest idea because despite what Doc Evans had told us, Buzz still had a lot of fight left in him. As I flopped over his legs, Buzz's knee flew up and smashed me in the jaw, sending a bolt of white light through my right eye and crashing me into Sonny.

Sonny pushed me away. "Goddamnit, hold him down!"

My bell had been rung, which brought me solidly into the moment. I wanted to scream in Sonny's ear, *How about we switch, I suffocate him and you get the shit kicked out of you.*

Instead, I again fell across Buzz's gyrating thighs, knees, and shins, this time grabbing the bed rail on the opposite side with both hands like I was holding on to a bucking bronc for dear life. I squeezed my hands tighter and tighter around the rails as my ribs and right thigh took sharp shots again and again. I held on as best I could with Sonny giving me encouragement: "It won't be long now, he's running out of gas."

The end came when Buzz heaved up, arching his back so that both of us rose with him, then flopped back down, dead. The machines went haywire, buzzing, blinking and flat-lining.

Sonny slowly lifted the pillow and mumbled calmly, "That didn't take as long as I thought it would," his tone oddly the same as Buzz's when he complained about blistering his hand after Sonny shot the lame horse in his corral. He pulled a sheet over Buzz's face.

A voice came from behind. Doc Evans had come into the room sounding like he was on rounds. He asked, "You boys okay in here?"

Later, in Doc Evans's office, I stared up at a fluorescent light and dirty white ceiling tile. I was a mess and in a shit-pot of pain. Doc had patched me up, then summed it up: "Looks like a broken jaw and a bunch of loose teeth – you'll probably want to see an oral surgeon when you get home. Most likely you'll have a shiner. Have Hope put a steak on it. Three cracked ribs we can't doing anything about and a deep thigh bruise from a charley horse." He popped two pills into my mouth and said, pressing a large bottle of pills into my hand, "Take one of these every two hours with water." Then came Doc's prescription for my cover story: "Looks like you took a nasty spill off Buddy this morning,"

I swallowed twice, the blood in my mouth helping to lubricate the pills. I closed my eyes praying for quick relief from the pain in my body and what had just happened.

The door opened. Sonny came in. Said that he and Clete were waiting outside. Doc said to hold on a minute or two so the pills could kick in; that the ride back to the ranch would be a rough go.

Sonny asked Doc, "Did you fix up Pete Farnsworth yesterday?"

Doc said, "Yep. Blue nearly tore through his right forearm. That boy should have known by now not to take anything from Buzz's truck. He tried to tell me it was some rig trash's pit bull gone rabid. Bunch of bullshit. If it'd been a pit, he'd have had no arm left. Besides, I've seen Blue's work before when he took a chunk out of Pete's arm working at the Lazy T."

The pills kicked in. I felt like I was flying off a cliff. Just before I passed out I heard Sonny say, "Don't worry, Doc, I'll finish what Blue started...

"Just give me time…

"I'm gonna nail Pete's nuts to his nose…

"The old man's, too."

Clete told me the next day that Sonny helped me out to the truck. I do remember that when we got to the Lazy T, Sonny carried me in his arms across the yard and put me in Clete's bed – me dreaming it was like Boo Radley ferrying Jem home after Bob Ewell clobbered him. Sonny left Clete to pull off my boots and cover me up best he could in my sleeping bag.

"You need anything, Squirrel?" Clete asked me, closing the curtains because the sun was coming up, sounding like he would've have run through a brick wall to get it. "Just tell me."

I lay still on my back, gripping and thumbing Doc's prescription, breathing carefully because of my cracked ribs. I was woozy and barely conscious, but I wanted to appear tough to Clete, like I can handle this, no big deal.

I said: "I got 'er."

# Chapter 16

## HOME

Beginnings and endings can happen quickly and unpredictably and coincidently. Back in June, in my college dorm room, in less than two minutes, I'd reluctantly crawled out of my sleeping bag and decided to journey to Wyoming for various reasons. Now, again, in less than two minutes, I was reluctantly getting out of my sleeping bag, this time to call it quits and go home. But this time around for one reason alone: Hope didn't want the college kid messing things up.

Around noon I opened my eyes because of voices. It was wild. Probably due to the medication, I'd been dreaming that the characters in *The Wizard of Oz* were standing around my bed just as they did to Dorothy after she came back from her bonk on the head. And in my dream they were still in the costumes of the Scarecrow, the Lion and the Tin Man. When I blinked a bunch of times, focusing on what was around me, I saw that it was actually Hope, Bit and Clete looking down at me.

Hope spoke first, all business, as if reading from a medical chart: "Henry, Doc Evans came out here this morning to tell us Buzz died last night. He said it was most likely a heart attack brought on by the trauma of his injuries. He also said you took a nasty fall off Buddy this morning. I called your brother Andy and he talked to your parents. They want you home immediately. There's a ticket for you at the Jackson airport for a flight this afternoon." She held up an envelope. "I have your wages. Clete will take you to Jackson. Best get a move on." She handed me the envelope, then dug out a cigarette from the breast pocket of her chamois shirt. Before she lit it, she gave me the hairy eyeball and warned me kindly, *"Doc said for you to lay low for a while, rest up. Best not to talk so you can heal."*

Clete twirled his hat in his hands.

Bit was standing next to her mother, jaw set in support.

I told them I'd be fine. No need to pack me off. Give me a couple of days; I could still drive a tractor.

But Hope said there was no time. My ticket was waiting for me and my parents were worried and wanted me home. She lit her cigarette and sucked hard, her face squinching up, the blazing red-hot coal delivering the message not to fight her. Hope told Clete to pull his truck around while she went to the house to get something that she wanted to give to me. Bit collected and packed my stuff as I did my best to ram my sleeping bag into a stuff sack. I got dressed in my Lake Forest clothes, and Bit helped me tie my tennis shoes then gave me a hand up. I hobbled to the door and stood on the stoop looking around the yard, the small log cabin house with a wisp of smoke winding out the chimney...the barn where I hung out with Buddy and milked the cow...the outhouse...the windmill...the work shed...the blue Ford 150...Bit's camel-colored El Camino...and the three-legged cat hopping back to the barn with something in her mouth. But no Buzz and no

Blue. I swallowed hard thinking train wrecks and final exams to keep my eyes from watering.

Bit came beside me, put an arm around my waist, mostly to steady me, but also to send a message that we had something together. (At least I think that's what I was hoping she was trying to tell me.) I had a brief flashback to the time at the Cowboy Bar when I was swinging her around the dance floor, our noses gently brushing and me inhaling wild and sweet. Anyway, I know she was trying to be light when she said, "Listen, Hank, maybe when things settle down and you're feeling better, come back and see us again. I know Mom would like that. And thanks for helping out. Buzz said you were a good hand...Sonny said so, too."

This being "a good hand" business was way out of whack. What Bit said sounded absurd, but I think she was fumbling with how to say good-bye (and so was I). All summer long I hadn't wanted to start anything with Bit that would interfere with my time at the Lazy T. But I was leaving and feeling brave and wanted her to remember me. I was also flying high again, the drugs and her closeness making me super-lightheaded and stupid. So I went for it. I pulled her even closer to me saying, "Do you want me to come back next summer?"

Bit inched closer, our bodies now in full contact. "I do," she said, "but don't say you will and then don't show up."

She looked up at me for a long time like *kiss me you fool so I know you're coming back*. I said *Yes I am* by planting a wet one on her lips the best I could with the bandage on my face. I knew this was all a little weird, considering I just helped put down her father, but what was I to do. I couldn't stop myself. I pulled back from the kiss, and looked back into the trailer. I said, "Make sure nobody sleeps on my saddle blankets while I'm gone," trying to sound Western cool like Buzz.

Bit smiled and looked away because I think she was about to cry. She was also skeptical. "How can I be sure," she said turning back, our noses now rubbing, "that you're not one of those dudes that comes out here with spurs and a ten-gallon hat then disappears back East to play golf?"

She had me there.

I thought for a second then leaned down and pulled my Cubs cap from my knapsack and put it on her head. Brushing her hair behind her ears, I gave her another kiss this time whispering something in her ear.

She whispered in my ear.

I whispered back.

She took off for the house, taking my knapsack with her

Clete pulled his truck around and pushed open the door on the passenger side door. I hobbled down and got in as he threw my gear in the bed. When we rolled around to the front of the house to say good-bye, Hope was standing on the porch holding Buzz's Akubra, her head bowed and her face full of thoughts I would have given a million dollars to know. She stepped down, walked over, and presented the hat to me through the open window of the truck, saying Buzz wouldn't be needing this anymore and he would want me to have it. I put it on and adjusted it, a remarkable fit.

Bit came up behind Hope and handed me my knapsack that now had in it a small parcel wrapped in brown paper that looked like it would have held a 5x7 framed photograph. There was a smile and a glow on Bit's face that I captured and tucked away with the parcel as I gently pushed it down next to my journal and zippered the knapsack closed. Clete found a station playing a corny Marshall Tucker song – "Heard It in a Love Song" – that we'd listened to on the radio outside the trailer all summer long, when we'd have our boots up, smoking, drinking beer, jawing. And that's how we headed out to Forty Rod Road. With Hope and Bit waving good-bye.

The ride to the airport was mostly a blur. Clete and I

tried to talk but I kept nodding off because I was exhausted, drugged out, and the motion of the truck and bright sun made it impossible for me to keep my eyes open. When we got to the airport, Clete carried my gear in as I hobbled along beside him. He asked the folks behind the ticket counter for a wheelchair, explaining with a wink and a smile that I'd been in a rodeo accident, which showcased his big crooked front tooth. That got a chair under me pronto, which Clete wheeled around the terminal with me in it, making me laugh, taking my mind off of what to say to him at the departure gate. I tried to give him back his Old Timer knife, telling him it was his, I was just borrowing it, but he wouldn't have it. I think we were both kind of stuck, looking for a way out; so, to avoid an awkward moment for both of us, I tore off a piece a paper from my journal and scribbled down my phone number in Lake Forest, palming it to him at the gate, telling him to call me the next time he was over at Eleanor's place.

On the plane, stretching out in first class the best I could, I sank into my aisle seat resting my head, wanting another pill to knock me out for the ride home. In the seat next to me was a rail-thin diva with long red fingernails and a bouffant hairdo, completely uninterested and unsympathetic.

The stewardess asked, "Can I get you anything before we take off?"

I was dying for a beer but didn't want Andy picking up Judy Garland on the other end, so I said, "Just ice water, please."

I lay my head back and fought drifting off. You would have figured I was down-and-out depressed on account of being beat up, Buzz and Blue dying and having to say good-bye to Clete, Hope, and especially Bit, so quickly. For sure, I was numb from what I'd been through, but in the end, I suppose, I processed Buzz's death and everything that had happened in the way they would have wanted me to. It was as Sonny had said: *Don't think on it too much out here.*

*That'll get you into trouble.* I was also floating in the clouds because of Bit and the kisses we shared and what she wrote in my journal when she took my knapsack to the house so she could sneak that picture of her on Blaze into it without Hope knowing – *Hank, I know you know how to write, so write me so I can write you back. I miss you already. Love, Bit.* She had also drawn a big heart under her name.

After reading that note a couple hundred times – and fingering the heart underneath – I finally closed my eyes, breathed deeply, smiled the best I could with the bandage on my face, and let out a long, slow exhale through my nose, rewinding my summer on Forty Rod Road, slowly passing out.

When we got to the gate at O'Hare, the stewardess was gently shaking my shoulder, asking if I needed a wheelchair. I said no, but could she please hand me my backpack from the overhead bin? She did, and also took down Buzz's hat and asked, clowning around and putting it on, "Is this yours?"

"Yes," I said. I took it from her and, tucking my hair behind my ears, put it on and gave her a painful smile. She said, "Cool hat." She stood aside so I could pass. As I did, she asked, "Stetson?"

"No," I said, tipping the brim with a wink, "Akubra."

When Andy spotted me limping down the jetway with a bandaged jaw, a shiner, and wearing a cowboy hat, his first words were the same ones I'd heard two months earlier: "You look mighty stupid, cowboy." Then he added, in his best Ricky Ricardo voice, shaking his finger at me: "Lucee, you got some 'splainin' to do."

I pulled out my journal and a pen, pointing to my jaw as I scribbled at the top of a new page for him to see. Andy read back to me what I had written: *Doctor told me to take it easy for a while, rest up. Best not to talk too much so I can heal.*

Andy understood. He's good about that kind of stuff.
He collected my bags.
We walked to the car.
The sun was going down.
We drove home.

# Chapter 17

## DINING ROOM TABLE ✳ POWDER ROOM DOOR

My first full day home I got a haircut – short to please my
father. I also spent a lot of time in doctors' offices having
my injuries poked at and opined over, the result being my
jaw wired shut for five days. My older brother Andy joked:
*What about his head, Mom, doesn't that need looking into?*
Andy's a real card. What he meant was what possessed a
Lake Forest preppy to ride a bucking horse. When Andy had
asked me *What really happened, Hoss?* I scribbled down in
my journal for him to read that I was thrown from a horse.
Big lie, but an effective alibi. I thought that would shut him
up. End of conversation. But no, Andy chose to inflate my
story, proudly bragging to everybody that I was bucked off
a horse in a rodeo. *A rodeo.* I'm a great bullshitter, but Andy
takes the cake. I also liked Andy's rodeo lie for obvious
reasons – it made me out to be a local celebrity around the
golf shop and Market Square in Lake Forest, and it was
good cover from what really happened, which I was pretty
twisted up about, so I laid low, self-medicated with pain
pills, and slept a lot.

It worked for the most part.

A couple nights later, I was seated at our dining room table with Andy across from me and my parents on either end, a couple of Zip codes separating us. In and around the room were the standard Lake Forest dining room furnishings: two baby sideboards under large gilded mirrors; an oversize oil painting of a great-great-great-relative; a chandelier; and, on top of the dining room table, a silver centerpiece sandwiched by two candelabra.

Normally, I thought of these family dinners as a forced march. Not now. My Wyoming adventure had elevated my status in the family pecking order from runt of the litter to returning hero. Before we sat down, Andy gave me a nudge in the ribs, telling me with all the muscle coming out of my Lacoste shirt that he'd want more strokes on the golf course. My mom, ever worried about my injuries, fussed over her little chick like a mother hen, making sure I was comfortable, well cared for and well fed – as much as I could be sipping nutrition drinks through a straw because of my wired jaw. Last, my father – usually glowering and dictatorial as he reigned from the end of the table – treated me now like an important client, or a relative he really cared for.

It was like I was a different person.

Because of my wired jaw, Andy had decided to liven up the evening by swiping a stack of chit books from the country club along with a bunch of those little pencils with rock-hard erasers. He instructed me to write on the back of the chit when I had something to say; unless, of course, I was planning on ordering a hamburger, shake and fries, then use the front.

I took a sip of my dinner, then wrote, tore off, and handed him my first message: *Mom's going to shit when she sees you stole these.*

Andy read it, said, "No she won't."

My mother said, "What's that dear? What are you passing to Andy?"

I threw Andy under the bus. I ripped off a sheet for my mother that read: *Andy broke into the club last night and stole a case of these and the manager saw him and is reporting him to the Board and the police.*

My mother, waving the chit at him, said, "Andy you didn't. Take these back this instant."

Andy asked to see what I'd written. He said, "Mom, I lifted three pads for Quasimodo here," giving me a nod. "How else is he going to communicate? As you know, he's not real expressive."

Andy gave me his dumb dog look.

I quickly drew a fist with the middle finger extended, blackening in the nail for effect. I folded the note and slid it across to him, flashing him a preview of coming attractions.

Andy studied my artwork. He said, "You know, Mother, I'm wrong. Hank does know how to express himself. He's just better with pictures than words." He passed the note to my father who had been demanding, "What is it you two are passing? Give it here." My father opened it. He harrumphed: "Well, a picture is worth a thousand words. I could use this at our next partners' meeting." He chuckled and slid it back to me saying he didn't know I could draw so well. My mom wanted to see it too, so I slid it down to her. She tittered, "Oh dear," tucking it in the corner of her placemat, adding with a laugh, "I could have used this today at the bridge table."

That was dinner: me chitting and them chatting.

For dessert we had Andy's favorite: Ding Dongs. Typical Andy, he helped himself to mine because of my wired jaw, jamming both into his mouth, giving me a gross chocolate smile. I mouthed back *bite me* as best I could. He gave me the finger then rolled up the two pieces of foil and fired it at me from across the table, nailing me in the chest. Both my parents demanded that we *Stop it*. While I was looking around the floor for the aluminum ball, my father asked me did I want to put my Wyoming earnings in my savings account. I said yes, standing up, faking a throw at Andy, making him flinch and cover up. I mouthed *pussy*, then hustled up to my room to retrieve the envelope Hope had given me when I'd left the Lazy T (I'd never opened it). My father did, taking out the check along with a note. He inspected the check: "I thought you said you were only making eight hundred dollars for the summer. This check is for a thousand." He slid it down to me along with the note. I unfolded it.

*Dear Henry,*

*Thank you for your help this summer. I want you to come back next year to help us out. We have work to do.*

*Sincerely,*

*Hope Stifel*

Mom asked, "What's it say?"

I slid her the note. She read it. "She has beautiful handwriting. That's so nice they want you to come back. Are you going back, dear?"

I nodded yes to my mother, reflecting on Hope's statement *We have work to do*. It was a twisted double entendre. If only Andy and my parents knew what she meant. Ever in charge and pulling the strings, Hope was coaxing me back to the Lazy T. Truthfully, I had little control; I had to return to Wyoming as much for them as I did for myself. But first I had to finish my story for Professor Gurney, or there would be no college and no Wyoming.

My father, clearing his throat, brought me back to the conversation. He was still confounded by the extra funds in my paycheck. "Why, Hank, did they pay you more than what they contracted for *and* you came home early?"

That led to an awkward silence with me tapping my pencil on the table. I looked at Andy.

Andy snapped his fingers for my pad and pencil. He scribbled a note to my father. My father read it: "They don't give it away, Dad. Hank earned it."

I snapped my fingers at Andy, then quickly penciled *Overtime* and held up the pad for my father to see.

He nodded – approving – sticking out his lower lip.

Technically, I was correct.

For the next couple of days, you could find me convalescing around the pool with our black lab, Winston, or in front of my mother's full-length dressing room mirrors, clad in fresh Brooks Brothers boxers, checking myself out after taking a shower in my parents' enormous bathroom that Andy and I still treated as our own. Ten weeks of ten hours a day had slimmed me down and hardened me up. My gut was flat and I could see my ribs. My nicked-up hands and fingers, along with my forearms, were thicker, stronger and tan. My face and neck were either burnt or browned. Working on machinery and bucking hay bales had shaped my shoulders and biceps. My hair was bleached out and somehow my eyes were bluer.

I liked what was looking back at me...a lot.

Four days after being home I got clearance from the tower that I was okay to go to a Cubs game. Andy figured a day in the bleachers sipping Old Style through a straw would do me good. He came up to my room as I was getting dressed. When I motioned with my hands *Let's go*, he asked, "Where's your Cubs cap?"

I tried to sign with my hands *Don't worry about it. Let's just go.*

Andy said, "I know you took that cap to Wyoming. *Shit, Hank, you lost it.* That was the cap Ron Santo gave to Dad. That was your favorite cap."

I pulled out and wrote on a chit *I didn't lose it. I made a trade.*

"For what?" he asked.

I made a rectangle with my fingers.

"A window," Andy said.

I tried again.

"A square?" he guessed.

Again, I fingered a picture frame – frustrated my brother was so thick.

"A parallelogram? A rhombus?" he said, running out of choices. "Come on, Hank, I'm growing a beard."

I wrote, *A picture.*

"A picture? A picture of what, Picasso?"

I waved my hands signaling a curvy girl. Andy was clueless as a toad. Frustrated, I dug in my bedside table drawer where I keep my *Sports Illustrated*s and handed over the picture of Bit barrel racing. I stood back with my arms folded, letting Andy absorb the reason Ron Santo's hat resided in Wyoming.

Andy looked at the picture for a full five seconds. Rubbing the edges with his thumbs, he said, "Holy shit. Good trade, Hoss." He looked at it again, then at me, his smile and my crooked grin hooking up. He weighed it in his hands as if it were gold. "I'd say you got the better end of that deal."

I reached for Andy to give it back. He held it up high, teasing me. "Just a second there, Ringo. You have to tell me name, rank, and serial number before I give it back."

I wasn't in the mood to spill my guts on country club chits so I furiously wrote and ripped off *Her name is Bit.*

"Bit," Andy read, fingering the note in one hand. "Do you get bit, Hank?"

I firmly pressed down on a dull pencil, shoving this in his face: *Short for Elizabeth ASSHOLE.*

"That's her full name," Andy joked, holding up the photo for another look.

I motioned, twirling my hand with *Don't be a dick. Give it back to me now.* I lunged, but Andy was too quick and tall for me.

We quickly digressed.

"I think Bit bit you, Hank? Didn't she?"

"Gibibach," I mumbled through a wired jaw.

"She did, didn't she?"

"Gibibachna," I said, my face red and getting redder, spitting out, "AnnyImnadkidning." And I wasn't kidding. I calmly walked over to the corner of my room and returned with my Stan Mikita hockey stick. I approached Andy with a firm grip ready to carve him up.

I jabbed at him.

He jumped back.

He handed it over.

Andy's not dumb.

*Once when I was thirteen and he was eighteen, I tried to tear apart the downstairs powder room door so I could kill my brother. It was summer and we both had friends over to swim. Andy thought it would be funny to trash my suit in front of everybody, girls included. After I yanked up my trunks, my eyes went wet with rage and revenge. Embarrassment ignited me. I was going to murder my brother. I chased him around the pool then outside into the yard. Because I could no longer run to my mother about my prepubescent problems, I ran and picked up a baseball bat that was lying in the grass. I didn't waste my breath yelling or screaming. Instead, I bore down, saving my strength for when I was to crush his skull. Andy kept checking behind him, thinking I'd tire out.*

*Andy's not only five years older than me, he's also a lot bigger, but I was fast and fueled by a deep dark fury: He'd crossed a line and was going to pay. I was wearing him down on the third pass around the house when he ducked in the front door and barricaded himself in the downstairs powder room. The lock clicked. Andy pleaded from inside for me to calm down, saying he was sorry, real sorry. I beat long and hard on the door, my bat doing my talking. Verna, our parents' housekeeper and cook, screamed from the kitchen, "Anny an' Hank, what you boys up to now?" I ignored her. She came from behind and caught my shoulder as I was switching from swinging to using the bat as a battering ram. She asked me what on God's green earth was I doing banging away like a crazy child on the powder room door.*

*I stopped my assault, winded, not wanting to explain my embarrassment.*

*Andy cracked the door, inching his head out. He said, "Oh hi, Verna. Hank's upset because I struck him out in our baseball game. I won't do it again. Promise."*

*I lunged at him with the bat but Verna had me pretty well wrapped up. She said, "Anny Chandler, you lying to me. Look at dat po boy's face. What's your father going to say when he sees dat?" She pointed at my assault of dents and chipped paint on the powder room door "He's gonna tan your hides." Meaning she wasn't taking the fall for this.*

*Andy stepped up. "Verna, Hank had nothing to do with this," he said, now standing outside the door, thumbing over the dents, but keeping an eye on Verna's hold on me. "I'll get some paint and fix it. Right away." (Andy's really handy, and he did fix it, with me helping him, finishing just as we heard our father's Mercedes roll down our gravel driveway.)*

*Verna turned me around and gave me a big hug in her plumpy middle, me being dangerously close to her large bosom. I was a little too old for this but Verna could not stop mothering us. Walking back to the pool, Andy stopped me in the den, said he was real sorry. He told everybody out by the pool that I would have surely killed him if Verna hadn't broken things up. In a weird way Andy was proud of me, and from that day on he was careful about pushing my buttons. (My parents have a lot of cool, expensive stuff in our house that someday will be Andy's and mine. I've never told this to Andy, and I won't either because I don't want to give it away, but I've got dibs on the powder room door.)*

# Chapter 18

## BIT'S LETTER TO ME ✻ MY LETTER TO BIT

On my fifth day home, a letter arrived from Bit. I was still in the process of writing her a long letter because I had a lot to say. Here is her first letter to me:

*August 2, 1977*

*Dear Hank,*

*I could not wait for you to write me. You didn't give me your address because I asked you to write me first so I could write you back. But I did copy down your address that was on the inside of your journal while I was in the house swiping that picture of me on Blaze that you wanted. That way I'd know, in case you never wrote me, where to track you down with a dull knife, or club you to death with a driver – that's a golf club, right? Either way your Cubs cap would be mowed, raked, baled and airmailed back to you. That's my way of saying I miss you.*

*I'm writing this at the Lazy T sitting in Mom's spot by the bay window, looking at her binoculars, books and an ashtray filled with cigarette butts. It's coming on midnight and she's asleep. Today was long, and she was worn out from the funeral and the party afterwards at the Cowboy Bar. I'm staying with her now here at the ranch. Sonny said he'd be down to help out Clete until the last bale of hay gets stacked. A lot of folks offered to come out and stay with Mom, but she said no, except to one. I'll get to that.*

*This all must be so confusing for you. Everything happened so fast with Dad's accident and you leaving. It's now come crashing down on me and Mom. I know you didn't expect this. All I can tell you is out here we live with accidents and tragedy every day, right outside the door. Sonny told me that God gives us all a coil of rope, and Dad ran out of his, like we all will one day. That's why we're so hardened and cynical about death. It doesn't mean we don't feel it. I think it just our way of protecting ourselves from the harsh world we live in.*

*Dad was buried at the cemetery up in the foothills behind town where everybody gets planted. Many of the ranchers from Sublette County were there. Sheriff Farnsworth and Pete were in the back row pretending to be solemn. Courtenay opened up the Cowboy Bar after and offered up to anybody to ride their horse in. Nobody did because nobody could do it like Dad. You know that. I miss him so much now I'm starting to cry again. I didn't think I had any tears left. I was raised around cowpokes and ranch hands and mountain men where crying wasn't in the cards. I picked up young that it's a hard life so turn off the waterworks; just get on with it. But it's impossible looking out at the hayfields knowing I'll never see Dad walking the ditches with a shovel over his shoulder, hear him play his guitar and sing country songs, and him and Mom laughing together, smoking, telling cowboy stories. I loved watching him rope, brand, and doctor a calf. I still see him and Blue driving away down Forty Rod Road, and always will. I told Mom I want kill Farnsworth with my bare hands. She assured me there's plenty of time for that.*

*You and I never talked about Dad's ways, and I'm thankful you didn't say anything. It must have been confusing to you because I know how much you liked my parents, and you struggled coming to terms with Dad and Dorothy Farnsworth. All I can tell you, Hank, is people aren't perfect, but if you love them, and they love you back, you make it work. Dad was what he was. Mom dealt with it best she could, usually with a sharp tongue, like when we were standing arm-in-arm over Dad's marker at the cemetery today, and she said, "Well, Buzzy Stifel, now when I come to town I'll know where to find you, and I won't worry about you being with another woman."*

*The funeral was all Mom. She didn't want the preacher from town mucking it up with Jesus and hymns and the Lord's Prayer. Reverend Sykes didn't know Dad from Adam. So, for the service Mom dressed up as a Lakota Sioux medicine man. She was beautiful in her buckskins and badger claw necklace and beaded headband, dancing around in her moccasins. She chanted in what people thought was the native tongue of the Lakota Sioux. It was beautiful, even though it was gibberish according to her. Nobody knew the difference. She was quite a sight twirling around with an old medicine stick with rattles on it, the wind blowing through the pines, and the sun shinning through. She gave Dad a great send-off.*

*At the Cowboy Bar after, Mom held court and got pretty drunk. She usually doesn't drink, so I was surprised when I saw two Scotch and sodas in front of her at all times, everybody volunteering to help her reload. All the cowboys in the county who rode with Dad came in and stayed late. I knew many of them from cow camp and branding, and they all told me the same thing – they loved Dad. It's funny, Hank, grown men – damn tough and hardened – were melting like butter talking about him. It made me cry and cry.*

*I was beat by the time Sonny came up to me at the end*

*of the night and swallowed me in a bear hug for about five minutes. He was real drunk and sad. He kept kissing the top of my head calling me Itty Bit – his pet name for me when I was a little girl. I wanted to cry but I didn't have any tears left. He didn't have to tell me how much he loved Dad and was going to miss him; that he was his best friend and there was none better. I knew because I could feel his tears dripping onto my scalp. Sonny asked about you. He told me how you were holding on for dear life when Dad was trying to buck you off. He said he wants you to come back next summer and help us out. Poor Clete's a mess. Losing Dad was like losing his father and best friend at the same time. And he misses your company in the trailer and out in the fields. He told Mom he'd stay on without pay for as long as she wanted.*

*This is what I aimed on telling you. At the end of the night, when the bar was almost empty, Dorothy Farnsworth came in. She was dry-eyed and serious. She went over to Mom. I heard her say she was very sorry for Mom's loss. She also said she loved Buzz and that she was sorry that she hurt Mom. Dorothy then kissed Mom's cheek and whispered something in her ear. Mom whispered back. Dorothy left. On the ride back to the ranch I asked Mom what she and Dorothy were whispering to each other back in the bar. Mom started laughing. I looked over at her and she had this wicked grin. She told me Dorothy's moving out to the Lazy T in a week to keep her company, that it will drive Farnsworth up a tree. Mom liked that, that she could make Farnsworth squirm. I don't know what she has up her sleeve, only that it's coming. Mom's told me stories over the years about the Lakota Souix being a vengeful tribe. I don't doubt her, and I know she wouldn't want to let the tribe, or Buzz, down. Mom will know what to do when the time is right, but I'm worried about Farnsworth – he knows we know. I'll stop there. I just can't wait for you to get back out here.*

*I have one last thing to tell you. You don't know but I used to shortcut across Forty Rod Road every chance I could to see Mom, but really I was hoping to see you. Mom knew I was up to something because she'd catch me looking out the window into the fields slipping in questions about you. She read me like an open book. But she wouldn't tease me. She'd just pretend she didn't know I had a thing for the cute, longhaired boy from the East. (Midwest, I know, but that doesn't sound right.) I can't wait until next summer to see you, meaning I want to see you sooner. I know you had a lot on your mind this summer and had your head down working hard. I was so worried at the end you'd slip away back East.*

*I had so much fun with you here at the ranch, and I can't stand it that you're gone. Work was not work when you were around, now it's just a chore. I wanted you to kiss me at the Cowboy Bar that night when we were dancing, but I knew you wouldn't because of Mom and Dad. That made me like you even more. Thank God you kissed me before you left because I know we shared the same feeling. Now, I can't stop thinking about you. If you've changed your mind about me you'd better change your address and get a haircut, because I'll come scalp you. I'm putting in another picture of me that Dad took last spring at roundup. It was one of his favorites, Mom's too. I hope you like it, and I hope you're healing from all your injuries and all that happened.*

*Write me back, Hank. I miss you very much.*

*Love,*

*Bit*

I looked over the new photograph of Bit with her long, loose black hair spilling out from under a wide-brimmed, white straw hat; neatly buttoned up in a well-worn man's blue jean jacket large enough to fit a sweater underneath and scarf wrapped around her neck. The photo captured the distinctive nose and ears and strong hands of her father; and the thin, finely shaped lips and watchful brown eyes of her mother; all riding tall atop a horse as calm as Bit was cool.

Reading Bit's letter over and over was if I was still sitting side-by-side with her on the front porch of the Lazy T overlooking the corrals and foothills toward the Wind Rivers, talking about our lives, families and friends. I could still hear her voice as I ran my finger over every word, every sentence. I read and reread her letter because I was afraid I'd forget what her voice sounded like; that her letter would become mere pen marks on a page.

Here is my first letter back to Bit:

*August 5, 1977*

*Dear Bit,*

*I had started writing you but put it aside when I saw your letter in today's mail. I was hoping to hear from you but did not expect to until I'd written you (you are a sneak). Believe me I went into overdrive when I saw your handwriting and the Cora postmark. None of the doctors I've seen came close to making me feel the way I did when I read your letter.*

*I'm still a bit of a mess, more from what happened to Buzz than what physically happened to me. Everything came on so fast, and Hope was right to ship me home pronto. All I did on the plane ride home was think about you, and that's all I've done since. So much of what I want to tell you about Buzz and Hope and Sonny and Clete and Blue and the Lazy T – and what happened – is in the letter I set aside. I will finish it tomorrow, I promise. For now, I want to wrap this up and get it in the mail.*

*I miss you,*

*Hank*

# Chapter 19

## THE BRIDGE TABLE * MEGAN MCCARTHY

Two days after Dr. Templeton unwired my jaw, I was feeling close to normal; my eye was no longer discolored and swollen, my Charley Horse had healed, and my ribs were on the mend. I'd been out running errands all morning when I tiptoed into the house because our driveway looked like a parking lot, which meant my mother's Tuesday afternoon bridge group was tabled and talking.

Our house is a three-story Georgian brick with two fireplaces and four gabled windows on the third floor that face a long, tree-lined driveway. The property abuts the Bogey Club, no more than a solid seven iron from our backyard to the eighteenth green. There is very little planting in front as my mother explained to me that a house should speak for itself. To the north is a three-car garage, above which Andy lived, and partied, rent-free. Out back is a fenced swimming pool and terrace surrounded by a yard big enough to play football, baseball, and hockey in the winter – when we would throw out a hose and flood the place. Now, as I made sure not to let the screen door slam, I crept up the staircase to avoid my mother's *Is that you Hank dear, come in and say hello.* I stopped at the top of the landing and listened. Cards were being shuffled and dealt.

My mother: "One spade."

Lemay Simmons: "Pass. Mary, what on earth happened to poor Hank. I heard from Lou he had an accident."

My mother: "Poor dear fell off a horse."

Dotsy Shapleigh: "Where was he on a horse? Two no trump."

My mother: "Jackson, Wyoming."

Shrimpy Watson's raspy voice: "I pass. At the Wentworths or the MacKenzies?"

My mother, hesitating: "Neither. No...I believe their name was Stifel. Four spades."

Shrimpy again: "Do we know them?"

My mother: "No, from what I've learned – Hank hasn't told me much – this was a working ranch. He came home looking like God knows what. His clothes took Verna a week and a box of Tide to clean. Dr. Templeton had to fix his teeth and wire his jaw shut. His ribs were broken and he's still walking with a limp. You don't want to see his hands they're so beaten up and scabbed over. And his face is so sunburned. They must have worked him to death. And I know they didn't feed him. I've never seen him so thin. Your bid, Lemay."

Lemay: "So sorry. Pass."

Dotsy: "How did he end up there? Four no trump."

My mother: "Apparently he wrote this man Buzz a letter and asked him for a job."

Shrimpy: "I pass. How did he know him? Were you and Peter okay with this? And Mary...please tell Verna she makes the most outstanding cucumber sandwiches."

My mother: "Oh, thank you, I will. I have to confess, we were skeptical about Hank's plans. You know he had a terrible time his freshman year. Five diamonds."

Silence

Dotsy: "Pass. Well…he's certainly grown up. I saw him in Market Square yesterday. I know you say he looks so thin and ragged, but Mary, he's also so handsome and rugged looking. Does he have a girl?"

My mother: "If he does, he won't say. I can't get any information out of him, or Andy. It's maddening. I know he had a girl last year, but it ended badly. You would think they would talk to their mother, but they don't. Everything seems to be on a need-to-know basis. It's like I'm living with the CIA. We can't even get them to play golf – and we all like to play golf. We have them for such a short time. It breaks my heart they want to make it shorter. It just makes me want to scream. Peter says they're just boys. I say they're not. I think I've raised two clams."

Lemay: "Pass. I agree."

Shrimpy laughs, coughs as she lights a cigarette: "My Alex has not spoken more than six sentences to me all year. How can he hold all those words in?"

Dotsy: "Trey does it too. The silence kills me. I know they're trying to torture me. Six spades."

My mother: "Would anyone like more iced tea?"

Lemay: "I would, please. So you say Hank doesn't have a girl. What about Megan McCarthy? I know she's always had a thing for Hank."

Shrimpy: "I pass. Megan's adorable."

Dotsy squeaked: "She's lost weight and her skin's cleared up."

Lemay: "I don't think she has a beau."

My mother: "You're so right. They always made such a cute pair. Hank will say no, but I'll insist he ask her out. It will be good for him while he's here. Boys always need a little goose."

They all agreed.

They all passed.

I was trumped.

I slipped away to my room for a cigarette and a few hours of writing, editing and typing before dinner, as well as contemplating what I could bargain for in return for asking out Megan McCarthy. Much of my time was now spent writing my story for Professor Gurney so that I could return to school (I lied to my parents about my time spent writing and typing Gurney's paper, telling them it was an extra credit project, which they ate up.) Telling stories comes naturally to me, but writing is akin to pushing a Chrysler up a hill with my forehead. That's why I had to spend countless hours writing and rewriting and editing and reediting, because if Professor Gurney failed me, my life would surely suck. I became obsessed, and that was good because my hard work prepared me for if and when I was to return to school. You should know there was part of my story that I obviously had trouble with and did not want to dwell on – meaning helping to kill Buzz. When you experience something like that, you dive deep into denial and silence, hoping it will sort itself out. The last thing I wanted to do at the moment was talk about it, much less write about it.

The bridge table was not wrong, Megan McCarthy was adorable. She'd been adorable since we were king and queen of the May Day parade in kindergarten. We were always on each other's dance cards, and were constantly being seated together at country club and family events. We were thought of as a couple in waiting, which is okay when you're thirteen and she's cute, but it becomes a bit of a problem when you get older and want to venture beyond your home turf. At the moment, for sure, my biggest concern was Megan McCarthy still had me in her sights, and the bridge table was helping her squeeze the trigger.

Normally, I don't give in to whom the mothers think I should ask out, but here I spotted an opportunity. I drove a hard bargain with my mother: I'd ask out Megan McCarthy if I could hitch a ride back to school with Tommy Childress – not one of her favorites. My mother cringed, but relented. Two nights later, I took Megan to one of the local hamburger spots, then on to a late-night place that wasn't quite yet buzzing. I was on my best behavior, directing questions to her, about her, painfully trying to follow her meandering stories. The loud music made it harder, and a bunch of times I had to fake it and laugh when I thought she'd said something funny because I wanted to appear polite and earn a solid report from my mother as I was dead set on riding back to school with Tommy Childress.

Truth be told, Megan looked hot. She'd prepared for our date: she had on tight preppy-pink shorts and a breezy blue summer button-up shirt – two buttons short of being all the way buttoned up. She was blond, tan, and firmly at her fighting weight. She was also out-beering me, which girls don't like if they are kicking it into gear and have you in their headlights, and you're jacking around in the breakdown lane as I was. Before the check came she toed me in the calf under the table and started reminiscing about us being king and queen of the May Day parade years ago. Later, driving her home, Megan, more than a little tipsy and nearly in my lap, was going on and on about how short I was at dancing school, how I only came up to her bust. She hammered home that point by turning sideways in the car and showing me – as if I didn't know – what a bust was.

When I dropped her off at her parents' house, I walked her to the front door. Before keying the lock she turned and put her arms around my neck and arched up on her Dr. Scholl's.

I squirmed around and looked down at my flip-flops.

She said to look at her.

I did.

That's when she can-opened my mouth with her tongue. I jumped and squealed as if I'd been jabbed with a pin, partially from surprise, partially because my jaw was still sore. Megan held me in place, her mouth now suctioned onto mine. I did my best to run my tongue away from her tongue, like a game of hide-and-seek or keep-away, but she was faster and caught me a few times. What could I do? So, I settled down to some French kissing because I had to come up with a plan, and you can't do that if you're playing defense in your mouth. I did not like the direction this was going. Coming up for air I panicked, abruptly stating *I have to go.* She protested and tried to rev up my engine. I backed away and said *I'm sorry.* Can you believe that? I said *I was sorry.* Boy, was I sorry I said *I was sorry.* I should have said I had VD. The look on her face could have fried an egg. I moved to my car, keeping an eye peeled in case she wanted to brain me with a flower pot. Instead, she went inside and slammed the door.

Believe me, I was up for messing around, but I try to think of myself as a monogamist (at my age, it's hard – double entendre intended). And I wasn't just thinking about Bit. This was a no-win situation. Denying Megan meant hell hath no fury like a woman scorned. However, I also knew this was a losing proposition because of the next day...and the day after...and the day after that. Do I call her? Then, let's say I don't for a week, which means I'm now paranoid as shit about running into her, which I will sooner than later in Lake Forest – believe me. You tell me what should be the first thing out of my mouth after *Hi Megan. What's new? Long time no see.*

To invoke Ricky Ricardo: *Ay carramba*!

The next afternoon my mother asked me in a chilly tone if we could talk; her face a howitzer pointed directly at me. Obviously, I had more than an inkling of what she had on her mind. I joined her in the den, sitting opposite, she on the sofa and me on the arm of a chair My mother was tense. My father was not home yet so she had not had a drink. She said, "How was your date with Megan?"

I said, "Fine."

She asked, "What did you do?"

I said, "I took her to The Pit, then O'Malleys. Why?"

"What did you do after that?"

I knew where this was going. "I dropped her off at home."

"Did you do anything?

"Mom, what's your point?"

My mother is polite but direct. "I heard that you were very forward with Megan."

I knew it. The bridge table had been burning up the phone wires – hell hath no fury, especially the mother of a scorned daughter. I said that was untrue and began to explain what really had happened. But it wasn't a fair fight: me against Mom, Megan, Megan's mother, and the bridge table. I was backpedaling when I shouldn't have been. I needed someone in my corner. Why Andy came in right then and there I'll never know. He sensed the tension. "What's up?" he asked.

I stood. "Mom heard I came on to Megan McCarthy in a bad way last night. That's so bogus. She was coming on to me. That's why I left."

Andy saw I was pissed, knew where I was coming from. He calmly tamped me down.

Still not believing me, my mother continued, "Hank, Mrs. McCarthy said you accosted Megan."

Andy sized up the situation. He stepped in front of me. "Mom, that's not true and you know it."

Mom gave Andy a look. He didn't back down. He said hold on a second, then disappeared.

My mom and I didn't say anything. I went over to the bookcase and fingered over titles, pulling out *The Godfather*, flipping to the dog-earred, sex filled page at the beginning of the book, reading it for the umpteenth time. My mother lit a cigarette. She rarely smokes, and usually with a cocktail. I wanted a cigarette but did not want to appear nervous.

Andy returned holding something behind his back. He

stated there are four reasons why Megan is not telling the truth.

My mother stubbed out her cigarette.

Andy said, "One, you know Hank. Two, Dad knows Hank. Three, I know Hank. And four, here." He handed over my new picture of Bit, which I had framed.

My mother sized up the photograph. She said to me, "Who is this, dear?"

I said, "My girlfriend."

"Who is she?"

"Elizabeth Stifel. I met her in Wyoming."

My mother studied the photograph. "She's quite attractive."

I didn't know what to say so I said, "Yes, she is."

My mother placed the photo in front of her on the table soaking it in. Then she went dark, her green eyes melting to a steely gray, her manicured nails clenching the arms of the chair; her bouffant, eyebrows, nose and chin now pointed and focused. My mother's origin is St. Louis, where manners and bourbon are poured straight. And though she may be a little la-de-da, she abhorred underhanded behavior and could be a jaguar when it came to protecting her offspring. Now that my mother knew the score, I could see she was set on defending me at the bridge table. I owed her for that and wanted to make her happy in some way. I had an idea. I said, "Mother, let me fix you a drink." I stepped over to the bar. Andy signaled "beer-me." Coming back, handing out the drinks – a healthy vodka tonic and lime for my mother – I took a hit off my beer then said, "Andy and I were wondering if you and Dad would like to sneak out tomorrow for a quick eighteen. We'll play a Scotch format. You get the warlord home by four and I'll pack up a few beers for us and a small carafe for you."

On cue, Andy followed my lead: "This time, Mom, it's me and Dad against you and Hank."

My mother's face returned, her eyes sparkled, her fingers

relaxed. She said, "Boys, I'd love that more than anything. It would be so much fun. For dinner, I'll have Verna make her special twice-baked potatoes and macaroni salad, and we'll grill steaks."

I said I'd check with the pro shop to see if we couldn't get off by four-thirty. Andy said we should be able to fly around in two and a half hours if Dad doesn't throw too many clubs. That made us all laugh and recount our favorite stories of Peter Chandler, cool, hard-nosed corporate attorney, throwing his putter with that helicopter sound. Now, basking in the glow of my mother's laughing face, I promised myself to spend my golf cart time with her talking about my summer in Wyoming – selectively of course – but especially about my new girlfriend. Somehow, I knew she would like that.

And she did.

And so did I.

You have to understand, I'm a momma's boy. So is Andy. We're the same that way except he doesn't admit it. I tried to hide it until my college friend Freddy Farr admitted to me last year that he, too, was a momma's boy, and proud of it. Freddy's a super cool, good looking guy from New York City who can get away with acting wealthy and sophisticated because he is wealthy and sophisticated; however, he's also down to earth and not a phony. Farr told me admitting you're a momma's boy also gets you girls' attention because they eat up shit like that because they think you're the strong, sensitive type. I think he's right. Besides, who am I to argue with Freddy Farr.

In addition to being a momma's boy, I'm also, simply, a boy; and, it's not right that boys frustrate their mothers by clamming up. For sure, we're torturing them. But sometimes we don't know how to form the words, nor spit them out. Mothers want to help us with our girl problems because they're female, like fathers want to help us by coaching how to throw a baseball or catch a football. But boys question

*What do mothers know?* We think they're ancient, out-of-touch housewives who for some reason married our fathers.

The next afternoon, on the fourth hole, with my mother as my playing and golf cart partner, I wedged open my mouth and spilled the beans about my love life, beginning with Bit. My mother acted nonchalant, but I could tell she was wetting her pants because our pace of play slowed and our golf game turned to shit. At first I didn't mention Janie Wallace because I wanted to move forward, not backward. So I told my mother about how I had a big crush on Bit; how I first got to know her because she and Polly Hamilton were good friends; how we hung out at the ranch and talked about Polly and Luke Danforth; and, how I really liked Bit, but I held back because I was afraid getting involved with her would screw up my time at the Lazy T. For obvious reasons, I purposely didn't talk at all about Buzz and Hope, but I did tell her about Clete, and how we'd become friends.

My mother's a romantic (that's where I get it). That's why she asked me at the twelfth hole *Did you kiss Bit?* That led me to telling her the whole story about dancing with Bit at the Cowboy Bar (which my mother lapped up with a spoon), and how later, outside the trailer when I was leaving, I finally got up my nerve to plant a wet one on her as we said goodbye. My mother was so caught up with my story that she ignored my father's waving arms, urging her to *Come on, Honey, hit your shot. The sun's going down.*

By the thirteenth hole I felt comfortable enough to really open up, explaining how I was a little girl-shy about Bit on account of how I'd smothered Janie Wallace, openly admitting how I was certain that my obsessive and insecure behavior blew up our love affair. My mother faced me, her expression composed and thoughtful. She asked a few innocent questions about Janie, which I answered, explaining to her how Janie had dumped me for another guy; how I couldn't blame her because I'd gone off the rails. It was a huge relief for me to let go, to be honest and own up to the breakup, even though it made me look away and go a little misty eyed. When I turned my head back around, my mother was looking at me with a pained expression that telegraphed she was dying to put her hand on my cheek and say, *Oh sweetheart, I know how it hurts.* But she didn't because I think she knew I was too old for that. Another reason she didn't say anything was by this time we were on the fringe of the fifteenth green and my father was blowing his horn: Mom and I were down by four in our match with three holes to play.

We were shit-out-of-luck.

Andy asked did we want to play in?

I looked at my mother and said *Absolutely.*

My mother rested her hand on my knee, giving me a soft squeeze with a sparkle in her eye. She then whipped around and addressed my father, firing a fingernail directly at him, demanding a rematch – same teams – claiming his scorekeeping must be faulty.

# Chapter 20

## CLETE * MY FATHER'S CHIT

Late one morning, after a week at home and two more letters from Bit, I was deep asleep having one of those fantastic dreams where I was running naked ahead of a stampeding herd of buffalo. I stopped just short of a steep cliff. I looked behind me. I had no choice. I dove off...falling... falling... falling. Then I said to myself this is stupid. This is a dream. I can fly. So I did. I spread my arms out and soared around like a hawk, diving up and down and around. Flying dreams are the best, and you never want them to end. This one did with my mother's gentle hand shaking me awake with *Honey, you have a telephone call. A man named Clete Nicholson is on the line.* (My mother rarely came into my room – I think for fear of infection and humiliation – and usually only to scout ahead before she'd send in Verna for an all-day sweep and scouring.)

I pulled on shorts and a T-shirt and grabbed my Old Timer knife from my bureau. My mother said I could take the call in her sitting room. I picked up and put the phone to my ear hearing kitchen noises from downstairs. I yelled as loud as I could *I got it, Mom.* My mother hung up. I put the phone to my ear hearing Clete's breathing and Eleanor Pfisterer in the background doing dishes in her kitchen. I knew exactly where Clete was: in Eleanor's small living room overlooking the mowed fields and haystacks, a quarter mile off Forty Rod Road, a mile from the Lazy T, sitting upright in her big brown Naugahyde Barcalounger, his hat off, not getting too comfortable because Eleanor would be eavesdropping from the kitchen.

I said, "Hi, Clete."

He whispered, "Hi, Squirrel. How you feeling?"

I propped the phone against my ear, opening and closing the Old Timer, saying, "No worse for wear," sounding and pretending as if I were still in Wyoming.

"You get doctored up okay?"

"Yeah," I said, feeling my face. "They fixed my teeth and wired my jaw for five days."

"How's everything else?"

"It's coming along," I said, knowing Clete was hinting at what happened in Buzz's hospital room. Even though I was struggling with it, and I'm glad he asked, I didn't want to dwell on it. I knew Clete was on the clock with Eleanor nearby, so I cut to the chase. "How was Buzz's funeral?"

He said softly, "Real nice. Hope put on her Lakota Sioux outfit and danced around with an old medicine stick that had rattles on it. She was chanting in some tongue no one could understand but somehow we all got the message. After at the Cowboy she held court. Stayed right up to the end. I don't think there was a rancher in Sublette County that didn't have somebody there." He went on about all of Buzz's cowpoke buddies and told me stories he'd not heard before. I didn't tell him Bit had written me about most of this; Clete wanted to tell me so I pretended like this was all new.

I asked, knowing the answer, "Farnsworth and Asshole Pete at the funeral?"

Clete lowered his voice even more so Eleanor couldn't hear him. "Yep, standing in the back. Farnsworth had those goddamn mirrored glasses on. He was telling everybody he was going to bring to justice whoever done this to Buzz Stifel. He's a low-down lying rat and if I'd had my 357 I'd've made Swiss cheese out of him right then and there."

I asked, "Do you think he knows we know…?"

Clete whispered, "He can't hide it, even behind his damn glasses."

"What about Asshole Pete?"

"Squirrel, he was as nervous as a whore in church."

"How about Sonny?"

"Real calm. I've never seen him more sober. You know how Sonny gets when he's got his eye on a chore."

"And Hope and Bit?"

Clete said, "It was tough on them, Squirrel. But the two of them played it perfect. Told Farnsworth they were so thankful that he was doing his best to find who done it to Buzz."

Neither of us spoke for a second or two. I looked out the window at Winston sprawled under the shade of a tree. I had to ask, "What happened with Blue?"

Clete took a couple of breaths and choked out: "Sonny and me fetched him out of the culvert the day you left. We scooped him up and wrapped him in one of Buddy's saddle blankets from Buzz's truck and buried him back of the barn. I never seen Sonny so upset. Said Blue didn't deserve this. I made a marker out of an old plank and a fence pole. Sonny wrote on the plank with some black paint just what Buzz would have wanted: *Blue – Goddamn Good Dog*. Yesterday we had a little ceremony. Bit and Hope and me were standing beside Sonny with that worthless three-legged cat setting beside us licking her stump. Sonny said 'Rest easy, Blue, we'll take it from here.' That's when Bear came scrambling under the fence and chased after the cat."

I was confused. I said, "A bear chased after the cat?"

"No, Squirrel," Clete said, "Bear's a whelp. Sonny showed up with her the day after the funeral. Joe Carney out at the Three Quarter Circle had a litter and Sonny took one for the Lazy T on account of Blue. I hope you don't mind, Squirrel, but she's bunking with me in the trailer."

I sat back on my mother's chaise, smiling. I clicked the knife shut – Sonny Skinner was a savior. I told Clete it was fine by me that the dog bunked in the trailer as long as she pees outside and checks the door at night. I could hear Clete chuckling and see his big crooked tooth. I could also hear Eleanor rattling pots and pans in the background, squawking in a loud voice: "Clete, is that a long distance call?"

Clete said away from the phone, "Yes, ma'am. I'm hanging up now. I'll call the operator for the charges and leave you the money right here by the phone." Then he whispered, "You coming back next summer?"

I promised him I'd be out as soon as school was over.

"I'm counting on it," he said. "So is Sonny and Hope. And you know Bit is. Time I got back to work. Sonny and I have some baling and stacking still to do."

I hung up, telling Clete, "Call me when you can. And next time call collect," explaining that's what parents are for.

I looked out the window at Winston now lounging on the top step of the pool, seeking relief from the hot and humid August day, following a fly, snapping at it with his snout. I rubbed the casing of Clete's Old Timer and stared out another window at a foursome finishing up on the eighteenth green of the Bogey Club. After they putted out and shook hands, I called Scott Hodges to confirm our match that afternoon. (Scott is my oldest friend and golfing partner. I love playing golf, especially with Scott, because our matches are competitive, but our time together is more about friendship than the scorecard – even though we both keep score. He was also the one playing with me a year ago when my father interrupted us on the tenth tee to tell me my friend Luke Danforth had died rock climbing in Wyoming – weird, you never forget where you are and whom you're with when you get hit with news like that.)

I was standing outside the pro shop waiting for Scott to show up for our match. Above me in the screened-in porch that overlooked the eighteenth hole, the practice green, and the first tee, I overheard my father talking with the other men in his foursome. They were winding down after their round, drinking, playing backgammon, shaking ice in glasses and dice in a leather cup.

Mr. Simmons said to my father, "Peter, what happened to Hank? LeMay told me something or other about him having an accident."

My father said, "He did, Lou."

Mr. Simmons asked, "What happened?"

My father said, "He was bucked off a horse."

"Where?"

"Wyoming."

"No kidding?"

Mr. Shapleigh asked, "What was he doing out there? Working on a dude ranch?"

"No, Wimmer," my father said, "he was on a working ranch."

"How did you get him that job?" Mr. Shapleigh asked.

"I didn't."

"You didn't?"

"No...he found it on his own."

"Good for him," Mr. Williams said.

Lou asked, "Peter, what was he doing on the horse?"

My father said, "Andy told me...Hank's been quiet about all this for some reason... that he was riding a horse in a local rodeo. I think he was riding what they call a saddle bronc. Anyway, he was thrown off and hurt himself."

Mr. Williams said, "Let me get this straight, Peter. Your

son got himself a job on a ranch in Wyoming and was bucked off a horse in a rodeo."

"Yes...yes, he was," my father confirmed.

Mr. Shapleigh said, "Well, Peter, you're not going have to worry about that one."

Silence

I next heard dice loaded up and shaking in a cup. I wanted to imagine my father nodding his head, sticking out his lower lip, looking into his empty glass with satisfaction.

The dice cup shook.

Lou said, "Let's roll for the drinks, I have to get home. We've got a party tonight."

My dad said, "No, no, I've got this round."

"No, Peter," Mr. Simmons said, "let's roll for it."

The four of them bickered back and forth only backing down when my father insisted: "Believe me, drinks are on me. Please give me that chit."

# Chapter 21

### SCOTT HODGES * ALISON HENRY

Scott Hodges and I were the last pairing to go off that afternoon. We weren't going to play a full round; we just wanted to get away, zoom around the course, play a bunch of holes, drink a few beers. Besides, I was still a little sore, especially in my ribs. Properly dressed in long madras shorts with solid color polo shirts, we teed off on time, both of us smacking drives down the middle of the fairway, then tipping our hats to the caddy master as we headed down the first hole – Scott in a purple Williams College hat; me in a red Chicago Blackhawks cap.

On the fourth hole, away from the clubhouse, the golf course empty, we slowed our game, switching to playing monkey golf in our bare feet – that means we could only use one club. We both selected seven irons. Normally, Scott and I are ten handicaps and play pretty even, but with monkey golf it really comes down to the putting. Imagine trying to get the ball in the hole with a seven iron after drinking a few beers while constantly laughing about girls and high times and stupid shit only twenty-year-old boys think is funny. We both five-putted a couple of greens. Then I had the great idea of putting using the handled end of the club like a pool cue. So, if you happened to be on the gigantic double green at the eighth and fourteenth holes at the Bogey Club at six o'clock on August 7, 1977, you would have seen two shoeless retreads lying prostrate with their golf hats turned around lining up putts like Willy Masconi and Minnesota Fats. I had an 11 on that hole, losing to Scott by a stroke. And it was a par three. We lost interest and track of the score after that, ending up at the halfway house under a tree because it was still sunny and hot. We had our shoes off and bare feet up on the dash of the cart, smoking, talking, finishing the last of our beers, the shadows lengthening, the temperature cooling.

Scott asked, "When are you heading back to school?"

I hedged, not knowing for sure if I was because I had not yet turned in Professor Gurney's paper. "I think the first week in September. You?"

He said, "I think the tenth. My parents want me to go back earlier, like today. You're lucky you didn't stay around this summer. After the deb parties and the Fourth of July, it died."

Scott and I grew up around the country club, at the Day school, and hanging out at each other's houses. I hate the expression "best friend," but Scott was my best friend and partner in crime. In terms of height, he's between my five ten and Andy's six two, and has the body of a cross country runner. He's got wavy, thick brown hair that the girls are always fussing with to get his attention, and mothers were always mussing up because he was "so darn cute." Like all of us, he plays sports, and would have been really good at any one if only he cared. He's quick as a whip, but only studies when someone is gaining on him. As for girls, he prefers Ginger and Veronica while I'm more Mary Ann and Betty (Think *Gilligan's Island* and *Archie* comics). My mother – like most of the mothers – always lights up when he's around.

Scott's a lot like my brother Andy: funny, clever, and always getting the part even though he doesn't know how to ride the horse.

For years, Scott and I have gotten into a lot of trouble, with his parents thinking I was the one stirring it up, and most of the time my parents thinking the same. Believe me, nothing stuck to Scott like it did to me. For example: The summer of senior year, he was sort of caught red-handed in Patricia (Pepper) Martin's second-story bedroom because her parents came home unexpectedly from their Lake Geneva house and spotted a ladder outside her window. Her father took it down and went up to his daughter's room to investigate. He gently shook Pepper, who was faking sleep and hoping her father would not look under the bed. He inquired about the ladder. She said that Scott Hodges washed the windows that day and must have left it behind. Mr. Martin said okay, goodnight, and left. Sensing something amiss because Mrs. Martin told her husband that Scott had washed the windows the day before, Mr. Martin marched back to Pepper's room to find her not in bed. He flipped on the lights. Pepper's head popped up from the floor on the far side of her four-poster bed. "Oh, Daddy, I must have fallen out of bed," she said, slipping back under the duvet as if she were exhausted and wanted him to leave. Her father – most likely tired and wanting to go to bed himself – said goodnight, again flipping off the light, forgetting about Scott's ladder, not seeing anything wrong. He also did not see Scott's hand shoot up, palming Pepper her undies; nor did her father see him shinnying down a drainpipe and hoofing it back to his house with only one tennis shoe, the other buried somewhere under Pepper's bed, which Mrs. Martin found the next morning. The story of the ladder and the stray tennis shoe quickly made him a legend on the cocktail circuit. I think it even helped his window washing business. If it had been me in Pepper Martin's bedroom, I would've been up on charges.

Now, I asked, "So no action?"

He lit a smoke. "Nothing. Anything where you were?"

I said, "Yeah, a little."

Scott perked up. "Farmer's daughter?"

I nodded Yep.

"Yowser," Scott said making a crude gesture that boys make when they are suggesting a home run.

I waved him off. "Nothing like that."

"Nothing like yowser?"

"No...she's definitely yowser...just not yowser yowser."

"So what's yowser's name?"

Believe me, I wanted to tell Scott all about Bit. But I was still unsure about the status of our relationship (God, I hate that word). I said her name was Elizabeth and that we met at the ranch. That we'd had a fun time together but the problem was I was here and she was there. I let it go at that. Scott understood. This way if nothing came of Bit and me I would not look like a dope.

"Where were you again?" he asked.

"Wyoming," I said.

"I know that."

"Near a little town called Cora. Twenty miles outside of Pinedale."

"Where's that?"

"An hour or so southeast of Jackson."

"Oh, okay," he said, now having a vague sense of where I had been. He took a bunch of drags, looking at his Marlboro. He then asked about my two friends at college, Boyle and Farr (we have this male habit of referring to each other by our last names). I told Scott I was rooming with Freddy Farr, and that Chris Boyle was living close by in an off-campus house. Scott goes to Williams College and had visited me last fall and met Janie Wallace. The six of us – including Boyle's girlfriend, Sally Swift – had all hung out together and had had such a marathon party weekend that we promised each other we were going to do it again the next year because we all had so much fun together. Scott really liked Janie. So did Boyle, Farr and Sally. And Janie liked them, a lot. Scott heard later through the grapevine that our relationship (uggh, there's that word again) ended up like a car crash. That's why I was surprised when he asked,

"How's Janie doing?"

I was paralyzed. What could I say? I didn't know. Janie wouldn't talk to me after we broke up. I have to admit, even with Bit in the picture, Janie still had her hooks in me; I couldn't help it. Janie and I had had a fantastic but screwed up love affair – meaning it was fantastic until I screwed it up. I'm mostly well-grounded, but I got knocked silly and stupid and started smothering Janie after falling hard in love with her – she was the first girl I ever really liked; the first girl I'd slept with; the first girl I'd told *I love you* – a deadly trifecta. It was good – really too good – for about five months, then it began to drive me nuts. I was worried it would end. Unfortunately, my nuttiness made that happen.

Believe me when I say Janie was hot and there was a line around the corner of guys wanting her phone number, which led to clingy, insecure, obnoxious behavior on my part. Stuff like calling her all the time (and hanging up when her roommate answered). Worrying about where she was and who she was with. Not wanting to leave her alone at parties. Paranoid about when she was talking too long with other boys. Always wanting to spend the night. I couldn't blame her that she punted me for another guy. I had it coming. I would have done the same. Safe to say I was still in love with Janie, and if she called me that night to meet up, I would have been up and out so fast all you would have seen is the phone bouncing around the floor with the backdoor wide open.

Now, I took a hit of my beer and choked out, "She's going out with another guy."

Scott nodded. He knew the score. He flicked his cigarette

butt far into the grass then gripped his seven iron, holding the club up in front of him, tapping the club face on the dash of the cart, his tapping telling me Farr or Boyle must have told him who Janie was dating and what had happened between us. Scott wasn't going to say anything. Why wreck the rest of our summer together. I respected that. I'd soon find out when I got back to school.

I stuck another smoke in my mouth fumbling around for a match, changing the subject, bringing up Polly Hamilton and going to see her about Luke's death.

Scott handed over a book of matches. "How'd that go?"

I lit my cigarette thinking about how much I should say, about my promise to Polly. I knew I could trust Scott. I said, "I was right. Something was up."

"You thought that," he said. "You told me Polly wasn't at Luke's funeral and the family was closing ranks about something."

I took a few drags, rolling the cigarette between my thumb and forefinger, thankful Scott was not pressing me for details (Scott had never really liked Luke that much; he thought Luke a little odd, and he was not wrong.) I swiped at a mosquito. I took a big drag then lay my head back, blowing the smoke up through the leaves of the tree. I confessed, "Luke had problems, Scott."

Scott knew where I was going. "I'm sorry. I liked him. He was a good guy." (This was Scott's way of saying I didn't have to say any more.)

The subject of Luke ended with me saying, "Yeah he was."

Climbing out of the golf cart and walking away to take a whizz, Scott asked over his shoulder, "How was your date with Megan McCarthy?"

I said okay, letting it go at that. I thought about telling

Scott how Megan tried to jump me. But why be a dick and rat her out. I know what it's like to be shut out. It sucks, and you don't want everybody knowing about it.

When Scott came back, he asked, "So what was it like in Wyoming?"

I said it was hard work, but fun.

He asked, "You going back?"

"Planning on it."

"You make any money?"

"A grand."

"Not bad. What were your hours?"

"Ten hours a day, six and half days a week."

"Wow. What's that work out to?"

"About a buck seventy an hour."

"Where'd you stay?"

"In a trailer."

He said, "Tell me again, you got bucked off a horse in a rodeo?"

I shrugged, like what's the big deal.

He asked, "What got you on the horse?"

I lied: "A handful of Budweisers."

"What did your parents say?"

"Mom was upset. Dad was sort of psyched."

"That you were injured?"

"No," I said, blowing a smoke ring, "that I was riding a horse in a rodeo."

Scott asked, "How are you getting back to school?"

I said, "With Tommy Childress."

"In his BMW?"

I nodded, blowing a smoke ring through a smoke ring.

Scott said, "That should be a kick. Your parents okay with that?"

I said, "No, not really," flicking my cigarette where Scott had flicked his.

He said, "My parents think he's Charles Manson."

Scott's parents weren't entirely wrong. Neither were mine. Skeleton thin, acne ridden, unshaven, greasy hair in his eyes – Tommy Childress was scary looking. He also had a bit of a fuck-you attitude that I liked and that I learned was his defense against not being a garden-variety preppy. No parents wanted their children hanging out with Tommy because they were afraid he would rub off on them. They were wrong. Once he trusted me, let me into his world and I got to know him, I quickly found out Tommy Childress was smart, funny, considerate, sensitive. Just like most bad boys.

I got out of the cart, something bugging me. Earlier in the summer Scott had had a serious make-out session with a girl whom I think had rung his bell – highly unusual. Scott has always been the one calling the shots with the girls. I sensed Alison had snuck up on him and he could not shake her. I moved to the front of the cart and took a few easy practice swings with my seven iron. In the middle of my back swing, I asked him, "You ever see Alison Henry again?" I held my follow-through, staring straight at him, waiting his response.

Scott hung his head, shaking it *No*; his eyes not meeting mine. I was right; Scott's armor had been pierced.

"Why not?" I asked.

"She went to Europe on some program," he said.

"Why didn't you call or write her?"

"I was embarrassed by what I did."

That was a first.

Now leaning on my club, I said, "What was she like?"

Scott threw his head back, looking up at the sky through the leaves of the tree, rattling off, "Fun. Pretty. Solid body. Good dancer. Smart...hey, she goes to Harvard!" He addressed me, pointing his club: "But she hates *your* guts.

You know her mother wants to strangle you for what you did. Making out with her daughter then disappearing to Wyoming for the summer. She thinks you're quite the rake."

Walking away to the halfway house to take a leak, I put my hands in the air with a *What can I say?*

(Here's the full Scott-as-me story. Follow carefully. I was invited to a deb party in Chicago but couldn't go because I was headed to Wyoming. So I gave the invitation to Scott and told him go as me, nobody would know because neither of us knew Alison Henry; she lived downtown on Lake Shore Drive. So what happens? Scott goes as me, Henry Thornton Chandler III, and, late in the show, ends up getting into a serious lip-grip with Alison on the roof of her building when the party is winding down. So Prince Henry (Scott) disappears after the party and the Princess Deb (Alison) calls my house after a week of radio silence wondering where is Mr. Wonderful. My mother clues Alison in that I'm in Wyoming and never went to the party. My parents put two and two together, figuring out Scott went as me and ended up making out with Alison. That put me squarely on the parental shit-list – thank God I was 1,200 miles away without a telephone. I did receive a sharp rebuke from my mother in a letter about manners and etiquette, and "we don't do that type of thing," but I could read between the lines that the bridge table was tittering and the foursomes were busting a gut. Typical: I took the fall and Scott skated away, as always, scot-free. And, I'm sure it helped his window washing business and fed his stack of invitations.)

When I got back to the cart, Scott asked, "You guys having a party again this fall?"

I re-gripped my club. "Yeah, late October."

He said, "Am I invited?"

I pointed my seven iron at him. "After what you did to me with Alison Henry? *Fat chance.*"

He said, "Good, in that case I'll bring her to your party."

That gave me an idea.

I said, "We gotta get the cart back to the pro shop. It's almost seven."

# Chapter 22

## PASSING GRADE * LAST SUPPER *
## COLLECT CALL FROM BIT

I finished typing my paper, ending my story for Professor Gurney's assignment where Andy and I drove home from the airport. I knew I was taking a risk including the part about me helping to kill Buzz, but that is what happened and I trusted Professor Gurney. I made a copy and sent the original special delivery registered mail to Gurney in Providence. Before handing it off to the woman behind the counter at the Post Office, I lightly brushed my lips against the envelope, looking beyond the fluorescent lights to the heavens above, sending up a silent prayer: *I don't ask for a lot, good Lord, but help me out on this one.*

A week later, my salvation was delivered to our house by Eddie, our mailman:

*September 1, 1977*

*Dear Mr. Chandler,*
  *I read, corrected and graded your composition, assigning it a C+ due to typos and grammatical errors. Otherwise, it was a solid story and did have the "redeeming" qualities I spoke*

*of. Mrs. Gurney also read your piece and felt it deserved a higher mark because you ably followed my directions, and I think – and don't repeat this – she also appreciates your drink recall, generous country club pour, and good manners. Taking that into consideration, the paper merits a B-, which I will record with the College, as long as we see your crooked smile back at the Faculty Club. Furthermore, I will confirm with the Dean's office that you are in good standing and should be encouraged to continue your studies for another year.*

*Sincerely yours,*

*Richard T. Gurney, Ph.D*

*Hallelfuckinglujah!*

I'd secured my ticket back to my sophomore year. And, I got a B-. Gurney gave *me* a B-. This was far better than a perfect score on the SAT's.

The only other interesting event in my life that summer, besides composing PG 13 love letters to Bit, and reading hers over and over, was that I taught myself to whistle like Buzz. No fingers, all lower lip and tongue. Having to listen to me blowing and blowing and blowing until I could produce a clear, clean blast nearly drove Winston and Verna crazy. Other than that, I'd run a couple miles here and there, do push-ups, sit-ups, chin-ups, and work on my chest with one of those contraptions with handles that has three springs that you pull apart; determined to return to school in fighting form.

Three days before pulling out for Providence, Farr phoned me from New York asking how was I getting back to school and could I bring a fridge for our dorm room. I said I was driving back with Tommy Childress, so no room in the BMW for a fridge, but I would bring the stereo and a black-and-white TV. Farr said okay; he'd supply the fridge and a hot pot.

My last night at home my mom made my favorite meal of spaghetti and meatballs. After dinner, while peeling open our Eskimo Pie desserts, the phone rang in the kitchen. Andy and I jumped up, nearly knocking over our chairs. My father palmed us down with a low growl. "Stay right where you are, I'll get it."

Once the swinging door closed behind my father, Andy balled the aluminum foil wrapper from his dessert and fired it at me from across the table, grazing my ear. I drew a bead, but he kept ducking behind the centerpiece. Struggling to hold back a smile while keeping an eye on the kitchen door, my mother clapped her hands, demanding, "Stop it. Stop it this instant. Both of you are too old for this type of behavior." She was right, of course, Andy and I were too old, but I know my mother still enjoyed it.

I said, "Andy started it," firing a missile that missed by a mile, hitting the oversized oil painting of my great-great-great-relative. Andy tsk-tsked his fingers at me. I was reaching for my father's wrapper to reload when the kitchen door swung open. My father barked, "Hank, there's a collect call for you from Bit Stifel from Pinedale, Wyoming. Keep it short."

*Holyshitholyshitholyshit.*

I pushed back my chair, discarded my napkin as if it were dirty laundry, and rounded the table in a 440 sprint, my mother's eyes sparkling up at me as she followed my path to the kitchen door. When she encountered my father's scowling face, her smile curdled to a frown. "For heaven's sake, Peter, it won't break you."

I didn't hear my father's defense as the door had swung shut and I was busy stretching the phone cord across the kitchen, burying myself in the pantry closet. I closed the door and turned off the light. I don't know why I turned off the light, maybe because I was nervous and insecure about talking to Bit for the first time in almost a month; nervous about what was going to happen between us. I felt around, lightly fingering boxes, bottles, and cans. Shrouded by darkness, hearing her soft breathing, I inhaled Bit's fragrance from 1,200 miles away and felt the heat of her body next to mine like when we danced at the Cowboy Bar and kissed goodbye outside the trailer. My mouth went dry. Mustering all the saliva I could, I said, "Hi, Bit?"

Bit said, "Hi, Hank. Was that your dad?"

"Yeah," I said, feeling along the wall for the light.

"Is it okay I called collect? You said to."

"Are you kidding? Of course it's okay."

"Your dad sounded upset."

"Don't worry, he's just not used to the telephone."

Bit said, "I miss you, Hank."

I exhaled. "Me, too. I miss you, too, Bit."

"Hank, I miss you a lot. More than I thought I would."

That made me dry-swallow and catch my breath. I gulped in a little air before I said, "I love your letters. Keep writing me. I can't wait to see you."

She said, "I will. I can't wait to see you too."

This led to a lot of goo-gooing and phone-petting, shit that I'm not ashamed of but wouldn't want played in public. It also stirred activity south of the border – if you know what I mean – something I was not comfortable with in my parents' pantry, so I doused cold water on a heating-up situation by asking if she was calling from Eleanor's.

"Yeah, I snuck over here because Eleanor's down at Mom's for dinner. I didn't want her listening in on what I wanted to tell you."

"What's that?" I asked.

"I got good news, I'm going to college in Laramie. Mom collected on a life insurance policy she had on Dad. It's not a lot, but it's enough to send me to school. I start in January. I'll be with Polly."

Bit's excitement could have lit up the pantry. She had wanted to go to college but Buzz and Hope never had the money. I hesitated, faking it as best I could: "That's great, Bit. That will be so much fun for you and Polly." It was great...for her...and for Polly and for all the cowboys coiling their lariats in Laramie. My stomach hit the deck with an *oh fuck* feeling, the same feeling I had when I was jealous and paranoid and stupid about Janie Wallace.

I found the switch and flipped on the light, now face-to-face with Captain Crunch and that Quaker guy on the front of the Quaker Oats carton. With the phone pressed between my ear and shoulder, I reached for and unscrewed the lid of a large jar of dill pickles, took one out, looked at it, juice dripping on the floor. I packed it back into the jar. I rubbed my hand on my shorts then flicked the light off, waiting for Bit to say something, not wanting to sound insecure. Bit's not stupid, she knew something was up with me because she said in a soft tone, "Hank?"

"Yeah?"

"I want to come see you. Mom said she'd pay for my ticket and Dr. Andersen said he'd give me some time off if I'd help out on Saturdays."

My mood flipped, so did my finger – over and over and over – on the wall switch, the pantry becoming a light show. I said, "Really, you'll come and visit me at school?"

She said, "*Yea-ah*," like she really meant it. "We can have our own little rodeo."

*Whoa, Nellie.*

I thumbed the light off because the pantry was heating up again and my thermometer was rising. I said, "My roommates and I are planning a big party in October. Can you come then?"

"Yeah. Tell me the weekend," she said as if she was writing it down. "Can I come early and stay late?"

I sank down on the floor next to a thin line of light

coming from under the door. I told her she could stay the whole semester as far as I was concerned. We cooed a little longer, then talked about Hope, Sonny, Clete, and how the new pup, Bear, followed Clete everywhere. We kept it light, nothing heavy. Nothing about Farnsworth. And nothing about Dorothy, which I found a little odd.

Bit caught me off guard when she asked me if I loved her. I said I honestly didn't know, but I'd like to find out. She said that was being honest, and Hope had always told her there was nothing wrong with being honest. She said she really didn't know either, but wanted to find out. We didn't say much after that, but didn't want to hang up either. That's when Andy snuck up on me, pleading through the door: "Hank, call her back tomorrow. Dad's about to bust a blood vessel."

# Chapter 23

## BONES ✳ THE NIGHT EARL ✳ THANK-YOU NOTE

When he turned eighteen, Tommy Childress's parents gave him a red BMW 320i; he was now twenty-one. The car had forty-three thousand miles on the speedometer, a stick shift, sunroof, black leather interior and a Dolby sound system (whatever that means). Tommy wheeled his "Beemer" around town with lead in his toe, wearing Vuarnet sunglasses, the sunroof open, music blaring. On the passenger side, under the seat, was a box that held a dozen cassette tapes – his "choice cuts."

Early as sin on a Sunday in early September, my mom was wringing her hands in our driveway as I jammed my duffel bags and stereo in and around Tommy's crates of record albums. Mom heaved a mother's sigh of *What did I do wrong* as she fingered our telephone number that I'd had monogrammed on the pocket of a new Brooks Brothers shirt, one of four she'd bought me for my return to school – two of which had "HTC III" on the pocket, which was, no surprise, her preference. Tucked in the top of my duffel was the fourth shirt, which I'd planned to give Tommy as a present from my parents for giving me a ride back to school.

Mom hugged and kissed me goodbye, whispering that the speed limit was fifty-five and call as soon as I got there. I gave her an extra squeeze, joking if it was okay if I called collect. Settling into the passenger seat, clicking my seatbelt, I advised Tommy to take it slow out of the driveway. He glanced up at my mother nervously waving goodbye in the rearview mirror, assuring me he wasn't a mental case, did I really think he was going to peel out and leave my mother with a mouthful of gravel?

Knowing Tommy, I wasn't so sure.

For those born and raised in the Midwest, having to drive to the East Coast – specifically, Providence, Rhode Island – on a regular basis was routine torture; a test of sitting up straight for long stretches; enduring someone else's music; subsisting on McDonald's hamburgers; dueling with semi trailer trucks at high speed; and, at the end of the trip, reeking like day-old garbage. Odds are you won't recall what you talked about flying past the cornfields of Indiana, the car plants of Ohio, up and down the hills of Pennsylvania, through New Jersey, over the George Washington bridge with the twin towers and the Empire State Building far down to your right, across the Bronx, and through the toll booths of Connecticut, hammer down all the way to Providence. But I did remember. And I'd do it again with Tommy Childress.

Since it was Tommy's car, he called the shots. He told me we'd leave early on Sunday to avoid traffic and drive the 960 miles straight through, figuring on 17 hours. We made the drive in three shifts; Tommy took two, I took one. He wouldn't let me pay for gas or tolls; said his parents gave him plenty of money and he intended to spend it. I did pay for three McDonalds stops with the extra cash my mother had palmed me in the driveway. Two hours into the ride, I woke after dozing off, sat up – a little drool on my shirt – and said, "Where are we, Bones?" (Bones is the nickname I'd given Tommy late one night when we were stoned and listening to jazz in his basement. It fit. He liked it. We went with it.)

He said, "Almost through Indiana."

I asked, "You okay?"

"Yeah," he replied, not looking at me, fingering his long greasy hair away from his face, curling it behind his ears.

We gassed up in Ohio at a truck stop where the restroom was advertising French Tickler condoms with special ribbing that was guaranteed to drive women crazy. I bought two. Bones asked me why two. I said no reason. Back on the road, I was studying everything on the condom packaging, even where they were made (Gainesville, Florida). I was curious if they had an expiration date, and how I was going to use them – figuratively, as a gag. After I put them away, Bones said out of the blue, "I like your parents."

I didn't know what to say. I wanted to say *They like you, too*, but that would have been phony, and both of us knew it. Instead, I rooted around for my Ray-Bans.

He continued, "They hate me, don't they?"

I said, "Why would you say that?" finding my glasses, cleaning them off with my shirttail, ducking the conversation.

He said, "Because they do. I freak out a lot of parents. I don't want to. I just do." He flipped on his blinker and blew past a semi hauling hogs to market in a pot-bellied trailer, testing the fuzz buster on the dash to make sure it was working.

I said, sounding sappy and sincere, "I don't think so. What makes you think that? As far as I know that's not true."

Bones snapped. He eviscerated me. "That's infra dig, Chandler. Don't prevaricate. You're not good at it. Keep it that way."

This was typical Bones. He didn't suffer fools lightly. He could also punish you with his vocabulary, and respected others who could do the same (William F. Buckley being one of his favorites).

I said, "Okay...okay," slightly embarrassed, shutting up, shutting down, wondering what infra dig meant, having a clue about prevaricate. I looked out at the cornfields, tuning out, tuning into the Grateful Dead's "Truckin" playing on the car stereo.

Tommy Childress was the youngest of six children in a household that had few boundaries or rules. I knew him from grade school and college. He lived a short bike ride from our house in a gray stone mansion that was more like a prison. I avoided his parents and did not really know his siblings, who were much older and had flown the coop. His dad worked for the family company, was loaded, and a big boozer. His mom had a lot of money, too, and was bit of a floozy. It was not hard to see why Tommy grew up like a weed, looked like a weed, acted like a weed. He was a rail-thin six-two who had to dance around in the shower to get wet (hence, my nickname Bones). My mother told me ad nauseam: *Why doesn't his mother take him to the barbershop, or the skin doctor, or Brooks Brothers, or Dr. Templeton, or feed him.* I told my mother it wasn't his fault he'd been dealt a shitty hand – long on money, short on love, last in line.

I think Bones felt bad about barking at me because he asked me about my shirt and the numbers over the pocket. I explained that my mother bought me monogrammed Oxford shirts, and that on one shirt I decided to stitch our telephone number for kicks. Bones thought that was funny. He then went on about how much he thought my mother was cool.

Fingering the hair behind my ears, I asked, being polite, "How are your parents?"

Bones corrected me: "Hank, I don't have parents. I have roommates."

I stared straight ahead through the windshield, thinking awkward but true.

He fiddled with the rearview mirror then checked his side mirrors. He said, "My parents haven't had sex in ten years."

I said, still staring straight ahead, "You don't know that."

Bones hit the gas to get around a convoy of trucks, the

Beemer vaulting past ninety. My head snapped back against the headrest. He said, "Hank, when my father throws me that nugget...that he hasn't touched my mother in ten years... with a fresh Pall Mall dangling out of his mouth while he's unscrewing a new bottle of Jack, and my mother's out...*who knows where*...I tend to believe him."

Bones throttled the car back to seventy-five. He ejected the cassette and handed it to me. "You're lucky."

Bones was right, I was lucky. I was also not stupid enough to say, *Oh, you don't know. My parents can be a real drag. They're always doing stuff like wanting to play golf, or making me sit down to a family dinner, or asking me shit like where am I going and who am I hanging out with.*

Bones continued: "Remember in high school when everybody had curfews? I didn't have one, Chandler. I was dying for a curfew. But my parents wouldn't give me one because *they* didn't have a curfew. So I gave myself one, so I had to be home like the rest of you."

I turned to him, bewildered. "So, you could have stayed out all night? Every night?"

"Yeah."

"That would get old."

"Yeah, real fast."

We didn't talk for two minutes – I know because I counted two green mile markers go by. The music stopped. The cassette ejected. I pulled out the box from under my seat and ran my finger across the tapes, asking, "What do you want to listen to?"

Bones said, "Your pick."

I asked, "Do you have any Night Earl?"

Bones reached over and fingered *That one* from the box.

I popped the tape in. Bones turned the volume up, tapping his fingers on the steering wheel to Taj Mahal's "Statesboro Blues". I thought *How fucked up is that, no curfew. He had to parent himself. Here I have two parents waiting up for*

*me to come home so they could tuck me in, and all Bones*
*had was an empty house with two absentee alcoholic parents*
*who didn't give a shit.* I fingered the cassette case, flipping
it over, reading the Night Earl's playlist: Taj Mahal, John
Mayall, Jeff Beck, Eric Clapton, Paul Butterfield, Lou Rawls,
Otis Span, B. B. King, James Cotton, Otis Redding, Wilson
Pickett, Sam Cook, J. J. Cale.

The Night Earl's real name is Earl Mitchell. Four nights
a week – Thursday through Sunday – he was the last DJ
standing at the campus radio station. Short, shapeless and
bald, he resembled an old fat penguin. He had wiry facial
hair and moley skin and wore thick black glasses, lime green
Tretorns, and ill-fitting, army surplus jump-suits open at the
collar. He was a sixty-three-year-old, grumpy introvert who
knew his music cold and would rather be left alone behind
a microphone, smoking Lucky Strikes, spinning discs and
stories into the night. His defining feature was a voice sanded
down and shaped by cigarettes and Scotch. A voice so full
and round it sounded like it was coming from the bottom of
well. A voice that could keep you up late at night, matching
you cigarette for cigarette as you plowed through European
history, Greek mythology, or typed English papers until he
signed off at two a.m.

At least the Night Earl did with me.

Bones had worked at the radio station since his freshman
year, broadcasting the news and weather, inching his way up
to his own time slot. He stayed late many nights to be Earl's
gofer around the studio and a student at his knee. From the
moment I first heard the Night Earl's show my freshman year,
I was dying to meet the mysterious late night voice few had
ever met, but many on campus had speculated about. Bones
knew Earl Mitchell's story, but out of respect had never told
anyone, always protecting him like a precious gem. Bones
made an exception with me halfway across Ohio.

We'd switched places and I was behind the wheel,

pushing the BMW at a safe sixty-four. Turning up J. J. Cale's "Call Me the Breeze," half-expecting to be shut down, I said, "Tell me about the Night Earl, Bones."

"Between you and me?" he said with a raised eyebrow, meaning *I can trust you, right?* "Earl doesn't like people knowing his past."

When I said, "Absolutely," the fuzz buster went off as if it was on fire. I hit the brakes. Up ahead two state patrol cars were parked in the median. I drove past them with my best choirboy profile.

Bones continued, "Earl Mitchell grew up in Woonsocket. Lived in the garden apartment of the house his uncle owned. You and I grew up in what, Chandler," – here Bones flipped his hand back and forth – "eight thousand, ten thousand, square feet? Earl Mitchell grew up in four hundred square feet with parents twice as large as ours."

I asked, "When did he leave?"

"As soon as he could."

"Did he go to school?"

"Yeah, high school. But all he wanted to do was play in the school band. Then he started doing gigs at night, so he mostly slept in class."

"What instrument?"

"Alto sax. His first love was Johnny Hodges."

I recognized the name. Bones had tutored me on the big names in jazz. I asked, "Did he ever play professionally?"

Bones pinched a zit on his neck then looked at his fingers. "Played in a big band that did shows in Providence and Hartford and New Haven. Never made it to the show in New York. Told me it was a big kick being up on stage, especially taking a solo. But it was hard work, long hours, little pay. Then his girlfriend Muriel got pregnant and he had to take a job with a company making costume jewelry, working the graveyard shift. Then he fell into a bad crowd and got busted in a drug deal."

"Did he go to prison?"

Bones kicked off his Topsiders, put his feet on the dash and started picking at his enormous, gnarly toes. "Fifteen years. No parole. Muriel left him. His son Norman works down in Groton as a welder on those nuclear subs. Comes up once a year to see Earl whether Earl wants him to or not."

That gave me the shivers. I couldn't imagine prison, didn't want to imagine prison. I didn't know what to say so I said, "Bummer," then cracked the sunroof to air out the McDonald's smell and Bones's feet.

Bones turned his head toward me. "Bummer is right. Earl told me it's why he doesn't sleep at night." He turned his head away, looking out his window at a series of road signs, the last two saying *Guns Don't Kill People. People Kill People.*

That gave me the willies. I swerved, avoiding some road kill – most likely a raccoon. I asked, "What did he do when he got out of prison?"

Bones said, "He DJ'd around town. Doing the late night stuff nobody else would do. Bartended. Gave music lessons. Gigged around with some of the local combos." Bones told me a bunch of other stuff about Earl, then went quiet, eventually nodding off. Three hours later I checked the gas gauge, close to empty. Bones had been awake for a bit but was radio silent. I didn't bug him. He stretched his arms and neck saying, "You want me to take over?"

I said, "Sure."

Around four in the afternoon we gassed up and switched seats at a truck stop in the middle of Pennsylvania. As Bones sped out to merge with the traffic, he asked, "You going out with anybody?"

I said, "Yes and no."

He laughed. "You said yes and she said no."

I grinned. "I've got a girlfriend, but she lives in Wyoming," (I'd not told Bones about Bit. Why? He didn't have a girlfriend, so why should I brag about mine.)

He said, "Holding out on me, huh. What's her name?"

I said, "Elizabeth. But she goes by Bit."

"A Western girl named Bit. You're something, Chandler. Didn't take you long to rebound."

I smiled, not believing I had. Bones knew about my breakup with Janie, but we'd never talked about it. Boys don't. Well...sometimes we'll toe around the edge, but we never dive in. It's too deep, and you know other guys don't want to hear about it, believe me. Besides, who wants their problems plastered all over school. I asked, knowing the answer, "You going out with anybody?"

He pointed to his acne. "With a pizza face like this? Fat chance."

I quickly changed the subject. Bones had flipped over and was playing side B of the Night Earl's playlist. I asked, "Is this Lou Rawls?"

Bones said, "Yeah...'Ain't Nobody's Business If I Do.' The Night Earl digs Sweet Lou from the South Side."

Two songs later, Bones asked, "You and Boyle and Farr having a party again this year?"

I said, "Yeah. Late October. You coming?"

He said, "Oh yeah, wouldn't miss it. Your party last year was a blast." Bones paused, thinking about something. "Can I help with the playlist?"

I said, "For sure," excited that he had offered and pleased to have his expertise.

He said, "Is Scott Hodges coming?"

I said that he was, then told Bones the story of Scott-as-me at Alison Henry's debutante party; telling him my plan to surprise Scott by inviting Alison to the party in October, but to keep it under his hat. Bones said no problem; he could do that.

Fifteen miles later, at the end of the tape, Bones handed me the cassette. He said, "You want to meet the Night Earl?"

I sat up, turned, dry swallowed; the look on my face clearly broadcasting: *You're fucking joking. Where and when?*

(I did meet the Night Earl, thanks to Bones, but he was not what I expected. Unfortunately, I had built up my expectations of Earl Mitchell; I should have left it to my imagination. I spent an hour with him late one Sunday night in the studio. He could have cared less that I was there paying homage to him. I could sense that I was just taking up space, getting in his way, asking stupid questions. For me, the Night Earl was best left in the dark; between my ears; between ten and two in the morning.)

Near midnight, Bones dropped me off at the entrance to the quad. I called Farr on the house phone to let me in, then pulled my gear to the curb. I opened a duffel and took out the fourth Brooks Brothers shirt and handed it to Bones.

He said, "What's this, Chandler? I put up with you for a thousand miles, now you want me do your laundry?"

I said, "Shut up, Bones. Put it on."

He finger-nailed away those annoying little pins and shook the shirt out.

I said, "This was my mother's idea to thank you for giving me a ride. She wanted to monogram your initials on it. I said no way." I pointed at the shirt pocket. "I thought that would be better. She agreed." (This was a lie, but so what.)

Bones looked at what was stitched on the pocket, the expression on his face awkward as if he were confused and didn't know what to say or think. He stripped off his T-shirt, revealing a bony structure barely supporting muscle and skin. He buttoned up the shirt, tucking it in.

Farr was now beside me, saying hello to Bones, grabbing a duffel, telling me all the doors were wedged open. I stuck out my hand: "Thanks for the lift, Bones. Let's do it again."

My mother called me a few days later, sounding slightly muddled. She said, "Hank, dear, I received the nicest...*the nicest, sweetest note* from Tommy Childress thanking me for a Brooks Brothers shirt that had BONES monogrammed on the pocket. Do you know anything about this?" I told her I had given him one of my shirts as a thank-you present for driving me back to school, and that I hoped she didn't mind. My mother agreed that it was appropriate, but she was possessed: "Hank, you should see this letter. I have it right here. This is such a lovely, lovely note. Let me read it to you."

I laughed *No Mom. Stop it*; now convinced that you can ax-murder somebody in Lake Forest, Illinois, but if you can write a halfway decent thank-you note, you'll never be convicted.

# Chapter 24

## BOYLE * LAST SUPPER * HARRY HOPE'S * JACKIE * DANTE

I have two good friends at college: Frederick McPheeters Farr and Christopher Andrew Boyle, Jr. Those are their full names and what was printed under their photographs in the college pig book. Farr's picture was in every girl's top ten; Boyle's mug shot could have been in the FBI's top ten; my photo was what Janie Wallace insisted was cute – she'd cut it out and put it in her wallet the morning after we "did it" for the first time. When Farr inquired about the cut-out picture of me in my pig book, I said Janie was now carrying it around in her back pocket. Boyle cracked: "Well, Chandler, that's one way to get into a girl's pants."

My roommate, Freddy Farr, grew up in New York City – 76th and Park Avenue, to be precise. Even though he hobnobs with the swells and the Studio 54 set, he's pretty Midwestern – if you catch my drift. By Farr (pun intended), he's the best catch of the three of us because he's tall, dark, and knows what he's talking about (Boyle and I tend to bullshit more). The girls love him because he's handsome, polite, and talks to all of them regardless – he's not a dick like most good-looking guys. Farr has a smoking hot girlfriend in New York named Sophia with a fancy Italian last name. He doesn't talk about her much and Boyle and I don't ask. If he wanted to tell us, he would.

My buddy Boyle is from Madison, Connecticut. He's built like a wrestler, walks like a wrestler, looks like a wrestler – in fact, he is a wrestler. He's never been in the society pages, but he made the sports pages a bunch of times in the 139-pound weight class and as a high-scoring crease lacrosse player. He can dance, too. But unlike Farr, who cuts a mean rug, both disco and ballroom, Boyle's moves are more interpretive, a blend of *Beach Blanket Bingo* and *Soul Train*. He's also a brain – like Farr – but does his best to disguise it, because he likes to surprise people who think of him as a dolt. He reads a ton, watches a boatload of TV, and dates Sally Swift, a super-cool girl who is way too good for him, which we tell him all the time.

I met Boyle and Farr in line for registration freshman year. We became fast friends because we all had gone to boarding school and had friends in common who told us to look each other up. It was in the same line that I met Janie Wallace. She was hanging out with her freshman roommate, a big-boned girl named Mimi Ryder from New Canaan, Connecticut, who wore Fair Isle sweaters, had great hair and big boobs. She'd had a crush on Farr from boarding school, so she invited him to a party in their room that first night. Farr convinced Boyle and me to tag along as his wingman and give him cover in case Mimi started drooling on him. Boyle and I didn't know anybody at the party so we came prepared with two cold six packs of beer so the girls would have to talk to us.

Mimi and Janie's dorm room, a cinderblock bunker with two of everything – beds, desks, chairs, dressers, mirrors and windows – quickly filled up. I ended up sandwiched between Boyle and Janie on Janie's prison-cell bed. Soon, the crowd crammed in, forcing Janie to rest her cute little behind on my knee to make more room. To review: Perrysburg, Ohio; tall and slinky; long dirty blond hair; a beautiful set; funky nose; talks out of the side of her mouth.

It was chemical.

It was electric.

It was magic.

Janie and I immediately bonded over the Midwest, a mutual friend named Sibby Watson, Johnny Carson, *Laugh In*, Van Morrison, *Saturday Night Live*, and *All My Children*. We agreed to dislike everything about Philadelphia, Jethro Tull, the AMC Pacer, Tiny Tim, *Saturday Night Fever*, the New York Yankees, and bell-bottoms. She insisted more than once – with me yanking her back down – "I must be crushing you." As I inhaled the lemony scent of hair, as I felt her soft, firm butt on my thigh, as I followed her quirky smile and absorbed the heat of her body, I was dying to say, *Yes, yes, you are crushing me, and please don't stop.* The next thing I knew we were meeting almost every morning for coffee and spending all of our free time together, much of it under the covers. That is until she went to Florida on spring break and fell for another guy. As you know now, my fault.

My second day back at school, after classes, Boyle, Farr and I drove to Harry's in downtown Providence. "Harry's" is short for the bar's full name, Harry Hope's – Harry Hope being the proprietor of the bar in Eugene O'Neill's *The Iceman Cometh*. Dante Romero, the owner, chose the name because of the cast of alcoholics and prostitutes that originally inhabited the place when he and his buddy Jackie Callaghan took it over. Dante is old – like maybe thirty-two. He's a mean six-one spread over a lean muscular frame with Donald Sutherland's beard, bright eyes and smirk (think *Kelly's Heroes*); except when he's angry at you for welching on a bet or falling behind with payments, then he's the shark in *Jaws*. Jackie Callaghan is Dante's childhood friend, bartender and bouncer; a beefy five-eleven under curly, strawberry blond hair (think a young George Kennedy). He has a great belly laugh, smile, and sense of humor; except of course when he's dealing with an unruly drunk or a punk selling something he wasn't buying, then he is a punching machine with iron fists. One is Italian, the other Irish. Both wore pinkie rings and gold chains. Both have scraped-up knuckles, crooked noses, tattoos, and countless scars. Neither have records. Both know good lawyers and the right muscle. Both have arrestingly high IQ's.

Harry's was a rough joint that Dante and Jackie were slowly turning around with the help of "legitimate" drunks like *Providence Journal* reporters, state workers and college students. They now have rock bands playing on the weekends, which drove away the professional drunks and pimps. The prostitutes were moving on, too, because business was drying up along with their free drinks. The strippers who worked the Voom-Voom Room three blocks away – "friends" of Jackie and Dante's – occasionally stopped by after work and on the weekends to dance and drink for free. This helped bring in the college students.

That's where we came in.

In search of a dive away from the hoity-toity haunts on College Hill, Boyle, Farr and I had heard about Harry's and decided to check it out one night early in our freshman year. Jackie was working the door collecting covers for the band. He quickly spotted us for who we were and where we came from – college snots venturing down from the Hill, crossing over to the other side of the tracks. Believe me, that's what we were doing, and we found it…and loved it.

At first, I was nervous, worried we were in over our heads and asking for trouble hanging out at a place like Harry's. But Boyle and Farr were cool. Oddly, Jackie engaged us in conversation at the door, not giving us attitude. Once Jackie and Boyle figured out they both wrestled in high school, he let us in with no cover. So, we drank as much as we could and left big tips. Before the night was over, Jackie had offered Boyle a bartending job, and once Dante Romero recognized that Christopher Andrew Boyle Jr. from the Connecticut shore could work the speed rail and handle the screwballs, Farr and I were In Like Flynn; often free beers in front of us. Why did they like us and we like them? Opposites attract, I suppose; but it was more than that. We got along because we didn't judge each other (similar to me and Clete). Also, we enjoyed debating books, movies, politics, sports and music. Clearly, Dante and Jackie needed us for comic relief and intellectual stimulation. Clearly, we needed them for comic relief and relief from college. Quicker than you can say *Give me a Narragansett and a shot of Fleishmann's*, Harry's became our go-to bar and the best sociology class we ever took; truly taught by tenured professors well-versed in the ways of Providence, Rhode Island.

From the outside, during the day, Harry's resembled exactly what was inside – a shabby bar serving sots and lonely souls who had nowhere to go and certainly did not want to go home. In the front window hung a red neon *Harry Hope's* sign, beyond which was a long, narrow room. The bar was on the right, video games and a jukebox on the left. Tables and chairs lined the walls. A small bandstand/dance floor was tucked in the back. The space was dimly lit and dirty, the only natural light coming through the dingy store-front window. Many of the ceiling tiles were water-stained or missing. Way, way back were restrooms where the boys never complained that the door didn't completely shut or lock, and the girls would scrunch up their noses, swearing they would hold it like a camel the next time.

It was not a place to take a date.

When we walked in Jackie was behind the bar, "Crossroads" was playing on the jukebox, and a cloud of blue cigarette smoke hung in the air. A handful of darkly dressed, misshapen men hunched over the bar, their hands wrapped around bottles of beer, cigarettes burning in ashtrays, their necks stretching up at the Red Sox game on the TV, the sound down. Jackie spotted us coming through the door. He greeted us with a downward shaking head and a beefy grin as he wiped down the bar and his hands, extending his meaty paw to Boyle, to Farr, then me, booming out in a robust Rhode Island accent, "You guys look like I need a drink."

We settled in on high-backed wooden chairs that could have stood some glue. Jackie drew three Narragansetts and poured four shots of Fleishmann's whiskey. We clinked glass then threw back the shots. Farr and I winced from the burn while Boyle smacked his lips.

Farr looked around. "Where's Dante?"

Returning the Fleishmann's bottle to a shelf next to the Jack Daniels, Jackie said, "The wop's out slapping around little Brucie again. He owes Dante a lot of money. Little prick thought he could run faster than Dante and skip town." We were familiar with Little Brucie and his problems: gambling, drugs, large libido, seven kids, and a wife who looked like a warlock. Boyle asked what would happen if Brucie couldn't make good. Jackie said that if Dante doesn't reset the clock, Brucie could find himself upside down in a garbage can with cinder blocks on the lid waiting for Monday's trash pickup.

What Jackie said was not that funny, but it was to me, making me laugh just as I was taking a sip of beer, which made me gag and shoot suds out of my nose. I rushed to cover up. Jackie stared at me. "What happened to your face, Chandler the third. You look a little lopsided. Like maybe Picasso rearranged your face or you fell out of a golf cart?"

Boyle shushed Jackie with an index finger to his lips, then looked around like he didn't want anyone to hear. He imitated Maxwell Smart from "Get Smart": "Chief, can we have the cone of silence?"

We joined Jackie, hovering close together over the bar.

Rubbing my cheek and jaw, I explained that I had been working on a ranch out West and got bucked off a horse and messed up my face, ribs and leg.

The cone of silence lifted. We sat back. Jackie straightened up, let out a laugh that turned the collective head of the bar. "A horse?" He looked at Boyle, then Farr, then me. "A horse?...Chandler the third on a fucking horse?" He pointed at Farr. "Why'd you let him out of your sight?"

Farr shrugged. "He slipped our noose, Chief. Ran off to Wyoming."

Jackie picked up a glass from the sink, inspecting it, wiping it clean with a bar rag. "Where the hell is Wyoming?" he asked.

Boyle folded his hands on the bar, looking left, then right: "Think, Chief...think. Think far, far away. Think beyond Pennsylvania. Think way west of the Mississippi River. Think Rocky Mountains. Think 'Home on the Range'...*Gunsmoke... Wagon Train...Bonanza...The High Chaparral.*"

Jackie rested his sandy-haired forearms on the bar, thick Irish muscle inked with tattoos and lined with scars, staring Boyle down with an arched eyebrow. "Listen up, Smart. If I had to think...*if I had to think*...I'd think about Sugar and Spice spinning around a pole at the Voom Voom Room." (Sugar and Spice were a couple of Dante and Jackie's stripper friends.) He slammed his hand – BAM – on the bar. "Why... Smart...why...would I think about a place that has more sheep than people?"

Boyle paused, holding up his index finger, forming his retort. He gulped air then belched so loud and long Jackie had to fan his rag at the wet air in front of Boyle's face.

Boyle slid his glass toward Jackie, meaning *fill 'er up*.

Jackie took Boyle's glass with a tilt of his head toward Farr and me, meaning *drink up*.

We did.

As Jackie drew three more, Farr discreetly palmed a twenty on the bar.

Jackie caught him. "Hey, what's that for?"

Farr shrugged his shoulders.

Jackie snapped up the twenty and held it to the light. "Don't try to pawn this off on me, Freddy Farr. This is counterfeit script. Nice try." He put the bill back on the bar, then placed Farr's new draft on top of it – Jackie's way of saying *Drinks are on me.*

Boyle tilted his head toward the back of the room. "We're going to hear about Wyoming and how Chandler the turd broke some poor ewe's heart. You join us?"

Jackie said, "Yeah, in a minute. When the game's over and these palookas drink up and screw."

We edged off our bar stools. Boyle – in his side-to-side jockish strut – made his way to a back table, pulling chairs around. Farr stalled at the bar, delicately wiping off his twenty, waiting for Jackie to turn his back. When he did, Farr folded and fingered the bill across the bar where you leave tips and change – Farr's way of saying *But I insist.*

I dug in my wallet for a single to feed the jukebox, punching my picks from memory. I followed Farr, floating on the bass line of Lou Reed's "Walk on the Wild Side," psyched to be back at school, psyched to be back at Harry Hope's, psyched to be back again with Boyle and Farr after my summer in Wyoming. Even though I'd only known them for a year, Boyle and Farr were my "fraternity brothers," though none of us ever joined a fraternity. When Janie asked me why we didn't rush our freshman year, I responded, "Why, we're already a fraternity…just a fraternity of three." Janie said, "Good point." Once we became friends, Boyle and Farr picked up quickly that I was unhappy at college and struggling with Luke's death, and that my affair with Janie masked much of my unhappiness. They didn't ask stupid questions or blow me off when the shit hit the fan. They stood behind me, giving me the support I needed. If anybody asked me what I remembered most about my freshman year (besides Janie

Wallace), I would say my friendship with Chris Boyle and Freddy Farr.

The reason we'd come to Harry's that afternoon – besides wanting to see Dante and Jackie – was to talk about our summers. Farr went first. Boyle second. I had the microphone last because my experience had not been so run-of-the-mill. They pretended to be interested in my yarn of cowboys, prairie dogs and pickup trucks, but what they really wanted to know was what Boyle asked me with a twirling hand, meaning *let's get to the important stuff, Chandler.* He said, "Okay...so farmer got a daughter?"

I said, "Yep."

"You get the daughter in the hayloft?"

I waggled my hand.

Farr said, "Is that a yes or a no?"

I waggled again.

Boyle said, "Ellie Mae got a name?"

I smiled, easing out, "Elizabeth...but she goes by Bit."

They both cocked their heads back, looking at me as if I'd just spit on the floor.

Farr leaned over the table. "Say that again, but slower this time."

"Bit," I said.

Boyle coughed in his hand: "Is her last name...O'Honey?"

Farr slapped his knee in mock laughter as I looked away, shaking my head. This was classic Boyle. Many ignored his humor because he was a jock and acted like a jock. Not so. Boyle was a master. To wit: Once in an American Lit class, the discussion was growing heated about Hemingway the writer and Hemingway the person, one girl claiming Ernest Hemingway was a misogynist. This caused a lot of grumbling among the genders as chairs shifted around lining up for a nasty free-for-all. Boyle sensed the tension – he really respected the professor, an older guy ill-equipped for what was brewing between the sexes – and raised his hand. He said, "Pardon me, Professor Cornwell, Ernest Hemingway was not a misogynist, he was a Methodist." The class howled. Crisis averted, the professor wiped his brow. Farr slapped Boyle on the shoulder, telling him that there was a call from the UN: Kurt Waldheim holding on Line 2 needing his assistance.

Now, Boyle and Farr both sat back mulling over that I had a new love interest and her name was Bit. Boyle socked me in the arm. "You score?"

I gave them a hand waggle.

"Okay, no score. But what?" Boyle asked, giving me the hand waggle back. "Single, double...come on?"

I clammed up, keeping my hand firmly around my beer.

Farr leaned back in his chair, cupping his hands behind his head, addressing Boyle, "I respect a man who doesn't kiss and tell."

Boyle did the same with his hands, leaned back and said, "I respect a man who brags about his exploits so I can live vicariously."

Farr asked me, "Any pictures Boyle can ogle?"

I held up two fingers; told them I'd show them later.

"Naked?" Boyle asked.

I said, "On a horse."

Boyle rubbed his hands together. "Naked on a horse. Better yet."

Farr rolled his eyes.

I said, "She a cowgirl. Barrel racer, too. Works as a vet's assistant in Jackson. Going to U-Wyoming at Laramie next semester."

Boyle asked, "When do we get to meet Lady Godiva?"

"Next month at our party."

They looked at each other, nodding, smiling.

Farr said, "You going back next summer?"

I nodded *Yep, for sure.*

Farr dinged my glass. "You look good, Chandler. I don't

know what you did out there, but you look good." He drained his beer.

Coming from Freddy Farr that was gospel.

Boyle gave my biceps a squeeze. "Take a look at these guns, Farr. Chandler's back to fighting weight." He clinked my glass, then killed his beer.

Coming from Chris Boyle that was golden.

I tried not to blush, but what Boyle and Farr had told me was heaven. The last time they saw me I was limping out of town on four flat tires: flunking out of school; Luke's death; my parents ragging on me; and Janie giving me the heave-ho. Now, I was back in school, Luke's death behind me, and my parents were suddenly a lot smarter.

But Janie was still a problem.

I downed my beer, then smiled my crooked smile, basking in the adulation of Boyle and Farr; a warm buzz running through my body as The Staple Singers 'I'll Take You There," cued up and filled the room.

# Chapter 25

## DON'T DO IT ✳ THE FACULTY CLUB ✳ PROFESSOR GURNEY

On my first day of classes I was edging around my dorm room in the late afternoon, killing time before my bartending job at the Faculty Club, alphabetizing record albums and shelving thick college textbooks that took up a lot of room and weighed a ton. Farr was at the library, which is where we did most of our studying. He and I agreed our room was best for sleeping and hanging out; cracking books was best done away from the distractions of a roommate, TV, and music. Once we got to know each other's class schedules and study habits, we figured out when each of us could be alone in the room, free to veg out, listen to our music at loud volume, or do the odd thing like spray a few blasts of your roommate's Right Guard under your pits, compare his Pepsodent to your Colgate, or slap slap slap on a bit of his Old Spice.

Farr was quietly serious and efficient in his study habits. Mine needed some honing; that's why rooming with him helped me focus. I've always been competitive with my friends, so rooming with Farr rubbed off on me, making me work longer, harder and smarter at my studies. It was sort of like being at the Lazy T and not wanting to disappoint anybody, in this case Farr, Boyle and my parents. I think, and most would agree, just rooming with Farr made me appear as if I was carrying a Four-0.

Outside the open window of our dorm room, fall was dancing politely with summer. Lynyrd Skynyrd's "Freebird" rang around the quad – a rowdy, shirtless crowd tapping a keg, out of the blocks early on a Thursday afternoon.

I lit a cigarette, then cued up and cranked The Band's "Don't Do It," mouthing lyrics I knew better than the Lord's Prayer and the 23rd Psalm.

*Oh, baby, don't you do it, don't do it*
*Don't you break by heart*
*Please don't do it*
*Don't you break by heart*

Farr and I had pushed our desks together facing the windows that looked down three floors and out over the quad. I pulled my desk away from the window so that I could sit on the sill with my butt on the ledge and my back against the jamb. Tugging on my hair, now long enough to finger behind my ears, I followed the kids walking back to their dorms. I gazed down. The ground below me was about half the distance that Luke had fallen when he killed himself. One night at Harry's, Jackie told us that falling from up high doesn't hurt you – that's the fun part – it's the last six inches that kill you. He made his point by smacking his hand *SPLAT* on the bar.

Jackie howled at that.

We all did.

I chuckled, peering down, convinced we're all closer to the edge than we know. This led to an existential crisis, and I wasn't even stoned. I had one of those what-if-this-happened-what-if-that-happened-what-am-I-here-for moments that are circular, confusing and disappear as soon as your roommate asks *Wanna another beer?* What weighed on me now was leaving Buzz at the Cowboy Bar. What if I had waited around and drove him back to the ranch. Would he still be alive? Was it my destiny to be in Wyoming to save Buzz? If so, I failed. Or would Buzz be dead regardless, eventually hunted down by Farnsworth and Asshole Pee? Why did I pick up the phone a year ago? I could have let it go; or said no, I wasn't the kid who wanted a job. Then I would not have had this problem. This existential business – and thinking about Buzz – was like a taking fifth class. I looked away, down, out over the quad. I mumbled *shit, shit, shit.*

*My biggest mistake was lovin' you too much*
*And lettin' ya know*
*Now you got me where you want me*
*And a-you won't let me go*
*If my heart was made of glass*
*Well, then you'd surely see*
*How much heartaches and misery*
*Girl, you been causin' me*

Even from three stories up, and at an odd angle, I knew who it was – I could pick Janie Wallace out of a packed stadium at three hundred yards: height, hair color, nose, tilt of the head, laugh, smile – little things you had a hard time shaking. She was thirty feet down and fifty over, bopping around like a fifteen-year-old, dressed in short shorts and my favorite Lacoste shirt that made her boobs stick out and bounce. She was dancing around her new boyfriend, Billy Flannigan, the guy Scott Hodges did not want to tell me about, the guy Janie would not tell me about last year when we broke up. Billy Flannigan – a chiseled, rugged, handsome hockey-jock-frat-boy – was built like a German U-boat and twice as menacing. He was also an asshole (just my opinion). I took a couple of deep breaths, then swallowed hard muttering again *shit, shit, shit.* It made sense: Flannigan was a hot-shot BMOC; Janie was a hot, hot, blossoming sophomore. I was nothing more than a minor inconvenience.

An uneasiness built behind my eyes – I squeezed them

tight, struggling to let it go. But there was still a big piece of me bouncing around with Janie on the path below, and that's why I forced myself to keep watching. Flannigan strutted along beside her in shorts and a T-shirt busting with muscles. Even from up high I could see he had that smug look of *look at what I've landed and am about to gaff.* Just outside his fraternity house, Janie stopped and tried to back-tap him in the butt with her foot. Problem was Flannigan was too tall, her shoe-tap landing on the back of his thigh. But Billy Flannigan had no problem back-tapping her cute little behind with his foot.

Here was the big problem: That used to be our routine.

They stopped outside his frat, talking, he nodding to come inside, she pulling away, being coy; he smiling and pulling back; she relenting, giving him a big kiss okay; he leading her in by the hand, the door closing behind them.

*But I been tryin' to do my best*
*A-you know I've tried to do my best*
*Don't do it*
*Don't you break by heart*
*Please don't do it*
*Don't you break by heart*

I left the window open; turned the stereo off; put on a pair of khakis, a white shirt and my cordovan loafers. I grabbed my smokes, hit the lights, locked the door, and headed to my bartending job at the Faculty Club, taking the long way, now carrying a full course load.

(For the record, I'm not a live-and-let-live type of guy. Even though I was responsible for the breakup, I was pissed and wanted revenge. That, of course, was the wrong thing to do, and that's where Boyle came to my rescue. I'd never take dating tips from him, but Boyle knew that when you're in a deep hole, reach for the rope, not the shovel. That's good advice. Two days later at the library, he caught me staring at Janie and Billy Flannigan from across the room, my body rigid with emotion that I had no handle on. He knew I was bottled up ready to explode, so he calmly put his hand on my shoulder and whispered in my ear: "Let it go, Hank. You can't do anything about it. She's moved on and so have you. Don't wallow in it. The best thing you can do is rise above it. You want to confound Janie. Really surprise her." I said yeah. Boyle said then show her what you're really made of. I asked how do I do that? He said simple, write her a letter and explain how sorry you are about how you acted and how you hoped you can still be friends. That's harder than it sounds, laying it all out on a page, but I did right then and there on white legal paper with a blue Bic pen with Boyle proofing my confession. I won't repeat what I wrote, but know it was honest, a tad droll, and flowed rather well. I sealed it with a kiss and mailed it that night.)

The Faculty Club is a stately, muscular red brick building that sits on a side street off the College Green – a patches-on-the-elbows type of place that the faculty retires to in the afternoons and early evenings. It has large, curved, single-pane windows and flags flying out front like an embassy. Inside, beyond the oak front door, is comfort. Ancient sofas and arm chairs welcome you, and dusty paintings of wise and learned professors follow you from room to room. I took the job at the Faculty Club because I liked bartending and needed the extra cash; it is also where I first met Professor and Mrs. Gurney my freshman year. She was why I took his English Comp class, convincing me I should not be intimidated by the revered taskmaster; he was why I was still at the university. They both were a big reason why I continued to write this story.

I clocked in. Dennis, the manager, greeted me in the kitchen, asking about my summer, commenting that I looked different somehow, pleased that I was back working behind the bar. Putting on my apron, I told him I had been on a ranch and had gotten a lot of sun. He said he was expecting a big crowd on the first day of school and was I ready for the rush? What he meant was to get the bar set up pronto, and did I remember what everybody drank? Funny, I can't remember the year the Magna Carta was signed, or the difference between igneous and metamorphic rocks, or how to use *lie* and *lay* correctly in a sentence, but I can remember precisely what the professors and their wives drank.

I had perfect drink recall.

*When I was growing up, my father once told Andy and me that in the army you should always be nice to the cook and the paymaster. Andy expanded that lesson to include Vince, the bartender at the Bogey Club. Vince – that's all it said on his name tag – was the locker room attendant and a bartender at the club for big parties on the patio that stretched out onto the pristine lawn beyond. Andy was always hanging around Vince, and I was always hanging around Andy. They talked sports mostly, and sometimes Vince would slide Andy a bruising comment about one of the members along with a Singapore Sling – sometimes two, if Andy had a girl in his sights. Normally, Andy didn't want me around, but he made an exception with Vince because I was his gofer – delivering plates stacked high with half-dollar hamburgers and shrimp cocktail intended to fuel Vince's two-fifty-plus, loosen his tongue, and ensure he'd supply underage drinks for Andy. One summer evening, during a big wedding reception for one of our cousins, Andy walked away with fistfuls of booze, leaving me with Vince. I was twelve. Vince was fortyish. A frumpy waitress named Joyce, wearing a black gunnysack-like uniform and a beehive hairdo, approached the bar with a lot on her tray and a mouthful for Vince. I kept low, sipping my Coke, my ears pricked like a German shepherd's.*

*Joyce barked, "Vinny, give me a Tabby, a Bulldog with three balls, Wilbur Nipping Mr. Ed, and Judy Garland with Missile Tits." She emptied her tray of dirty glasses and cocktail napkins as Vince whirled his magic, sending Joyce back into the ring in under two minutes. As she headed off in her orthotics, her tray poised high, I shifted closer to Vince, in awe.*

*"How did you do that?" I asked.*

*"What's that, young Chandler?" Vince said, wiping down the bar.*

*"What you just did," I said, not knowing how to explain it.*

*He ducked down for a burger, washing it down with two shrimp. He said with a mouthful and an eye out for the club manager, "It's our code."*

*That sounded cool to me. "Between you and Joyce?" I asked.*

*"That's right."*

*"Anybody else know?"*

*"No," he said shaking his jowly chin. "I don't think so." He chuckled. "I hope not." He wiped the sweat off his face with a towel, his blondish flat top glistening under the late June sun.*

*"What's it mean?" I asked.*

*He shook his head No way, giving my Coke a topper and a slide of ice from a scoop.*

*"Come on, Vince," I pleaded. "Tell me."*

*He shook his head again, buttoning his lip with his thumb and forefinger.*

*I was determined. I left and returned with a big plate piled high with burgers, shrimp and the last of the lump crab meat, telling anyone who asked that it was dinner for my Uncle Homer, my mother's fall-down-drunk brother who couldn't be trusted going through a buffet line.*

*I slid the plate across the bar. Vince's eyes unbuttoned his lip. He stowed the plate away as I leaned in. He said, "It's the way Joycie and me remember what everybody drinks. There's a word for it, but I can't remember. I'll think of it."*

*I was intrigued, like I was talking to Q in a James Bond movie about a new secret weapon. I asked, "How's it work, Vince?"*

*"Promise you won't tell?" he said, wolfing down another burger, then fingering the crabmeat into his mouth, wiping off the residue with three cocktail napkins.*

*"I won't," I insisted, looking around me, making sure no one was near.*

*He chewed then swallowed. "Tabby is a Tab with twist of lime for Mrs. McClintock – she's AA. The Bulldog with three balls is a gin martini on the rocks with three cocktail onions for Dick Masters – a real nutcracker. Wilbur is Sandy Williams – he only drinks light beer over ice – a little weird. Nipping Mr. Ed means Ed Jolley is drinking again but likes his vodka soda on the light side. Judy Garland is Jack Daniels in a snifter with a splash for Betty Hardin, and Missile Tits is Janet Shafer, she gets a chardonnay with her new pair."*

*Vince went through it one more time then said, "Now repeat back what I just said."*

*I did, with complete accuracy.*

*"You're a born bartender, Master Chandler," he said, finishing the plate of food and wiping off his hands. "I just wish I could remember what that word is. Joycie will know."*

Mrs. Gurney approached the bar and said to me, "Henry, do you remember your mnemonics from last year?"

Feverishly working the speed rail, I said, "I'm a little rusty but it's coming back." I looked up and flashed her my crooked smile while mixing a Lovey and a Thurston – my drink mnemonic for Mrs. Gurney and the Professor.

She reached across and laid a sympathetic hand on my cheek. "You poor dear."

"I'm okay, really," I said, blushing a bit.

She said, "I loved your story. So did Dick. You know he only gave out three B's last year. You should be proud."

"Thanks to you," I said with a smile, handing her a napkin, then her vodka on the rocks with a twist and a splash, and, for the professor, a Manhattan straight up with a cherry, light on the sweet vermouth.

Mrs. Gurney rolled her eyes. "Dick Gurney doesn't know how to form the letter A. He's only given out five in his career, and the last one went to Maria Mulhern who went on to win a Pulitzer Prize. He's more comfortable with C's and D's. I help him with the B's."

I looked up and saw a couple coming through the door I remembered from the spring semester: "Hawkeye Pierce" and "Hot Lips Houlihan" (gin martini straight up with a twist and a Dubonnet on the rocks) followed by "The Flintstones" (Scotch and soda with two olives and a white wine spritzer).

As Mrs. Gurney stepped away from the bar, she said, "Dick's over in the corner talking department politics. I'm his drink caddy tonight. I know he's dying to speak with you. Please come join us as soon as you can."

Soon wasn't soon enough, so I asked Dennis for a big favor: Could he watch the bar while I sat down with Professor Gurney because he wanted to talk with me about a story I'd written for his class? I let slip to Dennis that Gurney had given me a B. Dennis pumped my hand saying, *Gurney gave you a B? Go, Go* – as if I was Dorothy being granted an audience with the all-powerful Oz.

I sat down next to Mrs. Gurney on a red Victorian settee with big dimples and buttons, my spine ramrod-straight like my grandmother had taught me. Professor Gurney was to my right in a dilapidated, listing armchair. He had thick grey hair and eyebrows, a thick nose, thick lips, thick hands, a thick waist, and a thick voice. After talking briefly about my paper and how happy and healthy I looked, he asked in a low, growling whisper, mindful of the professors around us, "Did it really happen the way you wrote it?"

"Yes sir," I said.

He sat back, rubbing his gray stubble. He said, "I'm sorry...for your friend Luke and...and your friend Buzz."

I didn't know what to say, so I looked at my hands, rubbing them together like Buzz would have.

Professor Gurney said, "I would like to have met him."

I said, "You would have liked him, sir. He was the real deal."

"I bet he was. Those men are rare. How's his wife doing?"

"Hope is tough," I said. "She'll make it."

Mrs. Gurney said softly, "How's your friend Bit?"

I turned to face her. "She really misses her dad. But she's like her mom... tougher than new boots. She's coming to visit me next month."

Mrs. Gurney put a hand on my arm. "That's so exciting, Hank."

"Yes...yes it is." I tried not to blush.

She asked, "Are you going back to the ranch next summer?"

I looked down at my hands, rubbing them again, thinking about Buzz and what had happened. "Yes," I said. "Yes, I am" – as if there were no doubt.

Professor Gurney sat up, pushing himself closer to me, close enough so I could smell the bourbon on his breath. "Look at me, Mr. Chandler."

I did.

He said, "If you do return to Wyoming, I'd advise you not write about it. I've shared your story with no one. You have the only copy, and if I were you I would destroy it."

That was the best advice I never took.

# Chapter 26

## ALISON ✳ MELISSA ✳ JANIE

On a Thursday in the first week of October, Farr announced that he was going home to New York for a long weekend. He asked if I wanted to come along; he'd take me to Studio 54. I told him yes, but that I had a paper due; I'd train down the next day.

It was ten p.m. I was in our dorm room with the Night Earl on in the background, procrastinating, distracted by a phone call I had to make.

I dialed.

A female voice answered, sounding relaxed, like she was reclining in bed. I didn't have a script, so I winged it:

"Alison Henry?"

"Speaking."

"Hi, this is Hank Chandler."

"Who?" she said, as if she might have just shot up in bed.

I said, "Hank Chandler...from Chicago."

"Do I know you?"

"Yes and no."

"I'm sorry, I don't understand."

I said, "You know me as someone else."

She said, "And who might that be?"

"Scott Hodges."

"And he is...?"

I was tempted to blow a fastball by her and let loose with, *Let's cut the shit, Miss Snotty-I-Go-to-Harvard. He's the tall, dark stud muffin who twisted your pigtails. Remember? The guy you were playing tonsil hockey with on the roof of your building the night of your deb party. The guy you tracked down at my house because he never called you.* Instead, I threw her a curve:

"He is me and I am him."

She said, "This is real confusing."

I said, "You want to make it more confusing?"

When she spit out, "*No, I definitely do not,*" I sensed she was now up pacing the room with a stretched telephone cord as if she was a diva in an old Hollywood movie. I continued with my scheme, telling her we were throwing a bash and I wanted her to come down to Providence, bury-the-hatchet-and-smoke-the-peace-pipe type of thing.

She said, "Why should I? I don't know you, and I don't want to know you. You can't give me one reason why I should come to your party."

"Yes I can," I said. "Scott Hodges will be there."

"Is this a joke?"

"No."

"Well...that's not a reason to go to a party. That's a reason to join a convent."

"Want another reason?"

"Yes, please."

"He likes you."

"How do you know that?" she demanded.

"I don't know," I said, rather relaxed. "Call it male intuition."

"*Well,*" Alison huffed like a mother-in-training, "that's

a faulty sense. And why would his presence at your party possess me to drive all the way to Providence?"

I said, "Because you like him."

Alison Henry kicked up some dust. "I do not."

I teased her like a tattling ten-year-old: "That's not what your mother told my mother."

I sensed Alison was twisted up in her phone cord and backpedaling: "You're lying, she did not!"

I was enjoying this. I had her on the run, so I backed off a skosh. I said, "You're right, sorry, she didn't."

After a pregnant pause, Alison said, "Scott Hodges is a pig."

I said, "No argument here."

"And you're his friend."

"Guilty as charged."

Silence.

I flipped my Bic pen round and round visualizing Alison's cogs engaging. After half a dozen flips she said, "Well, Hank... if...if I did come, who would you suggest I come as? You're the one who started this whole charade by giving Scott Hodges *your* invitation to *my* party. Who should I come as to *your* party?"

Alison was making me sing for my supper. I thought about that for a second, my gears now spinning.

*Bingo.*

I laid it out rationally: "Well...you are coming to Rhode Island. And you are coming from Harvard. Let me think... Hmmm. How about Jenny Cavelleri? Yes...yes, come as... say... Radcliffe sophomore Jennifer Cavelleri from Cranston, Rhode Island. That would make it interesting, don't you think?"

Alison Henry of 1430 Lake Shore Drive, Chicago, Illinois, mulled that over. I think I heard her click her fingernail on her tooth. She stepped perfectly into character:

"When exactly is the party again?"

I said, "Saturday, October 27."

She said, "Oh, I can't make it. I'll be working at the library that night."

I said, "I completely understand. Sorry to bother you. Maybe some other time." I said my goodbyes and hung up.

Check: Alison Henry was coming to our party; I'd put money on it. I'd also send her a card the next day, a save-the-date kind of thing that she could use as a bookmark in her dog-eared copy of *Norton's Anthology of Poetry* while thumbing through Yeats and "Kates" – Scott Hodges on her lips, around her hips, and in her hair. If she was smart – hey, she went to Harvard – she'd see this as an invitation to get even with Scott, maybe even pull ahead. My male intuition also told me that Alison Henry would show up sporting a new haircut and have a friend riding shotgun for protection (turns out, I was right on both counts).

I returned to the work at hand, now knuckling down to my ten-pager due the next day. "No more, no less" is what my Greek Mythology professor growled at the class, drawing a huge 10 on the board and circling it, pointing: "Ten pages, not 7, 8, 9; not 11, 12, or 25."

My clock flipped to 1:54 a.m.

I was almost done.

I hit the carriage return on my Smith Corona, put in a new piece of paper, and typed my last sentence onto the top of...*Oh fuck*...page 9.

I turned off my desk lamp; the room now dark. I pushed back, stoked up my second-to-last Marlboro, put my feet up on the desk and looked out the window over the streetlights into the misty morning calm. I was tapped out; not another page left in me. Earl Mitchell was winding down his radio show:

*The clock on the wall is the winner after all. I'm leaving you with Duane and Greg and Barry...Dickey, Jai, and Butch. Now that's good company. I'm headed out for my eggs and beer.*

*Time to fly children...*
    *Ever Onward...*
        *Ever Upward...*
The Allman Brothers' "Melissa" cued up.
I drifted with them out the window.
The song ended.
My ears rang in the silence.
I turned the desk lamp back on and stared at page 9 for two flips of my alarm clock, searching for a solution.
*Ta-da.*
I grabbed my pencil and carefully erased "9" on the last page and typed in "10." I went back a page and erased 8 and typed in 9. I stapled the pages together, then hit the light. I imagined the Night Earl outside his studio, leaning over a wrought iron railing, flicking the last of his Lucky Strike into the moonless night like a shooting star. I did the same with my second-to-last Marlboro, flicking the glowing cigarette out the window, watching it jackknife into darkness. I fingered my last cigarette, debating whether or not I should save it for breakfast.

Opening the top drawer of my desk, I brought out a rubber-banded stack of letters. I opened the top one and read it twice. It was coming on two months since I'd seen Bit. Her letters were saying the same thing – or maybe I was just reading too much into it because it was late and I was feeling sorry for myself. I lit my last smoke, rereading two more letters, convincing myself that, in spite of her coming out to visit, our relationship (uggh) would fizzle like most summer love. Or that I might muff the whole deal like I did with Janie. That got me even more depressed and blue. I bundled and re-bound the letters, stowing them away.

Silence.
Stillness.
A light breeze drifted in the window.
My speakers buzzed.

My dorm room was dead, nothing doing except my insecurity about Bit and an aching desire to be with someone. I stared at the phone wanting to call her, but that was useless. We'd talked a few times since our conversation in my parents' pantry, but I didn't know if we would again before she came out for our party because it was impossible to connect with her at the ranch or at work. I picked up the receiver, unscrewed the mouthpiece and took out that round component connected with wires. I let it dangle around then packed it back together. I put my head down on my arms on the desk and closed my eyes.

A minute later the phone went off like a fire bell in the night. I shot up, the ringing reverberating through my ears, around the room, out the window. I lunged for the receiver, holding it to my ear, not saying hello. From the other end came a voice that I had prayed would call. A voice that I still craved and missed. A voice that had stopped me outside of class two days ago, telling me how much she loved my letter, appreciated my honesty and respected my integrity (her words, not mine). She had also given me a look as if she were seeing me for the first time all over again. Now, the voice pleaded softly, like she'd never left, "I'm at the front door, Hank. Please let me in."

I bolted up and out, sprinting down the corridor, my door left wide open and the phone banging around the floor.

I never made it to Studio 54.

# Chapter 27

## HARRY'S * THE DRAFT * BIT * SALLY * SCOTT

Before our big party on Saturday, we met at Harry's on Thursday afternoon just after five. Farr and I car-pooled downtown with Bones in his BMW. Boyle was already there talking with Jackie at the bar. Dante was around the corner tending to business. We set up in the back, pushing two tables together. Boyle brought over Narragansett drafts for the four of us. Jackie made himself a tall Scotch and soda and, for Dante, a cognac and Coke. Bones placed two pencils – sharpened to a deadly point – on top of a yellow legal-size pad of paper. The Zombies' "Time of the Season" was playing on the jukebox.

Dante strolled in wearing dark wire rim sunglasses and a mid-length brown leather coat. He took off both and sat at the head of the table, scooting in his chair. From his coat pocket he pulled out an eight-inch-high statue of a black woman. He took a sip of his drink. "This is Wheezie Jefferson," he said, "If there are any disputes that need to be settled, Wheezie here will be the referee." He pressed a hidden button releasing a shiny six-inch knife blade that shot out with a *ssssitttt* from the top of Wheezie's 'fro.

Farr pulled in his chair, giving Jackie a grin. "Game on."

Boyle looked at me saying, "I think we can agree to disagree without spilling blood."

Bones mouthed *What the fuck?* (He told me later that he thought he was in a scene from "Wait Until Dark." I explained he was right on, that Dante loved Alan Arkin in the movie, but thought Wheezie Jefferson, rather than Gloria, was a more appropriate name for his switchblade. Bones concurred, giving Dante points for his cinematic reference and originality.)

I introduced Bones to Dante and Jackie, telling them he was a good friend from Chicago who worked side-by-side with Earl Mitchell, explaining he was in charge of the playlist for our fall party. Jackie and Dante shook Bones's hand, impressed that he knew and worked with the Night Earl. They said they dug the Night Earl's radio show and had heard him gig around town since they were in high school.

After downing the first round of drinks, well into our second, we inched in our chairs and settled down to hashing out our musical preferences and prejudices. Jackie came on strong, purposely riding Boyle because he loved Mick Jagger: "The Rolling Stones blow and I'm not coming to your party if that's all you play." He glared at Boyle with a put-that-in-your-pipe-and-smoke-it.

Boyle fired back: "Who said *you* were invited to our party?"

Jackie – eyeing Dante's switchblade – replied, "My friend Wheezie."

Bones masterfully took command, stepping between them. "Okay, three Stones songs."

Boyle said, "'Satisfaction.'"

Farr said, "'Jumpin' Jack Flash.'"

Jackie said, "Booriiing."

I piped in, "What about 'Under my Thumb.'"

Dante said, "Love Bill Wyman's bass line."

Bones confirmed: "Okay, so we got three Stones songs, "Satisfaction," "Jumpin' Jack Flash" and "Under my Thumb." What about Springsteen?"

Jackie high-fived Boyle. "Now we're talking".

Farr gave me a smirk, knowing how to push Boyle's buttons. He imitated Jackie. "Booriiing. Try dancing to "Jungleland" sometime. It's worse than "In-A-Gadda-Da-Vida "

Boyle said, "Freddy, I got something for you," leaning back and reaching into his pocket with his right hand, pulling it out, his middle finger extended, giving it to Farr – if you know what I mean. Boyle then motioned to Bones as if he were at the plate with a bat in his hands. "Leading off the night, The Boss – 'Tenth Avenue Freeze-Out.'"

Bones – penning furiously – said, "Two more," throwing out suggestions: 'Rosalita,' 'Born to Run'...?"

I piped up, "Gotta be 'Rosie' and what about 'Spirits in the Night.'"

Jackie tippy-tap-tapped his finger tips on the table: "You got it, Chandler the third."

On a roll, I added, "What about Earth Wind and Fire?"

Boyle bounced up and screamed: "Ho, Lawd. Give us 'Reasons.'"

Bones said, "Slow down. Slow down," shaking out his cramping hand.

Dante – chewing on a piece of ice – said, "Sugar loves 'Reasons.'"

Bones said, "Live version, right?" looking around the table for confirmation.

Farr turned to Boyle mimicking a saxophone player. Boyle pointed at Farr: "Mr. Don Myrick on the alto horn. He plays so beautiful, don't you agree?" (This was not the first time Boyle and Farr had gone through this routine.)

Bones held up a finger: "One more from Earth Wind and Fire."

Boyle demanded: "'September.'" I promised Sally we'd dance to 'September.' It's her favorite."

Jackie sat back with his hands behind his head looking up at the ceiling, letting out a loud laugh. "Are you kidding me? You can't dance, Boyle. You're from Connecticut. You can barely walk and chew gum."

Boyle flipped Jackie off then rubbed his thumbs over the pads of his fingers, challenging him. "Five bucks. We'll see who's a better dancer at our party."

Jackie pointed at Boyle. "You're on."

Farr said, "Let's get back to business." He picked up Wheezie Jefferson, feeling around for the button. Dante leaned over and helped him. The blade zinged up. Dante said, "Careful, Frederick McPheeters Farr. I don't want you cutting yourself and bleeding blue all over my bar."

Farr found the switch; the blade disappeared. He said, "The blue blood from Park Avenue wants disco."

Boyle moaned. "Shit, no. Disco sucks."

Farr challenged him: "Girls like it."

Dante agreed. "Sugar and Spice love it."

I said to Boyle, "Hard to argue."

Bones intervened with a solution: "Tavares. 'Heaven Must Be Missing an Angel.'"

No argument from the table.

Bones said, "You need some Marvin Gaye."

Dante added, "And Al Green."

Bones pointed the tip of his pencil at Dante, adding, "The *Reverend* Al Green, sir. And I would recommend 'You Ought To Be With Me' and 'Let's Stay Together.'"

Dante palmed Bones's bony shoulder, complimenting him in a righteous tone. "Amen, brother Bones. I don't know how you found your way to Harry Hope's, but you're welcome back anytime in the house of the Lord."

Bones rolled his shoulders struggling to suppress a smug smile, as if he had been tapped by the teacher as the prodigy in the class. He asked, "Where's Tavares go in the lineup?"

Boyle said, "End of the night, then we'll be drunk enough to forget it."

Jackie asked, "You got a disco ball?"

I perked up. That was a great idea. All our friends would love it, dancing to a light show at the end of the party. I also knew it would impress Bit, because in my letters I told her about Farr and Studio 54. I even sent her a newspaper clipping of Farr and Sophia (she of the fancy Italian last name that I can't remember or pronounce) at some night club dancing under a disco ball. I asked, "Where can we get one?"

Jackie said, "The Voom Voom Room. Dante and I go dancing there on Monday nights with Sugar and Spice when they play disco."

Farr said to Jackie, "Hey, John Travolta, the party's at Boyle's house not the Voom Voom Room."

Jackie said, "No shit, Sherlock," then polished off his drink. He patted his stomach and belched. "Listen up, Einstein. Ditch your slide rule and protractor and pick up a pair of pliers and a screwdriver. I'll get you a ball. You guys set it up. You handle that?"

Boyle, Farr and I looked at each other, agreeing we could pull it off.

For the next hour and a half we hammered out and wedged in enough songs to fill two sheets of legal paper; Bones dulling his pencils to nubs, hardening the callus on his middle finger.

The playlist complete, Jackie asked, "You need help getting kegs?"

I said yeah, I was in charge of the bar, what would he suggest? He asked Bones for a piece of paper then scribbled down a name and an address. He looked up. "What else you serving?"

I told him we're making a punch for the girls.

He said, "You Girl Scouts *really* know how to make a punch?"

I shrugged my shoulders at Boyle and Farr. They shrugged back. Jackie wrote down some more, then handed me the paper. I read aloud the ingredients for a Pawtucket Leg Spreader, pointing at the last item, asking Farr if that was legal. He said it was if you poured it into the tank of a Formula One car.

Dante stood, fingering his beard, pondering something. "You have any security working the party?"

Farr – grabbing glasses to take back to the bar – said, "No, why?"

Dante put on his coat, pocketing Wheezie Jefferson. "Just asking," he said. "I'd be concerned if, say, Oliver Barrett IV gets out of hand and goes after Holden Caulfield with a squash racquet." Here he looked at Jackie at the end of the table, then us, then Jackie again. "If there's a problem, make sure you come get us" – waving his index finger between himself and Jackie – "come get Grosvenor and Winthrope." Dante giggled, his eyes lighting up at the thought of it. "We'll take care of it. Right, Grosvenor?" Jackie fingered an inch long scar on his cheek, chuckling.

Game over.

At just past eight, Boyle, Farr, Bones and I bobbed and weaved out of Harry Hopes' to Question Mark and the Mysterians' "96 Tears", the playlist complete.

Bones drove us back to the quad, then generously offered me the keys to his Beemer so I could pick up Bit. I flew to the airport with the sunroof open and Little Feat cranked. Farr had moved into Boyle's house for Bit's stay, bunking in the "attic suite." I'd sanitized our room and rearranged the furniture so the single beds made a double, belting together the bedposts with my mother's needlepoint belts. I wiped down the bathroom, did my laundry, and ditched the *Playboy*s. I cleaned up everything, even the dust bunnies under the bed. What I had not come clean on was telling Bit about my weekend affair with Janie. To mix metaphors, I was rolling the dice hoping I'd dodge a bullet. Did I feel bad spending a couple of nights with Janie? No, and here's why:

I'd learned to compartmentalize (this is a valuable concept I picked up in my Psyche I class). I was most likely in love with Bit, but I was still really nuts about Janie. I'd done some nosing around and found out from Janie's freshman roommate Mimi Ryder that Billy Flannigan had the morals of an alley cat, and Janie was having a tough time dealing with it. That's why she came knocking on my door the weekend Farr was in New York at Studio 54. She decided to fight fire with fire. So I became an attractive port in the storm, if you catch my drift. I also think Janie missed me because we always had fun together; I made her laugh and feel good about herself – and she the same with me. Janie didn't say anything to me about Flannigan's philandering, and I didn't ask. She also didn't pry as to my love status, and I didn't offer. We were in détente mode, our discreet rendezvous between us, confined to my room, snuggling under the covers watching black and white movies, our time together a mellow, romantic scene as if shot through cheesecloth. We said about three words to each other the whole weekend, our bodies, eyes, fingers, toes, and deep breathing doing most of the communicating. The closest Janie came to Bit and Wyoming was when she asked me about my injuries, running her hand over my face and ribs. I acted like a tough guy saying they were nothing and mostly healed.

Was this cheating?

I think not.

I rationalized it this way: Bit and I were barely in the pupa stage – we liked each other a lot and wanted to see what we would grow into. Janie and I had established a foundation of love and friendship. That's hard to give up. We were not starting anything new, nor, I might add, ending it either. We were merely backsliding for selfish reasons – we both missed and needed each other. But only temporarily. To wit, Janie announced she was done with me early that Sunday morning, kissing me on the forehead, walking out of my room without even turning around, the door clicking shut her only goodbye. She was headed back to Billy Flannigan, who'd figure out where she'd been, which would correct his behavior for about fifteen minutes.

Now, speeding down I-95, I shifted Janie Wallace from the front burner to the back, and Bit Stifel from back to front. I guessed (correctly, as I was soon to discover) that Bit wasn't a virgin and this was not her first rodeo. What I'd figured out about Bit in our flirting at the Lazy T, and in our letters over the last three months, was she didn't play head games. Bit was wild and sweet, my cowgirl wrapped in Wrangler. Tough. Cool. Tender. Smart. And that's what was racing through my head as I parked Bones's BMW at the airport and legged it into the terminal.

Bit's plane was on time. Eighty-two days, twenty-six letters and five phone calls later Bit was finally on my turf. Walking through the terminal door, she looked beautifully lost and wonderfully out of place. She was dressed neatly in Western garb, nothing fancy, as if she was going out to dinner in Pinedale (except she was wearing my Cubs hat). I slowly approached and blocked her path. She looked at me with eyes wide. She put a hand on my cheek. I forgot what I was going to say. Finally, fumbling, I said I missed her and asked if she was wiped out from her trip (she had traveled from Cora to Jackson to Denver to Providence in about ten hours). She put down her small back pack and placed her arms around my neck, kissing me long and hard enough to telegraph she was ready to go, assuring me I *missed you more*, then asking,

"Where am I again?"

I took off her Cubs hat so our foreheads and noses could touch. I replied, "The East Coast. New England. Rhode Island. Providence. Want a quahog?"

She said she didn't know what a quahog was, but how about a beer first to cut the dust, giving me a kiss that stayed with me until baggage claim (at which time I had to reload).

I said, "Two Narragansetts coming up."

She said, "What's a Narragansett?"

We walked away from the gate holding hands. (I'm comfortable with public displays of affection. Farr too, but not Boyle.) I explained, "It's beer brewed from the waters of the Scituate."

"What's that," she asked.

"A local river," I said.

"Is it cold?"

"The Scituate?"

"No, the beer?"

"Normally, yes."

"Do Easterners in New England drink warm beer like they do in England?"

An interesting question. I answered, "Only during blackouts."

"How far are we from school?"

"Twenty minutes."

"Where are we going now?"

"Back to the quad," I said giving her hand a squeeze. "I want to show you off to my friends."

Bit blushed. She stammered, "I...I want to meet your friends, too? What're their names again?"

"Boyle, Farr and Bones."

"Sounds like a law firm."

I thought about that. She was right.

She said, "What do I call them?"

I said, "Freddy, Chris, and Bones."

"Does Bones have a real name?"

"Yeah," I said, "Tommy Childress, but he goes by Bones."

"Where he'd get that nickname?"

"My mother," I said with a smirk.

In the car heading back to school, I popped in a special "Lazy T" cassette that Bones had made for Bit. I'd given him some suggestions, then he ran with it: New Riders of the Purple Sage, Pure Prairie League, Marshall Tucker Band,

The Eagles, James Taylor, Emmy Lou Harris, Bonnie Raitt, etc.

Our conversation in the car was mostly about Bit prepping for school after Christmas. It was not hard to see that she was excited about getting off the ranch and onto the college campus in Laramie, especially with Polly Hamilton, whom we were talking about as I pulled up and parked the car outside the quad. There was a slight nip in the air and you could smell the fallen leaves as we walked arm-in-arm into the quad toward the buzz of the party. There seated together on a brick wall outside the party, drinking beer from red cups, waiting for us, was the "law firm" of Boyle, Farr and Bones. Farr saw me first. He gave Boyle an elbow. Boyle looked around. So did Bones. We walked up to them. They stood. I introduced Bit.

That's all I needed to do.

I'm lucky. I don't have to worry about my girlfriend not getting attention from my guy friends, because my guy friends went of their way to watch out for my girlfriend because they knew I was sweating Bit fitting in, being from Wyoming and all, not a run-of-the-mill East Coast college girl. They quickly became her entourage for her stay, which attracted a lot of other girls' attention that night and that weekend because anytime a girl – especially a new girl on campus with a different look like Bit – has four guys hovering over her, it activates other girls' antennae, which is exactly what happened when Janie Wallace passed by us with Billy Flannigan in tow. I put my head down pretending I didn't see her, but I kept an eye peeled, noticing how Janie could not stop looking...stop looking ...stop looking...until she disappeared into Flannigan's fraternity house.

Sweet.

With the "law firm" now deposing Bit, I may as well have been a potted plant. They listened politely to her stories about Wyoming – ranch life, barrel racing and being a vet's assistant – but what they really wanted to know was

233

what Farr asked her: "Tell us how this knucklehead" – here Farr rocked my shoulder back and forth – "got into a rodeo accident. How did that happen?" Bit was prepared. She'd crafted a beautiful alibi (we'd spoken and written each other about my cover story, making sure we were in the same church, same pew). She put her arm around my waist and looked at me, calmly explaining that I was bucked off a tough draw named Lightning Strike in the local rodeo, and that the rodeo clown, Chester Higgins, had to decoy the bronc before he stomped me. Bones asked Bit, "But what possessed him" – pointing at me – "Henry Thornton Chandler III to get on a bucking horse in the first place." Bit gave me a squeeze, pulling me a butterfly's breath closer, saying she had dared me to do it. But she didn't think I would.

I gave my friends a shrug as if to say *It was no big deal*, like I'd do it again if I had to.

We hung out for a couple of beers, Bit now asking questions about the college and the campus. She asked me where was my room. I pointed across the quad, three floors up, the lights off and the windows open. I took Bit's question as my cue to walk back to Bones's car and retrieve her luggage, one of those old-fashioned suitcases with a big handle and locks on both sides that Bit had dug out of the barn. The "law firm" was in awe of the suitcase, but Bit appeared embarrassed, nervously asking if the suitcase made her look like she just fell off the turnip truck. Farr dismissed her insecurity, assuring her she possessed a piece of art that belonged in the Museum of Modern Art; that all that was missing were the London, Paris, and Rome stickers. Bones said her retro luggage reminded him of the suitcases of the big bands that traveled the country and the world. Boyle admired the luggage as if it were a classic car, rubbing his hands over the corners and fingering the locks. A couple of girls walking by noticed the suitcase and came over to *oooh and ahhh* over it. I didn't want to create a scene and have everyone on campus popping the locks on Bit's suitcase, so

I said it was time for us to go, big day tomorrow, gotta get a good night sleep, European history class at nine – that type of b.s. I purposely avoided looking at "the law firm" because if I did a big shit-eating grin would have dawned on my face that boys get when you know your friends are suppressing every bodily function because they know you're about to get lucky with a girl for the first time. And they don't want to give anything away.

Yeah, right.

Bit and I headed to my room holding hands with me swinging her suitcase back and forth and she shouldering her small backpack, her ponytail bumping off her back.

Inside my room, from the moment the lights went low and the stylus found Marvin Gaye's groove – "Let's Get It On" – we found ours. It was...

Slow...

Melodic...

Spontaneous...

Romantic...

Bit was my fantasy, think Katherine Ross in *Butch Cassidy and the Sundance Kid* when she shakes her head to let her hair down for Robert Redford. And we all know what happens after that. Bit and I helped each other strip, giggling as we fumbled through buttons, zippers and one tough clasp. I checked my racing heart, staying focused, determined not to go full tilt from a standstill. I took it slow, maybe too slow, because I was content taking inventory, running my hands over every bump and cranny of her body.

Bit urged me on...

She gave me the nudge to trot...

Then canter...

Then – *Whoa Nellie* – gallop.

Our ride ended in labored breathing, hands palming breasts and buttocks, noses nuzzling noses and ears, toes touching toes, sweaty skin sticking to sweating skin. After we cooled down, I pulled my unzipped sleeping bag around both

of us, still snuggling, kissing, giggling – both of us relieved
to have had that out of the way without any serious slip-ups.
There was not much talking. That would be for the morning.
We brushed our teeth together in the bathroom then slipped
back into bed, both in our undies with Bit wearing my Oxford
shirt – the one with my telephone number over the pocket –
she now proudly pointing, proclaiming "I got your number."
Before nodding off, I pulled the shades and turned on the
Night Earl as he was introducing Miles Davis's "Kind of
Blue"; the party in the quad fading fast.

Eighty-two days later...

Twenty-five letters...

Five phone calls...

*Hallelfuckinglujah!*

The next morning I let Bit sleep in as I went to my
European History class, a total waste of time because all I
did was flick my Bic pen around and watch the minutes tick
off the clock over the talking head of a bearded professor,
thinking more about sex education than higher education.

The minute the school bell set me free, I bolted back to
my room. Bit was clothed, on top of the bed watching "Let's
Make a Deal." She insisted we stay until we discovered what
was behind door No. 3. Turns out it was brand-spanking new
red Le Mans convertible. Too bad the couple (the husband,
poor bastard) had picked Door No. 2 – his and hers Schwinn
bikes. After that we walked to the mailboxes and student
union for a soda – Tab for Bit, Dr. Pepper for me. I tried to
look cool and nonchalant with Bit beside me. Bit asked me, as
a flood of girls came into the room, "When do I get to meet
*your old girlfriend?*"

I said, "Why? What does it matter," trying to recall if
Bit knew Janie's name, concluding Bit preferred *your old
girlfriend*, making Janie sound like a bad habit or a chronic
disease.

She said, scooting closer to me, our bodies glued together

as if we were Siamese twins, "Because I want to be make sure she knows there's a new mare in town."

I said, "Don't worry, we'll run into her."

"When?"

I shrugged.

"Where will we run into her?" she asked, tapping an index finger on pursed lips.

"Around here," I said, waving my hand around indicating the campus.

"Are you still friends?"

"I guess."

"Does she have a new boyfriend?"

"Yes."

"Do you know him?"

"Not really."

"Is he here?" she asked now checking out the boys in the room.

"No," I said, not looking around, now studying the ingredients on the back of my Dr. Pepper can"

"Do you like him?"

I huffed like stop it already. I said, "Well, aren't you the Chatty Cathy this morning?" (That's an expression my mother used on me when I had verbal diarrhea, before I hit puberty and cemented my mouth shut.)

Bit pulled away. She took a sip of her Tab. "What does she look like. Give me a hint. I'll see if I can spot her."

I said, "Keep an eye out for Farrah Fawcett."

She gave me an elbow.

I didn't want Bit to meet Janie, nor Janie to meet Bit. At least not right away. I admit I was being a dick, but I wanted Janie to suffer like I did when I knew she had somebody else and she let me twist in the wind. What I should've done was to march Bit right up to Janie and said *Janie I'd like you to meet Bit Stifel from Cora, Wyoming. She's my girlfriend.*

That's what I should have done.

Presto. No problem.

Yeah, right.

Now that I had the upper hand on Janie, I played it. I shouldn't have, but I did. Did I feel bad? No, I wanted payback. And I got it. Later that day an opportunity presented itself. I spotted Janie walking behind us on the college green. I put my arm around Bit then butt-tapped her with my shoe. Bit said *What the hell*? I said, "Sorry, it's an uncontrollable reflex, my foot just does that sometimes." Then I did it again. Bit threw her head back, laughing, her thick black hair cascading over her shoulders. When she butt-tapped me back, I gently spun and pulled her close, planting a full-on kiss, keeping one eye open and glued on Janie walking away with her head down and shoulders slumped.

Payback's ... a bitch.

Our party was set to go off on Saturday night, but we really lit the fuse at Harry's on Friday when Scott Hodges and Boyle's girlfriend Sally Swift rolled into town, our gang intact (Bones included). I'd made sure Scott did not blow off our party by guaranteeing him a big surprise. He asked me a hundred times what was the surprise. I told him to shut up, show up, he'd find out.

Here's the book on Boyle's girlfriend Sally Swift: she's from the stable born; grew up on a family compound in Chadds Ford, Pennsylvania, breeding horses, mucking out stalls, and fox hunting (tally ho!). She's tall, lanky, fit – horsey-looking, you might say – and often wears her long brown hair in a loose knot. At Harry's, when Bit and Sally figured out they both knew their horse hocks and forelocks, we had to shuffle the deck so they could sit next to one another – too much crosstown traffic according to Farr.

Weird thing about that night: For sure Dante and Jackie are rough nuts and twisted spokes who are constantly needling us about being entitled blue bloods – which we are – but they treated Sally and Bit as if they were precious gems. They couldn't get enough of these two horse-crazy girls talking equine, frequently interrupting them to ask a question about a subject as foreign as sailing or squash. Soon enough, Sally had Bit's jaw on the floor with stories of hounds, point-to-points, and women jumping over fences in skirts. Sally's mouth watered when she heard Bit's tales of barrel racing, leading a pack string, driving cattle with dogs, and shoeing horses. At one point, Boyle poked Jackie in the ribs joking that Sally and Bit should maybe get their own stall for the weekend. Jackie put a hand on Boyle's shoulder and told him in a Mr. Ed voice, "*Wilbur, will you close the door and leave the mares alone.*"

Another conversation was going on under the table. After Scott met Bit and figured out we were – indeed – boyfriend and girlfriend, he kicked me in the shin, mouthing *What the fuck, you're a douche for not telling me about her.* I mouthed back *What? What? What's the big deal?* (Surprising your oldest friend, who's supposed to know everything about you including your jock size, is always gratifying. It was also gratifying because Scott was clueless as to what was coming at him the next night at our party, as he was sure Bit was his promised surprise for the weekend.)

Toward the end of the night we went over the guest list for the party. Boyle, Farr and I had invited about fifty people, expecting a hundred to show. We attempted to level the playing field with boys and girls, making sure to invite the stretch-girls (hot girls we wanted to know better); and, selectively inviting jocks, not wanting whole fraternities to crash our party. I purposely did not invite Janie. Real dumb, I know. But I had my reasons. Mainly, I didn't want Billy Flannigan showing up with her, making me look like a turd at my own party. I knew Janie would be pissed being culled from the herd, but I figured she'd crash, which of course she did.

Scott scanned the invitation list, quizzing us about the girls who were coming and which ones were hot.

He'd stepped right into my snare.

That's why I banged the top of his full bottle of beer with the bottom of my Budweiser, announcing to the table, "Why do you care who's coming, Scott, you said you were bringing Alison Henry to the party. *Right?*"

Scott's beer bottle exploded with foam streaming out the top. He rushed to cover with his mouth. Bones sensed something was up. He leaned over the table, demanding of Scott, "Who's Alison Henry? Come on, 'fess up. Who is she?"

Scott shook his head, his cheeks bloated with foam. The point of his shoe politely found my shin under the table while the look on his face pleaded *Please don't say anything.*

I didn't.

I didn't have to.

Scott Hodges wasn't getting off "Scott-free" this time.

# Chapter 28

## THE PARTY ✳ SUGAR AND SPICE ✳ ALISON AND DAPHNE

Boyle lived in a great party house. For college living it was unusual: the house was clean, spacious and had not been trashed – mainly because one of his roommates was a girl who didn't take shit. The few houses around Boyle's house were occupied by a weird group of neighbors that we rarely saw or who infrequently complained about noise after ten o'clock. The house, three stories tall with brown weathered shingles, was located behind a grocery store off of the main drag that bisected the campus, set back on a side street under a couple of big oak trees. Six cars could be squeezed into the driveway in front of the house. The front door, which nobody ever used, faced the driveway. Off to the side was a door that led to the kitchen, which everybody used. Downstairs was a living room, dining room, sunroom, bathroom and kitchen. There were four bedrooms and two bathrooms on the second floor. The attic – where we would party sometimes – had a small room with lawn chairs, a table, and a dormered window. In the way back was a tiny spare bedroom Boyle called the "attic suite." into which Farr had moved for the course of Bit's stay. For the party, we'd moved all the downstairs furniture outside into the side lot except for the Ping-Pong table, which was pushed against the sunroom wall – one leaf down – on which the punch bowl and red Solo cups had been placed. The beer kegs were in the kitchen by the back door; the living room was for dancing. The sunroom, where we usually hung out, is where we were now, listening to Little Feat's "Fat Man in the Bathtub," smoking, testing the punch, sipping Budweiser, waiting for the party to begin.

We were set to go by eight; the crowd flowed in around nine. That's when Bones ejected the pre-party tape and popped in his playlist, Bruce Springsteen's "Tenth Avenue Freeze-Out" setting the pace. Because I was in charge of the bar and logistics, I checked on the kegs, the punch, and the toilet paper, making sure everything was up and running and flowing.

All systems go.

Bit and Sally Swift were chatting in the kitchen about Laramie and Bit's major, Veterinary Science (large animals, no cats or dogs) when I sidled up to them and put my arm around Bit. I followed their conversation but was more interested in keeping an eye on the back door on Dante, Jackie, and their dates, Sugar and Spice. (Boyle, Farr and I had huddled up before the party about making sure Jackie and Dante did not feel out of place, making sure everybody knew they were with us, making sure there were no questions. We asked Sally and Bit to be extra nice to Sugar and Spice, like they were just two of the girls.)

I topped off my beer in the kitchen and was hanging out with Boyle. The Beach Boys' "Good Vibrations" ended. The Spinners' "I'll Be Around" started up. Boyle put down his cup and started drumming his hands to the beat of the song on the kitchen counter with me keeping an eye out the back door. I put my hand out for Boyle to stop.

I said, "Party's here!"

Boyle stopped, looked up. "No joke," he said. Then he looked at me, grinning, and said it again, this time with a descriptive adjective: "No fucking joke."

Dante Romero and Jackie Callaghan walked up the back stairs and into the house as if they owned the joint; like muscle for the mob casing the joint for the Dons, or in this case their dates. Dante – nattily dressed in his mid-length brown leather jacket; black shirt open at the neck showcasing a gold chain; beard trimmed, and long brown hair slicked-back – was primed to party. Jackie followed, looking like he'd just emerged from a shower and a fresh shave; his short, curly, strawberry blond hair combed forward over his forehead; his beefy build bulging out of a short-sleeved Hawaiian shirt and a new pair of Wrangler jeans, 36/34.

Behind them, sashaying in side-by-side, were the showstoppers: Sugar and Spice.

Man-O-Manischewitz!

Sugar was downright adorable; an ebony Shirley Temple with bright eyes, curls, and dimples. Only difference was she had a body by Fisher. Her legs started just under her chin, and her lower three-quarters were poured into pink leather pants. Perky cupcake breasts were wrapped tight in a white tube top. From behind, her butt was flawless – carved marble buffed with a fine chamois. On her feet were off-white pumps with a red rose near the toe. She had a toothy smile that could melt ice and a voice so sweet it made you want to curl up and take a nap.

Spice was a bubbly platinum blonde with a high voice and a chassis showcasing 1955 bumper bullets. Farr nailed it: "She's Carol Wayne from *The Tonight Show*, maybe ten years younger and without the dimples." She wore revealing white pants and black stilettos. A red tank top – spaghetti straps straining against the cantilevered pressure – covered her generous upper half. Her body was not as tight as Sugar's, but it jiggled in the right places and at the right times. When Scott and I were getting them punch, he said: "I've seen cleavages before, but that's the Grand Canyon" – his emphasis on "Grand."

Sugar was twenty-two; Spice twenty-three – close to the same age as many of the other girls at the party. Big difference was Sugar and Spice were not college coeds; they were working girls. And that would be a major topic of conversation on the dance floor, behind drink cups, and in line for the girls' bathroom. The college girls wanted to know *what* Sugar and Spice did for a living. The college boys just wanted to know *where*.

Farr and Bones joined us in the kitchen. I made sure everyone had a drink then rounded up Sally and Bit – Harry's crew intact. Dante cleared his throat, introducing us to his date.

"This is Brown Sugar."

His date smiled at us. "Sugar...just call me Sugar. Brown Sugar is my stage name."

Boyle grinned, stuck out his hand. "Just call me Boyle. Christopher Andrew is my given name."

Jackie chimed in, "And this is Spice."

Spice squeaked, *"Hi,"* adding, "What a great house."

I stepped up, welcoming both girls, properly introducing them around as if they were royalty. Spice squeaked again, waving her hand, *Hi, so good to meet you,* her Rhode Island accent thick as stew.

"Sorry we're late," Sugar said. "We just got off work."

I asked, wanting to sound casual, "Busy night?"

"No, slow," Sugar said, shaking her head in frustration. "There was nobody in the club tonight. We were glad to get off stage and come here. Spice and I danced our butts off for nothing."

Bit piped up, sympathizing. "Sounds to me like you were rode hard and put away wet."

Sugar put her hands on her hips giving Bit some eye. "What's that mean, honey?"

Bit apologized, placing a hand on Sugar's arm, explaining it was Western slang for a horse being worked hard with no reward. Or, in Sugar and Spice's case, that they were having a bad day.

Sugar brightened, repeating the expression, rolling it around in her mouth like a piece of candy. She pointed a long, red fingernail at Spice. "Honey, tonight we was rode hard and put away wet."

They laughed.

We laughed.

The circle closed in, Harry's crew drinking as one.

A couple of minutes later Spice gave Jackie's arm a tug. "Come on, Jackie, I want to dance."

"Not to this," Jackie said. "I can't stand the Talking Heads." Jackie turned to Bones who had joined us in the kitchen, asking, "When are we going to hear some Earth Wind and Fire?"

Bones checked his list. "They're coming up."

Sugar asked, "What's the song?"

Bones said, "'September.'"

Sugar and Spice squealed, "We love 'September.'"

Sally Swift grabbed Sugar and Spice by their arms, squealing back, "I love 'September' too." She pulled Boyle by the arm. "Come on, Chris. Show them how you can dance."

A gleam sparkled in Jackie's eyes. He rubbed his palms together then pointed a finger at Boyle. "Let's see what you got."

Boyle pounded his chest, challenging Jackie. "I'm going to show *you*" – pointing back at Jackie – "how to dance. Five bucks you don't know who I'm imitating."

Jackie said. "You're on."

We moved to the dance floor in the living room. We put our drinks down on the floor along the perimeter of the room. Boyle stretched out his arms, doing a few deep knee bends, warming up, warning everyone *Give the man some room. Give the man some room.*

The few dancers on the floor backed away.

Dante whispered to me, "Nobody's going to get hurt… right?"

I said, "Best give him a wide berth."

"September" began.

Boyle launched himself onto the floor, arms folded over his chest, crouching, bouncing, kicking his feet out like a Cossack. He then scissored his arms out and in…out and in… while strutting his head like a rooster. It was a dance not seen before by anyone…anywhere…except…

Jackie put his hands on his head and cried out, "Oh my God. The man's a genius. It's Agarn teaching the Hekawis how to war dance." He said to the rest of us, "Come on you doughnut holes, didn't you ever watch *F Troop*. Get out there." Jackie followed Boyle. Farr shrugged at me and went along. I did the same, bouncing, kicking and strutting behind Farr, Jackie and Boyle. Bones dove in, bringing up the rear. Dante stayed out of it. More guys came in to watch; joining us; falling into line; dancing the Hekawi war dance; soon a conga line snaking around the room. The girls stood on the sidelines, no doubt wondering when we would ever grow up.

Two songs later, I was in the sunroom with Bit talking to Mimi Ryder and another girl, who were for sure checking out Bit so they could report back to Janie Wallace. Bit was holding her own with them when I spotted "Jenny Cavelleri" in the crowd looking around like she was here on business (which she was). She was also neatly dressed and groomed for an away game (which meant she was *really* here on business).

As my grandmother would say, Alison Henry was stunning – she was a prize; Scott Hodges was on to something. Her style was elegant, simple – faded jeans, black cordovan loafers, white oxford shirt underneath a faded pink cotton sweater. No makeup – no need. Her hair? – I racked my brain but couldn't recall who she looked like. Next to Alison, riding shotgun, was a tall thin girl whose expression might suggest she was pinching a walnut between her butt cheeks. I excused myself and slalomed through the crowd, applying my host face. I called out *Alison... Alison Henry,* holding up my beer cup to draw her attention. She acknowledged me with a grim smile, whispering something to her friend behind a cupped hand. Her friend nodded and racked her jaw as if it was a Winchester shotgun.

I approached, extending my hand, sincerely thanking them for coming.

Alison said, "Thanks for inviting me...us...Hank. This is my friend Daphne Murray."

I greeted Daphne Murray as if I were an ambassador. She grimaced, looking down on me as if I was an overflowing toilet.

I needed help on this one.

I had an idea.

But first I threw out the starter questions: How was the semester going? How's the football team? How's the weather? Do you want a drink?

Alison asked, "What are you serving?"

*Serving?* Shit, we weren't serving; we were spilling. I said, "Beer and punch."

Daphne butted in, insisting, "We'll both have beers," as if they had talked about this on the drive down, agreeing to drink beer because the punch was most likely spiked. (Hey, they went to Harvard.)

"Two beers it is," I said. "Stay right here. I'll be right back."

Alison cracked the weakest of smiles, giving me a little credit for being polite. She was also distracted, looking around the party. I left them, jockeying through the crowd bumping to the beat of Fleetwood Mac's "Go Your Own Way," periscoping for Bones. I found and buttonholed him on the edge of the dance floor watching a couple of the "stretch girls" dancing together. I rewound the story of Scott-as-me and the downtown Chicago debutante that I had told him about in the car, explaining I *really* needed his help.

He asked, "So where's Scott?" not catching my drift.

I said, "Somewhere. I don't know. I'll find him."

Bones said, "So why do you need me?"

I said, "To run interference for Scott."

"Who am I blocking?"

"Over there in the kitchen," I said with a nod of the head.

Bones arched up on his tiptoes, looking over the crowd. "Dorothy Hamill or the snapping turtle?"

I mumbled into my beer, "Bring a long pole."

He said, "Tell me again, why am I doing this?"

I explained that I needed him to neutralize the friend so I could surprise Scott with Alison Henry. Bones knew I was sweating it, desperate even. He went up for another look. Coming down he said, "Okay. Fifteen minutes."

"Fine," I said. "Then throw her back."

I returned to Beauty and the Beast with beers and Bones in tow. I introduced him as a friend from Lake Forest and tried to kick-start a conversation about Chicago. Alison was polite but acted more interested in perusing the room over the rim of her beer cup. Bones was doing his best to squeeze blood out of a rock with Daphne when Alison whispered to me *Where's the bathroom,* then quickly disappeared – solo – without Daphne. That never happens; girls always travel in packs to the powder room. Something was up. Now I was stuck between Daphne and Bones struggling to put two syllables together.

Bones – doing his best to be gracious – said to Daphne, "Have you ever been to Chicago?"

Daphne said, *"No,"* as if he had just asked her if she wanted an enema.

Bones pressed on. "Have you ever been to the Midwest?"

Daphne repeated, *"No,"* meaning stop it already.

"Why not?"

"Why would I? Just a bunch of rednecks in pickup trucks."

Bones blew: "Rednecks in pickup trucks? Where are you from?"

Daphne said, "Vermont."

Bones let out a long "Mooooooo."

Daphne snapped, "You're crass. Worse, you're infra dig."

*Infra dig?* – no way I thought. Nobody says infra dig. Except...

Bones tilted his head, the tiniest of grins dawning at the corner of his mouth. Daphne had struck a chord. He challenged her. "Bet you can't name three states that border Illinois."

Daphne backpedaled. "Yes, I can. Ohio, Utah, and Arkansas."

Bones let out a longer "Moooooooooo."

Now tapping her toe in frustration, Daphne gave it another shot. "Okay, okay. Wisconsin, Kansas and Pennsylvania."

Bones announced to the room in a game-show voice, "Time's up. One right. Tell us Don Pardo, what does the young lady from Harvard win...Tommy, she wins a wheel of Vermont cheddar."

Daphne's face blew redder than a blinking stoplight, every muscle twitching. She looked around for Alison. I was worried she'd crack her walnut and make a break for it; hunt down Alison and beat it back to Boston.

*Thank God for Dionysus.*

Just then a friend tapped Bones on the shoulder, asking when a Blondie song was coming up. Bones took the playlist from his back pocket, scanning it. "Two more songs," he said. Daphne asked in a demanding tone, "What is that you have there?" jabbing an extra-long bony digit at Bones's yellow legal pages.

He said, "The playlist for the party."

Daphne asked, "What are you doing with it?"

Bones shrugged. "I made it. I'm the DJ."

Daphne Murray's walnut hit the floor and rolled out the door. "I love music," she said, quickly adding, "not that I like what you're playing, but can I see it?"

They huddled together discussing and analyzing Bone's playlist, something brewing between them. I slipped away to find Scott, leaving them, oddly, agreeing about Jackson Brown.

I found Bit before I found Scott. She was holding up Jackie's beefy calf, demonstrating to Spice how to shoe a horse. I rubbed against her lightly; said that Alison and her friend Daphne had surfaced and that I had to find Scott. Bit said she was okay, giving me a smile that assured me *Do what you have to do* – I was discovering Bit was self-sufficient in party situations and not in need of much handholding. She also knew I was on duty and on a mission.

The party was now in full swing, the living room bouncing shoulder-to-shoulder to Elvis Costello's "Radio, Radio", everybody drinking; many smoking; an occasional joint floating by. I edged by a group from my Greek Mythology class who were backslapping each other on acing the ten-page paper that we had to write, complaining they could have written twenty. A funny kid named Ted Martin with a nose like a saxophone and the mouth of a fire hydrant stopped me and said, "Hey, Zeus, how'd you do on the ten-page paper?"

I told him I got a C+.

He asked, slightly perplexed, "How did *you* manage to get a C+?"

I shrugged. "Just lucky, I guess."

Ted Martin's mouth flopped open, but nothing came out.

I moved on, going up, over, and around the crowd, looking for Scott or Alison. No luck. Now I had to hit the can. The downstairs line had too many girls, so I bounced up the back stairs and stepped into the dimly lighted hallway.

I halted.

I pulled back.

I peered around the corner.

*Hosannah! Aphrodite had snuck in when I wasn't looking.*

At the end of the hall stood Scott Hodges and Alison Henry leaning against the wall, having a quiet conversation, their eyes and bodies doing most of the talking. I could see Scott was stepping up his game – Alison was gaining on him. I half considered walking up to them, being coy, saying, *Oh, hi Alison. Hi Scott. I'm so glad you two met. Scott, did you know Alison lives in Chicago? And Alison, Scott's an old friend from Lake Forest who loves going downtown to deb parties. Don't you Scott?*

But I didn't. Why be a dick? I left them alone and ducked into the bathroom. After peeing and washing my hands, I took pride in my grinning reflection in the mirror, pleased with myself, surprised to admit that this Cupid thing was sort of fun.

# Chapter 29

## JANIE \* WINTHROPE \* GROSVENOR \* DISCO DANCING \* BIT 'N ME

I rejoined Bit and gang in the sunroom, which now included Farr, who was telling stories about Studio 54. Soon after, Boyle came up to me and said,

"We got a problem, Houston."

I asked what's up, half expecting campus cops or a clogged toilet.

Boyle turned me aside. "She's hammered and hunting for you."

Instantly understanding who he was talking about, I said, "Is Billy Flannigan with her?"

"No. She's flying solo...and I mean flying." He nodded in the direction of the punch bowl.

I spotted Janie, weaving back and forth, spilling punch into a cup.

Bit said, "Who are you talking about?" looking around, more than curious.

"A friend," I said, putting my arm around her, giving her a tentative squeeze and a nervous smile.

Bit smiled back, giving me a little hip check. "An old friend?"

"Hmmmm" was all that I could muster. Unfortunately, I'd set myself up for this, and in hindsight should have manned up and invited Janie to the party; asked her nicely to leave Flannigan at his frat with his teammates. She would have understood. That would have been the easy way out. But it's not so easy when your emotions simmer on the surface of your skin. Janie knew about our party and that all *our* friends would be there. It's not a big campus. She'd seen Bit with me twice. I told you I should have just introduced them to each other and been done with it. But no, I was consumed with getting even. I knew Janie would crash the party. I just didn't count on her having one of those nights none of us are proud of and barely remember the next day. I'd been there before when Janie and I were breaking up. Now, she lurched toward us. Our circle widened, the conversation melting away. She ground to a halt in front of me. She looked at my arm around Bit then down at our well-worn jeans and cowboy boots.

"Hi, Janie," I said. "Good to see you." I then hand-waved between the two of them. "Janie, I'd like you to meet Bit Stifel. Bit, this is Janie Wallace."

I let out half a breath then held the rest.

Neither shook hands.

Clearly beyond repair, Janie weaved and splashed a wave of Pawtucket punch overboard. The circle took a step back, everybody checking their shoes. She slurred, "Thanks for being such a jerk and not inviting me, Hank. I'm so happy to be here with *your* friends and meet *your* new girlfriend. I thought you'd changed. But I was wrong. You're so fucking immature. I hope she knows that" – pointing her cup at Bit.

Sensing this was getting ugly fast, I said, "Janie, why don't we go outside."

She glared at me. "Why didn't you tell me you had a girlfriend? Why weren't you honest? Why do you have to be such an asshole? *Grow up!*"

Outside was not going to work.

I was not surprised by Janie's fury. She was pissed I had

not been on the level and opened up to her about Bit. Janie had showed up on my doorstep the night Farr went to New York because she still cared for me, was in love with me. And what did I do? I went out of my way to hurt her. Janie wasn't stupid, she knew I had been sticking the pin in, especially the butt-tapping and not inviting her to the party. This was a self-inflicted wound. Now it was her turn to inflict pain.

Payback...

Janie didn't scream, but it sure sounded like it. Just as Joe Jackson's "Steppin' Out" ended, she blurted out for the room to hear, " *Why didn't you tell me about her before you fucked me?* Janie's head wobbled, her eyes barely focusing as she again pointed her cup at Bit. "Don't you think I saw you with her? Why, Hank?...Why?"

I had no answer. I felt stupid small and stupid. I just wanted her to disappear.

The Beatles's "Twist and Shout" started up.

Farr came to my rescue. "Janie...wanna dance?"

Janie whirled toward Farr, splashing more punch on the floor. "No, Freddy, I don't want to dance." She glared back at me through red, moist eyes, losing her train of thought, struggling with what to say. "You told me your were only riding horses in Wyoming." (That was a pretty funny line. I doubt Janie remembered it the next day, but we did.)

I glanced at Bit. She was oddly calm, empathetic even. Her facial expression told me *You made this mess; you clean it up.* I was just about to say, *Janie I'm really sorry. I'm such an asshole. You're right. Please forgive me,* when Sugar stage whispered to Spice:

"Looks like somebody was rode hard and put away wet."

*Oh, shit.* Not what I needed.

I pretended like I didn't hear what Spice had said. Unfortunately, Boyle and Farr did. Boyle gave Farr a face as if he was due to explode, which made Farr put his head down, his shoulders shaking, sneaking a peek at me; which made me tense every muscle in my face as if I were giving myself a half nelson; which made Janie hiss, "*Fuck you, Hank,*" and throw her drink at me.

Well...part of her drink. Most of it landed on Bit.

Palming off my face, I said, "Janie, we really need to talk."

Bit confirmed, "Yes we do." She handed her drink to Boyle, wiped the punch off her face and shirt, then balled up her fist and said, "You're too nice, Hank," landing a hard right to Janie's jaw, sending her backwards in slow motion, her fall broken by the people standing behind her. She bumped to the floor appearing as if she was trying to remember what day it was.

Jackie said, "Solid shot."

Dante said, "I'll lay five to one she doesn't get up."

Spice squeaked, "Hank, you forgot to tell Janie that Bit could shoe a horse."

I said to Boyle, eyeing Janie being helped up and dusted off, "Do me a big favor, find Mimi Ryder and have her take Janie home." I grabbed Bit's hand and led her into the living room, Earth Wind and Fire's live version of "Reasons" just kicking in. Bit and I sort of danced around, not talking, her body stiff as a board; her hands like concrete. We stopped moving, now standing still. I had to say something. I whispered, "I'm sorry."

Bit looked me in the eye, all business. "You've got nothing to be sorry about, Hank. I'm the one who bopped her."

"No," I said, trying to be funny, "I was the one bopping her. I should have told you."

"So what happened?" she asked, not wanting any bullshit.

We started dancing again, Bit's body softening as I explained the circumstances that led to Janie giving us a punch bath. Believe me, I didn't cut my veins open and bleed all over her. That's not me, and Bit didn't want it. She just wanted me to tell the truth. I did, giving her the Cliff Notes version of how I was feeling that night when Janie showed up at my room – and why Janie showed up in the first place.

Presto, that did it.

Bit put her hand on the back of my head, massaging my neck and the curl in my hair, her hips now gently swaying to the music, our pelvises reintroduced. We were both a little drunk. She said, "Lighten up, Hank. That just the way it goes sometimes. You don't think I haven't been bucked off before and wanted to ride that horse again. Bit pulled me close. Our noses brushed. I inhaled wild and sweet. She whispered in my ear, "Hell, it makes you want to ride 'em more. Doesn't it?"

All I could say was, "Honestly?"

"Yeah," Bit said, her arms around my neck and her brown eyes locked in on my baby blues. "Honestly."

I said, "It really does."

We danced slow and close. I slid my hands gently down Bit's backside. She nosed my ear. "Nothing heats me up like another mare in the corral."

Whoa. Talk about going from the doghouse to the penthouse – this honesty thing honestly pays dividends. I lightly ran my hands over the back bump of her jeans. She pulled me tight to her body, tight enough to ignite activity below deck. She said, "What are you feeling now?"

"Honestly?"

"Honestly."

My cockiness returned. "Like maybe we should get something straight between us."

Bit threw her head back and laughed; knew where I was coming from. She slapped me on the flank. "Let's ride out of here, cowboy."

I looked at my watch: twelve-thirty. "I can't," I said. "The party's not over until two."

"Two?" she said, pulling me close for a deep kiss then coming up for air. "That's too long."

I didn't need to be Einstein to figure this one out. I said, "I know how to make time fly."

"How?"

I pointed upstairs.

Bit asked, "Is it safe?"

I dug out a key and dangled it. "Absolutely."

Bit gave me another slap. "Giddyup."

Boyle had put me in charge of the attic key in case anyone had a special need like Bit and I had now. We made our way through the crowd and snuck up the back stairs to the third floor, carefully avoiding Scott and Alison down the hall (they could have cared less), and locked the door behind us. The attic suite, where Farr was bunking for Bit's stay, was just large enough for a queen-size bed, a dresser, a window and a sixty-watt bulb. I turned off the light. Earth Wind and Fire's live version of "Reasons" floated up through the vent from below. Bit and I went at each other like two tornados. Normally, getting cowboy boots on is tough. But getting them off is even tougher. And getting them off in a blinding blur of wet lips, hot flesh and hungry hands is enough to pull a muscle. I don't recall what came off, or stayed on, in our little rodeo, only that we were holding on for dear life.

Bit and I returned to the party with a desperate need to slake our thirst and dim our glow. The party was roaring. The floor was slick and sticky from spilled beer and punch. Red solo cups dotted most surfaces; many half filled, many with cigarette butts floating in them. The air quality was lethal. Everybody was slightly hammered, a little high, talking loudly, repeating themselves. Bit and I were grinning behind our beer cups, giggling to each other. I groaned *Oh fuck* when I saw what was coming through the kitchen door.

Bit asked, "What's the problem?" like I'd forgotten something.

Of course what I'd forgotten is that Janie would stumble back to Billy Flannigan, and he would dispense the Gilligan twins to splinter our party. In the kitchen, a path cleared for them as if they were the Clanton Gang walking into a saloon. Pat and Mike Gilligan were Flannigan's line mates on the hockey team, and resembled an identical twin version of Vic Morrow in the *Blackboard Jungle*. Janie, thankfully, was not with them, nor Flannigan. Around campus, the Gilligan twins were legendary for crashing and breaking up parties by intimidating everyone or starting fights. Tonight was no exception. They strutted in wearing dumb smirks in tight shirts that showed they didn't care. Daphne and Tommy were at the keg. Tommy didn't see Pat Gilligan come from behind. Gilligan grabbed the nozzle and pushed Tommy away. Tommy was pissed but didn't lose his cool. He made the right move and put himself between Daphne and trouble. I needed help *Fast*. I told Bit to follow me, not wanting her in the line of fire. She asked if something was wrong. I shook my head, gritted my teeth, mumbled under my breath,

*Goddamn Ares had to show up.*

I said, "Do me a favor, go find Boyle and Farr. Tell them I need help with the keg in the kitchen."

Bit said sure thing, adding she was going to the bathroom. She disappeared into the party.

I found Jackie and Dante in the sunroom with Sugar and Spice. I said, "Grosvenor... Winthrope. We got a problem."

Jackie perked up. "Where?"

"In the kitchen. By the keg."

Dante and Jackie slammed their drinks, handed Sugar and Spice their cups, and walked single file through the party toward the kitchen. I followed behind not knowing what to expect, only that I started this and prayed it would not get ugly.

They stopped, now looking in the kitchen. Dante said to me, "The douchebag twins giving Bones and the girl a hard time."

I explained, "Janie's boyfriend sent his goons over because Bit slugged her. They're going to bust up the party."

Dante asked, "What's the name of the girl?"

I replied, "Daphne."

Dante repeated to Jackie, "*Daphne*".

Jackie went first.

The kitchen had cleared out. An early Michael Jackson song, I think "Rockin' Robin," was playing in the living room. Jackie swiped the hose away from Pat Gilligan and reached for Daphne's cup. He turned his back on the twins and said in a rarefied air, "*Daphne*, so good to see you again."

Dante came to stand beside Jackie, the twins now behind them, safely away from Bones and Daphne. Dante chimed in, "And Bones, what a surprise seeing you here. When was the last time? Newport?"

Mike Gilligan made the mistake of shoving Dante Romero in the back, saying, "Well, well, look what the cat dragged in. Some of the local colored."

I didn't see it.

I only heard it.

Dante's knife flicking open with a *ssssitttt*.

He pivoted, politely pointing the tip of the blade at Mike's nose...then the door. "This is my friend Wheezie Jefferson," he said in a back-alley, Rhode Island growl, his eyes now narrow, dead, dark. "Care to step outside and dissect your ignorance with her?"

Before Mike could answer, Jackie put down the hose and placed a hand on Dante's arm, huffing, "Winthrope, you silly goose, *put that knife away*. This is a college party. Here, use these." He pulled out two pair of brass knuckles, handing one to Dante.

Dante retracted the blade, the knife disappearing as quickly as it appeared, his upper crust returning. "I'm so sorry, Grosvenor. What was I thinking?" He slipped on the brass, flexing his fist, thumbing at the Gilligans. "After you."

Pat and Mike Gilligan were dumber than a bucket of pucks, but not thick enough to dance in the parking lot with two hooligans packing hardware. Pat Gilligan caught my eye and flipped me off, as if to say this is not over. They disappeared out the door.

Jackie pocketed his brass, complaining he never gets

to use them anymore. Dante filled up Daphne's cup, did the same with Tommy's. Boyle and Farr had come into the kitchen. Boyle had taken off his belt and wrapped it around his fist, ready to go if Jackie and Dante needed help. Jackie walked over and cupped his hand around Boyle's neck, giving it a friendly tug, acknowledging Boyle's courage. He said to Farr, "I know what Christopher was up to. What about you, Frederick?"

Farr reached down and removed one of his Guccis, brandishing it like a weapon. He said, "I had your back."

Jackie howled, "With an Italian loafer?"

Farr reached down for the other, now double fisted. "Both if necessary."

Jackie said, "You hear that Dante. The blue bloods had our back."

Dante was looking at door, making sure the Gilligans were gone for good. He turned with a giggle, his eyes now twinkling. "I would have loved sticking those pricks."

Jackie and Dante returned to Sugar and Spice in the sunroom. Boyle and Farr left to check out Marvin Gaye on the dance floor. I took up pumping the keg next to Bones and Daphne, hoping to slow my pulse, waiting for Bit's return from the bathroom. A bunch of kids spilled back into the kitchen buzzing about the dust-up with the Gilligan twins, wanting to know what happened. I told them Mike and Pat didn't like Budweiser beer nor the music we were playing, so they left.

Daphne – standing close enough to Bones to make you wonder – sipped her beer with a confused look, asking him, "Are Grosvenor and Winthrope friends of yours?"

Bones looked at me. "Yes…yes they are."

Daphne asked, "How do you know them?"

I stopped pumping the keg. "Tommy knows them because they're doctoral candidates in sociology." I caught Bones's eye. "Tommy's editing their joint dissertation."

Bones turned to Daphne, coughing up, "Darwinism and Deviant Behavior: Low Hanging Fruit at the Top of the Tree."

Daphne laughed. She tilted her head and smiled. She actually looked cute. She didn't believe our bull (hey, she went to Harvard). She chugged her beer. She handed me her cup, dismissing me as if I were the help. She touched Tommy's arm. "I love this song. Wanna dance?"

Bones said, "You like the Kinks? 'Lola' is one of my favorites."

"Lola" is one of my favorites, too, but not to dance to. That didn't stop Daphne Murray and Tommy Childress from being the only couple out on the dance floor, everybody else taking a beer, butt, or bathroom break. I peeked in on them: Bones, a whirling scarecrow, air-guitaring Ray Davies; Daphne, a limber Olive Oyl, writhing around as if she were performing the Dance of the Seven Veils; both, oddly, connecting from opposite sides of the room.

Soon after Farr tapped me on the shoulder. "When's Tavares playing?"

I said, "After 'Lola' and 'The Jean Genie.'"

He asked, "You ready?"

"Yeah. You got the tools?"

"In my back pocket."

"You got the flashlight?"

"It's on the stepladder."

"I'll go get the ball."

I hustled up to Boyle's room, giving Scott and Alison a heads-up whistle that the disco was starting. If they had moved since I last saw them, it was only closer together.

I found the disco ball that Jackie had borrowed from the Voom Voom Room and headed back downstairs. As David Bowie's "The Jean Genie" was ending, I climbed up the stepladder and attached the ball to a kitchen clock that I'd rigged to the light, the ball miraculously turning. I jumped down and dragged the ladder to the corner of the room, climbed back up, and hit the turning ball with a strong beam of light from a big, boxy flashlight you'd take on a camping trip. The party began flowing into room, *ooohing and ahhhing* at the light show, the last of the joints glowing and going around.

Bones hit play and turned up "Heaven Must Be Missing an Angel."

A light show shimmered over the dancers and swirled across the ceiling and walls. The whole room seemed to be moving. I held the light steady, below me a feast: Farr twirling Bit at the intersection of Park Avenue and Forty Rod Road; Justin boots sliding step for step with Gucci loafers. Next to them Dante spun Sugar; her smile twinkling like tinsel on a Christmas tree. Spice and Jackie were all business, as if they were facing off against John Travolta and Karen Lynn Gorney in *Saturday Night Fever*. Boyle, dancing with Sally Swift – her hair now unknotted and flowing – was showing off with some goofy Jackie Gleason-type moves. Scott and Alison stayed on the periphery, dancing close, occasionally executing a perfect dip. Daphne and Tommy were doing their best, but I think they preferred "Lola." Soon, everybody at the party was in the room packed tighter than a jar of olives, enjoying themselves like you should after two kegs of beer, plenty of Pawtucket punch, and an ounce of weak Mexican reefer.

It was a great party – my mother and grandmother would have been proud.

Tavares ended.

I stepped down.

Alison approached me. "Hank, I'm sorry, but we have to go."

I said, "So soon? The party's not over."

Daphne said to Alison, "Yeah. The party's not over." (I think her and Bones's fingers were touching.)

Alison – arms crossed and toe tapping – said, "Daphne, we have to go."

Daphne replied, "Oh, okay," knowing better than to argue with the driver.

I wanted to protest: *There's still more punch.* Instead, I said, "We'll walk you to your car."

Six of us walked out: Scott with Alison; Bones with Daphne; and Bit and me bringing up the rear, walking arm and arm. Bit was perspiring and loving the cool night air. I pulled her to the side and kissed her...and kissed her again. Up ahead, alongside Alison's car – a dark blue MG with the passenger side door open – Tommy Childress faced off against Daphne Murray, two and half feet of awkwardness between them. They lurched and staggered toward one another like two backhoes trying to say goodbye, fortunately their buckets colliding. On the driver's side, Alison yielded little, permitting Scott to kiss her cheek (but she did rise up high on her toes).

I looked at my watch: one-thirty. I thought: *Maybe the party's not over yet.* "Hold on a second," I said, like I'd forgotten something, now running back to the house. I returned with a slip of paper. I handed it to Alison. "Ninety-one-point-five on the radio dial. The Night Earl will see you back to Cambridge."

Alison thanked me, handing the paper to Daphne. They climbed into the car. The MG rumbled to life with a throaty growl. They roared away, the taillights disappearing down the street. The car braked, made a right turn, then headed up the hill and out of town, the engine and transmission singing a sexy duet in the early-morning calm.

Bones said to me, "Why did you have to go back to the house to write that down? You could have just told them."

I took out another piece of paper. I said, "Because you need to deliver this *right now*."

Under streetlight, Bones read aloud what the Night Earl would sign off to in twenty minutes. What the last of the party would dance to in the living room, calling it a night. What Alison Henry and Daphne Murray would turn up on the

MG's radio, car-dancing their way back to Boston; more than one trucker tooting his air horn. What the Night Earl would hear coming from behind him in the studio, outside leaning over the wrought iron, blowing a Lucky, wondering where he would eat and when he would sleep.

*The last spin of the night goes out to two brainy beauties in an MG beating a blue streak back to Boston. Tommy and Scott said they had a fun time and want to see you on the flip-flop. That's Hillbilly lingo for y'all come back now, ya hear. This is the Night Earl...out of air...leaving you with Jackson Brown's "Redneck Friend."*

*Swing easy...*

*Stay beautiful...*

*Love you madly...*

Bones said to me, "Well crafted, Chandler."

Scott said to Bones: "Ride like the wind, Tonto."

The morning after the party, Bit and I slept late, staying in bed until noon. I took her to Harry's to say goodbye to Dante and Jackie, then on to Boyle's house where we hung out all afternoon and evening, eating pizza, playing ping pong, killing what remained of the keg, replaying the highlights of the night before, especially how Sugar and Spice were the icing on the cake and thank the gods for Grosvenor and Winthrope. We danced around Bit bopping Janie – why stir it up? Scott Hodges and Bones were floating three feet off the ground, love butterflies circling their heads. Boyle tried all afternoon to beat Sally Swift at ping pong playing left handed, but never did. Poor Farr was exhausted, more than ready to check out of the attic suite and return to our room.

Around eight, Bit and I walked back to my room and fell into bed with our clothes on. I pulled the TV over so we could watch the *Sunday Night Movie*, Alfred Hitchcock's *Rear Window*. I fell asleep. When I woke Bit was gone; most likely in the bathroom. I sat up wondering what time it was – just past one. I turned off the TV and turned on the Night Earl, the volume low, McCoy Tyner digging deep into his piano solo on John Coltrane's "My Favorite Things." Bit returned. She stripped out of her jeans and shirt, down to her panties, her back to me. She opened my dresser drawer and pulled out my telephone-numbered shirt. She slipped it on, flipping her hair around. She turned toward me, buttoning up, leaving the top two open, the shirttail barely covering what mattered most. I slid out of bed and followed her lead, a few minutes later spooning next to her, gently rubbing her thigh, the only light coming from the stereo receiver and the light from under the door. The windows were open with a cool breeze floating in. I needed to know something before Bit went back to Wyoming. Something that had been bugging me since Sonny slapped my knee saying, *Let's go, Junior. Buzz told me you was a good hand.*

I whispered, "Bit."

"Mmmm," she purred, pulling my arm around her.

"Tell me something."

"Mmmm?"

"Why did Sonny pick me to help him with Buzz?"

Bit whispered, "He didn't."

I stammered, "Then who – "

"I wanted you, Hank."

I sat up. *"What!... Why?"*

"Because I wanted to see if you could do it."

I rolled away from her and looked up at the ceiling, rethinking the whole thing. I knew Hope had been pulling the strings. It never occurred to me that she'd let Bit pull mine. Bit turned to face me, her head now propped in her hand. She continued, "I wasn't sure. I liked you a lot. I wanted to see if you had it in you." She pulled me close with a hand on the back of my neck. "I don't want a boy, Hank. I want a man." She sealed it with a kiss.

We didn't talk anymore. I lay there listening to Bit's breathing, putting the pieces together. Weirdly, it made sense. Weirdly, I was okay with it. When I heard a police siren out the window, I checked the clock – one-fifty-five. The Night Earl was pulling the plug:

*I'm out of gas and leaking oil. I'm leaving you in good company. Two old friends stopped by to sing a song about a girl they once loved...*

*We've all been there...*

*Time for the Night Earl to fly the coop...*

Bob Dylan:
*If you're travelin' to the north country fair*
*Where the winds hit heavy on the borderline*
*Remember me to one who lives there*
*For she once was a true love of mine*

Johnny Cash:
*See for me that her hair's hanging down*
*It curls and falls all down her breast.*
*See for me that her hair's hanging down*
*That's the way I remember her best*

Bob Dylan:
*If you go when the snowflakes fall*
*When the rivers freeze and summer ends*
*Please see for me if she's wearing a coat so warm*
*To keep her from the howlin' winds*

Together:
*If you're travelin' in the north country fair*
*Where the winds hit heavy on the borderline*
*Please say hello to one who lives there*
*For she once was a true love of mine*

Despite being an avowed romantic, I throw "I love yous" around like manhole covers. I'd said it for the first time to

Janie Wallace. I would say it to only one other girl besides Bit Stifel (but that's another story). When Bob Dylan and Johnny Cash finished "Girl from the North Country," I gently pulled Bit's hair away from her ear, kissed it, then whispered, being honest, being truthful,

"I love you, Bit."

She pulled my arm around her as if she were hauling me back to the Lazy T. Hauling me back for what I had to do – this story not over yet. She whispered back, "I love you, too, Hank."

I didn't doubt her.

# Chapter 30

## BIT'N ME

Throughout the winter and spring, Bit and I fell into a comfortable routine of naughty love letters and long distance telephone calls. She was now at college in Laramie and I was working hard at staying in school, trying not to stress about her being around all those cowboys, trying not to be all paranoid and weird as I had been with Janie. A week after our party, I'd tracked Janie down and apologized profusely for my idiotic behavior and for Bit tagging her on the kisser. Turns out, Janie was the one who was embarrassed, mortified that the Gilligan twins were dispatched by Billy Flannigan to break up our party on account of her. Whatever, we reached a cease-fire and managed a smiling friendship, getting along nicely the rest of the year, and I think – and Janie would agree – a small spark from reigniting. I admit I was worried for a couple of weeks after the party that the Gilligan twins would track me down in a dark alley and administer a beating. Boyle squelched my fear by advising Billy Flannigan to call off his dogs; that if they laid a hand on me, Jackie and Dante would hunt them down and give them a private audience without appeal (Flannigan included); that Jackie and Dante didn't fool around.

Thank god for low hanging fruit at the top of the tree.

When school ended in early June, Bones and I drove back to Chicago with me mostly behind the wheel. We took off late because Bones had gone up to Boston the day before to say goodbye to Daphne Murray, and those long goodbyes will wear you out. After our fall bash, Bones found ample excuses to zoom to Boston. I never said anything. Why? So, I'd jinx it. One time I went along and we met up with Alison Henry on Beacon Street. I didn't mention Scott Hodges, nor did she. I pretended as if Scott and I had not known each other since kindergarten, played on the same peewee hockey team, and shared our first *Playboy* (he found it in his father's sweater drawer under Ben Hogan's book on golf). I knew Scott Hodges and Alison Henry were in the stew. Why stir it up?

Around midnight, before Bones came back from Boston, I'd placed a call to the Night Earl for a special request. Bones and I packed the car and took off at 1:30 in the morning; Bones palming me a mother's helper for the graveyard shift. Just over the Connecticut line, running hot with the hammer down, the Night Earl called it quits:

*The last turn of the table goes out to a Beemer burning rubber back to the Windy City. I know they got their ears on. I got my smokes, ready to blow. I'm turning the lights down low. Leaving you with my first love. A man who never blew an unsavory note. You'll recognize this one, Bones. Here's Johnny Hodges's version of Duke Ellington and Billy Strayhorn's "Satin Doll."*

*Keep the little one out of the ditches...*
*And the big one in your britches...*
*Say hello to Sweet Lou...*
*The Night Earl is over your shoulder...*

At the end of the song, before nodding off, Bones said to me, "You're a quick study, Chandler."

When he next woke we were in Ohio.

Bones dropped me off at home at just past seven in the evening. Both my mother and father came out to greet us in the driveway. My father shook Bones's hand and gave him a light slap on the shoulder as if he was Scott Hodges, sincerely thanking him for giving me a ride home. My mother placed her hands on Bones's cheeks, telling him with a loving eye that she liked his haircut; that he looked as if he'd put on weight; encouraging him to come back for a bite to eat after he settled in; that they wanted to hear about his school year. Cracking a smile, toeing at the gravel, Bones said he'd like that.

I had promised my parents I'd stay a week before flying out to Jackson, so when I told Mom my departure date she insisted my arithmetic was faulty, fingernail-tapping on her calendar that a week is seven days, not five. She was right, of course. So I made sure I was at her beck and call, especially for dinners and family golf. That was not too difficult because I had few other distractions – Scott Hodges being off my radar screen, playing away games at 1430 Lake Shore Drive, Chicago, Illinois.

Andy drove me to the airport super early the day I left for Wyoming. We'd stayed up late my last night, but not too late because I wanted to hit the ground running when my feet touched down in Jackson. For my trip, I wore my jeans with the split knees and one of my monogrammed HTC III shirts. (Note: I'd given my telephone-numbered shirt to Bit as a parting gift from our fall weekend because, as she accurately pointed out, she had my number. Also of note: When I'd arrived home from school, my hair was long enough to put into a ponytail. My father chided me for looking like a girl. My mother – pulling back and playing with my hair – kidded me that she always wanted a girl. Andy suggested I get a training bra. Bit warned me if I showed up at the Lazy T looking like Willie Nelson, she'd shear me with Hope's razor. So, I got a haircut; but I could still tuck it behind my ears.)

At O'Hare, shaking hands goodbye through the car window, the last thing Andy said to me was *You'd better not come back wrapped in plaster, Hoss.*

Andy's such a card.

Walking away backwards, shouldering my pack and knapsack, I gave Andy a hand salute saying, "I can't guarantee that, Ringo," then disappeared through the airport's double doors.

Settling into my airplane seat, I pulled out a new journal and wrote on the first page: *The Lazy T, June 10, 1978.* Underneath I wrote a bunch of inane garbage that you first record in a journal about who you are, where you are, and what you're thinking and feeling – the kind of tripe you scratch out later thinking *This is awful.* I drifted off to sleep dreaming about Bit and how this summer I was not worried about where I was going and what I was doing. I just wanted to get there. When we touched down in Jackson at a little past nine, I was wide awake and one of the first off the plane. Outside was cold and spitting rain. A low ceiling clouded the Tetons. I dug my hands in my pockets and hunched my shoulders as I angled toward the terminal. I spotted Bit watching me through a window. She was wearing my Cubs cap with her ponytail underneath, packed perfectly in blue jeans and a tan corduroy jacket, waving, smiling.

I smiled, waving back, picking up the pace.

Inside, we modestly kissed and pawed at each other, shaking a bit as if we were dogs in heat. I waited until the parking lot to back her up against the hood of her camel-colored El Camino for a proper hello. Bit reciprocated. She flipped me around and pinned me against the car, laying firm she was just as happy to see me. That's when Bear, the new ten-month old black and tan mutt with white paws and floppy ears, jumped up and began running around inside the car, barking her head off. Bit let her out and settled the pup down by having her sniff me (I must still have had some of Winston on my jeans because the pup wouldn't let it go).

Buckling up with Bear sitting upright between us, her small pink tongue peaking out and panting, Bit flipped the ignition switch, revving the engine. She spun out backwards then floored it out of the parking lot, the back tires spitting gravel, swerving onto the highway, fish-tailing, gunning it, driving like an Italian high on meth. Clete had warned me that Bit only used the brake as a footrest. He wasn't joking. I put my arm around Bear, holding her steady.

Ten miles south of the airport Bit slowed for the stoplights and pedestrians in Jackson. The tourist crowds were light on account of it being early June and the inclement weather. The rain had stopped, but the sun was still having a difficult time poking through. I was hungry and considered a stop at Dog n Suds, but thought better of it. When Bear curled up between us for a snooze, I asked Bit about her being back at the ranch since returning from school. She said it was a little claustrophobic with three of them in the house; explaining to me she was now bunking with Hope in her parents' double bed, Dorothy having taken over her bedroom. That bugged Bit, and I could understand why. I wouldn't want anybody sleeping in my bed, especially if it meant that I was shoved off into my parents' bed. She told me in a tight-lipped way that after Dorothy had moved in the Lazy T had taken on a different look and feel. As if Dorothy had co-opted the place. Bit explained that with Sonny's help, Hope and Dorothy had built a lean-to against the barn for the tractors, mowers and rakes. They also tidied up the place, giving it a women's touch, with rock paths and some potted geraniums. When Buzz ran the ranch, the outside looked like a yard sale of machinery and tools – Buzz never put a tool back and only parked a machine where it came to rest. It was a mess – but it was his mess. I asked what Hope thought of all this. Bit didn't answer right away. I turned and saw that she was struggling, her eyes narrowing and boring a hole through the bumper of a car in front of us.

She said, "I guess Mom's okay with it."

I asked, "How do you feel?"

Clenching the steering wheel, her jaw set, she said, "It doesn't set right."

I changed the subject, asking about Clete, who had come up from Florida in late April to help out with roundup, branding and irrigating. Bit said Clete had been a big help, really pitching in to fill the void left by Buzz. She said Sonny had cleaned up his act and was now spending more time helping out at the ranch, drinking less, keeping Dorothy and Hope company. (I recalled what Clete had once told me about Sonny, that he stayed relatively sober when he had his eye on a chore – in this case, watching over Hope and Dorothy and Bit and the Lazy T.)

I asked about Farnsworth and if he'd caused the Lazy T any problems.

Bit pressed her top teeth into her bottom lip.

I asked, "What's up?"

She said, "You can't say anything. Promise me. Dorothy doesn't want anybody to know."

I promised.

"Farnsworth got hold of Dorothy one night in town. Said he wanted her to move back to town or else. That the town was talking and he said it didn't look right her shacking up with the widow of Buzz Stifel. Dorothy told me him to go to hell, so he slapped her around pretty good."

"When did this happen?"

"Just after I left for school," Bit said, keeping one hand on the wheel, the other rubbing Bear's head, her lips pressed together in a pained look

I stupidly asked, "What'd she do?"

Bit snapped at me, "What could she do, Hank? Go to the police!?"

That shut me up and got me thinking about how Farnsworth held all the cards – and the keys to the jail – being the law in a small Western town where everybody knew the consequences of what happens when you crossed the line, or in Dorothy's case, stepped out of line.

We rode in silence. I changed the subject, asking her about school, comparing our spring semesters. I filled her in on the "law firm" and how Scott Hodges was in love with Alison and Bones with Daphne; and that Jackie and Dante wanted her to come back to Providence. She told me again – though I'd heard it before and read about it in her letters – about her first semester at Laramie; how she loved her classes and being with Polly Hamilton and her boyfriend Joe Alexander. When she went on about meeting new friends and the bar scene at school, I reached over and turned on the radio, keeping the volume low.

An hour or so later, Bit slowed, not using her blinker, and turned off 191 onto Forty Rod Road. We bumped over the cattle guard. I quickly located Gannet Peak in the distance as if it were an old friend. Bear popped up sniffing, knowing we were close to home. Through a long, spidery crack in Bit's windshield, I honed in on the Lazy T – the top of the windmill, the green tar paper roof, the bold outline of the barn. Weird, I had this out of body experience like I was in an old western movie, slowly approaching my Western outpost; not knowing what to expect, anticipating a new adventure. I rolled down my window, breathed in through my nose and out through my mouth, wetting my lips.

"God, it's good to back," I said, not taking my eyes off the Lazy T, "especially with you." I turned to look at Bit.

Bit palmed the steering wheel with both hands, straightening out and stretching her arms and shoulders. She stared straight ahead. "You sure you're not going to miss playing golf?"

I said *Nah*.

"What about all those fancy pants parties you go to?"

"Seen one, seen 'em all."

"What about Scott Hodges and the law firm?"

"They're big boys. They can get along without me."

"What about that old girlfriend? You gonna be pining away for her out here in the hay fields of Wyoming?"

"Not with a new mare in town, I won't."

Bit smiled showing no teeth. "Good answer," she said reaching over and grabbing me by the shirt, pulling me in tight for a mushy kiss, squishing Bear between us, almost running the El Camino into the ditch.

We drove through the gate under the Lazy T sign. Hope and Dorothy had come out onto the porch to greet us. Hope stood with hands on hips, her neatly cropped head of salt-and-pepper hair now a little more salty than peppery. Dorothy was beside her leaning against a porch pole, arms crossed, not a mile clicked off her speedometer. The sun had come out, but the air was still cool. I edged open my car door. Bear – not waiting – jumped over me and headed for a drink from the big metal dish at the end of the porch. I pulled my pack from the bed of the El Camino and walked toward Hope. She gave me a look I'll not forget. My mind raced back to a letter I'd written her after Buzz died; a letter not rambling nor sentimental, just flat out telling her how I felt about both her and Buzz, and how I blamed myself for not driving him back to the ranch that night. Now, Hope waggled a finger at me, saying, "Henry, Bit promised me you were getting your ears lowered before you come back out here."

Making an exaggerated gesture of tucking my hair behind my ears, I said, "You should have seen what I left on the barbershop floor."

When Hope said, "Well, from what I see you still have plenty to leave behind," I was standing a step below her on the porch, our eyes locked in as she wiped her hands on her apron. She ticked her head toward the trailer. "Get your gear stowed then come have something to eat. Clete's out irrigating. You and him patch fence this afternoon. Bit, you come give me a hand with dinner."

Hope turned and went into the house.

Bit followed.

Dorothy had not moved. She pulled a strand of hair from her face that the wind had blown awry. She shielded her eyes from the sun. She drawled, "How's it feel to be back at the Lazy T, Hank?"

I faced her, squinting, saying, "It's like I never left."

Dorothy eyed the new shed and spruced-up yard. "We made some improvements."

I looked around. "I can see that."

She said, now purring more than drawling, "You grew so much in a year, Hank. I'm so glad you came back."

I didn't know what to say to that because she was giving me a look like she really meant it. This was weird; something was up. Dorothy Farnsworth had always been polite to me, but now she was being way too friendly, flirty even. I dry-swallowed. I felt funny.

I slung my pack over my shoulder, avoiding further eye contact, and turned to look out over the corrals and foothills toward the Wind Rivers. I mumbled just above the whisper of the wind, "So am I. So am I," turning, kicking my way to the trailer, crossing the plank laid over the stream, now chewing on a new twist to a new chapter.

# Chapter 31

## THE NEW LAZY T ✳ FREDDIE SAUNDERS ✳ BINOCULARS

I changed into ranch clothes, then snooped around the trailer. Spic and Span had erased dirt, dust, and grime. Gone, too, was the aroma of dung and diesel. The old boxes of clothes had been put away and the table where Clete reloaded his 357 shells was neat and tidy. The salt licks were still in the tub in the ripped-out bathroom, but you could tell by the smell that Clorox had been run around the place. The windows were scrubbed squeaky clean and the sun was shining through. The scarred and stained white linoleum floor was somehow white again. My new bed – a mattress that Dorothy had donated from her place in town – was made up with sheets and blankets and two pillows. The windows were even decorated with flowery makeshift curtains, and Hope's lamp now sat on a small wooden table. The saddle blankets I had slept on the previous summer had been moved to the back bedroom for Bear's benefit, the pup no more than an arm's length from Clete.

Walking back across the yard to the house, I pulled on my blue jean jacket because it was still chilly. I buttoned up taking stock of the whole place; even the outhouse had not escaped the beautification program, the roof now painted white and the structure nicknamed – I would come to learn – The White House. What had not changed were Buddy the horse (now joined in the corral with Bit's horse Blaze), and the three-legged cat licking her stump sitting directly in my path – still ugly, fat, mangy, menacing – so I cut her a wide swath as I continued to the house.

Not much had changed inside the cabin as far as I could see. Clete sat smoking and reading an old Jackson paper. He'd come in from irrigating, was washed up and plunked down in what had been Buzz's spot by the bay window. He didn't get up. I didn't expect him to. He smiled, his big, crooked front tooth a far better greeting than a hearty handshake. He stubbed out his Marlboro asking me about my trip and the traffic coming down from Jackson, as if I was just gone for the day. I said it was a breeze, joking about our record time with Bit behind the wheel. He got up and clomped toward me, guiding me to the table with a firm hand on my shoulder. "Let's get some meat put back on those puny college bones."

The five of us squeezed in around the table with Clete at the head. I sat next to Bit and across from Dorothy and Hope. We dug in: chicken fried steak covered in gravy, mash potatoes, tomato and cucumber salad, buttered bread, and iced tea. At first, the meal was quiet, just the sound of knives and forks scraping plates – I think all of us getting used to this new arrangement. Clete broke the silence, chewing on his food. "Bit told us about that wild party she went to at your college. Said there was a lot of rock and roll music being played. Mighty strong alcohol being drunk. Said there was even marijuana cigarettes being smoked. Is that right?"

I shook my head slowly with a downward tilt, acting seriously confused. "I don't know anything about that, Clete. The only party I remember taking Bit to was at the library where we celebrated the new edition of the *Encyclopedia Britannica* with doughnuts and cider."

Hope whispered, "Save me Lord."

Dorothy added, "Boy's full of more shit than a Christmas turkey."

Bit turned toward me. "So, Sugar and Spice are librarians?"

I corrected her. "Apprenticing...apprenticing librarians."

Hope sat back and folded her arms over her chest. "Bit told us things got a little out of hand. Said she had to set down your old girlfriend."

"An unfortunate incident," I hedged, "of a spilled drink."

Bit dragged out, "Yeeeah, and most of it on me."

I calmly continued, "This old...ex...friend was upset because Bit kept hogging all the punch."

Bit elbowed me hard. "I was not. I was drinking beer. That punch would've killed an Indian."

Bit and I went back and forth about the party and her weekend in Providence with me blurring and softening the details as much as possible. I was relieved that everyone was comfortable with Bit and me, if you know what I mean. Hope stood to clear the dishes, instructing Clete and me to get a move on; we had work to do; to take the blue Ford and patch the fence along Forty Rod Road for the afternoon. Clete squeezed his eyes shut tight a couple of times like he does when he's thinking or has something to do. He pushed back, stood up to his full six-three, palmed his tan cowboy hat from the counter and walked out, leaving the door open. I edged out and followed, grabbing a toothpick, giving Bit my see-you-later eye.

(Later that night after supper, Bit and I talked awhile sitting side-by-side on the porch, waiting for the cover of darkness so we could sneak off into the hayfields. It had been a mild winter so one stack remained standing in the fields, about three hundred yards from the house. Great thing about hay: it's relatively soft; you can hide a blanket between the bales; and, binoculars can't see through it. For the rest of my stay, when we were not eating, sleeping, milking, irrigating, haying, or just fixing shit, Bit and I would rendezvous there, or in the barn, way back in the loft where she'd made a soft bed of saddle blankets on top of a mattress of hay, next to a candle hot-waxed to the top of a small stool. The Lazy T was always a tight, cozy fit. Now, it just got tighter and cozier.)

Clete and I drove away down Forty Rod Road with Bear in the back of the truck. The sun was out and the day heating up. About a quarter mile from the house we pulled over and parked. Clete let the tailgate down. I grabbed a box of staples, work gloves and the fence stretcher (think a metal device with clamps on the ends and a handle that you push down to tighten the barbed wire). Clete grabbed two pairs of fencing pliers and his gloves. We edged into the culvert then up the other side to the fence line. Bear stayed put, resting her head on the side of the truck, her black-and-white floppy ears relaxed, watching, supervising.

A barbed wire fence takes a beating over time because the wooden posts and wire get ripped up by snow and ice, as well as antelope, cows, and an occasional mule deer passing through. Our job was to make sure that the posts were solidly in the ground and that the wire was firmly stapled to the posts. Every so often we'd have to replace a post. Normally, patching fence is a bore. Not so with Clete. We were not far from the ranch, just about the place where I first met Buzz. Glancing back at the house, I kidded Clete about Hope watching us with binoculars through the bay window. "We still within range?"

Clete turned his back to the house. He smiled down at me, yanking on his gloves. "Hush now, Squirrel, or she'll hear you."

I pulled on my gloves. Pressed a finger to my lips.

As we tightened wire and hammered in staples, Clete filled me in on what he knew: since Buzz's death, folks from Pinedale and Sublette County rallied around Hope, helping out at the ranch, making sure she had plenty to do and didn't have to cook too much. Dorothy moved in a week after the funeral, quietly with no fanfare but it was the "buzz" around town (so to speak), and a burr under Farnsworth's saddle. That pleased everybody. I asked how all the women were getting along under the same roof. Clete said so far so good. When I asked about Bit and how she was doing being back home, Clete shrugged his shoulders, something bugging him. I said, "What's the matter, Clete?" thinking the problem was inside the log cabin house.

He said, "'Cause you're going out with her, Squirrel, there's something you should know…"

I stopped hammering. "What's that?" I asked with that *Oh shit* feeling building in my stomach.

Clete hesitated. "Freddie Saunders's back in town."

I didn't recognizing the name. "Who's that?"

"Freddie and Bit went to high school together. Had a thing going for a while. They broke up but I think she's still stuck on him. He's a couple years older. His daddy cowboyed with Buzz and Sonny – Sonny could tell you more. After high school Freddie left out of here…first working the rigs down around Kemmer…then down to the Gulf."

I asked, "When did he get back?"

"Hope told me two weeks ago."

"Where's he now?"

"Up in the Basin working for his father's cattle operation."

"You know him?"

"A little…"

"What's the problem?"

Clete hesitated. "He's not my type of company."

"Why not," I asked, now curious because Clete liked everybody and everybody liked Clete.

He stopped hammering. He straightened up and pushed back his cowboy hat. "Now this ain't traveling back to Bit?"

"I promise," I said, holding my palm up like I was swearing on a bible.

"He just ain't on the level. Drives a big fancy pickup his daddy bought him. Borrows money and don't pay it back. Picks on the smaller hands. Always angling for others to buy his drinks. Always trying to steal away another man's girl."

I went quiet thinking about this, hammering staples again. Bit never told me about Freddie Saunders. That stung, but I let it go. I had a suspicion she had a backsliding problem like me – she'd hinted around it. It also explained why she was so forgiving when we were dancing around at my party, when I came clean about Janie Wallace. I asked, "Why's Bit stuck on him if he's such an asshole?"

Clete moved to the next post, rocking it back and forth, making sure it was secure. He paused, plucked his Red Man pouch from his back pocket and put a wad of tobacco in his cheek, rolling it around, packing it down with his tongue. He spit. Shook his head. Then dragged out, "Shit, Squirrel...I...don't...know..."

I asked for his chew. I dug in the pouch, fingered a good-size chunk and packed in my cheek, then spit. I took a stab at it. "Sounds like Freddie Saunders was her first and he's the bad boy she can't quit."

Clete picked up the fence stretcher and attached it to a post. I moved to help him. We both bent over, grunting, groaning. Clete pressed down hard, the handle snapping shut. I hammered in staples to secure the wire. Clete took off the stretcher. He raised up, wiped his forearm across his brow and said, "I don't like to admit this, Squirrel..."

I straightened, took off my hat and palmed the sweat from my brow.

"What's that?" I asked.

"That college you go to..."

"...Yeah?"

"It's not wasted on you."

# Chapter 32

## SWISS CHEESE

Behind the barn, near the wooden cross that marked where Blue was buried, Clete had set up a wall of old hay bales about fifteen paces away in the sagebrush. In the middle of the wall he'd spray-painted a white target approximately the size of Sheriff Darryl Farnsworth and tacked small paper bull's eyes over his heart, testicles, and between his eyes. Along either side of the wall were staggered bales that provided shelves for beer bottles, as if we were at a shooting gallery at the fair. This was our practice range, where we went sometimes after supper and on Sunday afternoons to blow off a few rounds, drink beer, smoke, talk. Bit had no interest in our games or guns, leaving us to our play, preferring to stay in the house with Hope and Dorothy; read, play cards or watch TV.

Clete let me shoot his hand gun a little the summer before, but I was uncomfortable with it. Not this summer. Now I wanted to learn how to handle a gun and hit a target. It had been a fantasy of mine for a while. I also felt as if it might be in my best interest. I was not wrong.

Our first day out, while Clete loaded his 357 he'd

nicknamed "Swiss Cheese," I asked him, "Could you shoot Farnsworth?"

He spun the cylinder. "I'd like to think I could. But I don't know." He clicked the cylinder shut and took aim.

BANG – a Budweiser bottle exploded.

He fired again – BANG – nothing this time but a small thud and a wisp of dust from a hay bale.

"Shit, missed high," he said, adjusting his feet with the gun at his side. He looked at me. "I've never shot a man. Never aimed a gun at one neither, much less wanted to pull the trigger. I don't know if I could." He aimed the gun with both hands at the target, mouthing *Bang*. "But I dream about it every day – killing that low-down sonofabitch." He stopped, let the gun rest at his side, thinking, slowly shaking his head with a lost look, saying, "When I come up here in the spring for round-up I was talking with the other hands about Farnsworth. They told me about one of the younger cowboys – I think his name was Curt – got run in by Farnsworth and Asshole Pete on some bullshit charge. Spent a couple days in jail. When he come out he wasn't the same."

That gave me the shivers.

Clete looked at me with a confused look. "Just wasn't the same," he repeated, his voice drifting off. He readdressed the target, his eye and jaw set. He squeezed off four quick rounds, all landing inside the outline of Farnsworth, one hitting the target over the heart. Clete broke the gun open and shook out the shells, putting them in an old box for reloading. He handed me the gun. "You think you could shoot Farnsworth?"

I took off my cowboy hat and hung it on Blue's cross. I thumbed bullets in the gun. I told him I didn't think I could do it either, even though I, too, had thought about it – gunning down Farnsworth – all school-year long. I admired the 357 – the grip, the barrel, the trigger, the hammer, the weight. I positioned my feet, aimed, and fired Swiss Cheese at Farnsworth. I don't think I even hit a hay bale. Clete came beside me saying I was way high and to bring it down a tad or they'd be picking up bodies over at the Three Quarter Circle. He adjusted my hands, head, stance. Told me to relax, flex my knees a little, breathe, squeeze the trigger, feel the shot. That helped. After five more rounds, I was homing in, but my arms went heavy and my ears were ringing. A 357 weighs more than it appears and kicks like a mule. Clint Eastwood makes it look easy shooting with one hand. It's not, and I was using two. I thought hitting a beer bottle only fifteen paces away would be child's play. It's not, and I'm a pretty good shot. At least I thought I was. It took three weeks of practice for the muscles in my hands, forearms and arms to be strong enough to hold the gun up properly and pop off six rounds in a row without the kick of the revolver throwing me off.

That's when I said to Clete, "I got 'im."

Clete walked over and inspected the targets. "You sure did. Right through the heart," he said, taking it down and putting up another. He handed me the spent one. "Put that in your journal, Deadeye, case anybody asks if you can shoot straight."

I did just that.

# Chapter 33

## TRAILERING HORSES * ITTY BIT * CO-DEE * FREDDIE SAUNDERS

Two weeks into my summer, Sonny had to make a delivery to a dude ranch outside a town called Dubois on the other side of the Wind Rivers; about sixty miles away as the crow flies, but more like 150 miles and a four-hour drive each way as the route was around the north end of the Wind Rivers. Because of the distance and mountain roads, Sonny had asked to borrow Eleanor Pfisterer's Chevy 4x4 to pull Buzz's trailer, a much better choice than the blue Ford or Sonny's ancient truck. Eleanor okayed Sonny driving the horses over, but didn't trust him driving back after a long day on the road, a fresh wad of folding money in his pocket, and a slew of Budweiser signs along the way tempting his thirst. She insisted on someone else driving her truck home so it didn't end up nose down in a ditch. Hope told Eleanor that I could go with Sonny; she could spare me for a day.

Early that morning, after breakfast, I drove the blue Ford and Buzz's horse trailer over to Sonny's, figuring to help him wrangle the horses, but he'd already had them all lined up and hitched to the corral ready to go. Sonny was sitting on the front porch of his two-bedroom shack whittling a stick with a large jackknife. I pushed the truck door open with my boot saying, "Morning, Sonny," trying to sound Western cool and nonchalant.

He kept whittling.

I said, "How you doing today?"

Sonny grunted, pitched the stick into the yard. "Older and uglier, Junior." He folded his knife shut with a click, stood, went into the house, returning with a steaming cup of coffee. He handed it to me almost smiling. He appeared to be in a good mood. He must have had a good night's sleep because he didn't smell like booze and was neatly dressed in washed jeans and a pressed red cowboy shirt with white snaps. The wispy, sandy-colored hair on his large square head was slicked down and combed. I took a sip of coffee. It was truly awful. Like hot water run through smelly gym socks. I forced the hot black liquid down my throat, smacking my lips, "Mmmmm, mountain grown."

Sonny said, "Huh?"

I raised the cup. "It tastes mountain grown."

Sonny rumpled his brow. "Mountain grown?" He looked at the Wind Rivers, shaking his head. "Don't think so."

I corrected him. "No," I said holding up my cup, kidding him, "It's mountain grown coffee. It tastes like Folgers."

Sonny said, "Could be. It come out of a can."

I said, "A red can?"

He said, "I guess. It come from Farson's store. Biggest one they got." He clomped down the steps past me, heading to the horses tied up at the corral. "Let's get a move on, Junior. Trailer needs to be hooked to Eleanor's truck and these money-makers loaded up. Got a long day ahead of us."

I put down my coffee to help Sonny unhook and reconnect the trailer to Eleanor's truck, then led the four horses in and tied them off. When Sonny went back into his shack, I ducked behind the trailer and emptied my bladder, as well as my coffee, on some sagebrush, relieved to be rid of both. I opened the truck's passenger-side door and looked inside. Sonny had set his clean, white straw cowboy hat on the bench seat between us; on the dash, in front of the steering wheel, he'd placed a half carton of Camels with his dented silver Zippo wedged between two packs. The front door shut and the screen door slammed. I looked up. Sonny bumped down the steps with both arms full, approaching the truck with a manila folder and two six-packs of Coors under one arm, a rifle and a box of shells under the other.

I took off my jean jacket and cowboy hat and climbed in.

He handed me the cold six-packs through the driver's-side window, then opened the door and hung the rifle on the gun rack in the back of the cab, stowed the shells under his seat, and carefully slid the folder (horse paperwork, I figured) under the cowboy hat that separated us. I didn't ask how he was going to keep the beer cold because I don't think he cared – but I did. So I told him to hold on a minute while I rummaged around for some old newspaper that I'd seen in the truck bed to wrap up six of the cans, wedging them under the passenger seat so they would not roll around. I put the other six-pack on the floor of the cab, doubting it would be drunk. Sonny asked if wrapping beers in newspaper would keep them cold. I said most definitely; I did it all the time at school. He thought about that as he fingered the ignition key, carefully turning over the truck's motor. Taking off the parking brake, pressing in the clutch while guiding the stick shift into first gear, he mumbled, "That college you go to..."

"Yeah?" I said, putting on my seatbelt.

We pulled out.

Sonny didn't finish his thought.

On Forty Rod Road, just outside his place, Sonny eased the load into the dip in the road. The truck splashed through some rain run-off, then Sonny gunned it up the other side, the horses shifting around in the trailer, the engine laboring.

Back on the flat, we moved right along, Sonny angling and bending the truck and trailer around the trouble spots in the road. I lay my head back, wetted and sealed my lips, settling in for a quiet ride; maybe getting in a snooze, figuring Sonny would not want to talk with *Junior*. He tooted the horn as we passed by the Lazy T, Dorothy and Hope outside hanging laundry; they waved back. We made the turn onto 191 and headed north to Jackson. Sonny settled his big frame into his seat, minding the speed limit, getting comfortable with the load behind us.

A couple minutes later he surprised me. "You heal okay from that whuppin' Buzz gave you?"

I turned and sat up. I'd been daydreaming about Bit and me meeting up the night before in the barn. I stripped myself away from Bit – choosing my words carefully as I mimicked Sonny's clipped, gruff tone (I admit, I'm a suck-up and a copy cat) – and said, "Didn't take too long." I rubbed my chin, adding, "Jaw was wired shut for a while but my charley horse healed quickly. Ribs were the worst."

Sonny gargled up a mouthful of phlegm, rolled down his window and let fly. Cranking up the window he said, "Getting your ribs busted ain't no fun. Can't do nothing 'cept let 'em heal." He reached across the dash and pulled out two Camel straights; one went on his lower lip, the other he handed to me. Sonny giving me one of his smokes was better than a palm on the pate from the Pontiff. I took the smoke, holding it between two fingers, tapping the end with my thumb, asking an obvious question, "You break ribs?"

Sonny popped open his Zippo and lit his smoke. He closed the lighter and tossed it to me. "Buncha times," he said. Smoke shot out his nose. He took another drag and breathed out, "Sometimes getting throwd. Mostly after in a fight outside the bar. Either way felt the same." Gazing straight ahead down the two-lane highway, no cars around, he chuckled at a long-ago memory I could only fantasize about. He said, "Nothing CC and soda can't heal. Know what I mean, Junior?"

For sure, I was intimidated by the man. Who wouldn't be? He was stronger than Magilla Gorilla and as predictable as a tornado. Nearly a year later, I could still feel his enormous hands lifting me off the ground and slamming me against the wall, promising to enlarge my rectum with the tip of his boot if I didn't keep my trap shut about who jumped and beat up Buzz Stifel. But what he said now, *Know what I mean?* was his way – I think – of acknowledging what happened when we were together in Buzz's hospital room. If there was one person I could talk to about Buzz, it would be Sonny Skinner. But I would not, not now. Buzz had been Sonny's oldest and best friend. If Sonny wanted to talk, he would. It was not my place to bring it up. If the roles had been reversed and I took Scott Hodges's life the same way, I wouldn't want anybody talking about it, not even the guy holding down his legs.

This is weird to admit, but I never grieved for Buzz or Luke, but I did have a bunch of strange dreams that I'll tell you about soon enough. I know I was supposed to grieve, but I never did. And I can't fake it. And I can't explain it. I didn't even squeeze out a tear or two for appearance's sake. Granted, if Andy or my parents died I'd be a blubbering puddle, so don't think I have a heart of stone. It's just that this death thing is a mystery to me, and I repeat, I can't fake it. For instance, not too long ago at a funeral in Lake Forest, kneeling on one of those needlepoint cushions at the Blessed Black Labrador Episcopal Church (Andy coined that one), I did my duty and prayed to God and Jesus and the Holy Ghost. Andy elbowed me when I sat back in the pew, asking me did I pray for the person who died and hoped they went to heaven, blah, blah, blah. I was honest; I told him I prayed for the Cubs to win the World Series. He said he'd done the same.

Now, looking over at him, I said, "I know what you mean, Sonny," lighting my Camel with his Zippo, clicking the lighter shut and blowing a big hit of smoke toward the windshield.

I handed back his lighter and cracked my window.

When a hippy-looking VW bus plastered with liberal bumper stickers chugged passed us, Sonny gave them the finger along with a two-minute rant that skewered Jimmy Carter, Robert Redford and Jane Fonda. I noticed for the first time that his middle finger was bent at an odd angle. I asked what happened. He said he mashed it in the hay baler last summer after I'd left; that Doc Evans froze it that way so he wouldn't have to cut it off. He said he couldn't feel anything in the tip, which actually helped his guitar playing. I said I didn't know he could play the guitar. He said he played a little, that Buzz taught him enough chords to be dangerous. That singing came naturally to him, which his mom made him do in the church choir growing up.

I asked, "Where did you grow up?"

"Kemmer," he said. "Grew up in a house with five brothers. My mother couldn't handle all the fighting so she mostly took to her bed. Told us to fetch her only if there was blood. Come up here at sixteen for a ranch job and to get away from my dad. Fell in love with Hopie and bird-dogged her for three years. She was living with her folks on a ranch south of Jackson. I had my sights set on marrying her but Buzz come riding along and scooped her up. Can't blame her. Didn't hold it against him either. I stood up for Buzz at the wedding. Figured if I couldn't have Hopie, I wanted Buzzy to. That way we'd all be together. 'Bout a year later, I got myself hitched up to a red-haired tornado named Dixie Master – "

" – That was her real name?"

"Yep. Why?"

I grin-laughed, holding it in.

He said, "What's so funny, Junior?"

I said, "Nothing, Sonny."

He said, "Something's got you. Tell me now."

"Her name sounds" – here I paused because it sounded so immature, and I was embarrassed to say it – "like dick master."

He said, "*Dick master?* Huh. Never thought about that." He shook his head chuckling at my suggestion. "Well, believe me, she wasn't."

I said, "I'm sorry. I didn't mean to insult your wife...I –"

Sonny waved me off. "Insult her all you want. She's gone."

"She left you?"

"Died, too."

"Oh," I said a bit red faced. "I'm sorry about that."

"I should be, too," Sonny said. "Got some kind of cancer. Dropped her like an anvil. We had our problems. No secret around town I like a woman with a big can. Problem was her mouth was twice as big and we lived in a small cabin. Made it through two tough winters holed up with her nagging me about quittin' cowboying and rodeoing. Take an honest job working in her father's feed store is what she wanted. We'd fight then make up – that make-up sex's the best, Junior. That ended one day when I finally woke up and told her 'Dixie take your tongue out of my mouth I'm kissing you goodbye.'" Sonny drew out another smoke and lit up. He flipped the Zippo shut, tucking it back into the carton of Camels. "Told the judge I couldn't take it no more. Dixie and I were ready to kill each other. I pleaded with him, 'Just let me keep my cabin, my horses, my pickup and my gun. She can have the rest.'"

Sonny's eyes twinkled.

I prodded him. "What'd the judge say?"

Sonny coughed, rolled down the window and spat. Rolling up his window he said, "Judge told me, 'Sonny Skinner... somebody beat you with the stupid stick again. That's all you got.'" He sucked hard on his cigarette, the Camel crackling hot. He blew a long stream of smoke at the windshield that filtered around the cab.

I cracked my window.

"Judge wasn't wrong," he continued, turning, smiling, showing me a mouth full of amazingly white teeth. "That's all I got." He looked straight ahead, mumbling, "That's all I've ever had."

Sonny's mouth was well oiled and running quite well. I quickly changed the subject, wanting to know more about his friendship with Hope and Buzz. "So you homesteaded your place at the same time as Hope and Buzz?"

"Yep, around fifty-eight."

I faced him and made the mistake of sounding like my father, like a prosecuting attorney. "About when Bit was born. Am I right?"

Sonny said, "You ask a lot of questions, Junior."

"Sorry," I said, sitting back.

Sonny turned the table on me and started asking the questions. "They teach you that in college?"

"What?"

"Ask a lot of questions?"

"Yeah, I suppose."

Silence

Sonny said, "Hopie told me you like to write. You gonna write a book about all this?"

"I could, I guess? Think anybody'd read it?"

"I know Hopie would. She says reading books teaches us about humanity. Gives us hope."

I said. "That's a pun."

He said, "What's that?"

"A play on words."

"What's that?"

I explained what a pun was and how he had used one.

He said, "You learn that in college."

I nodded.

He shook his head. "I'd never make it."

I confessed, "I almost didn't."

"I thought you was a smart kid. What happened?"

I shrugged. "Didn't make sense to me."

"Does it now?"

"Starting to."

He said, "Hopie told me that's why you come out here. You was unhappy with your life. Wanted to figure out what happened to that boy killed up at Hamilton's camp. He was a friend of yours?"

"That's right."

"You get it sorted out?"

"I think so."

Silence.

Sonny braked for the car ahead of us turning off for gas. Clutching, shifting, accelerating, he said, "You and Bit courting?"

That made me squirm. "No," I said.

"Whatcha doing then?"

"Dating."

"What's the difference?"

"I don't know."

"You fixed on marrying her?"

What Sonny said was like pointing a double barrel shotgun at my chest as if he was a father wanting answers – answers I had not thought about; did not want to think about. I had a panic attack worrying about what if Bit was pregnant right now and I had to marry her. Don't get me wrong, I loved Bit and she loved me, but not in that way – for me at least. Bit and I had never talked about that. We were just kids having fun – playmates not life mates. Would Bit have an abortion? Wow. Again, we never talked about that. I didn't know. I wasn't sure. I had no fucking idea. Clete told me out here they play for keeps, meaning if you're using live ammunition and hit the bullseye, you get married, no questions asked, no matter how young. I went mum and must have turned white as a sheet because Sonny slapped me on the thigh. "Lighten up, Junior, I ain't her daddy. But she's my Itty Bit. Always will be. Don't forget it. With Buzzy gone, everyone's got to go through me now."

I struggled to mask my anxiety, sipping air and wetting my lips so my voice would sound normal. "So...so... you were telling me about Bit...."

Sonny continued his story. "Yep, Itty Bit come along and caused hell for me and Buzzy."

"How's that?' I asked.

"Hopie wouldn't let me and Buzzy go to town if Itty Bit wasn't down and asleep. Said we couldn't run off have our fun. Leave her with a screaming baby."

"Hope didn't like going to town?" I asked.

"Didn't much cotton to drinking," Sonny said. "Didn't like to dance or fight neither. She'd rather hole up read a book."

Sonny paused, checking his side mirror as a passenger car pulled out to pass us.

"So me and Buzz had to team-rope that little rug rat every Friday and Saturday night. It was hell in the summer when the sun wouldn't go down and neither would she. Me and Buzz had to take turns holding her in our arms, walking her around the cabin. Or outside with her on our shoulder. Or lying in the crook of Buzzy's arm riding Cody. Beautiful little two-year-old roan. Itty Bit loved the horses, especially Cody. That was her first word." Here Sonny formed the word like a one-year-old girl would: "Co-dee. Co-dee."

Sonny laughed at himself as he drifted deeper into his story.

"Hopie nearly wet her pants watching us. We were desperate with thirst. Buzzy riding bareback in the corral with Itty Bit in his arms. Not even a bridle on Cody – goddamn that was a good horse. And me following behind, walking and strumming Buzzy's guitar. Singing a lullaby I'd made up just to get that little varmint to shut her eyes."

Sonny paused, palming the wispy hair on the top of his head, then gently massaged an indentation just above his ear with his crooked index finger, an indentation about the size of a quarter, camouflaged neatly by his hair. This is where Sonny got kicked in the head by a bronc; just before Buzz jumped in the ring and dragged Sonny away before the horse would have most likely stomped and killed him. It's hard to see at first but obvious once you know it's there. Sonny smoked the rest of his cigarette, rolled down his window and dropped it out, his voice now soft, almost humming: "Yep. Me strummin' and singin'...Bit in the crook of Buzzy's arm... looking up at him with her big beautiful brown eyes...fightin' to stay awake...riding round and round in the corral cooing, 'Co-dee, Co-dee'...Hopie laughing hard enough to pee."

Sonny's eyes turned rheumy. He went quiet and turned inward as if he wanted to be left alone. I looked away, counting telephone poles, minding my own business. After what seemed like an hour, Sonny said to me in a soft, sincere tone, as if he was confessing, just like he did in the hospital room before he smothered Buzz, "You know, Junior, I'm gonna kill Farnsworth. I ain't afraid to die neither. Either Farnsworth goes to hell or I go to heaven and get to be with Buzz again. That way I won't have no more bad dreams. Be able to sleep at night." He looked my way. "Know where I'm coming from?"

It's really strange talking with someone in a dream that you know is dead, and they know they're dead, and you're carrying on a conversation like it's a Sunday social. What I'm about to tell you is really weird, and I'd never told anybody about my dreams about Buzz for obvious reasons. One time I dreamt I followed Buzz riding Buddy into the Cowboy Bar with Blue perched on Buddy's rump, a grotesque grin on Blue's snout and his red tongue hanging out. The bar was packed, everyone rooting Buzz on as he rounded the room. Buddy stopped by the bandstand, lifted his tail and dropped a mound of road apples on the barroom floor. Buddy flubbered his rubbery lips at me, sounding like Mr. Ed, saying, *"Hank will ya clean up that shit,"* And there I was with an elephant shovel in my hands, trying to scoop up the manure, but only able to pick up one road apple at a time, running around the bar not knowing where to dump it, and the one road apple always rolling out of my shovel as everybody in the bar jeered at me with ugly distorted noses and mouths, and me trying to apologize but my words frozen, nothing coming out of my mouth. That dream was strange enough, but the most bizarre – and I've never told anyone this one either – was one time I dreamt Buzz and I were irrigating together and he told me to kill all these prairie dogs swimming around the flooded ground around our feet, which I tried to do but my feet were stuck in mud and my shovel felt like it weighed five hundred pounds and the prairie dogs were jetting around faster than guppies, and I was swinging in slow motion and Buzz was getting madder and madder telling me *Can't you do anything right; why don't you go back to college* as he whipped out his gigantic dick and started killing gophers with his enormous schlong, which he then aimed at me after killing all the prairie dogs, nailing me in the chest with a hot shot of urine at the exact same moment my brother Andy was – in real life – pouring water on me in my bed at home, telling me it was dinnertime – *Wake up* – at which time I bolted up and screamed simultaneously at Buzz and Andy *What the fuck.*

Believe me: Flying dreams are much more fun.

I repeated back to Sonny, now knowing we were in the same church, same pew, "I know where you're coming from."

Five miles later a souped-up Chevy pickup *varoomed* past us going close to eighty. Both our heads popped up. Sonny growled, "Sonofabitch Freddie Saunders."

*Freddie Saunders.*

I leaned forward and followed a black pickup with orange cab lights, twin tailpipes running up the side, and mud flaps with reflective outlines of sexy girls – Freddie Saunders was obviously a hotshot with a need for speed. I acted ignorant. "Who's he?"

Keeping one hand on the steering wheel, Sonny extended his crooked index finger over the dash. "His daddy has a cattle operation just yonder outside Bondurant. Freddie was working on an oil rig in the Gulf. Moved back here little while ago. Most likely couldn't handle the rig-work – or got shit-canned."

I stupidly stated the obvious. "He sure likes to drive fast."

Sonny groused, "Thinks he owns the road. Same as his old man."

Up ahead, the pickup weaved in and out, trying to pass a semi truck. Again, another stupid question: "Do you know his father?"

"Wish'd I didn't," Sonny said. "Buzzy and I knew Charlie Saunders back when we were riding saddle broncs on the circuit. Charlie thought he could rodeo and fight and drink like us, but he couldn't. His boy there," Sonny again pointed up the road toward Freddie's truck, "thought he could ride too, but he's a yella-belly chicken shit. Tries to hold himself out as a bronc rider, but he'd always find an excuse not to ride."

Sonny paused, paying attention to a slow-moving Winnebago up ahead that was turning off for gas. I paused, too, digesting what Sonny was telling me, connecting the dots with what Clete had told me about Freddie Saunders and Bit. Freddie was definitely a bad boy and Bit definitely had a bad-boy problem. Now I realized why Bit was so empathetic toward me about my backsliding problem with Janie Wallace – she had one, too.

Sonny continued, "Charlie Saunders was always jealous of Buzz. Had it in for him."

I said, "Why, I thought everybody liked Buzz?"

Sonny said, "For the most part, but there were a few who didn't favor Buzz, and Charlie tried to do something about it with a gun." I put the pieces together quickly. I recalled what Clete told me my first day at the Lazy T last summer, that Buzz had had guns pulled on him by jealous husbands, and Charlie Saunders must have been one of the them. I concluded, "Charlie must not have been a good shot."

Sonny snorted, "Charlie Saunders couldn't hit the broadside of a barn with a bass fiddle. Wasn't even man enough to duke it out with Buzz. He should have known that if you pull a gun you'd better use it. And use it quick before the other feller makes you eat it."

"What happened?" I asked.

"Buzzy took the gun away from Charlie, then slapped the shit out of him. Embarrassed him bad in front of the whole lot of us. Never was the same. Heard he took it out on his wife and kids. Took it out on me and Buzzy, too, always telling everybody around here what a great rancher he was and what a bunch of dirt famers we were. Then Bit started dating Freddie in high school – none of us liked that boy – but what could you do? Freddie went out of his way to be all sugar and nice to Buzz and Hopie and me, but we could see through that glass full of shit. He was bedding Bit to get back at Buzz for banging his mother and for all the shit he had to eat from his daddy."

"So why did Bit…" here my voice trailed off.

"Bit…Bit had a blind spot," Sonny said. "Freddie's a good looking boy with a line of bullshit as long as your arm."

I asked, "Did Bit know that Buzz fooled around with Freddie's mother?"

"Bit knew," he said in a sympathetic voice. "Bit knew. But you forget when your blood's running hot. All I know is that boy is a bad seed." Here Sonny warned me: "He's the jealous type, too. Be careful."

Freddie Saunders and his black truck had long disappeared around a bend.

Out of sight.

But not out of mind.

# Chapter 34

## DUBOIS * CLEMENTINE * THE FATES

We made the turnoff at the Jackson junction around ten
o'clock and headed east on Highway 26 toward Dubois. I
stayed quiet, not wanting to distract Sonny too much because
of the winding and hilly roads. We rolled into Dubois around
noon and headed to the A-Bar-A dude ranch about three miles
outside of town. We wound our way down a small, narrow
gravel road that passed by the stables and corrals and emptied
out at the base of a small box canyon with a large open field
surrounded by cabins, a lunch hall, the main lodge, and small
replica covered wagons where the wranglers and kitchen
staff slept. Bull Dunlap, the corral boss – built like a five-
foot-seven block of granite with a handlebar mustache and a
dirty-white felt ten-gallon hat – greeted us. It was obvious
he and Sonny had known each other since Creation and had
swapped horses and tall tales as well as bar tabs. Bull invited
us to stay for dinner which we did – Sonny entertaining a
long dinner table of about twenty dudes and their families
with his cowboy stories. When Sonny's sober and on stage,
he's downright funny and charming. All the kids at the table
(mostly eight to fourteen-year-olds) had their mouths open

catching flies listening to Sonny go on about wrestling a grizzly bear to the ground after the bear yanked him off his horse because he would not get out of the bear's path. Sonny said he and the bear became good friends and, to this day, he goes up to the mountains and visits the bear, even stays overnight. A little girl in a pigtails and freckles sitting next to him asked what was the bear's name. Sonny tilted his hat back and thought about that while the little girl looked up at him, waiting. He said, "Sweetheart, her name is Clementine and her eyes are as brown as yours, and one day I plan on marrying her." This surprised all of us because, I think, we were expecting it to be a boy bear. The children thought the story funny and cute, especially the girls, while the adults had to rethink it.

After lunch, we headed home with me in the driver's seat gently guiding the truck through the gears, getting used to the clutch. Sonny began rummaging around under his seat, unwrapping two beers. "We done good, Junior." He waved a small brick of tens and twenties at me. "The bar's now open."

He offered me a cold one.

Sonny had been too good for too long, He needed to cut loose. I understood now why Eleanor had me come along as his chauffeur home, but I was uncomfortable drinking and driving, especially pulling a trailer in the mountains. I didn't want to be a downer and not join in on his celebration, so I took the cold can of Coors and put it between my legs and nursed it like it had to last the four hours back to the ranch. I figured with Sonny in a partying mood, why not spice it up and play some music to shorten the long ride home. I pulled a cassette of country music out of my jean jacket that Bones had made for me before I left for Wyoming. Picking up speed leaving Dubois, I made a motion to slide the tape into the player on the dash, asking Sonny if it was okay.

Sonny'd already crushed his first beer and was well into his second. "Knock yourself out," he said, lighting up a smoke, then exhaling, "Just none of that hippy music, Junior."

I'd not listened to the tape so I had no clue as to what Bones had mixed up for me. I pushed the tape in and turned the volume low in case he had decided to somehow classify Led Zeppelin and ZZ Top as Country. When I heard "Gentle On My Mind," I turned it up. Sonny – tapping his fingers on the dash – leaned over and turned it up some more. "I didn't know you liked Glen Campbell, Junior."

"Sure," I said, checking my mirrors, tucking my hair behind my ears. "'Gentle on my Mind,' 'Wichita Lineman,' 'By the Time I Get to Phoenix.'"

"Well, shit, College boy, you surprise me." Sonny held up his beer can to toast me. I clinked cans then took a sip. Truth be told, I'd surprised myself – I can't believe I recalled those three songs. I was now feeling cocky enough to joke with him. I said,

"Sonny?"

"Yeah, Junior?"

"Can I ask you something?"

"What's that?"

"Did Clemetine have a big can?"

Sonny laughed. "She did have a big can. She could also cook, screw and sew, and didn't mind if I hung out with other bears." He looked out the window. "I make up stories all the time for kids. Buzz used to take me up to Hamilton's camp with him so I'd tell those little varmints funny bedtime stories. You ever heard 'Moose Turd Pie'?"

I shook my head *No*.

Sonny said he'd tell me someday. He downed his second beer and opened his third. He flipped through his brick of cash. I pulled down my visor because of the sun and checked my mirrors again, pretending to be busy. Sonny placed the cash in the manila folder between us. He groaned, "I gotta piss like a racehorse. Pull over there."

Up ahead was a wide shoulder with sloping woods on both sides of the road. I eased the truck and trailer over and stopped. Sonny kicked the door open with a grunt; a beer can clanged onto the pavement and rolled away. He unbuttoned and leaned against the bed of the truck, tilting his hat back, letting out a long moan and a longer pee. A car zoomed by with a toot of the horn. Sonny doffed his hat. As he was repacking his jeans he stopped, staring up into the pines. He said quickly, quietly, "Junior...Junior..."

I replied softly, "Yeah, Sonny?"

He motioned with his hand, his voice now steady: "Hand me that rifle. Real slow."

I reached behind me for the Remington on the gun rack. I lifted it off and carefully handed it to him as he kept his eye on something up in the pines. He quickly thumbed bullets into the rifle, eased back the bolt, seating a round, then aimed. He took his eye off the target – blinked – then refocused.

I stayed still as stone.

BANG.

He threw back the bolt and fired again.

BANG.

"*Goddamnit,*" he said, lowering the gun.

"You missed?"

"No," he said, squinting. "I think I got him."

I didn't know what "him" was and I couldn't see because the trees and brush were thick. I got out and went around to where Sonny was standing. He ejected the shell and thumbed on the safety. "Goddamnit, I think I got him. That's meat in the pot. Take me through the winter. Come on, Junior."

I followed him up into the trees. About thirty yards in I saw "him" – a big buck mule deer. Sonny handed me the rifle, said to put it back in the truck and open up the trailer – we had another passenger.

I did as I was told.

When I trekked back up the hill, Sonny was opening his jackknife. I watched him gut and bleed out the mule deer. He wiped the blood from his hands on his pants saying, "Get a good hold, we're dragging him to the trailer." I did – get a good hold – and we pulled the mule deer down by his antlers through the trees, down the hill and into the trailer. We were breathing hard and sweating when Sonny closed and latched up the back gate. He walked to the passenger side of the truck saying, "Lucky we had this trailer, otherwise it would have been tricky explaining to them Fish and Game snots how a gutted mule deer jumped in the back of a pickup truck." He dug around the floor of the truck and pulled out two beers from the second six-pack, which was warm. He cracked open and handed me one. "Good job, Junior."

I took a sip. "It's warm."

Opening and draining half of his, Sonny said, "Yeah, but it's wet. Let's get a move on."

I told him to hold on a minute so I could take a leak (and pour out most of my beer).

Back on the road I asked if he'd ever bagged a mule deer like this before, meaning illegally without a permit. Sonny said he had a bunch of times. I asked had he'd ever been caught. He said, "Twice. Buzz was with me both times. First time Buzz told the cop that it was road kill. Cop said, 'What about the bullet hole in his chest?' Buzz said that was to make sure the mule deer stayed dead. Another time... same cop... I said, 'What mule deer, officer? Oh my God, Buzz, what the hell! Did you know there was a mule deer in the bed of the truck?' Buzz said, 'No, Sonny, but by God thank you officer for telling us. And Sonny, whattaya say we dress this critter out when we get to the ranch and give this nice officer twenty-five pounds of mule deer steak and ten pounds of jerky. We wouldn't want that to go to waste.'"

Sonny finished his beer and popped another. He was feeling good, lubricated; and had a fresh wad of money in his pocket and a freezer-full for the winter. The mule deer tale led to a stream of other stories about roundups, rodeos, cow camps, branding, bar fights and mountain men; stories I was glued to as if I was a twelve-year-old back at the dude ranch in Dubois, or around the fire at Hamilton's camp, ears pricked, eyes wide, my jaw an inch off the ground. When we made the Jackson junction and were on the home stretch, Sonny yawned, said, "You liked Buzzy, didn't ya?"

Right then and there I could have cut open my veins and bled Buzzy Stifel all over Sonny. But he didn't want me turning sappy, so I just said, "Yeah," as coolly as I could, turning my head to catch his eye, adding, "*A lot.*"

Sonny caught my drift. He looked out his window. "Funny, you coming out here last year and all that happening. I bet you wasn't expecting that when you signed on." He paused and looked over at me. I could see Sonny was tired from the long day, the beer, the travel, the sun. He leaned his head back and tilted his hat over his eyes. "That's the way it goes sometimes. Life don't lie…Life don't lie."

Soon I heard soft snoring.

I mulled that over for the rest of the ride – *That's the way it goes sometimes. Life don't lie…Life don't lie* – and what Sonny had barked at me the summer before when I couldn't pull the trigger to kill his injured horse: *Don't think on it too much. That'll get you in trouble out here.* That got me to thinking about the Greek Mythology paper I'd written on the Fates. In a nutshell, I had argued that we cannot control our destiny. Our lives are preordained no matter what we do, because if we try to change our fate, then that is our fate. That as humans beings we are trapped and must accept our destiny because it is inalterable, no matter what we do. Consequently, we can't get trapped into worrying about it. We just have to do it. That's our fate. At least that's what I argued for almost ten pages.

Recall, however, I got a C+.

# Chapter 35

## DINNER WITH DOROTHY AT THE DEW DROP INN

In the first week of July, on a Saturday night just before haying was to begin, Bit said she had to meet some high school girlfriends in town and would likely spend the night. Coincidently, Hope was going over to Eleanor's for dinner and Clete was headed to Jackson to hear a band play at the Silver Dollar Saloon. That left me and Dorothy at the ranch for supper. Sizing up the situation, Dorothy said to me, "Hank, wouldn't it be smarter if we went to the Dew Drop Inn for dinner and I paid, rather than staying at the Lazy T and both of us suffering through my cooking."

I said that sounded fine to me, not wanting to decline Dorothy's invitation. That would have been rude even though I felt awkward about going out to dinner with her alone. Let me explain: For the month that I'd been at the Lazy T, Dorothy had been super nice to me (too nice according to Bit), sharing stories with me about growing up in the South and her being a debutante and all. From what I pieced together, Dorothy was born into a well-to-do Savannah family on the downslope of prosperity, her upbringing, finishing school, and pretty looks her only dowry. I deduced (and Bit agreed) that was why Dorothy was always flirting and acting coquettish – she was trying to impress me and others with her upbringing because she was insecure about her reduced circumstances. Hope brushed off Dorothy's behavior – I think because she found if harmless – but it bugged Bit.

One evening on our walk through the hayfields, Bit had her knickers in a knot because Dorothy had been going on and on at supper about her past, directing much of the conversation toward me. Just before the haystack, Bit punched me in the arm, imitating Dorothy's southern guile, "'Oh Hank, don't you love dressing up in a tuxedo and go to a coming-out party. You must look so handsome. And the parties are so gay." Bit stopped me just as we turned the corner of the haystack. We'd been holding hands. She spun in front of me, pointing a finger. "All she does is butter you up like a Thanksgiving turkey. She's up to something, I know it."

Bit was not wrong. Dorothy was up to something. I'd felt it the minute I'd stepped out of the truck the first day, when she ran me over with her Mrs. Robinson eyes. At the moment it was not in my best interest to get into a lot of speculation and discussion behind the hay stack about Dorothy's intentions, because that's a waste of good hay; so I massaged the situation with humor, putting my hands up under Bit's fleece and t shirt, lifting it over her head, saying, "I thought for sure another mare in the corral would heat you up."

Bit undid her bra and shook out her hair. She placed my hands on her breasts. She said "Another mare, yes. But not the old gray mare. That just pisses me off." She gave me a firm kiss, which was the pistol shot for let the games begin. She bulldogged me to the ground, both of us kissing and laughing. After our brief rodeo, tucking the blanket way back between two hay bales, we dusted each other off and picked hay out of our hair and off our backsides. We walked slowly back to the house, the sun down and the stars peeking out. I put my arm around her. With Dorothy living at the house and now part of the everyday conversation, I felt comfortable enough to ask her a burning question: How did she deal with her father's infidelity and carrying on with Dorothy.

Bit explained to me in a clinical way that her dad was just that way; something he was born with and couldn't help, as if he could naturally sing or do long division in his head. Bit admitted it was hard seeing them in town together and how it hurt her mother. It was confusing, but what could she do – she loved Buzz and Buzz loved her. She talked to Sonny about it, and he told her that Buzz loved Hope more than anything; that the other women were romps in the hay and had no hold on him; that Buzz would never leave her mother, and that if he did, Sonny promised he'd marry Hope in a New York minute.

Bit kicked at a rock on the ground.

She continued, saying she'd rather have Buzz as a father than some faithful deadbeat who treats his family like shit. She asked me, "Any of your friends have a dad like Buzz."

I told her about Bones's mother and father and his screwed up family life. How Bones said it was embarrassing and how he resented them for it.

Bit said, "That sounds a lot worse than what I got. What about your parents, Hank? Are they still faithful to each other?"

I kicked at the dirt. "As far as I know," I said. "They seem happy and in love. Andy and I talk about it, and he told me that he's never seen or heard anything to suggest they weren't. If somebody tried to break up my parents' marriage, I'd want to hurt that person."

Bit stopped me with an arm across my midsection just as we passed underneath the Lazy T sign. Up ahead, through the bay window, I could see Hope reading and Dorothy watching TV. Bit turned to me. She said if Dorothy had ever tried to break up her parents' marriage, she'd have broken her neck. I didn't doubt her.

I kiddingly asked would she do the same if I Dorothy tried to break us up.

Bit said she'd break my neck.

Again, I didn't doubt her.

Then I asked her a question in an academic tone that pertained to both of us: "Is backsliding when not married infidelity?"

She gave my ass a slap, saying, "It is when you're dealing with me," then reached for my hand.

Is backsliding when not married infidelity? – that's what I was mulling over as I watched Bit's car zoom away down Forty Rod Road toward town. I headed to the house for a quick shower and shave so Dorothy had time to get dolled up (Dorothy could keep a mirror busy, while Bit and Hope were content dragging a brush through their hair and washing their faces). I dressed in clean clothes, combed my hair, deciding not to wear a hat. Killing time waiting for Dorothy on the porch outside the house, I filled Bear's water dish and emptied food scraps into the three-legged cat's bowl. I noticed a growling whirlwind of dust moving my way from 191. When I saw it was a truck...when I saw it was a big black truck... when I saw it was a big black truck flying by with orange cab lights, twin exhaust pipes running up the sides and sexy reflective girls on the mud flaps...I leaned against the porch post, crossing my arms, crossing my legs, speculating: Freddie Saunders and Bit were headed in the same direction, and both liked to drive fast and use all of the road. That got me asking myself a question, and who was walking out the cabin door saying, "Who in tarnation was that ripping up the road," was just the person to help me answer it.

I uncrossed my arms and legs. I lied: "I'm not sure."

Dorothy sashayed down the porch. I was still leaning up against the post following Freddie Saunders's cyclone of dust to town. Sewing her arm through mine, she purred, "What a beautiful evening, Hank. My you look sharp. Let's take my car. You drive."

"Yes ma'am, "I said as she gently tugged on my arm, guiding me to her green Bonneville. I opened and held the door for her. As she slid in she said, "That's so polite of you, Hank. Thank you." Dorothy Farnsworth's time in front of the mirror was well spent. She was smartly dressed in jeans, a blue and white country shirt with aquamarine snaps, simple black cowboy boots, and a red bandana tied around her neck – she had cleaned up nicely and was prepared for our dinner together.

The Dew Drop Inn is twenty-five miles north of the ranch on 352 and abuts the foothills of the Wind Rivers. It is a large, rectangular roadside restaurant that has a pool table, juke box and bandstand. Elk-antlered chandeliers hung from large round ceiling logs. A large moose poked his head out of one end-wall. Fury animal hides and trout with lures in their mouths decorated the side walls. Out back were small cabins where hunters, fishermen, and families would stay overnight. The Dew Drop Inn, unlike the rowdy Cowboy Bar in Pinedale, catered to a mostly older crowd and vacationers with children. We slid into a booth by the window facing the road as Dorothy waved at two old cowpokes named Shorty and Slim – one was short and the other slim, no joke – and they waved back. They were nattily dressed and shooting a game of eight ball as if every shot was life or death. The place was only a third full and nobody was dancing to Patsy Cline's "Walking after Midnight."

A waitress came over to take our order.

She handed out menus. "Dorothy Farnsworth, it's been a month of Sundays."

Dorothy put on her cat-eye glasses and looked up at a waitress who could have been Flo on the TV show "Alice." "Ruby, it's been longer. What keeps you so young?"

Ruby smacked her gum. "Straight whiskey," she said

with hands on her hips, "and straight shootin' men."

Dorothy glanced down. "Is that on the menu?"

"The whiskey is," Ruby said tilting her head toward me. "The other ain't, but looks like you're doing okay."

Dorothy winked at me. "This is Hank Chandler. He's helping out Hope at the Lazy T."

I stuck out my hand and stood the best I could, saying *Good to meet you.*

Ruby gave me a once-over, cracking her gum at my curling hair and preppy looks. She said, "What'll you have, Mr. Hank Chandler helping- out-Hope-at-the-Lazy T."

I turned my palm up to Dorothy in a gesture of *ladies first.*

Dorothy said, "It's Saturday night, Ruby, how about a Stinger?"

Ruby held her hands up in defense. "Whoa there, Dorothy. Ernie's okay with whiskey and water and scotch and soda. A Stinger could send him off the reservation. You gotta tell me what's in that concoction?"

Dorothy was stumped. Even though she was a bartender at the Cowboy, I knew she was over her head. I stepped in: "Ruby, tell Ernie it's two and a quarter ounces of brandy. Three quarters of an ounce of white crème de menthe. Shake and pour over cracked ice."

Ruby, writing furiously, repeated back the ingredients and instructions, adding, "And for you?"

"Coors, please."

"That I got cold." Ruby turned to go, gliding away in her red polyester waitress dress and white sneakers, running her pen into her hairdo, acknowledging who was coming through the door, giving them a friendly wave hello, telling them to sit anywhere.

Dorothy's face lit up. She said, "Hank, I'm duly impressed. How did you know how to make a Stinger?"

I explained that I bartended at the Faculty Club at

school, and that Stingers were not uncommon (I'd never nicknamed one before, but now a *Dorothy Farnsworth* came to mind). While we waited for our drinks, Dorothy and I talked about ranch stuff, how haying was going, how long I'd stay at the ranch, the new dog Bear, and how Hope was getting on without Buzz. Ruby returned with our order. We clinked glasses with me avoiding Dorothy's big eye. Her drink disappeared faster than if the glass had a hole in the bottom. Soon her hand was in the air motioning to Ruby across the room she was ready for round two.

I didn't like where this train wreck was headed.

Well into her second Stinger, Dorothy's head popped up for air. She asked, "How are you and Bit getting along?"

I sat back, slightly surprised. I said fine.

She said, "You know where she is tonight?"

"In town."

"You know who with?"

"Her girlfriends," I replied. "Polly Hamilton and Jen someone."

Dorothy ran her finger around the rim of her glass, then licked it. "You know about Freddie Saunders?"

I blinked twice saying nothing.

She continued, "Buzz hated that boy. Hope, too."

Again, I said nothing, looking at Dorothy with a slightly bored expression like tell me something new.

"You know what Buzz did to Freddie's father, Charlie?"

"Sonny told me."

Dorothy said, "Bit's a fool to be around Freddie. He's trouble."

"Then why'd she date a guy like that?" I asked.

"Because she's stupid." Dorothy laughed. "Just like me."

I wanted to say *How did you and Darryl meet?* but Ruby was now standing over us, asking, "What looks good tonight?"

Dorothy put on her glasses; studied her menu. "Hmmm," she said running her finger down the menu, pointing, "I'll have the strip steak rare with a baked potato and a side salad with the house dressing." She took off her glasses and put them in a soft red case.

I didn't even look at my choices. "Same," I said handing over the menu, wanting to get back to the conversation.

"Another round?" Ruby said.

Who was I to stop forward progress? I twirled my finger signaling *Bring it on*. When Ruby walked away, I asked, "How did you meet Darryl?"

"You really want to know?"

I sat back, nodded my head yes, curious as to what would come out of her mouth after two Stingers.

Dorothy sighed. "I'm a cliché, Hank. I was the head cheerleader. He was the handsome captain of the football team. I got pregnant. We got hitched. I married down. I kept house while he kept losing jobs, sinking to being a lawman in Savannah. Then we came here."

"Why Pinedale?"

Dorothy slurred, "Why? Because he got a job." She looked up at the ceiling, reciting: "Why? To start new. Why? To save our marriage. Why? Flee embarrassment. Escape my family. Forget I made a mistake. Stop the fighting and abuse. None of it worked." She looked at me, "How much do you *really* know about Darryl Farnsworth?"

I admitted, "Not much."

She gave me a dark stare and said, "Keep it that way," as if it was a warning and she wasn't fooling.

I caught her drift; I changed the subject: "How did you meet Hope?"

Dorothy picked up her drink and wiped off the table underneath it like a good bartender would do. "We met at the Mountain Man museum in town where she was a docent. I was looking for something to do so I volunteered with her. We both liked books and movies and got along together. She became my new best friend and I became hers. Then we broke up."

"Because of Buzz."

She nodded.

"What happened?"

"I couldn't stay away from him."

"What did Hope — "

" — What could she do? This had been going on a long time. Buzz had a reputation with the ladies...a well-deserved reputation. I was lonely. Darryl was working all the time, and when he wasn't, he was either drunk or abusing me about bills. I took the job at the Cowboy Bar so I could get out of the house. Make some of my own money. That's where I met Buzz. When he died...when he was killed...I told Hope I was sorry for what I did. I still wanted to be her friend. That's why I wanted to move in with her. Help her out and drive Darryl crazy at the same time."

I didn't say anything.

Dorothy sat back, breathed in then placed both her hands flat on the table. She looked out the window at a car's headlights pulling in, acting as if she had a mouthful of words and needed to spit them out. "Hank, I don't belong here. Neither do you. I know you're having your fun being a ranch hand. Being a cowboy. But that won't last. Neither will you and Bit. It won't work and you know it."

You think I would have been stung by what she said (that's a pun). But Dorothy was not wrong. I loved Bit and what I was doing, but it was temporary. I wasn't stupid. Bit had her life; I had mine. Dorothy was not wrong.

She continued, "You and Bit are in love right now. But it won't last."

"Why not?"

"They won't let you."

"Who won't?"

"Freddie Saunders. Or any of those boys in town or down at Laramie. They're jealous about their women. Bit's no exception. She's a beautiful and popular girl around town.

They're clannish and protective —"

"— Like the South?"

Dorothy let go a wicked smile. "They'd like nothing better than to stomp your butt in the parking lot of the Cowboy."

"You know that for a fact?"

She bobbed her head *Yes*. "That's what I heard."

Silence.

I didn't doubt Dorothy. Being a bartender in a small town meant she knew what was brewing on the other side of the taps. I stayed quiet, sensing she was getting to the point of the conversation (and being a little melodramatic).

"There's only heartache ahead, Hank. Bit's in town tonight with Freddie Saunders. I saw his truck go by. So did you."

We stared each other down; George Jones's "He Stopped Loving Her Today" the only words between us. Dorothy reached across the table and caressed the top of my hand. "I know it's upsetting Hank." When I looked down she gave my hand a light squeeze that lasted longer than I was comfortable with. "I know what you're going through," she said, slowly taking away her hand, stumbling with her words, "I can help."

I said, "So what do you recommend I do about Freddie Saunders?"

She shook her head. "Don't wrestle with a pig, Hank. You get dirty. Besides, the pig likes it."

I downed that pearl with swig of Coors. She was right. She toed me under the table with the tip of her boot. "Remember when we first met. I snuck up and surprised you behind the bar."

I pulled my boot away from hers. "I was looking for a pen."

"And look what you found."

I didn't know how to respond.

She said, "You seemed mighty confused."

I said, "I didn't know where to find a pen."

"No, I mean about seeing me...and Buzz...together."

"I was confused."

"What did you think?"

"To mind my own business."

"What did you think now?"

This was more than weird – Dorothy holding my hand and toeing me under the table and asking *What do you think now?* I knew what she was fishing for. I had to pick my words carefully. Had I thought about Dorothy Farnsworth in the biblical sense? Damn straight I had. She was the older, experienced woman I'd fantasized about since I was old enough to fantasize (think Letters to *Penthouse*).

I picked at the label on my Coors bottle. I looked her in the eye and gave an honest reply. I shouldn't have, but I did. I wanted her to feel good about herself. I said, "I had a crush on you."

Dorothy put her napkin on the table and inched out of the booth. "Let's have a dance before dinner." She held out her hand. I slid out of the booth feeling a lot older than I was as many eyes followed Dorothy leading me by the hand to the empty dance floor. Patsy Cline's "I Fall to Pieces," had just cued up. She turned with flair. My dancing school manners kicked in. I put right my hand on her waist, my left up high. Her left hand rested on my shoulder brushing my neck and hair. As we gracefully swung around, she said, "I love your hair, Hank. It's cute long."

I didn't have a comeback except *thank you*. No way I was saying something stupid like your hair is really beautiful, even though I know women like to be complimented on their hair. I could feel Dorothy's fingernails on my neck tickling the ends of my hair. I could smell her perfume and was eyewitness to quite a nice view of her gold locket swinging pendulously. I led, but Dorothy was doing all the dancing, her shapely behind broadcasting plenty by the looks we were getting, especially Shorty and Slim who had stopped their game and were resting on their pool cues, watching us. The song was soon over. When we walked side by side off the floor, most eyes were still on us as we made our way back to our booth and dinner, which Ruby had brought out. We cut at our steaks and mashed our food around, not talking much; Dorothy's fourth Stinger brimming, untouched. She excused herself to go to the ladies room leaving me to contemplate wrestling a pig. She came back. "Hank, I think it's time."

I said, "Yes, ma'am," relieved she was calling it a night, three Stingers and we're out. I asked Ruby for the check and paid. (My parents had strongly impressed upon me a gentleman always pays, which I impressed upon Dorothy, who relented with a "That's so sweet of you, Hank," while giving my bicep a squeeze.) We walked out into a cool, clear night, the mountain air refreshing. Dorothy stopped to find the car key. "Here," she said pressing it into my palm, weaving slightly.

Funny, I thought, it didn't feel like the Bonneville key. I opened my hand and looked down – looked up – in my hand the key to Cabin #3 at the Dew Drop Inn.

# Chapter 36

## LETTERS FROM HOME * HAIRCUT * GUNDERSON'S MEADOW

The next day, Sunday, Clete and I walked to the house from the fields for dinner after mowing hay. We'd seen Bit's El Camino coming down the road kicking up a cloud of dust. She tooted her horn, which meant get to the house for dinner and help bring in the groceries. Clete and I picked up on a conversation we'd had that morning about how long Dorothy would stay at the Lazy T. Clete flushed a wad of spent Red Man from his check with two fingers, flinging the brown mess in the high grass. He wiped his hand on his jeans. He said, "Most likely until Hope don't want her no more or Dorothy moves on."

"GODDAMNSONOFABITCH," I screamed, slapping the back of my neck with a cupped hand to catch whatever bit me. I looked at my balled up fist and slowly opened it, inside a horse fly. Clete said *Give it here.* I carefully transferred the fly into his hand. He pinched the large green-eyed bug between his thumb and forefinger, then plucked off its wings, throwing the fly to the wind, telling him, "Now walk home, you cocksucker."

I rubbed the bite on my neck asking Clete why doesn't Dorothy talk about her son Pete.

Clete wiped his hands on his pants. He said, "I think Dorothy's disappointed in him."

"Why's that?" I asked.

He said, "He's not much to talk about. You seen that. Pete's just one of those boys that don't fit in and's easy to hate. Gets it from his old man. Thinks he knows it all and bullies you if you don't believe him. Likes to hide behind that uniform of his. Thinks he's funny when he's fooling with you, but he ain't. He just don't get it. Best not bring him up around her."

I said, "I won't say anything."

Clete gave me a tap on the shoulder.

I looked up at the sky and over at the Wind River Mountains. The day was hot, no breeze; big fluffy clouds hung still against a blue backdrop. We kicked our boots through the dust and gravel on Forty Rod Road, passing underneath the Lazy T sign. A scab on my index finger from a cut had opened up and was now bleeding. I rubbed my bloody finger on my jeans, adding to the canvas of dirt and grease and grime. Normally washing our clothes meant Clete and I would have to go to town in our spare time and sit at the stinky, hot Laundromat. No longer. Because of Bit, our work clothes found their way into the washing machine located in the bathroom in the house – one of those coin operated jobs that Buzz bought for nothing and Hope fixed and rewired so you didn't have to put in quarters. The best part was Bit would line-dry our jeans and work shirts outside by the corral, so when you put them on they were cardboard stiff and smelling like whatever was in the wind that day.

In the yard, we hoisted the groceries out of Bit's El Camino, lugged them into the house and put them on the counter. Inside one sack was a mess of mail I was dying to rifle through to see if I had any letters from Boyle, Farr,

Bones or Hodges – I'd mailed them corny Western postcards when I first arrived so they'd write back and tell me what they were up to. Clete and I retreated to the couch by the bay window leaving Dorothy helping Hope prepare dinner while Bit unpacked the groceries. Once, I tried to catch Bit's eye, but she pretended to be busier than she really was. When she was folding up the groceries sacks she shot me a look that told me I was in big trouble. What the hell, I thought, what flew up her nose? Wasn't I the one who should be in a snit about her going to town and meeting up with Freddie Saunders?

We sat down to eat. When we finished and were kicking back for a smoke, Bit – who was sitting across from me, not next to me, and had barely uttered a syllable all meal – stood and went rummaging through the sack for the mail. She stomped back with five letters in her hand and a note of sarcasm in her voice: *"Hank, you're a mighty popular boy."*

I reached across the table for the letters.

She said, "Not so fast," looking around the table to draw attention.

I faked laughed, motioning with my hand *Come on, give me my mail.*

She ignored me, saying, "This one comes all the way from New York City. I bet that would be your friend Freddy Farr."

She handed it over.

I put it on the table, acknowledging that she was correct, waving my hand for the rest.

Nothing doing.

"This letter," she said, "comes from Connecticut. I bet I know who that is from."

I played innocent. "Christopher Boyle, perhaps?"

She smacked the letter in my hand. "That would be my guess, too. And this one is from Lake Forest, Illinois." She held the letter for me to see the author's name of the pressed-down printing of a number two pencil.

"That would be Bones," I said reaching over.

"Yes," she said. "*Bones* is all that is on the return address."

I placed the letter on my stack.

Bit continued, "This one is also from Lake Forest—"

"—Scott Hodges," I said reaching across and snatching it.

"This one," Bit said holding up the last letter, "smells funny." She tilted her head and gave me a look like a dog will when you make a squeaky sound with a play toy.

"Funny how," I asked, imitating her curious dog look.

"It's fishy," she said. "No... no...not fishy, it smells more like that knock-out punch you had at your party." She handed it over. She dared me. "Why don't you open it, Hank, and read what she has to say." Bit smiled that hard smile girls will give you when they have you cornered and want you to try and get away. But I wasn't running. This was my doing. I'd written Janie Wallace hoping she'd write me back. Why? Simple. To get even with Bit for Freddie Saunders. I tore open the envelope and unfolded a sheet of white notebook paper, both sides filled with small print. Hope, Dorothy and Clete pulled their chairs in. I patted down my pockets like an absentminded uncle, explaining that I didn't have my reading glasses so they would have to excuse me if I read a little slowly - this gave me time to make up what I was about to say.

*Dear Hank,*

*How are you? I am fine. How is your summer going in Wyoming? I'm having fun in Perrysberg, even if it is without you. If you get tired of riding horses in Wyoming, why don't you come to Ohio for a ride. Say hello to Clete and Hope and Dorothy and Sonny, and tell Bit no hard feelings for slugging me. That punch packed a punch. If you catch my drift. See you back at school.*

*XO*

*Janie*

I said to the table, "Well, that was very nice of Janie to write me, don't you think."

The table stayed out of it.

"That's not what it says," said Bit, waving her hand in a *Give it here, I don't believe you,* motion. "There's a lot more writing on the back you haven't read. Let me read that."

I turned the letter over, appearing dumbfounded. "Oh my God, you're right." I snapped the paper in my hands. I held it up to the light. I cleared my throat. "P.S... I forgot, tell Bit to say hello to Freddie Saunders for me. I know what great friends they are even though he bucked her off and she wants to ride him again." Finished, I theatrically folded and slid the letter back in the envelope, taking my time. I looked up to see Clete puckering, Dorothy smirking, Hope grimacing, and Bit stalking out the open door into the yard toward the barn.

I didn't want to be a jerk; I was just being defensive... and stupid. As I was soon to find out, I fucked up again and it would cost me.

I trailed Bit out to the barn, adjusting my eyes to the dim light as I entered. She was in the way back beyond Blaze's stall. She was moving around with her head down. I approached slowly, not because of the light or because I was nervous. I approached cautiously because Bit had a large pitchfork in her hands – she was mucking out a stall. I passed by Buddy who had his head out and was flubbering his lips, wondering what was going on. I gave his neck a gentle pat thinking this was my mess and I had to straighten it out pronto. I remembered what Hope had said to Bit about *nothing wrong with being honest.* I made that my shield as I walked slowly toward her as she came out of the stall with a pitchfork full of soiled straw. I said, "Bit, I'm sorry. I only wrote Janie because I found out about Freddie Saunders when I first got out here and I was trying to make you jealous. I figured he was the guy who bucked you off and you wanted back on. Then, I saw his truck fly by last night headed to town and—"

" —and what Hank," she said, pitching the hay on a manure pile.

"I thought the worst."

"Which is?"

"You were fooling around with him."

Bit gritted her teeth. "I went to town to see my girlfriends, Hank. Not to see Freddie Saunders."

"But I saw —"

" —Freddie Saunders is no concern of yours. He's an old boyfriend...*that's all.*"

I felt something weird on my face – I'd walked through a cobweb that was hanging from a dim, dusty light bulb above me. Waving my hand around, brushing off my cheek, I said, "Did you... see him?"

Bit huffed, "Hank, he's hard to miss in Pinedale, Wyoming, at the Cowboy Bar on a Friday night, and he's looking for me. I was there with Polly and Jen when he came in. I knew he'd come to town. I told him *No* I didn't want to dance or be with him and that got him mad. I had to tell him out back in the parking lot about you, and that he and I were over. Then he stormed away and went down to the Corral Bar and most likely got drunk. That's all that happened."

I said again, "I'm sorry," feeling kind of low, wanting to hold her in my arms and make up, but Bit still had a steel case look in her eyes and a pitchfork in her hands. I had work to do.

She said, "You *should* be sorry...writing old girlfriends... were you just trying to piss me off?"

Again, I went with honesty. I said, "I was worried. I was jealous. I did a stupid thing. I'm sorry."

She jammed the pitchfork in the ground. "Did you run back to Janie Wallace after I left you in October?"

"No."

"You promise?"

"I promise."

"Well you're acting like you're still in love with her."

I didn't know what to say.

Bit said, "I'm thinking she's right about you."

That stung.

Bit was about ten feet from me, her gloved hands wrapped around the top of the pitchfork, gathering herself. Blaze had poked her head out to see what all the commotion was about. I picked out a lump of sugar from an open box of sugar cubes on a milking stool and held it out to Blaze with an open palm. Her rubbery black lips nibbled it up. I ran my finger down the white strip on her nose. I had to get out of this fix. I had an idea. I said, stroking Blaze's neck, "Let's go for a ride."

"Right now," Bit said.

"Right now," I said. "Your mom will let us take the afternoon off."

Bit stripped off her gloves, putting the pitchfork to the side (thank God). "Where do you want to go?"

"Your call," I said pinching another lump of sugar from the box, walking back and palming it to Buddy.

Bit hesitated. She stomped her foot. "No, I'm not going."

"Why not?" I asked.

"I'm still mad at you. I could scalp you."

I thought about that – scalping me. Bit was really pissed and for good reason. I'd questioned her love with my immature behavior. I'd be pissed too. I put on my thinking cap: What could I do or say to prove I was truly sorry?

Shazzam.

It was so simple.

I took off for the house with Bit saying *Where you going?*
Not looking around, I said, "Evening the score. Put the tack
in the truck then meet me in the yard. We're going for a ride."

I came out of the house with a sheet, a chair, and Hope's
razor; followed closely behind by Hope, Dorothy and Clete.
Bear and the three-legged cat joined in, circling the chair I'd
put in the middle of the yard.

I sat.

Hope tied the sheet around my neck.

I handed the razor to Bit saying *Have at it.*

Bit said, "Hank, you don't have to do this."

Hope laughed. "Yes he does, Bit. Now get to work."

Dorothy said, "But he has such beautiful hair."

I reassured myself, "It'll grow back."

Clete took off his hat and palmed his crew cut, giving me
a preview of coming attractions, saying, "It sure does."

Bit positioned herself behind me. She ran her hands
through my hair, tickling my neck. She whispered in my ear,
"This won't hurt a bit", as she turned on and held the buzzing
razor close to my ear. I didn't flinch nor close my eyes. I'd set
myself up for this and was going to take it like a man. I told
her, "A little off the top. Even up the sides. Leave it longer in
back. And trim the sideburns."

My haircut lasted a full five minutes with a lot of coaching
and kibitzing from the sidelines. Bit moved around me like a
novice sculpture, unsure, trying to even out and smooth over
her creation as more and more and more of my long, curly,
sandy locks slid down the front of my sheet. The expressions
Oooooooh and Oh nooooo on Hope and Clete and Dorothy's
faces were unmistakable. When it was over I didn't rush to a
mirror and scream out in horror. Rather, I rubbed the bristle
on top of my head, put on my hat, and said, "Ready to go for a
ride." (Great thing about Wyoming, there are few mirrors, no
reason to look into one, and everybody wears a hat. What did

I care what I looked like as long as Bit was looking back at me. Now, I figured, every time she'd eye my lopsided-crew-cut-scalping, she would bear witness to how much I loved her. Truth be told, getting shorn the way I did made me feel more like a genuine ranch hand than a wannabe preppy cowboy.)

I hooked up the trailer. Bit loaded Buddy and Blaze. I let down the tailgate and whistled for Bear. I asked where are we headed. Bit said to drive to the Dew Drop Inn and park behind the restaurant by the cabins; she had a special place to show me; that we were riding bareback up into the mountains to Gunderson's Meadow. The five of us pulled out of the Lazy T with the horses clomping around. Bear stood on his hind legs in the bed of the truck sticking his nose into the wind. Bit sat next to me on the bench seat, her hand resting lightly on top of my thigh. I wanted to put my arm around her, but thought better of it because I needed two hands on the wheel hauling a trailer, but we did hold hands as much as we could.

I parked the truck and trailer behind the Dew Drop Inn; Bit ran in and told them we were going for a short ride. I unloaded the horses and put on their bridles, looking over my shoulder, praying I did not run into Ruby. (By the way, NOTHING HAPPENED – are you kidding? No way I was going through Cabin door #3 with Dorothy Farnsworth.)

Holding the horses, I watched Bear nose around the grounds, marking her territory and lightening her load. Bit came out with two full water bottles, which I packed in my knapsack. We tied our jean jackets around our waists, then Bit gave me a leg up on Buddy because he's a big horse and getting on bareback is hard, especially if you're not used to it and the horse is moving around not being used to you. Bit grabbed Blaze's main with the reins in her left hand, swung, jumped, scissor-kicking her legs in one fluid motion onto the horse's back like you see Indians do in the movies, the horse not moving a muscle nor batting an eye.

She tied her hair in a knot and reset my Cubs hat. She smiled, said *Ready*.

I said *Lead on*.

We followed a narrow trail behind the cabins up into the woods that slowly gained elevation. The horses heated up quickly. Bear followed behind, shooting off into the woods whenever a fresh scent tickled her nose. As we climbed, I squeezed my thighs around Buddy's flanks and gripped his mane with one hand for support. I noticed his tail stopped swishing and went up. I smelled and heard road apples hitting the ground. Up ahead, Blaze had stopped to pee with Bit leaning forward to give the horse's kidneys a break. I followed closely behind Bit because it's erotic watching a girl ride a horse bareback. She was telling me how she and her friends would make this thirty minute ride to Gunderson's Meadow in the summer and hang out, maybe pack a lunch. Soon our horses were really sweating and our jeans were wet and sticky with horsehair plastered to our butts and inner thighs. Believe me, you never forget skinny-dipping nor riding bareback.

After a half hour of switchbacks, we came to a small clearing that overlooked a large meadow about a quarter mile long and half as wide with a small lake in the middle that fed a stream. We were at the top of a huge bowl looking down, about fifty feet above the floor of the meadow with tall pines and firs surrounding us. We dismounted on a grassy ledge and unbridled our horses so they were free to forage. Bright sunshine shone down on the meadow like we were in an opera box at the theatre overlooking a stage with a spectacular mountain view as the backdrop. Below was a herd of Angus and Herefords – too many to count – grazing, drinking, suckling, with cowbells clinking and a melodic mooing moving around the meadow. Time had no bearing in Gunderson's Meadow; description inadequate. Bit didn't say *Isn't this beautiful. Don't you just love it.* She let the vista speak for itself. I opened my eyes and shut my mouth. I breathed in pine and earth and grass and sunshine. I breathed out looking down on sunlight twinkling off the lake as if it was electrified. I found a level spot and sat with my back against a tree. Bit sat between my legs, my upper body her support as I lightly wrapped my arms around her. After ten minutes of no talking, she turned sideways, took off my Cubs hat, curled up and lay her head on my thigh using her jacket as a pillow. I lightly stroked her hair. Soon she was asleep and I was left to my thoughts.

Something happened then and there that doesn't happen to me that often. I had an epiphany. That's a fancy college word for a moment of clarity. It wasn't like the heavens parted and a chorus began to sing. More like my mind was free and clear. It was a bit paranormal, as if I was looking down on myself from above. I closed my eyes then open them as a gentle breeze wrapped around and through the conifers and pines. Bear's nose twitched; her ears perked; her eyes narrowed; her upper lip inched up showing teeth. She growled. I followed her quivering nose to a spot a couple hundred feet away at our same elevation. Hidden in the trees and high grass was a wolf sitting on his haunches scanning the meadow. He caught our scent. He looked our way. His head was beautiful and calm; his nose long and dark; his eyes yellowish green with jet-black pupils – still and calculating. I knew what he was doing. He was patiently waiting for a stray he could cull from the herd. Bear's hackles went up readying to bark. I calmed her down with a pat, whispering *It's all right. Let him be.* Bit fidgeted between my legs, pushing her butt flush to my thigh. When I looked around, the wolf was gone. As is he'd never been there.

I rested my head against the tree; fully awake, fully aware. I could feel it, like plates subtlety shifting in the earth. My time in Wyoming was drawing to a close. Dorothy was right: Bit and I were not built for the long haul together. We could fake it for a while but our different lifestyles and

backgrounds would rattle us awake. We both knew it. I had
to break it off before it turned sour. Leave on a high note.
I had to wrap up our love affair with a bow and a kiss that
would say *I'll love you forever*. That's what I had to do, and
I now had an idea how I could tie it all together and make
that happen, and that's what I was feeling and thinking, and,
to this day, it is why I believe Bit took me to Gunderson's
Meadow.

# Chapter 37

## ITTY BIT'S SONG ✳ COWBOY BAR ✳ FARNSWORTH ✳ DOC EVANS

A week later, on a Sunday night, it rained hard enough for us to stop haying for a couple of days. Sonny was now taking all his meals with us at the Lazy T as he was helping out on the hay crew by running the baler. You'd think we would have liked a break from twelve straight days of haying, which we did for half a day or so, but soon cabin fever set in and we were getting on each other's nerves. The real reason we were jumpy was Rendezvous was coming up at the end of the week, which meant the anniversary of Buzz's death. Sonny never mentioned it – none of us did – but it was on our minds and rubbing us raw along with the hard work and long days. Two nights later, after an awkward supper with the only conversation being forks and knives scraping plates, Sonny bolted up and paced around the cabin ready to jump out of his skin. Hope asked him what was the matter. Sonny said he just needed to go to town.

Hope said, "What's got you, Sonny?"

"Same thing that's got you, Hopie," Sonny barked, slamming his fist on the counter, " 'cept you don't show it."

Hope said, "Settle down."

Sonny pointed at Hope. "You goddamn settle down – "

"Settle, Sonny – "

"It's eating a hole in me, Hopie."

"Me, too."

"Don't act like it."

Hope said, "When the time's right."

"When's that," Sonny said, throwing his hands in the air. "We're running out of time."

I spied Hope nodding at Bit, then at the guitar in the corner by the deep freeze. She said, "You're no good to anybody all riled up, Sonny. Calm down."

Bit went over and came back holding out Buzz's guitar. "Before you go, Sonny, do one thing for me."

"What's that?" he groused.

"Sing me a song."

"I don't know no songs."

"You know one."

"Come on, Bit," he said, like leave me alone already.

"Sing me a song, Sonny. You know… my song."

"It's been too long… I can't remember it."

"Yes you can," – Bit humming a little – "You remember."

"Nobody wants to hear that."

Bit said, "Hank would."

"Junior don't need to hear no nonsense lullaby."

I stayed out of it.

Bit continued holding out the guitar. Not giving an inch.

Dorothy spoke up. "I want to hear it, Sonny. Play it for me."

Sonny reluctantly took the guitar from Bit, then tried to hand it back, mumbling as if he was confused, shaking his head *No*.

Hope – not kidding around – said, "*Sing it, Sonny,*" her arms wrapped around her chest with a fresh smoke between her fingers, now looking out the bay window at Buddy and

Blaze necking in the corral. She turned. She stared Sonny down. She blinked, her taut expression evaporating, her tone now sweet, almost pleading. "Sing it for me, Sonny," she said, as if there was no way in hell he could refuse.

I stood up.

I inched closer.

Sonny sat down on the couch with the guitar on his knee. He felt around the neck for the chords. He coughed, cleared his throat, then mumbled and hummed, his voice thick and as sweet as honey. He plucked at the strings with his crooked middle finger, locating the notes. He rolled his shoulders, shook out his hands, reset them on the guitar, readying to play.

I don't recall how the song began because Sonny was a little rusty and his rambling voice disguised a lot of the lyrics as he rolled into the first verse. But that didn't matter. I knew the origin of the song because of what Sonny had told me going to Dubois the day we trailered his horses. The lullaby was about Sonny singing and plucking Buzz's guitar as Buzz held Itty Bit in the crook of his arm riding Cody around the corral; Hope looking on, laughing – Buzz and Sonny desparate to get Itty Bit to close her eyes so they could go to town. I picked up bits and pieces of the lyrics, some poignant, some endearing, some ridiculous, some funny. Like the Lazy T, the song was improvised – rough, tender, beautiful, harsh. Like the Lazy T, it was about Bit and Hope and Sonny and Buzz.

Except Buzz wasn't here anymore.

That's what the song was really all about.

When he finished, Sonny stood, walked to the corner of the room and set the guitar down as gently as you would a sleeping baby. The expression on his face was oddly calm, but a slow burn lit his eyes. Hope was still staring out the bay window with her arms wrapped around her body, not much left of her smoke, a pile of ash around her moccasins. Dorothy had silently moved to the sink, her head hanging down and her hands busy re-washing clean dishes. Bit was beside the open door that Sonny had just slipped out, her eyes red and wet. Clete sat by the wood burning stove, bent over looking at the cabin floor, nursing a smoke, rubbing his hands together. He stood, palmed his hat, and swooped out past Bit, tailing Sonny, sucking me up in his draft as he said, "Squirrel, we're going to town."

I glanced at Bit. Her nod said *Go*. I was almost out the door when Hope – watching Sonny's truck taking a sharp turn onto Forty Rod Road toward Pinedale – said, "Henry..."

I stopped, my cowboy hat in my hands.

She inhaled the last big hit off her cigarette as she followed Sonny's truck, the flaring red coal reflecting in the glass. She exhaled, "Watch over those boys."

"Sure thing."

Launching off the porch I whistled a quick blast, looking around the yard for Bear. Her headed popped up from the bed of Clete's red Chevy with a quizzical look, one ear up, the other bent. I gave her a quick pet before hopping into the passenger seat of the idling truck. Clete shoved the Chevy into gear and peeled out after Sonny.

On the drive to town, Clete was mute. All he did was smoke and stare at Sonny's one working taillight ahead of us. Turning on to 352, I told Clete that I was okay driving back to the ranch if he wanted to tie one on with Sonny. He acknowledged me by tipping the brim of his hat. I figured, given the circumstances, the best thing I could do would be to stay stone sober and let Sonny and Clete "go to town," my job being, as Hope told me, to watch over both of them, meaning make sure they get home okay. I took this as my charge and was determined not to fuck it up.

We parked in the back lot of the Cowboy Bar next to Sonny's truck – Sonny being halfway to the back exit of the bar with no sign of waiting for us. Clete stowed Swiss Cheese under his seat as I checked on Bear's saddle blanket and water dish. I followed Clete through the backdoor of the bar. Being a Tuesday night, there was nothing doing except a Merle Haggard song on the juke box, a table with older couples nursing drinks with straws, and Sonny alone at his spot at the end of the bar. He had a Coors and Courtenay – the owner of the bar – in front of him; his hat was on the bar and his hands were folded over one another. A cigarette burned in an ashtray beside him. He and Courtenay were quietly talking. Courtney nodded his head then moved down the bar near the cash register and made a phone call. When he hung up I approached and ordered a double Wild Turkey and Coke, a Coors, and asked for two dollars in quarters, leaving my change from a twenty on the bar for the next round. I did not acknowledge Sonny six feet away – nor him me. Both Clete and I knew when to let Sonny be. I joined Clete who was racking pool balls. I picked out a cue and chalked it. While Clete broke the balls, I pumped a bunch of quarters in the juke box playing every song I recognized, starting with Dolly Parton's "Here You Come Again." One of the older couples upped and moved to the dance floor, laughing, feeling frisky, leaving their friends tapping fingers on the table to the song, heads swaying back and forth. Clete and I shot five games of eight ball – not talking much. Over the next hour and a half Clete nervously pounded five doubles like lemonade, shredding my twenty in no time. I nursed my beers, or emptied them out when I went to the men's room. Around nine-thirty Clete was blubbering and couldn't see straight, so I led him out to his truck where he lay his six-three across the seat with his boots sticking out the open window and his hat pulled over his eyes, telling me he was just taking a snooze, come get him in a while.

I checked on Bear, then went back inside, burying myself in the darkest corner of the room, keeping an eye on a hunched-over Sonny – I'd never seen him drink so little. Around ten o'clock the screen door opened and slammed. Big cowboy boots thudded in. I followed the beefy figure through the dim light of the bar.

Farnsworth.

Sonny perked up.

He patted the chair next to him.

Farnsworth – his high hair perfect and his dog shit brown uniform pressed and creased – took off his stiff white straw hat and placed it on the bar and sat next to Sonny. Courtenay put a drink in front of Farnsworth. I took my feet off the chair in front of me, stubbed out my smoke, staying still in the shadows. Sonny and Farnsworth were quietly conversing, nodding their heads as if they were coming to an understanding. They didn't talk long. Farnsworth downed his drink; Sonny let his be. They made ready to go; Crystal Gayle's "Don't it Make Your Brown Eyes Blue" just ending.

Change of plan: I was not driving Sonny home. I had the feeling he was driving me…somewhere.

I quickly snuck out the back door, hotfooted it to Clete's truck and opened the driver's side door and felt under the seat, removing Swiss Cheese, making sure it was loaded. I shut the door then put my finger to my lips shushing Bear's whimpering, pushing her back down, flinging my cowboy hat in the bed of the truck. I jumped in the back of Sonny's truck, lay down and pulled a sheet of green canvas over me just as the back door of the bar opened and shut and Sonny's size thirteen boots crunched toward me. He pulled open the creaky truck door and got in, the ancient seat springs groaning under his weight. The engine coughed to life on the third try. He found reverse with a *clunk*, backed up, then ground the gears into first, heading out to Main Street toward the ranch.

The ride was brutal. I lay scrunched up on whatever tools and machinery parts were in the bed of the truck. I held the canvas snug around me with one hand because I didn't want it flapping in the wind sending a signal I was a stowaway. My other hand held Swiss Cheese between my legs. I ran my hand over the familiar smooth and jagged contours of the 357, at home with handling the gun. My immediate thought was *Could I kill Farnsworth?* I didn't know. I had no intention of shooting Farnsworth. I had a feeling Sonny and Farnsworth were going to square off, so I'd grabbed Swiss Cheese as my insurance policy because I did not trust Farnsworth, meaning what if he had Asshole Pete laying in the weeds readying to ambush Sonny. For sure I wasn't sure what I was doing. But I was sure as sugar about one thing: If I pulled it, I had to use it.

As I lay in the back of Sonny Skinner's fifty-two Chevy wobbling down the road on four bald tires, one taillight working, the lone headlight struggling to illuminate our path, I had an existential moment. I realized now—from the moment Buzz first called me in my dorm room, waking me up from a late night college slumber, asking me, "You the kid wants a job?"—I'd been following destiny. Buzz's call to me was the journey that would shake me from my silly self-loathing and self-indulgent despair. That meant I was supposed to be in the back of Sonny's truck heading for a showdown, just as Bit meant for me to help put down Buzz. Sonny said it, "Life don't lie." And it doesn't. This was my life. I had no control. I was just holding on. That brought me solidly in the moment. I peeked through the tarp at brilliant stars illuminating a deep blue moonless sky. The night was cool; I could see my breath. I was cleared headed and calm as a kaleidoscope of thoughts ran through my head. I thought about everybody that was important to me and how much I loved them. This then stirred up the whole notion of heaven and hell and which direction I was headed if this night didn't turn out right. I thought that maybe I should've prayed more to Jesus and the Almighty when Andy and I were kneeling at the rail instead of pulling for the Cubs. That made me start humming – I swear to god – Bob Dylan's "Knocking on Heaven's Door." It's a really beautiful song and quite appropriate for the moment.

I also thought I should have gotten a better grade on that Greek Mythology paper.

The truck slowed, vibrating more than normal, angling to turn. I pulled the flap back over me and stretched out my legs to get some feeling going. We bumped over a cattle guard and glided to a crunching stop. I knew where we were. I arched up and peeked through the glass over Sonny's shoulder. There, beyond the cracked, dusty windshield, illuminated by the truck's lone headlight, was a brown police cruiser in front of the Cora Store and Post Office. Standing beside the cruiser's open door was Farnsworth taking off his hat and jacket. I ducked back down, pulling the tarp over me as Sonny kicked open his door, the rusted hinges screeching bloody murder. I propped my head to listen.

Sonny approached slowly. "Farnsworth, I'm gonna send you to hell on the ends of my fists."

Farnsworth laughed. "Just like Buzz Stifel tried to do."

"You jumped him you sonofabitch. You and that worthless shit stain son of yours. That wasn't a fair fight. Then you left him out here to die. Worse, you left him to be a vegetable."

Sonny stopped walking. I sat up and peered out at two imposing silhouettes standing ten feet apart; the only light coming from Farnsworth's open car door.

Farnsworth chuckled. "I was just bringing him down to your level Sonny... dumb and worthless as the old cow pie that you are. Buzz Stifel had it coming. You can't cross the law. I saw to that. Pete had nothing to do with it."

Sonny said, "You're a lying coward. I saw Buzz's hands and face. That was a two-man job. And you strangled and shot Blue. You shot a man's dog, you yellow-bellied sonofabitch."

"Shut up you old drunk."

"Funny...ain't it," Sonny said now stripping off his long sleeve blue work shirt; a white T-shirt underneath, flexing his hands, rotating them around like a bare-fisted prize fighter would.

Farnsworth rolled up his sleeves, flexing and balling up his fists, not taking his eyes off of Sonny. "What's that?"

"Dorothy told me you should've been born female. That the only pleasure Darryl Farnsworth gives a woman is when he zips up and leaves." Sonny held up his bent-up middle finger for Farnsworth to see. "My finger's bigger than your dick, and it's for sure made more women happier. Makes you sort of think, don't it?"

Farnsworth motioned with his hands for Sonny to come at him. "It's Sheriff Farnsworth to you, you shit-kicking cowboy. Now come on over here Sonny so I can shut your damn mouth."

Once the fight started I hopped out of the truck and crouched behind the passenger side fender with Swiss Cheese in my hand. Before me two large, strong men wrestled and struggled to throw the other to the ground. They clutched and grabbed and gouged, fighting for an advantage, trying to kick out the other's legs. There were many punches thrown in close. Believe me, it's not like the movies where fights are roundhouse events, fun and entertaining. Real ones are brutal and ugly and make you want to look away – you want them to stop. This one did when Farnsworth fell back, slipping, his hand finding a fair size rock. When he regained his balance and swung, the rock in his fist smashed against the side of Sonny's head. Sonny crumpled to the ground not knowing what hit him, blood streaming into his eyes and down his face. Farnsworth walked over, stomped him in the thigh and ribs a couple of times with the tip of his boot, ground his boot into Sonny's hand, then slugged him again on the side of the face.

With Sonny down and dazed, Farnsworth walked over to Sonny's truck, opposite from where I was squatting. I saw his boots underneath the truck as he rooted around in the bed looking for something. He walked back to Sonny with a shovel held waist high, saying, "Before I kill you Sonny Skinner and bury your worthless bag of bones out here, I wanna know something."

Sonny sat up mopping the blood off the side of his face with his shirt.

Farnsworth jabbed him with the shovel. "You killed Buzz in his hospital room. Didn't you?"

Sonny said nothing.

Farnsworth whacked Sonny on his knee with the shovel. "Didn't you?"

Sonny grimaced and grabbed his knee. "Yeah, I did."

"I should've run you in for killing Buzz. Who was with you? You had help. I heard there were three of you in Clete's truck. Was it Clete?"

Sonny didn't respond.

"Tell me."

Sonny spit.

Farnsworth kicked Sonny in the ribs.

Sonny grunted, "Go to hell".

Farnsworth squared himself, set his feet, then raised the shovel high above his head. *"Tell me who was with you goddamnit."*

Sonny stared Farnsworth down, not flinching. He wasn't going to give me up. He lay his head back and looked up in the starry sky, as if he was content to go to heaven and be with Buzz again. I'd seen and heard enough. I stood and let out a long, high-pitched whistle.

They both turned and looked my way.

I stepped from behind the truck and walked toward them with Swiss Cheese held out in front of me with both hands. I stopped fifteen feet from Farnsworth. Planted my feet. Breathed calmly in and out. I found my target. I cocked the hammer. I said, "I helped kill Buzz Stifel."

Farnsworth lowered the shovel – focusing – barely recognizing who I was through the darkness – probably because of my new haircut. He shook his head. "Bullshit, boy."

I reassured him in a calm voice, "No, it was me."

He sneered, dismissing me. "You ain't got the sack, Sweet Pea."

I didn't say another word. Instead, I slowed my breathing, closed one eye and squeezed my finger just enough to feel the pressure of the trigger. Farnsworth wasn't buying it. What Farnsworth did next – rise up on his toes, hoisting the shovel high so he could swing it down on Sonny's head with a killing force – was enough for what I had to do. I had no fear. I was not shaking or afraid. The 357 was in my hand cocked and ready, and I intended to use it. Farnsworth was no more than a target for me to aim at and fire – he was not flesh and blood. And, let's face it, I'm not dumb. I'd watched enough *Dragnet*, *Hawaii Five-o* and *Perry Mason* to know you can shoot someone in self-defense and to prevent a killing. Farnsworth was going to kill Sonny. Then me. I had no choice. It was simple. I shot him.

BANG.

I shot him *again*...BANG.

And *again* BANG...and *again* BANG...and *again* BANG...and *again* BANG.

I shot him until I heard the cylinder turn with a *click*. Farnsworth fell backwards. Dead. His arms and legs spread out. Mouth open and eyes staring up into the starry abyss. My ears rang. I brought the 357 to rest at my side, feeling the heat and the weight of the gun, inhaling the gunpowder smoke. The ringing in my ears dissipated as I heard Sonny kicking at the gravel, struggling to stand. He limped over to inspect Farnsworth. He said, "I think one would've done it, Junior. But I like your style."

I hesitated, not knowing what to say. You think I would have said something cool like *Dirty low-down sonofabitch had it coming* or *That'll teach him to mess with the Lazy T* or *That's for Buzz*. Instead, I said what I was truly feeling, "Shouldn't done that to Blue."

Sonny, now standing in front of me, said, "Ain't that the truth." He took the gun out of my hand, opened up the cylinder and dumped the spent shells in his palm, putting them in his pocket, telling me as he wiped the gun down with his shirt, gripping it so there was no doubt as to the fingerprints, "All that schooling you do done you good, Junior." Then, sounding as if we were in the fields and he needed me to do a chore, he said, "Take my truck and drive to Eleanor's. Call Doc Evans's house and tell him to get out to the Cora Store. Tell him Sheriff Farnsworth had an accident and to bring a body bag. Wait fifteen minutes – go out for a smoke or a take a leak, I don't care – then call the sheriff's department and tell them to get Pete out here, tell them his dad had an accident. If Eleanor asks – which she will – tell her we were driving back from town and spotted his police car and I asked you to call Doc Evans and the sheriff's office. Then get back here."

I repeated Sonny's instructions back to him so I had it right, then drove to Eleanor's house confident Sonny knew what he was doing. You think I would have been a mess after shooting a man – I wasn't. I had a job to do and was simply following Sonny's directive.

I rapped on Eleanor's door. She pulled back the curtain, saw it was me and let me in. She was in in her bathrobe, slippers and a hairnet, wearing glasses that made her look like an owl. I could hear *McCloud* on in the background. I asked to use the phone. She asked why. I said that Sherriff Farnsworth had an accident at the Cora Store. She asked if he was dead. I said I didn't know for sure, only that Sonny told me to come here and make the call. I phoned Doc Evans at home and told him the situation, quietly telling him, because Eleanor was eavesdropping, to bring a body bag. Doc said to sit tight; he'd be there in twenty minutes. After hanging up I dawdled about, asking to use the bathroom, taking my time, watching a little *McCloud*. After fifteen minutes, I asked to use the phone again, calling the sheriff's department. They said they'd send Pete out right away. I left the house with Eleanor following me to the truck, pulling her robe tight around her, telling me that Sheriff Farnsworth deserved to die for what he did to her husband Gene. That she'd gladly go to his funeral just to make sure the bastard was dead. I agreed with everything she said as she waggled her finger at me through the open window as I struggled to start Sonny's truck and get it into gear.

Returning to Cora, bumping across the cattle guard, the truck's headlight shone on Doc Evans zipping up a big, black body bag. Coming north on 352, about a mile away, was a red and blue light show – Asshole Pete. I got out and approached. Sonny told me to keep my mouth shut; he and Doc would do all the talking. The only reason I was there was because I was driving Sonny home when we saw the sheriff's car at the Cora turnoff. The ground around the body bag was smoothed over, no sign of blood or struggle.

Asshole Pete drove up leaving the emergency lights spinning like he was so important. Doc walked over, standing tall in his white hat, trimmed mustache, shiny black boots and buttoned coat – the real law in town – and ordered Pete to shut the damn lights off.

Asshole Pete did as he was told then addressed Doc Evans. "What's going on, Doc? I got a call something happened to my father."

Doc said, "Pete, your dad had a massive heart attack. He must not have been feeling well and pulled over here in Cora. He's dead. I'm sorry."

"What's he doing here?" – Pete pointing at Sonny.

Doc said, "He and the boy found your dad on their way home."

Asshole Pete tilted his hat back and said to Sonny, "What happened to you?"

Sonny said, "Tripped and fell coming out the bar."

Asshole Pete nodded *Sure, I bet*, then eyed the bag on the ground. "Is that him there?"

Doc said *Yes*.

Asshole Pete said, "You shouldn't have moved him."

Doc said, "I'm the coroner. He was dead of a heart attack."

"Can I have a look?"

"Suit yourself."

Pete walked over, knelt down, unzipped the bag. He zipped it up. "Tell me what really happened, Doc."

"Your dad had a heart attack, Pete. That's all."

"That's murder," he said pointing his finger at the body bag, "Six bullet holes ain't no heart attack."

Doc Evans was close enough to Pete so that when Pete reached for his gun, Doc grabbed his arm, pushed up his sleeve and thumbed a big ugly scar. He said, "That ain't no pit bull either."

"What're you saying, Doc?"

Doc held Pete's arm with a firm grip. "I'm saying I swabbed and doctored your arm the night Buzz was beat up and Blue was killed. I also swabbed Blue's mouth," he said pointing to the culvert where Blue was found, "and sent both to the FBI lab in Cheyenne. You know what come back?"

Pete spit out, "A bunch of bullshit, I bet."

"No. A match."

"That ain't nothing."

"No, Pete, you're right. It ain't nothing. It's forensics. You're a lawman. It's just like matching a bullet with the gun it come from. That's called ballistics. You and your dad jumped and beat up Buzz Stifel, and you strangled and shot Blue. But not before that dog took a piece of your arm with him. That places you here at the night of the murder. You want to explain that to the judge? You and your dad had plenty of motive. Think on it. You get convicted – dollars to donuts you will – then you get to spend the rest of your life down in Rawlins with boys you helped put away. If you do get off, you'll most likely lose your job and be run out of town on a rail. You got one choice, and I recommend you take it son or your life is going to turn to manure real fast. I guarantee it."

The blood ran out of Asshole Pete's face faster than he could roll down his sleeve. He circled the dark, lumpy body bag twice then looked away at the Wind Rivers. Doc Evans spoke up as if he was just handed a news bulletin: "Sheriff Darryl Farnsworth was found dead in his police car at the Cora Store by Deputy Sheriff Pete Farnsworth. It is assumed that Sheriff Farnsworth must have pulled over not feeling well. Doctor Wilbur Evans pronounced Sheriff Farnsworth dead of a massive coronary. Sublette County and Pinedale, Wyoming, have lost a loyal law enforcement officer. Deputy Sheriff Pete Farnsworth will assume the duties of sheriff until the next election."

Asshole Pete buttoned up his sleeve...and his lip.

# Chapter 38

## A FISTFUL OF SHELLS

By the time Sonny dropped me off at the Lazy T it was past midnight. Clete had obviously woken up and driven back to the ranch because he was now asleep in the trailer. Sonny told me, "Go to bed. Don't wake anybody up or say anything. I'll handle it."

I wanted to sleep but I was wired. So I stayed outside by the fence Clete and I'd built, chain smoking cigarettes and downing the three beers Sonny gave me from his fridge. I followed car and truck lights a mile and a half away on 191. The beers finally did me in around one-thirty. When I went to bed, I was still fully clothed, only my boots off, lying on top of my sleeping bag. Bear must have sensed that I was tied in knots because she came down from Clete's room, jumped up on my bed and curled up beside me. I stroked her head and coat. She licked my hand. I shut my eyes, slowed my breathing, the only sound in the trailer being Clete's soft snoring. I lay as still as if I was dead in a coffin like Farnsworth would soon be; and that's the way Clete found me when he came down the hallway at sunup to take a leak, pulling on his jeans, scolding

Bear for being a whore for sleeping around. He left the trailer door open for the sunshine to pour in. When he came back I was stripping out of sweaty, sticky clothes wanting to take a shower. I toweled off with a T-shirt then re-dressed in clean work clothes. Not saying a word.

Clete said, "My melon feels like it was squashed after them double Turkeys. Why'd you let me reload like that, Squirrel?"

I said, "It's the only way I could beat you at pool."

He said, "You drive Sonny home?"

"Yeah."

"Any problem driving his truck?"

"You kidding? I don't know how Sonny drives that truck," I said pulling on my boots. "The gears don't mesh. The brakes are for shit. The tires are bald. And keeping it on the road with no power steering almost broke my arms. I think he'd be better off with a rickshaw."

"What's that?"

"A Chinese automobile."

Clete thought about that looking out the open door into the yard, buttoning up a work shirt with good size tear in the elbow that he'd butchered sewing up. He said, "Sonny's truck's here. Was he in bad shape when you took him home?"

I said, "No."

Clete scratched at his stubble. "Funny...didn't seem like he was drinking much...just jawing with Courtney was all I remember. Seems to be he lost his thirst."

I didn't say anything as I gathered up the clothes I wore the night before, along with my sheets and pillowcases – I wanted everything washed clean. Clete saw what I was doing and said he'd take care of milking the cow if he could slip in a few things. I said for sure. After he jammed in his work duds, I swung the laundry bag over my shoulder, walked out and stood on the stump looking around the yard. Sonny's truck was parked next to Bit's El Camino. He was most likely inside the house poking on a Camel and sipping a cup of coffee by the stove, filling Hope in on our night. I flung the bag onto a lawn chair and went around the corner to take my morning pee. Coming back around, Clete was adjusting his hat, waiting for me. He said hold on and went back in the trailer for my cowboy hat. When he handed it to me I said, "That bad?"

He said, "Maybe best if Hope evened things out."

I said, "No. Let Bit's work stand on its own. I don't want her nose out of joint."

Clete tapped me on the shoulder, then headed to the corral to milk the cow while I walked to the house with the laundry bag over my shoulder, not knowing what to expect on the other side of the open door that now let the morning in. I entered slowly. Bacon sizzled in a skillet. Hope's biscuits were stacked high on a plate with knife and butter nearby on the kitchen table that was already set up for breakfast. Sonny was, indeed, sitting by the wood-burning stove with a mug of coffee and a Camel burning. Hope was poking at the bacon, dressed neatly in jeans and a tan chamois shirt, her hair properly brushed and pulled back. She looked at me and said, "Henry, put that laundry on the washing machine after Bit's done in the bathroom. I'll get to it after breakfast. Sonny said the hay's dry enough to rake and bale so get some coffee and breakfast, then let's get after it."

I poured a cup of coffee; took a seat across from Sonny. I lit a smoke so I didn't have to talk. The nicotine was calming. I blew on my coffee not wanting to look at anybody. Bit came out of the bathroom and hustled into Hope's bedroom, not saying *Hey Hank*, like she usually does. Soon she came to sit beside me, reaching for my hand, giving me a tiny smile. I sat back waiting for this story to unfold; waiting for what my role would be. It did when Hope cracked an egg with one hand on the lip of the skillet, plunking the orange orb and gelatinous goo into spitting grease.

"Henry, Dorothy had to go to town. Her son Pete came out early this morning and gave her the sad news about Darryl." Hope cracked another egg. "As you know, Pete said Doc Evans told him his father had a massive heart attack. Most likely he was dead before he hit the ground." Hope deftly deposited three more eggs into the popping grease then hit them with three grinds from the pepper mill before covering the skillet, wiping her hands on her apron, continuing, "Doc said nobody could have saved him. Pete said he appreciated what you and Sonny did, finding him, letting him and Doc Evans know as soon as possible. The funeral will be Friday, before Rendezvous. I know you didn't know the sheriff personally, but I think it would be nice if you joined us for his service at the cemetery."

"Sure thing," was all I said.

That was all anybody said until Clete came in from the barn with a full pail of milk, bragging nobody could beat what he was now pouring through a strainer into a large pickle jar, screwing on the lid and placing it in the refrigerator. Sonny had not moved, the bruise on the side of his face from the fight now red and purple and mottled. His knuckles were scratched up and swollen. He flexed his hands a few times. I wondered if he had any broken ribs and how bad his knee was hurting, but I wasn't going to ask because it's always embarrassing falling and hurting yourself coming out of a bar – you just don't want to talk about it; but Sonny did talk about it because Clete got a good look at him and said, "What the hell happened to you, Sonny?"

"Slipped and fell coming out of the bar," he growled.

Clete nudged back his hat, his hands on his hips, looking around at all of us, not believing.

Hope shoveled eggs onto plates recounting for Clete exactly what she had told me.

Clete gave me a look.

I kept stone-faced.

Clete said, "Farnsworth's really dead?"

Sonny said, "Dead as a doornail."

Clete said, "I can't believe it."

Sonny said, "That's why we got funerals."

Clete said, "I gotta be honest...I wish I had a hand in killing that sonofabitch."

Sonny said, "Don't you worry," reaching down to the floor, coming up with Swiss Cheese. "You did." He handed Clete his gun. "Load that up and put it back in your truck."

Clete took his pistol, looked at it for a full five seconds. He said, "Right now?"

Sonny said, "After breakfast. Don't want your eggs to get cold."

Clete placed the 357 on the counter next to the coffeemaker, taking down a cup and filling it up, his hat still set back, smiling, exposing his big tooth, happy to be in on it now; holding up his cup, asking *Anyone want more coffee?*

When you shoot and kill someone, a paralyzing feeling comes over you for a couple of days. I shut down and mostly kept to myself because I questioned what I had done and who I was. My chest tightened making it hard to breathe, and I avoided conversations at the dinner table because my mind was clotted. At night, I'd turn off my light so I wouldn't have to talk with Clete. Bit kept giving me an eye like *Are you okay,* touching my arm, saying *Do you want to talk about it.* I shook my head looking away saying *Not yet,* telling her I was confused and couldn't explain it, much less go behind the haystack. I spent more time hanging out with Buddy and Blaze in the barn. Clete cut me a wide swath, so did Sonny. I could sense Dorothy wanted to talk with me, but I avoided her. Hope was the only one who acted like nothing had happened.

On the third day after gunning down Farnsworth, I was outside in the work shed sharpening sickles for the mowers when Hope came from behind and touched my shoulder, making me jump.

"Henry."

I shut down the grinder, excusing myself to go around the corner for a second, fingering out a wad of chew, coming back to find Hope running her finger across one of the sickle blades I'd sharpened. I thought she'd come out to say something like *Thank you for what you did. That was really brave of you. Buzz would have been proud. Blah, blah, blah.* Then give me a meaningful hug and head back to the house. End of conversation. Wrong, that's not Hope Stifel. Instead, she reached into her pocket. She pulled something out. She thrust a balled up fist at me, then slowly opened up her hand, her palm extended out flat as if she was a magician showing me what she'd conjured. I gazed down at the six spent shells that sent Sheriff Darryl Farnsworth to hell on a sled of lead. As slowly as she opened her hand, she quickly shut it tight with a wicked grin and cackle; a grin and cackle so wicked it made me smile because I knew where she was coming from. What Hope held in her hand and in her eyes was my salvation. Her salvation. Our salvation. She tucked the shells in her jeans pocket and turned to go. I followed her slow swaying gait back to the log cabin, the three-legged cat hopping alongside, keeping her company. She walked into the house and shut the door, not looking back.

I came around after that.

That night, sipping beers after another long day haying, watching the sun go down, Bit and I sat and talked on the porch about what had happened at the Cora Store. I was not emotional. I sat whittling a stick with my Old Timer and told her what I had done and how I felt about it. Once I got it all out I was about a hundred pounds lighter. I looked at Bit, who was seated with her back against a pole, her boots touching my thigh. She drew her feet up and wrapped her arms around her knees and gave me a meaningful look girls will give you after you've splayed open and spilled your guts about something that shows you're vulnerable like everyone else.

She said, "Hank, I'll say this once: What you did was brave and selfless. You saved Sonny. Someday you'll look back on this and it won't be a burden. Mom shared with me your letter about how you felt about Dad and not protecting him. You couldn't have stopped it. Dad's luck ran out. Farnsworth killing Dad was wrong, but you killing Farnsworth was right. It doesn't matter that he was a lawman. He was bad. What you did was good. I know you've been carrying around guilt on account of not giving Dad a ride home that night. You shouldn't have felt guilty, but you did. Most would have let it go. But you didn't. You couldn't. You cared. That's who you are and why I love you." Bit stopped, her eyes welling with tears. She said, "You avenged Buzz and Blue's deaths. They can now rest in peace. And so can we." Bit stood, extending her hand to me. "And I need to make love to you right now, even if I have to drag you to the barn by the little hair you have left on your head."

What Bit said made me go a little misty and blurry eyed. This is bizarre, but right then and there I thought I saw Buzz coming out of the house putting on his black cowboy hat, blasting a quick whistle, cutting a path to the Blue Ford as Blue raced him from the work shed, arriving just as he pulled down the tailgate for Blue to jump in; shutting and rocking the gate back and forth with Blue perched on his front paws, panting; caressing the dog's face in his hands, mumbling what he always did; turning, flashing me his wonderful smile, then driving away, disappearing down Forty Rod Road.

Or maybe I just dreamt it.

Anyway, my mind cleared.

I could breathe again.

I accepted Bit's hand, ready for the barn.

I'll be honest with you, I don't like talking about the down-and-dirty details about girls I've slept with. Why? It's private stuff, so why would I write about it either? Likewise, as a twenty-year-old, grappling with sex is confusing enough because it can be so many things: Passionate. Routine. Innocent. Gentle. Emotionless. Exciting. Quick. Languorous. Mistaken. Inevitable. What Bit and I shared that evening in the barn – with a candle burning bright – was ethereal (that's an eight-dollar word that means out of this world). Bit was clearly at the helm, guiding me, kissing me, caressing me, moving me out of my clothes with ease. I had no control over this rodeo. Bit made love to me that night for many reasons: for avenging her father and Blue's deaths; for who I was; for what I'd become; because she truly loved me; and— as if it was —for the last time.

# Chapter 39

## FARNSWORTH'S FUNERAL ✳ RODEO AT THE COWBOY BAR

Sonny and Clete had made sure earlier in the summer that I was well aware of who Freddie Saunders was before I met him. I was positive I could've picked him out of a lineup, or a photograph, or by walking into the Cowboy Bar, and told you *He's the one; he's the blowhard; he's the guy who picks on smaller hands; he's the one who'll steal your money and your girl; he's the one who'd cut and run; he's the one who won't ride a bronc.* And that's just what happened the Friday night of Rendezvous when Bit and I made our entrance and fought through the crowd to set up shop by Sonny at his place at the end of the bar. Freddie Saunders was in the middle of the bar flapping his gums about being a derrick hand on an offshore oil rig in the Gulf. I tapped Clete on the shoulder, glancing in Freddie's direction. Clete nodded *Yep.* To mix sport metaphors, I was prepared for my face-off against Freddie Saunders; I knew how to play the shot.

But first, Farnsworth's funeral.

The service was at ten o'clock in the morning up at the cemetery behind town in the foothills of the Wind Rivers where Buzz was buried. The Lazy T showed up all showered, shaved and dressed appropriately, sitting strategically in the front row, as if we were family and emotionally attached to the deceased, which we were...in a negative way. Opposite us, Dorothy Farnsworth – dry-eyed as a gecko, her air of indifference proof any tears or emotion had long ago left the station – sat next to Asshole Pete. Pete's face and body language were clearly being tested because, I think, he did not know who he was supposed to be: Darryl Farnsworth's grieving son, his loyal deputy, or the new sheriff in town. Clearly, he was failing all three.

The hole had been dug and the thick cedar casket, wrapped in the state flag, rested on a dolly behind which the Reverend Myron Sykes stood tall and bald. He was pontificating with a bible in one hand and brimstone in the other, rallying us around the ludicrous notion that Sheriff Darryl Farnsworth had done the work of Jesus by being a shepherd to all in Pinedale; counseling, soothing, assuaging our fears and anxieties as he did his best to serve and protect, and that when the good Lord took him into his heavenly kingdom, he did so because Sheriff Farnsworth was ready to walk with Jesus, to help the Almighty enforce the laws of faith. Amen.

*Amen* murmured the fifty or so assembled.

Not Sonny Skinner. He mumbled to Clete beside him, "Jesus Christ, what a bunch of bullshit." Hope, on the other side of Clete, leaned over and shot Sonny a look that could have knocked a bird out of a tree at twenty yards, shushing him. Bit, sitting on the other side of Hope, suppressed a laugh, giving my knee a squeeze. I covered her hand with mine, squeezing back.

I told you I'd had trouble figuring out death and funerals. Not so with Darryl Farnsworth. It's hard not to be tickled to death at the funeral of a man whom you despised and had a hand in killing. That's why Sonny, Clete and I had arrived late at the funeral as Hope was pursing her lips and Bit was mouthing *Where the hell have you been,* and me whispering apologetically *It's Sonny's fault.* (When Clete and I'd swung by Sonny's place to pick him up, he was in the middle of a pre-funeral celebration, insisting we join him in a cold one, which we did, Sonny telling us he'd never been to a funeral sober and was sure as hell not starting with Farnsworth's, which led to another beer, then climbing into Clete's Chevy with me in the middle and Bear in the bed, rocketing to town on Waylon Jennings and Willy Nelson's "Goodhearted Woman," which led to another beer, which tasted really good, good enough to put a bit of a buzz on the brain and a stupid grin on my face, which Bit noticed, which I tried wiping off by licking my lips, which she had better luck erasing with a kiss, which got me just as hot as the temperature that sunny morning. That's a long rambling sentence – I know – but I'll let it go because of the three Budweisers.)

More important, before we left the Lazy T that morning I had asked a rather obvious question: "What would the undertaker think laying out Farnsworth, eyeing the six bullet holes in his chest if cause of death was from a massive coronary. Clete said he'd not thought about that. Sonny said *Good question, Junior.* Hope said not to worry, Doc Evans had arranged for the body to be put in a coffin immediately and nailed shut – that's what his son the new sheriff and his ex-wife wanted, and who was he – the undertaker – to argue with the coroner, the family, and the law.

When it came time to place Farnsworth in his well-earned resting spot six feet under, Reverend Sykes asked for four volunteers to help lower the casket into the ground. Sonny surprised me. He jumped up. Slapped me and Clete on the knee. "Let's git after it boys. The sheriff needs a hand." I was unsure if he was referring to Farnsworth, or Asshole Pete, who'd now solemnly stood and moved to grasp one of the straps placed under the coffin to lift it up and lower it into the grave. I caught Clete's big front tooth breaking out in a smile as he looked across the casket at Sonny, something brewing.

On the count of Sonny's "One…two…three," the four of us carefully picked up the coffin and moved closer to the hole in front of those assembled. Suddenly, Sonny lurched… lost his balance and grip…letting go of his strap…Clete, too. The coffin tilted down, falling into the hole, forcing me to let go, leaving Asshole Pete holding the proverbial bag. The casket fell to the bottom sending a plume of dust up as Sonny clutched his leg, crying out, "Goddamn trick knee," quickly apologizing to Reverend Sykes and those in attendance.

Hope covered her face, rivulets running down, staining her face. When the dust and tears cleared, Reverend Sykes asked us to come forward and throw a scoopful of dirt on Sheriff Darryl Farnsworth as a final goodbye. We did, with Sonny pitching in a healthy two.

As the congregation headed back to town – Bit and Hope included – Sonny, Clete and I hung around graveside for a smoke. When the coast was clear, we unzipped and pissed out three Budweisers apiece on top of Farnsworth, nearly floating his boat; flicking our butts in his hole as a final farewell. Walking away, Sonny put his arms around both me and Clete, saying we done good, drinks are on him; and now that we know where to find Sheriff Darryl Farnsworth, feel free to unburden ourselves on him anytime. Jesus would approve.

We went back to the ranch and had a lazy half-day of haying then returned to town for the Friday night celebration before the Rendezvous parade and rodeo the next day. Dorothy stayed behind keeping Hope company and, I think, laying low because she didn't want to have to lie to everyone about her ex-husband. Last year during Rendezvous I had ducked in and out of the bars, staying on the periphery because I felt out of place and didn't want to be a weight around Buzz or Bit or Clete's neck. This year I felt on stage as the anniversary of Buzz's death swirled around us; Farnsworth's death was on the town's tongue; Bit firmly on my arm, and Freddie Saunders waiting in the wings.

Polly Hamilton found us at the bar, her face lighting up when she saw Bit and me. I'd not seen Polly since I met with her at her family's wilderness camp last summer when I went to talk with her about my friend's death. I removed my Cubs cap – Bit had loaned me Ron Santo for the night because me wearing a cowboy hat around real cowpokes was not in the cards. After giving Polly a brush-on the-cheek kiss and a light hug and a *Good to see you again, too,* I reached around to shake the hand of her boyfriend, Joe Alexander, a cowboy-handsome guy built like he could bulldog anyone in the bar to the ground, but wouldn't want to because he was a mellow ride who got along with everybody and everybody got along with him.

The bar was packed, smoky and loud; the band playing a rowdy Jerry Jeff Walker song; carrying on a conversation was near impossible, which caused a lot of head nodding and shouting. Bit had her hand around my waist, anchoring me as she and Polly talked back and forth about Laramie, the Lazy T, and the Hamiltons' Wilderness Camp. Joe, Clete and I politely listened, sipping beers. It was not hard to see the other cowboys in the bar looking at us. It was not hard to see we were with two of the prettiest girls in Pinedale, Wyoming. It was not hard seeing Freddie Saunders glaring at our group, lit up with me in his headlights. It was not hard to see him make his move toward me once Bit and Polly departed together for the ladies room, and Joe Alexander was pulled away by an old timer wanting to hear about Wyoming's football team.

Really, it was not a fair fight, for either of us. Freddie Saunders was a full head taller; a beefy boar with thirty more pounds of obvious muscle; but seriously, a mental midget – albeit a handsome one – who could not fight his way out of a wet paper bag. That was my advantage. I was prepared. I'd learned from the best. My father had counseled me that in close quarter negotiations with a bigger, stronger opponent, establish an advantage by acting friendly, then knock him off balance so that your adversary is thinking about something else other than kicking your ass. That was good advice. My mother taught me that when dealing with a difficult person in an awkward social situation to pound him with politeness. Again, good advice. Boyle taught me *If you are going to get hit, hit the other guy first.* Farr added, *Then, run like hell.*

Freddie brushed past, enough to turn me. I looked him square in the eye and said, "You're Freddie Saunders? Charlie Saunders's son, right? Your dad has that great spread in Bondurant? You're a good friend of Bit's from high school? I've seen your black Chevy. Really cool truck. Good to meet you."

He looked down at my outstretched hand and reluctantly shook it. He said, "Who are you?"

I said, "Hank Chandler from Lake Forest, Illinois."

He grunted, "Where's that?"

I replied, "Halfway between New York and Connecticut."

Freddie had to think about that. He and Clete acknowledged each other as if they were ex-spouses. I made small talk about Rendezvous, pretending like I knew what I was talking about, asking him if he would be riding in the parade or the rodeo. He said both. I asked what event in the rodeo. He said bronc riding, acting cocky, like what else.

Bingo.

I smiled.

Freddie sensed something and didn't like it. He asked me, "What're you doing here?" meaning in this bar, in this town, in this state, and why do I have to be looking at you right now?

I said, "I work at the Lazy T."

He laughed. "Doing what?"

I was honest. "Tearing up machinery and generally

getting in the way. Right, Clete?"

The spotlight turned on Clete. He played the straight man perfectly. "Nothing I can't fix, Squirrel."

I reached in my pocket and pulled out a small wad of money, along with those two French Ticklers with the special ribbing that was guaranteed to drive women crazy that I bought at the truck stop when Bones and I were driving back to school. I'd thrown them in my Dopp Kit and forgot about them until Gunderson's Meadow. I'd never thought a condom could ignite a bomb, but it did when Freddy looked down as I was peeling off a twenty, making sure he saw not one, but two. I slapped a bill on the bar saying, "I'm buying, what're you having Fred?"

Freddie Saunders gave me a look as if I'd just jammed my finger up his ass and he didn't appreciate it.

Bullseye!

I cut back on the attack, handing him a fresh beer, keeping him off balance by asking questions about working on an oil rig as a derrick hand; complimenting him by saying it sounded like rough, dangerous work. It wasn't hard to see Freddie Saunders wanted to throttle me in a New York minute, but he couldn't right now because of Sonny and Clete and Bit, who had now returned with Polly, and whom I now had my arm around feeling her body go stiff as a board.

The band was on break.

Polly asked me about school. I explained that it was going okay; that the highlight was when Bit had come out to visit.

Freddie interrupted, "Where's that?"

I said, "Where's what?"

He said, "Where you go to school?"

I said, "Providence."

He said, "Where's that?"

I said, "Rhode Island."

He said, "Where's that?"

I said, "New England."

He looked at me as if I were a fresh turd. He decided to play with me. "I don't *think* I know where that is."

I looked around at the faces of those who were anticipating my response. I said, "Well, Fred, think the United States. Think the Eastern seaboard. Think about two-thirds the way up. Think Connecticut. Think Massachusetts. Think somewhere in between."

Polly smirked.

Bit press her lips together. She pinched me, holding back what she wanted to say, waiting for the moment when the band returned and we were on the dance floor, after she'd pulled me by the hand through the crowd like a frustrated mother hauling a ten-year-old boy away from a scrap he'd started. As we turned to dance she slapped me on the back – but it may as well been on the cheek – warning me, "Hank, don't mess with Freddie. Don't. Mess. With. Him. Okay? He's my problem."

I said, giving her a twirl, "It's okay" – not one of my best moves because Bit was a little twisted up and not in a spinning mood.

"No it's not," she insisted.

We danced around with a bunch of shallow breaths between us.

"You don't know him. He's not a good person," she whispered in my ear, pulling and twisting a tiny sprout of hair on the back on my head, again repeating, "He's my problem," then adding in a sincere tone as she pushed me away and looked me in the eye, "Not yours."

He was both of ours, but I kept my trap shut.

Bit surely had a problem, I knew that, but now as the problem came into focus I knew why. On the surface, Freddie Saunders was a handsome hunk with a full head of wavy brown hair, a chiseled jaw, captivating brown eyes and a toothy smile that could melt resolve. In a word – my grandmother's words – he was a charming, naughty boy that girls could not resist. But underneath it, he was a bully, a lie, a cheat – just what Clete and Sonny had warned me about. For sure, the book didn't match the cover. For sure, Freddie had his hooks in Bit, and it wouldn't take much for her to hop that ride again.

It was getting late, close to midnight. The band had stopped playing. Bit and Polly were catching up with high school friends at a table. Clete had disappeared down the street to the Corral Bar. I was sitting next to Sonny enjoying his stories while keeping an eye on Freddie slowly smoldering at the opposite end of the bar. When Bit disappeared to the bathroom, I turned to Sonny and said, "I gotta do this," tilting my head toward Freddie. "I'm going outside to check on Bear." Sonny's eyebrow arched up. He thoughtfully nodded, catching my drift. I walked through the thinning crowd out the back exit of the bar. I didn't have to turn around to see Freddie Saunders downing his beer, cracking his knuckles, following me out.

Out back, there was a couple getting into a pickup leaving three trucks in the dimly lit parking lot. I'd just reached in the bed of Clete's truck to pet Bear when I heard the screen door slam and boots crunch toward me in a slightly drunken pattern, a voice slurring,

"Why don't you go back to New England, you faggot?"

I did not turn around when I said, "I intend to."

"When?"

I looked up watching this dark figure approach, backlit by the exit sign of the bar. I said, "Soon as I'm ready."

"Not soon enough for me."

"Tough shit."

"What'd you say?" he said, now within hands reach.

I turned and squared off with Freddie. "When would you like me to go back, Fred?"

He reached out and grabbed me, lifting me off my feet, spraying me with his Coors breath. "How about right now. Say I give you a pretty send-off."

I looked at his mitts on my shirt then up at him, smirking. I played to my strength, rubbing the nub of our confrontation in his face: "You and Bit went out in high school."

"What's it to you?"

"She dumped you."

"Fuck you, faggot."

"You still like her, Fred."

He tightened his grip on me. "That's my business. And it's not Fred. It's Freddie, faggot."

I could have cracked wise and said, *Pardon me. So it's Freddie Faggot? Not Freddie Saunders. So sorry.* But I didn't because I had to be careful not to write a check on my alligator mouth that my preppy ass couldn't cash. I paused for effect. I said, "But she likes me now."

He said, "You don't know what she likes."

Freddie was partially right and wrong. I was not going to get all chummy with him and have that discussion of why he was right and wrong and why I was wrong and right. I was more concerned with the immediate consequences of swallowing my teeth, so I said, "Let's settle this like men."

"That's what I aim to do," he said.

"Good, here's how we'll do it."

That confused him. He was readying to punch me but stopped when I said, "You and I will ride for her."

That confused him even more. "What do you mean ride for her?" he said lowering his fist (thank god), but still keeping a hold on me.

"You mentioned to me that you ride saddle broncs. Right?"

"Yeah."

I'll bet I can stay on a bronc longer than you. If I do, you leave Bit and me alone."

"And if I win?" he said removing his hand from my shirt, wiping off his nose with the back of his sleeve. "What if I win, *faggot*?"

I backed up a couple steps, straightening my shirt, dusting myself off, looking him in the eye. I said, "Peter Pan flies back to New England."

I had him cornered. Freddie was confounded. Quickly, he concluded that it would be a whole lot easier kicking my ass in the parking lot rather than getting on a horse that terrified him. His eyes narrowed. He breathed in half a parking lot of air, coming at me with open fists, grabbing me again, cocking his arm back, leaving me looking down the barrel of five, hairy kicked-up knuckles.

*Help me Lord, this is going to hurt.*

Preparing myself to be knocked into the middle of next month, I was miraculously saved by a deep Divine voice demanding an answer: "What'll it be, Freddie?"

Freddie turned.

I looked around him.

Sonny said, "Man challenged you. You owe him an answer. What'll it be?"

Freddie reluctantly released me saying I was full of shit, I'd never climb on a bronc's back. Sonny said I was due an answer; let's see what tomorrow brings. Freddie pushed me away, walking past Sonny to the back door of the bar, boasting he'd see me tomorrow in the ring...if I showed...if the faggot had the balls.

I said, "The faggot will go first, thank you."

Freddie pivoted, now walking backwards toward the exit sign, pointing at me. "I'll believe it when I see it. You'd better show." Then he disappeared inside, leaving me and Sonny leaning against Clete's truck with Bear propped on the side rail, wagging her tail and panting. Sonny reached in and poured water from a jug into Bear's bowl He took a swig himself, washing out his mouth, spitting out a stream that darkened and dampened the dust around our feet. He said, "You know what you're doing, Junior?"

I nodded yes, calmly laying out my plan and why I had to

do it, not getting too heavy on him, explaining what had come over me in Gunderson's Meadow.

Sonny thought on it for some time before saying, "Okay, here's how it'll work. I'll make sure you're in the program for the rodeo. Make sure of your draw and get you set up. I'll be working the chute. No more drinking tonight, and none tomorrow. You got to be clear headed."

I said I understood.

He reached into his pocket for his Camels and shook out two, handing me one. He flicked open his Zippo and lit up – first me, then him. He clicked the lighter shut, palming it to me, telling me to tuck it into my pocket for good luck like he used to; the only time he forgot was when he got kicked in the head.

I felt the weight and rubbed the dimples of Sonny's lighter, sliding it into my front jeans pocket. We smoked in silence then went back into the bar to collect Bit and Clete – Freddie Saunders gone – calling it a night and one long day.

# Chapter 40

## HOME

For obvious reasons, I had a hard time getting to sleep that night not knowing what I was doing or what to expect. My thrashing around and lighting up a smoke to get back to sleep was enough for Bear to pad her way down the hall, hop up, curl by my side, lick my hand. I stubbed out my smoke and petted her until I fell asleep.

When Clete opened the trailer door to let in the morning sunshine and the smell of dew on the sagebrush, I was already up and dressed in my cleanest work clothes, adjusting my cowboy hat. I followed him out across the plank over the stream to the house, then to the barn to keep him company as he milked the cow. I told him what happened the night before with Freddie; what I'd planned to do and not to tell Bit. Clete said the same thing Sonny had said to me, "You know what you're doing, Squirrel?" I said I had a pretty good idea. Clete said he would be on the top rail by the chute just in case.

Breakfast was a quiet affair, except for Dorothy who was chattering on, wanting to know what was going on in town, fishing around for info on Freddie Saunders. Bit was hung over and not talking. Clete kept his head down. Hope had something on her mind and was smoking, not eating. My appetite was limited to caffeine and nicotine and staring out the bay window toward the mountains. A couple of times I looked over at the cracked and faded 8x11 photograph of Buzz thumbtacked to the wall above the freezer, riding a bronc in the 1950's. Perfect form, leaning back, hand held high, boots spurring the horse, just like you see on the license plates in Wyoming or on the blinking red sign above the Cowboy Bar.

The rodeo ring in Pinedale is located just outside of town, up the hill toward the cemetery. It's a sturdy structure built in the 1930s from crude mammoth logs about six feet high that are pitched slightly out to protect the riders when they crash into them. You can sit on the top rail and watch, which is where most of the kids hang out, while the older folks sit in the small grandstand under cover. The man on the microphone sat in a rickety wooden booth near the chutes, broadcasting through big, black air raid-type speakers connected to lights on top of pine telephone poles. Grey dirt carpeted the arena giving off an aroma similar to what you'd smell if you ducked your head inside a horse trailer. There was a flurry of activity by the stock pens where cowgirls were pinning numbers on the backs of the cowboys' shirts, wishing them good luck with a handshake, hug, or kiss. I asked Chester Higgins, the rodeo clown, to pin mine on, telling him who I was and whom I worked for. He gave me the once-over, skeptical, certain this was my first rodeo. He wheezed through a cigarette pinched between his teeth, to stay loose and that if I got bucked off to get away from the bronc (duh); he'd move in to distract the horse away from me. Watching him limp away in his bowler hat, Jack Purcell's, baggy pants, suspenders, and an oversized red bandana floating from his back pocket, I prayed he had some backup. (Thank god, he did.)

It was not hard spotting Freddie Saunders. He was dressed and strutting around like a peacock. He avoided eye contact with me; and I with him. I wanted this over and was not into small talk; my stomach would not allow it.

The parade long over, the town was split between the bars in town and the rodeo grounds. I'd decoyed Bit earlier by telling her Clete and I wanted to go up and see the rodeo and would be back soon. She had not seen the program printed that morning with my name in the fourth spot of the bronc riders followed by Freddie Saunders. Bit told me later Polly got hold of one and had run her finger down the participants and stopped under my name asking *Is this a misprint?* Apparently Bit took the program, studied it, and was up and out faster than a jackrabbit with Polly in pursuit, hoofing it with both arms swinging, head still, a serious expression on her face like those nurses you see in the beginning of a "Mash" episode as they're hustling with all their might to the helicopter pad to save a life. In my case, Bit was running to save mine, yelling at the top of her lungs, "Get off that goddamn horse. Get off that goddamn horse god damn you." That's what I saw and heard coming up the road as I sat atop Lightning Strike, following Sonny's instructions to hold on to the rope with my right hand, hold my left up high, keep my legs loose and don't worry "marking the horse out," whatever that meant, now hearing my name come over the P.A.:

The fourth rider up, Hank Chandler from Lake Forest, Illinois, is on Lightning Strike.

Sonny slapped me on the back. Clete, perched on the top rail nearby, gave me a solemn nod. Chester Higgins threw away his smoke, placed his hands on knees, ready. Lightning Strike's ears perked. His nostrils flared and his breathing revved. I raised my hand signaling I was ready, and – don't ask me why – I whistled and yelled *FORE* just as the chute door swung open releasing a thousand pounds of kicking, twisting, bucking muscle; all wound up and ready to explode.

Imagine teeing up a golf ball and driving it straight up in the air, having it land five feet in front of you. And you ask yourself "How'd that happen?" as the other three in your foursome are checking the shine on their golf shoes, holding back a moan. That's similar to what happened when Lightning Strike spun out of the chute bouncing on both front and back feet at the same time, which made me feel like I was awkwardly between bounces on a trampoline. Then the horse kicked his hind legs up and out with such force it sent me into orbit like Andy used to do on the same trampoline in our back yard, when he would time my bouncing and double-bounce me so high my stomach could not catch up, and I'd fly up higher than I'd ever been before. But not as high as Lightning Strike propelled me on that Rendezvous Saturday, high enough – I'm sure – for me to have executed a double gainer with a twist in the pike position. I did not stick the landing, instead planting myself with such force that the crack from my shoulder was heard, according to Clete, from Casper to Kalispell; my face submerged in three inches of dirt; my body frozen with shock and pain.

I could not move. Did not want to move.

The first hands on me were Bit's. She turned me slightly, asking the obvious. I spit out dirt, moaning I was okay. She cleaned my face and mouth. Doc Evans was now by Bit's side telling her he'd take it from here. He helped me to sit up. Bit stood, looked down at me, then at the rider-less horse next up in the chute. She swiveled her head and took off running, following Freddie Saunders' black Chevy peeling away toward town, now screaming at the top of her lungs from the top rail of the corral, "Get back here you yellow-bellied bastard. Get back here and ride you chickshit sonofabitch. I never want to see you again. You're dead to me." (I'm not positive Bit said that last part, but I wanted to think so.)

It took me a while to gather myself and limp out of the ring with Bit and Doc Evans' help; Clete followed with my cowboy hat in hand. Sonny, who'd jumped in the ring with Clete to help Chester Higgins, was now back at his post by the chute. There was concerned applause, which I tried to acknowledge, but there was really nothing to acknowledge or talk about, so I'll skip ahead to when I was sitting up in Doc Evans's examination room; him kidding me: "Didn't I see you in here last year around this time?"

Squirming and flinching at his touch, I said, "I keep getting bucked off, Doc."

"That happens young man. Just keep getting back on. Just keep getting back on." He examined me some more. "I can't do much for you. Just give you something to hold you over until you get to Jackson where they'll set your shoulder. You broke it."

I promised him I would – keep getting back on – as I watched him maneuver on one of those stools that has wheels on the bottom and spins around so the doctor can push himself around the room to get whatever he needs, in my case diving into a rusting, white metal drawer, rooting around, wheeling back with a large vial and a larger syringe. He married the two, pulling out a voluminous amount of liquid, promising me quick relief just after tapping the syringe and giving the plunger a nudge, sending a squirt of pure heaven into the air. He swabbed my arm, paused, looked at me — Doc Evans was known around town for handing out healthy prescriptions. Here was mine: "Now let's see if I got this right, young man. Buzz saved Sonny some years ago from being a vegetable by jumping in and hauling him out of the ring. You and Sonny saved Buzz from being anything but the cowboy he truly was. Then you saved Sonny from being murdered and buried out around Cora because he was trying to save himself. Then Sonny goes and jumps in the ring today and saves you from most likely going home in a box because you wanted to save Bit from that road apple Freddie Saunders." He chuckled at himself. Chuckled at me. Chuckled at the whole chain of events, shaking his head, now jabbing me with a needle as long as your arm, thumbing the plunger, propelling me into the land of the bunnies. I closed my eyes, whirling, feeling warm and fuzzy. My pain melted away as I heard Doc say, "Everybody saving everybody. Damn near enough to set Reverend Sykes's head to spinning. Looks to me like you're going home."

Home.

Going home.

I told you those drugs will mess with your mind, especially the amount Doc Evans pumped into my veins. Now in la-la land, flat out on my back, eyes closed, I imagined that I was Tooter Turtle, spinning around in space, pleading with Mr. Wizard:

*Help me Mr. Wizard.*

And Mr. Wizard saying, *Drizzle. Drazzle. Drazzle. Drome. Time for this one to come home.*

Home.

Come home.

Time for this one to come home.

When I next opened my eyes, I was looking up at Bit looking down on me. She was caressing my head, brushing my bristle, her facial expression at the intersection of concern and anger, like my mother's when I fell off the jungle gym after she told me to be careful up there. I blinked and blinked again. I said, "I think I stayed on longer, but let's go to the replay."

She said, "There'll be no replay."

"Why?"

"Because I want to kill you, goddamit."

"I – "

" – Why, Hank?"

"I – "

" – Doc said you're going home."

"I – "

" – Said you broke your shoulder. I gotta take you up to Jackson Hospital so they can set it in a cast. That you gotta go home tomorrow. Why Hank?"

I had to answer her. But I didn't want to tell her what was running through my mind. That our worlds were too different. That long distance love was harder than Chinese arithmetic. That I did not want to hold her back or fend off all the cowboys in the state of Wyoming. That I was done with being a ranch hand, and how – let's face it – Bit was not going to learn to play golf, nor cotton to my preppy life. So I told her what was in my heart:

"Because I love you."

Bit drove me from town to Jackson in her El Camino in the slowest time ever recorded. Despite the drugs, I was uncomfortable and in pain so I didn't talk much, and Bit didn't either. When she wasn't steering the El Camino around bends, she searched for and found my left hand, squeezing, massaging my palm and fingers. At the hospital, a doctor and two nurses wrapped my entire torso in warm, gauzy plaster, holding my right arm up and in front of me, supported with a fiber glass pole attached to my midsection. My left hand was free, but mostly useless because I'm right handed. Loading me up in Bit's car was comical, so was driving back to the ranch as motorists passed us, gawking at the guy in the passenger seat encased in a plaster barrel with his arm suspended in front of him, mouthing – I'm sure – *What the hell happened to him?*

Hope and Dorothy and Clete were on the porch when we pulled in under the Lazy T sign. They watched me struggle to extricate myself – with Bit's help – from the car. When I was upright and moving toward them with adequate dexterity, again with Bit's assistance, Hope spoke up, "Henry Chandler, you know what this means?"

I said, "My parents are suing you for everything you have."

"Wouldn't blame them," Hope said, waving her hand around the Lazy T. "They can have it all."

"How about we call it a draw," I said. "I'll settle for a

smoke, some supper, and a mess of your biscuits."

"A draw it is," Hope said slapping her hands together then putting them on her hips. "I had to call your folks and explain what happened."

"What'd they say?"

"I spoke with your mother. She said 'Oh poor dear. Not again.'" Hope laughed. "We talked for a while."

"What about?"

"The only thing we've got in common."

I thought about that, wanting a smoke, pinching the first two fingers on my left hand together, practicing to hold a cigarette. "When's my flight?"

"Tomorrow at eight. First class ticket is at the American counter."

Bit left my side and shot into the house.

That night, Bit slept with me on Clete's bed in the trailer. Clete and Bear took up quarters on my bed, even though Bear came sneaking back when she heard Bit and I talking and giggling after the dust and tears had settled on my heading home. I told her I'd never heard her swear so long and loud as she did at me and Freddie Saunders. She said she'd heard cowboys yell a lot of things coming out of the chute like YEHAA and YAABOY, but never FORE. I explained on the golf course that meant watch out, heads-up. She said never a truer word had been yelled coming out of a rodeo chute. I asked if I scored any points from the Russian judge for style and form. Bit shook her head, her hair floating around my face as she kissed me, saying my performance resembled a rag doll that had been pitched high in the air. This lead to a bunch of whispering with me on my back and my wing in the air and Bit curled up on my left side, reminiscing about our first dance at the Cowboy; Bit coming out to visit me at school and bopping Janie; making love for the first time in my dorm room and our last time in the barn; scalping me and our ride to Gunderson's Meadow; Farnsworth's funeral;

how Sonny and Clete hopped into the ring the moment I was launched, waving their arms, blocking Lightning Strike from killing me; how Sonny ran full force into the horse with his shoulder; how he and Clete chased the horse out of the arena as Chester Higgins – wheezing and coughing – ran to catch up, his handkerchief falling out of his back pocket. It was getting late, but neither of us wanted to fall asleep because we'd have to wake up. We kept on talking and talking. Soon after taking another of Doc Evan's pills with some water – Bit propped up on one arm, her fingers gently massaging my scalp, telling me about Cody, the first horse she ever rode and took care of – I closed my eyes and nodded off.

We had an extra early wakeup call from Hope who came out before sunup to roust us with a strong beam from a flashlight. Bit and I had not moved. I was on my back with my wing in the air, and Bit was still clothed and wrapped around me. Hope said for us to get a move on, there's coffee and biscuits in the house. I dressed with Bit's help. She and Clete said go to the house, they'd packed my gear. I stood on the stoop outside the trailer door looking around the darkened yard, then began a slow, careful walk to the light in the kitchen, mindful of my balance, smelling the pine smoke drifting out of the cracked cinderblock chimney with the rusted TV antenna; gingerly crossing the plank across the stream for the last time, feeling the chill because I didn't have a jean jacket big enough to fit over my body cast. On the horizon, the stars were fading in a morning sky that welcomed the sun climbing up over the Wind Rivers. I looked back toward the trailer, Bit and Clete hard at work with my belongings.

(Because I did not have a hand in packing my gear, I didn't know until I got home that there were four mementos from the Lazy T carefully wrapped and tucked in amongst my clothing.

375

1) Swiss Cheese, holstered and cleaned, but not loaded;

2) Farnsworth's Sheriff star, polished and buffed;

3) Sonny's silver dented-up Zippo, gassed up with half a flint;

4) A Hope Stifel handmade badger claw necklace with a pendant of six spent 357 shells set in silver and turquoise – a real beauty.

I would put these treasures in the trunk in my room that contained the only copy of my story for Professor Gurney, along with Buzz's Akubra and Clete's Old Timer, securing it with a new padlock that only I knew the combination. The last memento traveling back with me from the Lazy T was originally mine, and that I tucked in my knapsack just after Bit removed it from her head at the airport.)

At the departure gate, Bit and I held hands and kissed as much as we could. When the announcement came for first class to board, Bit looked at me and said, "I know you know how to write, Hank." She did not cry nor get sappy on me. That's not Bit. "It'll grow back," were the last words she spoke to me as she put a hand on my cheek, just before I swung my wing around and headed out across the tarmac. Halfway to the plane I turned to see Bit standing in front of the same window as when I had arrived in June, this time hands in her pockets and a thousand-yard stare on her face. At the bottom of the stairs leading up to the plane, I gave her a left-handed wave goodbye.

She waved back.

The stewardess – who'd been sent down to help the passenger injured in a rodeo accident – said to me, "Take my arm, Mr. Chandler." At the top of the stairs, I stopped and looked down at the window again, but Bit was gone. As if she'd never been there. I blinked, and blinked again; then looked away at the Tetons, making sure they were still there.

The stewardess named Jane asked, "Are you okay?" as if I had seen something.

I had seen something – felt something, too – but can't for the life of me describe what it was. It was mystical. Or maybe my cast was just too tight. Or I was having a backdoor rush from Doc's painkillers. I don't know. I locked in on Jane's blue eyes, red lipstick, cute round face, dyed blond hair, and leprechaun green uniform, feeling her fingernails on my arm, now catching my breath. I said, "I'm not sure," as if maybe I'd had a vision. Then I disappeared through the door of the Boeing 707; Jane behind me, reminding me, *You don't have to pay for drinks in First Class.*

Like I didn't know.

At O'Hare, walking off the jet way, I immediately spotted Andy directly across the concourse leaning against the wall with a look of disbelief. I thanked Jane for escorting me, assuring her I was in good hands, then made my way over, careful not to clothesline any travelers hustling to their planes, and came to a stop in front of him, my casted arm not three feet from his chest.

Andy said, "Shit, Hank, you promised."

I shrugged, giving him my What-the-fuck-sorry-to-disappoint-you look.

He said, "What the hell happened, Hoss?" reaching for the knapsack in my left hand.

I said, "Got bucked off a horse in rodeo, Ringo."

He pointed. "No, your hair."

I rubbed my hand over my bristle. "Do you like it?"

He gave me a full once-over saying, "Sure, if you're in line to be electrocuted."

We turned and walked to baggage claim with me saying, "Do you want to sign my cast?"

Andy stopped me, putting a hand on my wing. "Seriously, Hank, with what, a paint roller? You're a walking billboard. How are you going to explain this to Mom and Dad?"

I shrugged. "Slowly, I guess. One word at a time."

We walked in the middle of the concourse with most of the travelers flowing around us like we were boulders in a stream, the adults trying not to stare at me and the kids glued to the college kid sporting a prison Princeton, encased in a body cast with his arm up and out, bent at the elbow, flying in front of him.

Waiting for my pack at baggage claim, Andy asked, "So what's up next year, Hoss, a body bag?"

I didn't say anything because there would be no next year. Andy knew something was up so he changed the subject, kidding me, "I'm not giving you any more strokes, you realize that don't you?"

I said, trying to smile, "I can beat you with both arms in a cast," but my smile was tired. Andy knew it. He laid off.

In the parking garage, Andy threw my backpack in the trunk of his Volkswagen Rabbit. He helped angle and wedge me into the front seat that had been shoved back to accommodate my cast. Getting on a seat belt was not going to happen, so Andy dug around in the truck and came back with a red hockey helmet, plunking it down on my head, not snapping the strap because that's the cool way. He hustled around to get in while I, with my left hand, managed to unzip my knapsack and root around, pulling out Bones's country cassette. The knapsack was still open with my Cubs cap peeking out. Andy saw it. He's not stupid – there was a reason Ron Santo was back in Chicago. He started the car. Before he put it in gear, he gave my knee a light tap and said,

"You okay, Hoss?"

I stared through the windshield at a gray cinderblock wall. For sure I was blue over Bit, beat up, still bothered by Farnsworth, coming down from the drugs, not knowing what next. Then, a strange feeling came over me. It was so simple. Sonny was right – *life don't lie*. This was my life, my journey. And, I'd come full circle. Every beginning has an end, and every end has a beginning. But it's not about the beginning or the end, is it? It's about the road you've traveled. And in my case, it was Forty Rod Road. That sounds corny and stupid, but that is exactly what I was thinking staring at a water-stained cinderblock wall in Section C4 of the dark and dank parking garage at O'Hare International Airport.

My crooked smile returned.

I glanced sideways, adjusting Andy's red hockey helmet with the strap dangling down, leaving no doubt as I said to my brother,

"I got 'er, Ringo."

I handed him the cassette, telling him last song on side B.

He slid in the tape, hit fast forward, found the selection, pressed play.

We drove out of the garage, heading home under bright summer sunshine.

Me, Andy, Bob Dylan and Johnny Cash.

Now that's good company.